KILLING IT SOFTLY

KILLING IT SOFTLY

A *Digital Horror Fiction* Anthology of Short Stories

DIGITAL HORROR FICTION

DigitalFictionPub.com

DIGITAL FICTION
PUBLISHING CORP

Anthology copyright © 2016 Digital Fiction Publishing Corp.
Stories copyright © 2016 the Authors.
All rights reserved. Edition 1.01
ISBN-13 (paperback): 978-1-927598-50-4
ISBN-13 (e-book): 978-1-927598-49-8

Contents

Foreword—Suzie Lockhart	vii
Torn Asunder—Rebecca Snow	1
Lambent Lights—H.R. Boldwood	11
Nosophoros—Christine Lucas	22
What the Rain Brings—Gerri Leen	38
Taking it for The Team—Tracie McBride	61
Here We Go Round—Rie Sheridan Rose	71
Songs for Dead Children—Aliya Whiteley	82
Music in the Bone—Marion Pitman	93
All of a Heap—Jenner Michaud	111
Traitorous, Lying, Little Star—Suzanne Reynolds-Alpert	126
Truth Hurts—Carole Gill	138
A Trick of the Dark—Tina Rath	149
Abysmoira—Airika Sneve	159
Skin Deep—Carson Buckingham	184
Orbs—Chantal Boudreau	205
Rule of Five—Eleanor R. Wood	215
Guilty by Chance—Nidhi Singh	226
Ecdysis—Rebecca J. Allred	246
Coralesque—Rebecca Fraser	257
The Funhouse—Jo-Anne Russell	268
Graffiti—K.S. Dearsley	279
Complete—Amanda Northrup Mays	290
Ellensburg Blue—M.J. Sydney	305
Abandoned—Rose Blackthorn	319
The Call of the House of Usher—Annie Neugebauer	341
Ravens—Elaine Cunningham	354
Foxford—Sandra Kasturi	375
The Root—Jess Landry	385
Long Time, No See—Sarah Hans	399
Saving Grace—Lillian Csernica	413
Millie's Hammock—Tory Hoke	430
Changed—Nancy Holder	445
More from Digital Fiction	470
Copyright	471

Foreword

Suzie Lockhart

I must admit, when I was first presented with the title 'Killing It Softly', it gave me pause. I wondered if it sounded a bit, well, sexist? But then I realized the title held a sarcastic tone, because the irony is: *these stories are anything but soft!* Women authors instinctively knew that, because the short stories flooded in.

And because 'Killing It Softly' is a reprint anthology, the submission call lured the best of the best. Making decisions about which stories to feature in this anthology was an excruciating process, because practically every one we received was well above the fray!

Finally, however, the selection of dark and dangerous tales was complete, and what we ended up with was a *'Best by Women in Horror'* anthology.

The mere prospect of writing an introduction for this anthology was so intimidating that I almost convinced myself it wasn't necessary. *What could I possibly say*, I thought looking through the list of amazing authors from all over the world now gracing the pages of 'Killing It Softly', *that would be worthwhile?* I mean, with authors such as: Rebecca Snow, Carole Gill, Carson Buckingham, Tina Rath, Gerri Leen, Elaine Cunningham, and Nancy Holder gracing the pages of this book—just to name a few—well, if you're a lover of the horror genre, you get the picture. I mean, some of these women are award-winning authors; members of the Horror Writers Association; some have appeared in anthologies edited by Ellen Datlow and P.C. Cast; others have appeared in Stephen Jones's 'Mammoth' books of horror; and some—already best-selling authors—nonetheless answered the call.

I was moved when one of the authors thanked me for giving female horror authors a voice. One of the reasons I wanted to do this

Suzie Lockhart

anthology was because I felt, as a female horror author of dozens of short stories myself, that we were an under-represented, and sometimes misunderstood, group.

I want to thank the wizard behind the curtain, Executive Editor Michael Wills for offering me this opportunity, and S. Kay Nash for all her hard work as Copy Editor. Being Managing Editor for an all-female anthology was something I've longed to do since I had a story of my own appear in 'Mistresses of the Macabre' a few years back. Now, watching this amazing book come to life will be another goal I can cross off my bucket list...

Suzie Lockhart attended The Art Institute of Pittsburgh after graduating, but the gnawing urge to write always remained. After discovering the innate ability for macabre storytelling, Suzie embraced her inner-creepiness. Her middle son, Bruce began writing chilling tales, and they teamed up. Five years working together have yielded nearly 50 short story publications, in dozens of paperbacks and eZines. The pair have also edited several anthologies, including two top ten Preditors & Editors™ Readers' Poll Awards.

Torn Asunder

Rebecca Snow

Charlotte's eyelids trembled. Her fingertips flinched, and her nose twitched. Something fluttered from her nostrils. The scents of cinnamon, sandalwood, and cedar wafted through the close air. Uncrossing her arms, she flexed her hands and brushed the detritus from her face. With her eyes wide, she saw only white flecks of total darkness. She blinked to clear her vision and craned her neck as far as she could turn, but the pitch black remained.

Lifting to her elbows, her head collided with a hard surface, and she fell back onto satiny cushions. She opened her mouth to cry. Instead of a shrill yell, she gagged on wads of oiled cooking spices. She reached between her teeth and pried the debris from her cheeks. Her next shrieking effort brought forth no more than a muffled choke.

Charlotte shed her long evening gloves. She could not recall having donned them. The thin hide caught at her knuckles. Exploring the snags in the darkness, she caressed several recognizable stone rings. She slid off the hindering metal jewelry and tucked it into her bodice before she freed her hands from the confining goat skin. Her naked palms trembled as she pressed forward and found a solid wall of wood.

Spidering her fingers to the place where the stitched fabric seams met the boards above her, she ripped until the threads rent from another wooden wall. She rapped against it and heard an echoless knock. As she searched her clothing, she discovered the shape of her grandmother's locket draped around her neck.

Charlotte kicked her legs and encountered the same wooden prison below her waist. She shoved with all her strength, grunting with the effort. Employing her knees in the endeavor, the process succeeded in tearing a piece of her skirt but nothing more. She drooped back into the satin folds and coughed a hissing sob for help.

A memory formed in her clouded brain. She remembered a man's smiling face leaning over her. A single gold tooth gleamed like the evening star. The recollection faded as her stomach grumbled. She thought of the moist richness of a slice of jam filled cake. Reaching to her left hand, she felt a small metal band and wondered if the man had been her husband.

She picked at the buttons on the unfamiliar taffeta dress she wore. Straining her mind, she believed the texture of the embroidered designs resembled the garment that hid in the deepest corner of her wardrobe. The fashionable gown was to be worn in the event of her death.

Charlotte gasped as much as her throat would allow. She released the buttons as if they had stung her. The wooden box, the aromatic spices in her mouth and nose, the funeral clothes, all her significant jewelry, each piece clicked into place like a puzzle, and she understood. Thrashing her fists, she pounded on the hard surface above her. Rasping shouts fell from her uncooperative lungs.

Charlotte's mind flashed. Her father would not have buried her in anything but a security coffin. He had made an order with the cabinetmaker. A string was to be attached to one hand and one foot. The line would be secured to a bell on the surface. When the lead was pulled, the bell would ring.

The buried woman patted her wrists and felt along the lid of the coffin. No filament presented itself, and the hole to allow the cord entrance was missing. Not knowing how long she could survive, she attacked the bare wood with her fingernails. Splinters pierced the delicate skin under her nails as the tips peeled to the quick.

Her stomach gurgled, and she dropped her hands to her sides. A memory of a banquet seeped into her head. Platters of food sat on every surface, her pastel wedding gown shimmered in the moonlight, and the man's golden grin reappeared. His smile had made her squirm before it faded into her deepening hunger. The unsatisfying thought of watercress sandwiches remained.

Scrambling her hands through the folds of fabric, she seized one of the long gloves and bit into the wrist. She gnashed her teeth, ripping the kid gloves to ribbons. Aside from the saltiness of her dried sweat, the clothing had no taste. The chewing calmed her mind, and her father's face filtered through her thoughts. Papa's wicked grin alongside the gold-toothed man and a sideways glance down an alleyway flickered like a magic lantern show at the New Richmond Theatre. A purse, bulging with banknotes, fell into her father's hand.

Charlotte's ravenous insides felt as though they twisted in knots, though the memory of her father's transaction endured. She gnawed at the remaining tatters until a vision of a whirling dancer interrupted. She imagined a meal of stewed mutton and beef tongue instead of tanned hide gloves as her teeth gnashed into the tough leather.

A small vibration thumped through the ground. Charlotte froze, trying to discern the thud's reality. After a moment, she felt another tremor. She kicked at her wooden prison and coughed a feeble yell. Growing still, she lapsed into silence as she envisioned the gold-toothed man wrestling her to the cobblestones. The deserted park on Libby Hill overlooked the James River. The sunset sky transformed from dull orange to dusted sapphire as Charlotte struggled against her attacker, her husband, as he wrapped his hands around her throat. As his grip tightened, her memory congealed.

The coffin shuddered as debris crept through a thin crack in the wood and onto Charlotte's face. She swept the loose earth away with the back of her hand as a hard knock sounded above her.

"Fred," a man's deep voice said. "I think I found 'er."

A series of metallic scrapes followed.

"Good job, Henry," a second voice said. "Now alls we got to do is get 'er out and over to Ole Chris."

A heavy thud sounded above her face. She flinched but remained silent. Her stomach lurched under the constraints of her corset. Her cravings grew. The memory of a dripping mouthful of ox heart at Ford's Hotel eased the pain, but the imagined meal did not satisfy her all-consuming appetite.

"How much do you think he'll give us for 'er?" Henry asked. "She ain't been under but a day."

A brisk sweeping sound followed a series of grunts.

"Better be more 'n last time," Fred snorted. "'Specially since he's been askin' for a woman to cut up at the college." A shuffling boot scraped the wood. "Even so, this one'll have some pretty baubles for us to make up the difference."

Charlotte closed her eyes to protect them from the falling soil. Her mind raced with questions. Where had she been buried? Did her father know she was here? Why had he taken money from the gold-toothed man? Why had her husband tried to kill her? What was his name? In a matter of moments, she believed she would know the answer to at least one of her questions.

She squinted as a sliver of lamplight shot through an imperfection in the wood. Her stomach grumbled at the sound of a stomping foot. She thought of tearing into a rare steak and watching the blood drip down her arms. The coffin lid splintered at her waist.

"Hand me the crowbar," Henry said.

Something clattered above her.

"Watch it," Henry hissed. "You almost took my good foot off."

Having eaten her gloves, Charlotte had none to wear. She folded her hands on her chest and closed her eyes. A cracking of pine preceded a small dirt avalanche. She hazarded a peek from behind her long lashes and saw the stocky form of a man fold the split planks into a packed wall of earth.

"Hey, Fred," the man said, pointing to the wood he had removed. "Looks like this one was still kickin'. We got claw marks."

A second head appeared above her and squinted to where Henry gestured.

"Only three nails missing. Couldn't have been too alive." Fred adjusted his cap and wiped a filthy handkerchief across his face. "Well, strip her and haul her out. We got two more stops to make before we head to Baker's."

Fred's words speckled Charlotte's face with flecks of spittle before he disappeared from view. She wanted to wipe away the slobber, but she remained motionless, thinking of slaughtered meat. Henry grabbed the lantern and shone the light on Charlotte's prone form.

"Fred," he said. His deep voice turned up in a question. "She don't look like a scared rabbit like the other scratchers." Squatting on a thin ledge of dirt, he pressed his ear to her breastbone. "But she's got no heartbeat." He felt her pale forehead with his calloused touch. "And she's clammy cold."

Charlotte's stomach rumbled. On instinct, she wrapped her thin fingers around his forearm and pulled his burly muscle to her mouth. Henry's saucer eyes bulged. He shrieked when Charlotte jammed her teeth into his gristly tissue.

"Hush down there," Fred said from his perch. "You tryin' to wake the dead?"

Glancing into the pit, a string of curses flew from his tongue. He leaned into the hole and clung to Henry's collar. The frayed fabric tore, and Fred fell back into the empty graveyard. He shot to his feet and took a last look at Henry's flailing free arm before he fled into the shadows.

Charlotte's grip strengthened with each hunk of flesh she devoured. Henry stopped screaming a moment after she plucked his arm from his squirming torso. His body lay in a heap next to her as she ripped through tendons.

By the time Charlotte's hunger diminished, she had made a meal of most of Henry's organs. The dead man's brain had been a challenge, but she had managed to snap his spine and saw through his neck muscles with her teeth. She had scrambled from her grave and smashed Henry's skull on a white marble slab, exposing the gray matter. Spooning her cupped hand into the cavity, she dug out his lobes and slurped them like snails. She squatted on her haunches and licked her fingers as her father's face blinked into her mind.

With her thumb in her mouth, she glimpsed the dark stains on her white lace cuffs. She lowered her hands as if she were approaching a skittish animal and stared at the chunks of carnage swaying from her sleeves.

She peered into the open trench. The lantern rested next to Henry's remains. Charlotte croaked a scream, remembering her part in his destruction. She thrust her hand to her chest. No telltale thump of a beating heart met her fingertips. Henry had been right; she did not live. Her husband had not *tried* to kill her, he *had* killed her. She had become a monster.

Pieces of a picture trickled into her thoughts like drizzle on a drought-ridden streambed. Thomas, her husband, held a needle to her throat. The man had stolen her away from their wedding feast under the guise of a connubial kiss and stabbed her in the neck.

Jolted by the memory, Charlotte whirled. *What had been inside the syringe? Had the shot made her hunger for flesh?* The nearby holly trees hid her from the surrounding city. Marble tombstones scattered the landscape. She staggered past a large wrought iron cage and toward the sound of rumbling water.

The James twinkled below her in the moonlight. Charlotte fell to her knees. She recognized the view. The end of her father's street looked out on an identical idyllic scene. Her stomach protested as the hunger returned. She rose to her feet and gazed at the statues and tombs. Just beyond the gates of Hollywood Cemetery, her father slumbered in his Oregon Hill home.

Skirting the marble angels and obelisks, she traversed the night. Though her hunger drove her forward, she ducked behind a large rectangular stone as a large black dog trotted past. The idea of ingesting the four-legged creature repulsed her. The mongrel took no notice of the shadows that held her. When she unfolded from her hiding spot, Charlotte glanced over her shoulder and noticed the dog had vanished.

The closed iron gate blocked her exit. She shook the bars, but the lock held fast and rattled in protest. Placing a low-heeled boot between the metal staves, she grasped two of the finials and hoisted herself over the barrier and onto South Cherry Street.

Carriage wheels clattered in the distance, and Charlotte clung to the darkness against the fence. She could recognize the porch steps from where she stood. A lantern flickered in the parlor window. Her father had not retired for the evening.

A knot in Charlotte's gut bent her double. She wrapped her arms around her middle and waited for the piercing pain to pass.

"Excuse me miss," a voice whispered from a nearby alleyway. "Are you all right?"

Charlotte straightened as if she had been a marionette yanked up by the strings. She squinted toward the stranger but made out no more than a furtive form. Her hunger fogged her mind, but she waved away the question and nodded into the gloom. Turning on her heel, she strode toward the familiar veranda.

The five wooden stairs creaked as she climbed. Covered in Henry's drying blood, she reached out her crusted fingers and cranked the bell. Footsteps approached. The latch rattled before the door jerked open, banging into the wall.

"Where have you been?" her father shouted, turning away from the doorway. "We've got to go get her. The shovels are in the..." His gravelly voice trailed into silence as he turned and saw his daughter's soiled figure. "You," he croaked. "I should not have doubted Thomas." He stepped back and beckoned her into the room. "Come inside. You must be starving."

Charlotte lunged at him with a vigor she had not possessed in life. Tearing at his clothes, she bit into his shielding wrists and clawed at his face. He toppled into the hall table and sent a silver candlestick sliding across the surface. He stretched his arms toward the polished holder as Charlotte cinched her fingers into his hair and snapped back his head. Her father collapsed into a heap. His body twitched. Charlotte fell on his carcass and indulged her appetite with his entrails.

As she lifted the ornate silver cylinder to bash in his skull, a scuffling step sounded at the open door. Forgetting the delicacy encased in her father's head, she stiffened and took a measured turn. A gold-toothed grin gleamed from the entryway.

"Charlotte," Thomas mewled, holding his grin. "What have you done?"

Charlotte snarled and stepped toward him. Thomas shut the door and edged around the wall. He backed into the parlor and rounded the horsehair sofa, using it as a barrier between them. Charlotte stalked into the room and glared at him from behind her gore-drenched bangs.

"Now, Charlotte," Thomas said. "Calm yourself. Your father only wanted what was best for you."

Charlotte hurled the candlestick. Thomas ducked as the projectile sailed past his head and crashed into the velvet-papered wall. A smirk bloomed on his face when he saw a pout form on her blood-stained lips.

"I met your father after a lecture at the medical college," Thomas spoke as if comforting a tantruming child. "I had been asked to speak on the possibilities of eternal life."

Charlotte took a single step closer to the fresh meat. Thomas tensed but continued to talk.

"Your father requested that I join him after the discourse to discuss my findings in more depth."

Charlotte scowled and tilted her head as if listening or taking stock of her prey.

"I told him I had made strides in perfecting a chemical formula that would make death obsolete. My success rate among four-legged mammals intrigued him." Thomas cleared his throat and waved a dismissive hand. "Still, my colleagues insisted on my insanity." A crease burrowed between his bushy brows. "With only the human trial remaining, they still refused to sanction my study." Thomas glanced at the pile of man on the floor. "But your father understood. He believed." His metallic tooth shone in the flickering light. "And look at you, a success." A frown darkened his eyes as he tapped his thin lips. "I may have to adjust my ratio calculations for two-legged mammals. You seem to have developed quite an appetite for long pig."

Charlotte sprinted around the couch and slid into the dense lace curtains covering the front window. Her sticky skin and torn nails snagged the eyelets. A single panel spat from a rod as she tried to free herself. Thomas chuckled, strolling to the front of the sofa. Charlotte flung the drape aside and whirled to face him.

"Dear, since your father is dead, this house and its contents are mine." Thomas crossed his arms over his chest. His brocade waistcoat strained across his rounded shoulders. "As are you. I paid your father a handsome dowry to have the privilege of taking you as my wife." He looked from her grimy face to the torn curtains and the dented wall. "I would appreciate your taking better care of my possessions." The bridge of his nose wrinkled to a sneer. "And wash yourself, you resemble nothing more than a wild beast."

Charlotte's stomach protested its famished state. She sidestepped the lamp-topped table and growled. Her ruby-stained teeth glistened. The discarded drapery tangled in her boot heel. As she approached the edge of the couch, the trailing fabric snared the insubstantial table. The glass globe atop the lamp shattered as it fell, and the room dimmed before the glowing wick ignited the spilled oil. Flames snaked across the carpet to the remaining curtains. Charlotte crouched to pounce as her husband backed away from the rising heat.

Thomas shrieked when gnarled knuckles wrapped around his ankle. Charlotte's father glowered from where he lay in the oozing remains of his own innards. The older man's teeth ground together as he tried to pull Thomas down to the floor. Shaking his leg, Thomas attempted to dislodge the corpse's grip.

"How do you still live?" Thomas muttered as he tugged his foot. "You received no serum." He relaxed his pull as his mind toiled. His eyes grew to saucers. "Charlotte's saliva must have transferred her eternity along with her malady to you, old man."

In reply, the consumed man's jaws snapped at the empty air.

"What have I done?" Thomas asked the rising flames.

The blaze flared as it enveloped a framed portrait. Thomas glanced up to see Charlotte's accusing likeness blacken to ash as it stared from the wall. With his opposite heel, Thomas pried the dead man's hand from around his leg. He took a step backward as boughs of fire flicked around the doorframe and into the entrance hall.

"Forgive me," he whispered, taking a second step back as the parlor ceiling collapsed.

Thomas spun toward the closed door and into the waiting arms of his hungry bride.

Rebecca Snow is a Virginia writer who enjoys weaving her real world into her fictional fabrics. When not scribbling, she enjoys photography, herding cats, and travel to anywhere there isn't hot weather.

Lambent Lights

H.R. Boldwood

There is no rest for the wicked. This morn, I awoke to a symphony of saws and hammers that heralded the raising of my gallows. No doubt by midday the news had spread through the city more quickly than consumption. *The Graveyard Ghoul to swing! Ian Bates dies on the morrow!* The merchants of Baltimore surely bustled in the streets, hawking their wares like draggletailed harlots. *Sundries for the hanging! Parasols for the ladies. Hats for the gents. Penny candy for the babes.* I'll wager that upon the lighting of the street lamps, the town cronies raised a toast to my impending demise.

So quick they are to see me dangle at the end of a rope…and so blind to the truth.

Moonlight bleeds through the iron bars of my cell, spilling across first one stone and then the next pursuing me relentlessly. I conceal myself in the shadows, certain beyond all reason that the Angel Gideon, sword held high, rides that light like a stallion. Patient as Job, he is waiting to pass judgment upon me.

Without question and for just cause, I shall be found lacking. But I should not stand alone. Let me be clear. It is not forgiveness I seek whilst idling in the shadow of the hangman's noose. It is vengeance against the demon seed who put me here.

It was well past midnight on June 3, 1830, when wearied by my duties as night watchman at The Westminster Hall and Burying Ground, I leaned against the carriage gates to enjoy a paste cigar and partake in some mindless woolgathering. From the corner of my eye, I spied a lambent light at the edge of the property.

Having served as the cemetery's watchman for nearly a decade, I speak with great authority on the matter of these mystifying lights. These ghostly will-o'-the-wisps are sentient beings, at best mercurial, at worst malignant, and have lured many a man to his damnation. We both ply our trades in the dead of night, these lights and I. In that regard are we kindred, and so, we afford each other easement as we go about our business. Given the fickle nature of these fiery sprites, I am wont to grant them a wide berth.

However, on this particular night, the shimmering specter beckoned me, refusing me respite until I answered its call. Senses keen and nerves a-tingle, I grabbed a mucking shovel from the gateway and proceeded into the burying grounds. Then came an unexpected sound that chilled me to the bone. It was a nearly imperceptible ringing in the distance. *Steady now*, I thought, *'tis likely your ears deceive you, nothing more.* I continued on my way to where I'd seen the ghost light, whence came the sound again, only stronger. Without question, it was a bell with resonance and reverberation and not the result of fitful hallucination. My anxiety grew.

To a watchman on duty, a knelling in the night could carry horrific implications; implications that made me shudder.

The ringing magnified one hundred fold—a banging, clanging, pealing appeal; a demanding, commanding call to action that could not be denied. Upon discovering its source, I stopped in place. My dread had proved well founded.

The sound that had beckoned me was the tolling of a safety bell from atop a freshly dug grave! I drove the shovel deep and threw the dirt aside, scarcely allowing myself to consider the untenable truth. *The occupant of this grave was still alive.* "I'm coming!" I screamed. "Hold fast!"

The shovel was far too small for the task but the only tool at hand. Faster and harder I shoveled and heaved, calling out, "I am almost there!" Soon, I began to hear a muffled thumping from beneath the dirt, and moments thereafter, a frantic voice screaming from within the coffin.

Breathless, and with arms that had given their all, I raised the shovel high and brought it down like the hammer of Zeus upon the lock, breaking it free. I threw back the lid to the casket. Its occupant sprang upright like a demented jack-in-the-box!

Ne'er in my life had I seen such a sight. The man gulped air as if to inhale the sky; his eyes so wide they might have popped, his skin more pale than a bloodless corpse. The cord that stretched from inside his coffin to the bell above ground remained in his hand. Adrift in a fugue, he continued to yank it reflexively, causing the bell to toll again and again. One by one, I pried his fingers free. He grabbed at me with such forceful desperation as to dislodge the buttons from my jacket. A croup-like cough burst from within his chest. I handed him my handkerchief and waited for his lungs to clear before moving him.

Once stabilized, I led the exhausted man to the caretaker's shanty and placed him in a chair beside the desk. He shivered in spite of the warm summer night. I laid my jacket across his shoulders, and he began to babble.

"God bless you, Sir. Thank heaven you appeared! I hadn't long left. You saved me from a fate more gruesome than I could ever have imagined. My name is Angus Winchell. How may I repay you? I don't

H.R. Boldwood

even know your name."

"I am Ian Bates, the watchman of Westminster Hall," I said. "You're safe now, Mr. Winchell. I suggest you rest and pull your wits about you. Perhaps then you will explain how you came to be…buried alive." I shuddered at the sound of those words, pulled a flask (reserved for medicinal purposes) from my back pocket and poured him a shot. It vanished, as did the next. So pallid he was, with eyes that looked feverish and over-bright.

"Mr. Bates, I assure you, I am of sound mind despite what you may come to think. Mine is a preposterous tale defying all explanation; still, it is the truth. I will swear to it on my mother's grave."

"How utterly appropriate," I said, taking a goodly swig from the flask. Leaning back in my chair, I placed my feet atop the desk and sighed. "This entire episode defies explanation, Mr. Winchell. The prospect of a more implausible tale boggles the mind.

"There could be no story without Malcolm Fletcher," he began, "the most villainous lout ever slipped from a mother's loins. I rue the day I met the double-crossing bastard. We shared a coach and several bottles of whiskey while traveling from Charleston to Baltimore. He was a bright man, affable enough when he was in his cups, but as fate would have it, a taciturn tyrant when abstinent.

"The fool that I am formed a partnership with him before his sobriety surfaced. We opened The Winchell Fletcher Trading Company." He raised his brows. "Perhaps you know of it?" I shook my head, and he continued. "Fletcher saw to the daily operations. I avoided him like the plague, simply supplying the capital as needed. We split the profits evenly. All was well and good, until he decided he no longer needed my money and wanted to buy me out."

"The thankless bugger!" I said.

"Wasn't he, though? I told him absolutely not, and if he did not agree, it would be I who bought him out. We did not speak for days; then suddenly, he appeared in my office, hat in hand, offering me a glass of Hermitage Burgundy. He admitted that he had wronged me and lamented his odious behavior. Tired of the quarrel, I accepted his apology. We toasted and agreed to allow bygones be bygones. But moments later, I fell ill.

"My sight blurred, and my belly boiled as if brimming with acid. I twitched like a festering corpse. Numbness quickly spread, beginning in my extremities, then progressing to my core. Unable to breathe, I collapsed. My last waking moment found Fletcher straddling me, flashing a serpentine twist of rotted teeth.

"'By now, you realize there was poison in your glass,' he said. 'But do not despair, Winchell. It will all be over soon; and then, you will become fodder for the worms. Pity. This was all so unnecessary. You should have accepted my offer.'

"When next I opened my eyes, I was surrounded by an obsidian darkness, confined so that my head could barely raise, arms and legs pinned at my sides. Thoughts muddled in my aching head. When the veil of confusion lifted, my dilemma became morbidly clear. Reason departed and madness ensued. The sound of my screams filled my ears. The more panic prevailed, the less air remained. I found the cord and pulled, praying the bell would be heard." His voice cracked. "I was about to give up hope when suddenly, you appeared like an angel. I owe you my life."

"But the poison!" I cried. "How did you survive?"

He offered a wry smile. "I can only surmise that Fletcher had a less than optimal grasp of alchemy."

"Astonishing!"

"I ask you, Mr. Bates, has ever a more horrific torture been inflicted upon a man than Malcolm Fletcher visited upon me?"

Opportunity dangled before me like low-hanging fruit. I seized the moment. "Mr. Winchell, this Fletcher character as much as killed you. Consider the torment he wreaked upon you. Justice must be served."

He hesitated as if pondering my words. "Aye, but what justice? What punishment befits so heinous a crime?"

"Why, death, of course! Swift, merciless, and discreet."

His eyes grew wide. "What are you implying?"

"Biblical equity. An eye for an eye." I pulled my Barlow knife from my boot and thrust it to the tip of his chin. "Justice dispatched by the very angel that delivered you from the jaws of death. Even God could find no quarrel with that."

Winchell gulped. "You would…perform such a service?"

"With proper motivation, it is possible."

"Money is no object, Mr. Bates, if that be what motivates you."

I wet my lips and leaned closer. "Do tell."

"What say you to twenty guineas?"

"Twenty? To the man who pulled you from the worms? Surely, you can…"

"Fifty! Fifty guineas are yours. You have only to accept."

Not wishing to appear eager, I brought the discussion to a close. "There would be significant risk involved with such an endeavor. I shall take the matter under advisement."

He gathered his legs beneath him and moved toward the door. "Consider my offer, Mr. Bates. Surely, a watchman like yourself could make use of such a tidy sum. I shall meet you at the carriage gates tomorrow at midnight expecting your response. I leave you now to your conscience."

Odd, that he assumed I had a conscience. I am not now, nor have I ever been, a virtuous man. The road to hell may be paved with good intentions, but its stones are aflame with avarice. I have spent my lifetime skipping across those red-hot coals. Truth be told, this would not be my first undertaking of a nefarious nature. I have done dark and damnable things. My services are available—but always at a cost.

True to his word, Winchell approached the gates at the stroke of twelve. "What say you, Bates?"

"Aye. I will do as you ask. But the cost is sixty guineas. Up front."

"Ridiculous—that's highway robbery!" "Perhaps, but there is something more I want."

Winchell's face blazed. "More, you cheeky bastard? What more could there be?"

"You must leave Baltimore. There can be no one to tie this deed back to me."

"You needn't worry about that, Bates. Once you have completed your duties, I will raid the coffers of The Winchell Fletcher Trading Company and disappear like smoke in the night. I will give you half the bounty now and the balance upon completion of your mission. You are experienced in these matters. Surely, you understand I would be a fool to pay you in full now, only to have you renege. That would never do. Are we agreed?"

"We are," I said, with a vigorous shake of his hand.

"Listen carefully. Fletcher is as round as a barrel and hasn't a hair on his head. He walks with a decided limp and carries a gold-tipped cane." He bit his lip and fidgeted with the cuff of his sleeve. "I do not wish to tell you how to do your business; however, I might make a small suggestion. He is as predictable as the moon. Each night, he stops at The Cork and Stein to wallow in his nightly bottle of scotch. When he leaves at closing, he stumbles down Alesford Alley toward his home on Beaumont Street. Alesford is dark and quite secluded," his voice softened, "the perfect place for misadventure.

Tomorrow night, report for your shift as usual. Slip from the burying grounds unnoticed and secret yourself in the alley before the tavern closes. Commit the deed and abscond under cover of night. No one will be the wiser. You have no ties to the man. With a modicum of care, you shall ne'er be discovered."

I nodded my approval.

"Good man," he said, clapping my shoulder. He placed the money in my hand. "I shall meet you here at the gates at 3 a.m., with the balance of your bounty. Until then." Winchell tipped his hat and walked away, fading like a phantom into the night. I finished my rounds and left the cemetery at shift's end to spend the day plotting the commission of my crime.

At one o'clock the following morning, I skulked, Barlow knife in hand, through the barren streets of Baltimore. The mouth of Alesford

Alley yawned like a bottomless abyss before me. I picked my way through a sea of garbage and inhaled a bitter blend of urine and vomit. A discarded stack of crates offered suitable concealment. Finally, Fletcher stumbled into the alley and wandered past my hiding place. I snatched him from behind, clamped my free hand over his mouth, and drove the blade deep into his back. He gurgled as his lungs filled with blood. Death took him quickly. I dropped his body in place and emptied his pockets as if he had been waylaid.

While scurrying from the scene, my heart near skipped a beat at the sight of a flickering light that danced at the end of the alley. The muffled sound of a child's cough caused me to sigh in relief. No doubt some guttersnipe warmed himself o'er a pile of smoldering tinder. I stifled a curse and chastised myself. *Every flicker becomes a ghost-light. Your nerves betray you, Nancyboy.*

I hurried back to the burying ground and counted the minutes until my meeting with Winchell. He did not arrive at three o'clock as agreed, and so, I continued to count the minutes until four. When still he had not arrived, my heart began to race. Having no recourse, I waited and watched the clock strike five. Winchell was nowhere to be found. I bellowed and shook the carriage gates is if to tear them asunder. Whence came six o'clock, the end of my shift, I traveled home both furious and baffled by his absence. Then I collapsed into bed where I tossed and turned until exhaustion claimed me.

I awakened to a knock upon my door. It was Constable Hightower. He questioned my whereabouts the previous evening. It seemed a local business man had been murdered in Alesford Alley.

I leaned against the doorjamb and yawned. "I was in the commission of my duties as watchman at Westminster Hall, as I am every night."

His eyes narrowed. "Perhaps you arrived for work but left during the night."

"I assure you, I did not. Why would you suggest such a thing?"

"It appears the criminal left behind some evidence." He swept past me into the parlor. "We found a handkerchief."

"And?"

"It bears the monogram, IMB. Ian Michael Bates. That is your name, is it not?"

"Yes, of course it is, but I have no embroidered handkerchiefs. They are far too costly. Clearly, this belongs to some other man who shares those same initials."

"I considered that myself, you see," said the constable, "until I saw your coat hanging on the banister. Its buttons are missing." I followed his eyes, first toward the coat, then down into the palm of his opened hand that held two buttons identical to those on my coat.

An ugly picture began to emerge. My teeth clenched as I recalled Winchell tearing at me from the grave, ripping those buttons free. The memory of handing him my handkerchief nearly brought me to my knees. The swine! He had likely paid some scullery maid to stitch my initials on my own handkerchief.

But why was Winchell set to frame me, when I could so easily point the finger of guilt to him? He must have had an accomplice. Someone had to bury him. But who? An even darker question lurked in the corner of my mind, a question too unsettling for thoughtful deliberation. Before I ever heard the ringing of that damnable bell, I had been lured toward Winchell's grave by the ghost lights. I believed them to be colleagues, if not allies. Might they have betrayed me and lured me to my doom? If so, they could rest assured I would not go quietly.

Once taken into custody, I sang like a canary, quick to implicate Winchell. I even took the constable to the cemetery and showed him Winchell's grave, but it now contained the body of a woman who had been buried more than two weeks past! Dear God! Had he displaced the poor woman's body for want of an open grave? Clearly, he reasoned I would hear the bell and dig him up. He must have returned the woman's body to the ground whilst I was dispatching Fletcher. Such depravity eluded even me.

Unwilling to yield, I demanded that the constable investigate The Winchell Fletcher Trading Company. To my dismay, he found no record of either Angus Winchell or such a company having ever existed in Baltimore. Malcolm Fletcher, the man I murdered, had been the owner of a local milling operation.

"Impossible!" I screamed, punching a hole in the wall of my cell. Who was this monster that so sorely fixed my fate? Why had he driven me to murder?

I dropped to my knees, baffled and beaten, certain only of having been duped. Humiliation haunted me, but curiosity consumed me. What had this demon gained from his manipulations? It occurred to me that I may never know. Therein lay madness.

As if the nails in my coffin were insufficient, at trial, Fletcher's wife, Madilyn, a winsome woman with a heart-shaped face, drowned the judge with tears from her emerald eyes. Other than my testimony, I had little by way of defense. The court's decision came quickly and without mercy.

Thus, it comes to pass in this eleventh hour that I, a dead man walking, still grasp for the answer to this gruesome riddle.

The sun has yet to rise and already an angry mob demands its pound of flesh. I climb the gallows' steps to oblige them. From atop the platform, I scan the sea of faces on the ground below, finding not a benevolent soul among them.

But he is there, the monster I knew as Winchell, standing among the horde. His eyes lock with mine; a wicked grin consumes his face. He turns to the woman beside him and brushes his lips against her hair. She tilts her head upward, triumph beaming from her heart-shaped face. It is Mrs. Fletcher; her emerald eyes no longer brimming with tears as they had in court but with forbidden love for the man at her side.

The irony is sweet. I, the instrument of their duplicity, will swing alone.

As the noose slips over my head, I catch a fleeting glimpse of the will-o'-the-wisps migrating through the early morning fog; their tiny flickers burning brighter, closer. They come to claim my blackened soul, for God above will not.

The trap door opens and at the snap of the rope, I am transformed. I no longer fear the wrath of Gideon's sword. I no longer seek the solace of shadows in my cell.

I am a lambent light seen from the corner of the eye, a flickering harbinger of doom, waiting for the cur who ruined me to breathe his last. He will see my flame glowing in the distance, coming ever closer, blazing ever hotter until it swallows him whole. And I will revel as I descend into the bowels of hell, dragging his wretched soul behind me—for vengeance will be mine.

H.R. Boldwood, a Pushcart Prize nominee, was awarded the 2009 Bilbo Award for creative writing by Thomas More College. Publication credits include, *Bete Noir*, *Toys in the Attic*, *Floppy Shoes Apocalypse II*, *Pilcrow and Dagger*, and *Sirens Call*. Boldwood's characters are often disreputable and not to be trusted. No responsibility is taken by this author for the dastardly and sometimes criminal acts committed by this ragtag group of miscreants.

Nosophoros

Christine Lucas

Damned cockroaches would conquer space alongside mankind.

Every time that thought crossed her mind, Anna Mathews felt tempted to shred her diploma in genetic engineering and flee the Earth Central Research Station. She checked the latest results. The skin cells with the recombined DNA resisted radiation but were still sensitive to intense heat. She leaned back in her chair, her heart heavy and her neck aching. In the dark corners of her mind, a huge, black cockroach clicked its mandibles, mocking her.

She glanced through the observation window. Major Hazelwood lay on the narrow bed inside the scan chamber, his face calm, his pulse and breathing steady. Anna turned on the speaker. "Just a few more minutes, Major."

Astronaut John Hazelwood, her test subject: tall, fair, handsome, father to a six-year-old boy. Also a volunteer for the New Human Project and the first of his species with human-cockroach recombined DNA—the first to survive this long. Back on Earth, there had been other subjects; common folk—starving folk—signing up for a meal and a roof over their heads. All dead now, their files sealed, accessible only to those who needed to know. Anna didn't *want* to know.

Hazelwood looked up and flashed his perfect smile at her. "Okay, Doc."

Her skin prickled. She'd never go back dirtside.

Anna had been born in the slums of Earth where the damned bugs roamed freely everywhere, driving rats out of their holes and pigeons from their nests. Brown, black, some winged, some not, small and big, the cockroaches thrived in the aftermath of the 21st-century nuclear fallout. They had adapted much faster than humans, and no pesticide had proved effective for long.

The computer printed another test result: the bone marrow cells showed some minor irregularities, mostly in shape. Otherwise, they were normal with the added bonus of increased resistance to radiation.

Damned bugs.

Anna's childhood memories crawled with cockroaches, ever-present, ever-hungry. They scurried along her pillow when she opened her eyes in the morning, their bites haunted her sleep. She'd find their cooked corpses in her food and their nests in the pockets of her clothes. Often she'd dream of them, legions of black critters crawling all around her, on walls, floors, up her limbs and over her face, disease-bearers, and harbingers of death.

And Earth Central had assigned her this particular project. No way to get out of it now.

Anna clenched her jaw. She had worked hard to get out of the slums—even lied in her application where it asked about phobias. She had kept the whispers in her head a secret, the chirping of countless bugs inside the folds of her brain, their voices louder after every little bite on her arms and legs. The Earth Central Space Station orbiting their radiated, bug-infested planet was sterile and pest-free—until now. Damned bugs had found their way here, even in DNA form.

On the wall over the main computer screen, a lab tech had placed the reprint of a famous 21st-century painting: the image of a distorted, monstrous cockroach, flashing a crooked human smile and yellow vampire fangs, slouching through a street littered with gutted corpses. The artist had titled his work *Nosophoros*, the Greek word for disease-bearer. Anna shuddered. How fitting.

She sipped her bitter, tepid coffee, instinctively checking her cup for floating bugs, and willed the disturbing image to the edge of her consciousness. She checked Hazelwood's vitals on the screen: all values within normal range. The deep tissue scan was almost over. She turned the speaker on again.

"Almost there, Major. I'll be with you in a minute."

He nodded without looking up.

Anna doubted he had been told the specifics of the project. No sane person would agree to *that*, but she wouldn't be the one to tell him. There were other volunteers subjected to different combinations. Other creatures had been found resistant to radiation and heat: some types of bacteria, as well as the tardigrades, the tiny bugs commonly known as water bears.

And she had been assigned to the damned bugs.

Green light flashed, and the system unlocked the door to the scan chamber. Anna picked up Hazelwood's chart and entered.

"So, Doc, what's the verdict?" He sat up, the perfection of his face marred by tiny wrinkles of worry around his mouth. "Everything okay?"

You have roach DNA in you. She flipped through the pages. "Yes, although this is uncharted territory for all of us. Your bone marrow and skin cells react as expected." The tests showed the presence of new elements in his bloodstream, mostly immunoglobulins, but no need to alarm him until she knew more. "Anything to report? How have you been sleeping? How's your appetite?"

"I sleep like a baby. But I'm hungry all the time." He frowned. "I also dream of food a lot."

A swarm of roaches cleaning the meat off a dead dog's bones within minutes.

Anna ignored the disturbing image in her mind, struggling to keep her face straight. "That's normal. Your body needs the extra energy to cope with the changes."

"Okay. Any estimation how much longer until we're done?"

Oh boy. "Why?"

He looked away, the dimples in his cheeks adding to his boyish expression. "My son has been authorized for a visit. I know this goes against protocol, but it's my boy's sixth birthday. I haven't seen him since he was three—since his mother…" He looked away. "I'd like to see him, and not through a glass wall."

"You've checked with your commanding officer?"

"He said it's up to you. As long as it doesn't compromise the project…" His voice trailed off, a note of longing lingering in the air.

She clutched the chart on her chest. "I'll see what I can do."

The cockroach inside her head hatched a black, quivering egg and scurried away.

Even the soft light of the station's cafeteria hurt her tired eyes. Anna removed her glasses and rubbed her temples. She should have denied Hazelwood's request on the spot.

Damn that smile!

When she was younger, fresh out of the academy, she had hoped that one day her husband would look like him. Twenty years later, she had come to accept that astronauts didn't date lab rats. Even if lab rats hooked up, usually with someone of the same caste, those assigned to space stations didn't get breeding permits. Their genes had been exposed to too much radiation.

He had a son. What did she have?

Inside her mind, the cockroach egg throbbed, ready to burst. She sipped her iced tea to wash down the bitter taste in her mouth and nibbled her pie. Space had proven a harder environment than mankind had ever guessed. Low gravity gnawed away their bones, radiation burned their gonads, and the unfathomable emptiness between stars claimed their sanity. *Perhaps we shouldn't be out here.*

The roach egg at the back of her mind burst, and countless little bugs emerged, scurrying all over the walls of her skull, creeping between her meninges, crawling around the folds of her brain, fleeing through her ventricular system into her spine. She hid her face in her palms, resisting the urge to start banging her head against the table.

"Dr. Mathews? Are you all right?"

The familiar voice scattered the baby roaches into the depths of her unconscious mind. She looked up at the balding head towering over her.

"Dr. Delamora?" She put on her glasses, her fingers shaking. His team worked on the tardigrade DNA. Concern furrowed his brow over his bespectacled eyes. "Thank you, I'm fine. Just a bad headache." She managed a weary smile. "Too much caffeine, not enough sleep."

"I can relate." He smiled back, his skin stretching over the angles of his ascetic face.

"I-I need to return to my work." She started gathering her charts and notes.

"A moment of your time, please?" Without asking her permission, he sat on the empty chair next to her.

"Okay."

"Everything going well with your part of the project?"

"Fine so far. Why?"

"How can I say this?" He looked away, tracing spirals on the immaculate surface of the table, the nail of his index finger visibly chewed. "The tardigrade project has encountered certain…problems. I'd like your professional opinion." He pushed his glasses up on his nose. "Will you walk with me?"

"Sure."

Anna followed him to a lab similar to her own, her curiosity piqued. They passed the analysis area, where bored assistants monitored the results of scans and tests of various biological fluids. Blood cells, skin cells, and sperm were checked on a daily basis under extreme conditions of radiation, heat, and cold. She tried to get a sneak peek of the results, but he picked up his pace. In less than a minute, they reached the living quarters of the test subject, and Dr. Delamora led Anna to the observation room. When he turned the monitor on, she almost dropped her notes.

"Meet Captain Michael Brown, twenty-nine years old, first of his class in the Space academy." Bitterness edged Delamora's voice.

Anna leaned closer to the screen. That man sitting at the edge of the narrow bed couldn't be in his late twenties. He could very well be one of those ancient mummies she'd seen in documentaries—a *breathing* mummy staring back at her. His skin had an ashen shade, and his head resembled a skull too much for her comfort. His white overalls hung on him as though made for a man twice his size. The monitor displayed lowered vitals; pulse, respiration and blood pressure were just a notch over critical. Still, his ECG waves were close to normal.

She shuddered. That unfortunate man was fully aware of his condition.

"We cannot keep him hydrated." Dr. Delamora shoved his hands in his pockets. "His skin loses moisture faster than he can replace it through his digestive system, and intravenous infusion cannot exceed a certain limit without compromising renal function. The only time he maintains a minimal level of hydration is inside a full bathtub."

"Like the tardigrades," Anna whispered.

"It would seem so. However, his skin cells show rapid deterioration. Apparently, they cannot adapt fast enough to the increased moisture exchange. We have reached the conclusion that this hybrid is not suitable for interstellar travel." He cleared his throat. "He is not viable at all."

Inside Anna's head, a swarm of roaches laughed hysterically.

She avoided eye contact. "What do you want from me?"

"Protocol dictates that the decision for subject termination must be brought to vote before the Chief Engineers' committee. I'd like your support."

She blinked. "You want to kill him?"

"He'll die anyway. We'll just end his suffering."

She straightened her shoulders. "Has he been told?"

"At his condition, he's incapable of rational thought. Terminating him *is* the humane approach."

Her fingers tingled, and she resisted the urge to punch him. "I will not consent to murder. Inform him of his choices first, and then you might get my vote." She headed out without looking back.

On her way to her lab, Anna authorized Major Hazelwood's family visit.

Anna watched her subject and his son until her stomach knotted up. She'd never have this. After the boy's departure, though, Major Hazelwood showed increased levels of anxiety. He slept little, spoke little and paced the length of his quarters over and over again, day and night.

Allowing the visit was a mistake. Then the image of Dr. Delamora's unfortunate subject sprang to her mind. Preserving some level of Hazelwood's humanity couldn't be a mistake. She glanced at the latest results: thicker skin, rad-resistant bone marrow and blood cells, elevated adrenaline levels. Nothing abnormal, given the circumstances.

Right?

Much to her relief, the bugs inside her head kept their distance and silence. She picked up the chart, put on her blank, professional face and knocked on his door. She found him doing sit-ups on the floor, wearing only his underpants.

"Good morning, Major." *You're not sixteen. Focus.* She managed to keep her gaze on his face.

"This is a space station. There's no day and night." His dry tone only added to her uneasiness.

"Right." A pair of roach antennas waved out of the shadows of her mind. "So, how are you feeling today?"

"Is this a joke?" He stopped and sat up, resting his elbows on his knees, his blue eyes cold and mirthless. "You keep me locked in this fucking room! How do you think I'm feeling?"

Instinctively, she took a step backward, clutching the chart on her chest.

He brought his fist down on the floor. "I want out! I want to run, eat real food, and play ball with my boy!"

"Perhaps we can arrange another visit. You had a good time, right?"

"Right." He looked away, his jugular pulsating wildly in his neck. He breathed in, his struggle to maintain his self-control evident in every muscle of his body. "Forgive my outburst, Doc. The visit was too short. I miss him. And I'm not sleeping well."

Focus. "I see."

"And I have these weird dreams."

She gulped, his musky scent too close, his almost naked body too hard to ignore. "What sort of dreams?"

"Cockroaches, whole swarms of them."

His words chilled her more than any cold shower could. She forced her voice to remain steady and her face blank. "Yes, that's weird."

"Why would I dream of *bugs*? They've never scared me. When I was a kid, I had fun stomping on them."

Crime and punishment. Inside her head, the cockroach stood still, its antennas barely wavering, as if monitoring the exchange.

"I'll prescribe a mild sedative." She made a note on the chart. "It will help you sleep better."

"Thanks, Doc." This time, he smiled.

She nodded and hurried out of the room. Her throat burned, and she went in search of a cold drink.

Her chief assistant found her by the beverage dispenser in the empty cafeteria. Droplets of sweat crowned his forehead, and his frown promised nothing good.

"Dr. Mathews? I have some bad news."

What a surprise. "Something wrong in the test results?"

He shook his head. "No, everything is within acceptable limits—so far."

"Meaning?"

"The health officer of the dirtside terminal just sent us a contamination alert." He wiped his forehead with a crumpled tissue and shoved a paper in her face. "Our subject's son has the flu. The symptoms manifested during the flight home."

"What?" She snatched the paper from his trembling hand. That meant the boy was an asymptomatic carrier during his stay on the station. "We scanned him on arrival, right?"

"Yes, but apparently it's a new viral strain. Our scanner's software just received the update."

"How bad is it?"

"The usual: sore throat, low fever, the sniffles, perhaps some chest complications for normal humans. But there's no telling how our subject will react. The viral DNA might not interfere with the recombined DNA at all."

Did roaches catch colds? "He has elevated adrenaline levels, right? Perhaps that will boost his immune system enough to ward off the virus." She eyed the beverage dispenser. A beer would be *so* good now. Or a shot of tequila. Instead, she pushed the button for a lime soda.

"I read an article on a new anti-viral drug that—"

"No," she cut him off. "Anti-viral drugs rarely help with the flu, and their side-effects aren't worth the risk in this case. Pack him with vitamins and monitor his vitals more closely. If he as much as sneezes, call me, day or night. Is this understood?"

He nodded and trailed off. Anna watched his hurried walk down the hallway until he vanished through the sliding doors. Only then did she collapse on a chair, her head throbbing.

The eerie silence of the roaches inside her head couldn't be good.

Anna didn't get much sleep over the next few days. Major Hazelwood eventually developed flu symptoms: low fever, joint ache, and conjunctivitis. Nothing alarming in itself, only those symptoms were accompanied by escalating mental and emotional aggravation. His nightmares worsened, his fits of rage became more violent and frequent, and his appetite waxed to ravenous levels.

She glanced at the observation screen. He had been pacing the length of the room for two hours straight now, his eyes wild, his fists clenched. Her stomach knotted up.

The latest analysis results didn't shed any light. She flipped through pages and pages of printed material. The chemicals in his feces were probably the result of his digestive tract adjusting to his new DNA—cockroaches excreted similar substances. Same with his newly developed photosensitivity. She leaned back in her chair, her mind racing. Could this explain her own reaction around him? How her pulse quickened, how she blushed like a schoolgirl every time he looked at her? Cockroaches emitted airborne pheromones to attract mates.

Lovely. The roach inside her head snickered. *Go to hell.*

When she checked the screen again, Hazelwood sat at the foot of his narrow bed, his shoulders slumped, his face in his palms. Good grief, was he crying? Subjects often experienced breakdowns after increased periods of stress. Anna sprang to her feet, turned off the screen and hurried to his quarters through the deserted lab area.

The silence crushed her chest. She had sent all her exhausted assistants to get a good night's sleep, taking over the night shift. She couldn't sleep anyway. Her nights crawled with roaches.

It was dark inside his quarters. The light through the open door outlined the furniture and his hunched form. She clenched her teeth. *You cannot hug him. You cannot kiss his cheek. You cannot smell his hair.*

"Dr. Mathews." Neither a question nor a statement. An invitation.

"A-are you okay?" She cursed her girlish stuttering.

He looked up. "It's all clear now." She heard the smile in his tone. He offered her his hand. "Please, don't stand there. Am I that intimidating?"

Yes. "No, of course not." Her voice rang less steady than she'd hoped. She shifted her weight from one leg to the other.

"Come sit with me. We need to talk." He patted the bed right next to him. A cold edge lined his soft voice.

She glanced over her shoulder. "Perhaps I should call a med tech. You sound troubled."

"You'll do no such thing. I need *you*. Please?"

"I'll call in a tech to do some tests—"

"No more tests." His voice hardened. "I know what you did to me."

She bit her lip. "You do?"

He patted the bed again, his voice softer now. "Please."

"Very well." *Walk slowly. Step lightly. Don't anger him.* The door closed behind her, and butterflies fluttered in her stomach—no, not butterflies but huge, winged roaches. Tasting bile, she pulled a chair and sat facing him.

"I *do* scare you, then." He leaned forward, his gaze burning her face, his scent intoxicating.

"No." Yes. She gulped. *It's the pheromones—just a chemical reaction. You are stronger than this.* She met his gaze. "What do you think we did to you?"

"I don't think. I know." He chuckled. "The cockroaches in my dreams have told me everything." He tapped his right temple. "They're with me now, in sleep and waking. And they've told me interesting things about you too."

"Wh-what?"

"They speak to you too. They have chosen you."

The blood drained from her face. *Cockroach DNA.* The memory of countless bites from her childhood prickled her skin from head to toe. Was that what the bugs had been doing? Injecting their genetic material in her, bite after bite? Tasting bile, she started to get up, but his hands grabbed her knees and forced her back down.

"*Sit.*"

"Major, you need—"

"Shut up!" His grip tightened. "You've made me less than a man but more than a bug."

"Pl-please, I-I—"

He grabbed the sides of the chair and pulled her closer. "I said, *shut up*. You'll finish what you've started." His knuckles brushed her cheek, his body heat too close, his scent highwiring her resolve.

Please, stop! She pressed her legs together until her muscles hurt. "No." *Yes. No. Yes.*

"Yes."

"No!" She pushed him back and sprang to her feet.

He was faster. She had barely turned around when he caught her wrist and pulled her down, pinning her to the floor.

"No!" She struggled under him, trying to knee his groin. He was stronger.

He sniffed her face, grinning. "No? I can smell it. Your body says otherwise."

"I'll scream."

"No, you won't." Another sound came from his throat, a low chirp that made her skin crawl.

Inside her head, the cockroach came forth, chirping back.

"Yes?"

Anna said nothing. She couldn't—only wept.

He licked off her tears.

No one will believe me.

She scrubbed harder, to cleanse her body from his foul smell. Even if they did, he was more valuable to the project than she was. They'd send her back dirtside, and get someone else to complete the project.

Crouched inside the shower, she hid her head under her arms.

The camera had recorded only blurry images and muffled sounds. He could always argue consent. They'd dump her to the bug-infested planet and send him to the stars. The flow of water ceased, having reached its five-minute limit.

Inside her head, a pile of throbbing roach eggs awaited. Fiery jolts of pain made her womb contract. She shivered. Blood tests were pointless. The bastard had passed on his new DNA.

And she was carrying his brood.

Anna shuddered anew, chill added to her terror now. She couldn't let the fucking bugs win. Abortion was not an option—no facilities aboard and too many questions to answer. And he could always find another candidate.

She grasped the shower's door handle and pulled herself up. She had no firearm experience, even if she could find one. He'd disarm her in a blink. Poison? The labs were packed with toxic substances. But they were also packed with antidotes and trained technicians. She needed something faster.

Her skin welcomed the warmth of the bathrobe. Her soul would never find warmth again.

Warmth. Fire.

Her mind raced. She sat at the edge of the bed, mechanically combing her wet hair. She couldn't get hold of a lighter nor an accelerant without raising suspicions. Unless…some explosives weren't hard to cook. She tossed the comb aside and called in sick for the next few days, blaming the new flu strain for her absence.

That night, she dreamed of two roaches fighting. The victor dined on the corpse of its fallen enemy.

Two days later, Anna sat in the cafeteria, enjoying a beer and their biggest hamburger—loaded with carbs, fat, and cholesterol. She licked her greasy fingers and grinned, aware of the curious and disapproving stares of her colleagues. But she had reason to celebrate.

It had been *so* easy. The labs carried all the ingredients she needed: nitric acid, sulfuric acid, and glycerin. She snatched a pinch from here, an ounce from there, while politely checking on their projects and making small talk. Mixing them in the privacy of her room was trickier, but she managed without blowing herself up. Sipping her beer, with the deadly vial of nitroglycerin resting in her coat's chest pocket, Anna waited for the station's personnel to turn in for the night. Hopefully, the blast doors would close and isolate the living quarters. Even if they didn't, all wars had casualties.

Inside her head, the roach eggs still throbbed, but hadn't burst. The little monsters hadn't come out of the shadows since her rape.

During her hunt for glycerin, she had visited Dr. Delamora's lab. His proposal for his first subject's termination had been outvoted. Now the unfortunate captain spent his days in a water tank, swimming back and forth, his emaciated body barely resembling his former self. His eyes, dark and bulging in his thin face, watched everything without any hint of emotion. Still, when she walked by the cell housing his tank, something gripped her mind: a few words, loud and clear inside her skull.

Don't let this happen to anyone else.

She'd never know if the recombined DNA made him a telepath, or if this was how tardigrades had been communicating all along.

His words had steeled her resolve. When the last person left the cafeteria, she drew in a sharp breath and walked down the corridor to her lab. She had only the night tech to deal with but expected no trouble there.

The observation station was empty. Terror gripped her heart. Had he seduced another woman? She reached for the switch, her fingers shaking, and turned the screen on. Half a heartbeat later, she wished she hadn't.

Oh God. Oh God.

Her last supper threatened to come right out. On the observation monitor, Major Hazelwood crouched over the still body of the night tech.

Cockroaches were cannibals. How had they overlooked that? He looked up at the camera, his face covered in blood, a strip of flesh between his teeth. His grin loosened her bladder. She sought the support of the chair, her vision blurry.

Breathe. Breathe. Finish it.

She glanced at the grotesque image on the wall, the distorted body of the grinning roach. *Nosophoros: disease-bearer.* The bug inside her head came forth, chuckling. Others followed, a legion of black forms, crawling out of the folds of her brain.

I will not help this plague to reach the stars.

She turned on the terminal and accessed all the New Human Project files she could, deleting everything. Once finished, she stood upright, squared her shoulders and straightened her lab coat. With her head high, she made her way to his quarters. The doors slid open, and the sickening sound of teeth on bone welcomed her. He looked up, blood dripping from his chin.

"Hello, honey." He raised a thigh bone. "I'll share. Come on in."

"Murderer."

He shrugged. "As you wish." He broke the bone in half and slurped the marrow. "It's good. In your condition, you need all the nutrients you can get."

"Bastard." Before he could say one word, she turned on all the lights.

He cried out and covered his eyes. "Turn them off!" He slouched to the far wall, covering his head with his arms. "It hurts! Turn it off!"

"No." She stepped in, walking around the gutted corpse and the blood. "I've brought you a present…honey."

He peeked between his arms. "You did what?"

"Your brood will not reach the stars—not if I can help it."

"It's too late, honey." He grinned. "We're already there."

"It ends here." She took out the vial and held it to the light. "Nitroglycerine, enough to blow a hole in this part of the station."

His face twisted. "Bitch!" He lunged at her.

Inside her head, the roaches screamed.

Anna dropped the vial.

Christine Lucas lives in Greece with her husband and a horde of spoiled animals. A retired Air Force officer and mostly self-taught in English, she has had her work appear in several print and online magazines, including the *Other Half of the Sky* anthology, *Daily Science Fiction*, and *Space and Time Magazine*. She is currently working on her first novel, and in her free time she reads slush for ASIM.

What the Rain Brings

Gerri Leen

I slammed the door shut, closing us off from the drenching rain.

"It's out there." Vadner paced in the shelter with the never-ending energy of someone trying to pretend he was not very, very spooked. "Why the hell did Gideon send us here?"

"Nothing's out there but the woods," I said as I poured fresh water into our cooler. "And Gideon sent us here because this planet is what he wants surveyed."

"Not that he'd tell *us* that." Calla ran her hand over her close-cropped hair. "You're the only one he ever talks to."

"That's because I'm in charge, and he's an elitist." I tried to move past them, but Vadner put his hand on my arm.

"There's something out there, Meilan." Vadner looked over at

Calla. "Tell her it's out there."

Calla stared hard at the door, as if she could see through it if she just looked long enough. "Vadner can feel it. He tested high in psi."

I tried not to laugh. "If Vadner has any psi ability, then why didn't he give us an inclement weather warning?"

"I can feel it, too," Calla said.

She was full of feelings, all right, most of them for Vadner. It was against regs for teammates to have an affair, but that didn't stop them. Not that I was going to report my mission mates. I'd been young once, too, young and in love with life and adventure and the man in the next bunk. But that had been a long time ago.

"There is nothing out there." I walked away from the door, away from the rain, which, unexpected as it was, was normal rain—healing rain that would bring precious moisture to the plants keeping us alive while we were on this planet. It would fill the rain barrel on our roof, so we could take baths again, and make the stream flow strong—the stream that I'd dipped our container into just a few minutes ago so we could make pot after pot of tea to keep us company as we wrote up our survey reports. Or as I sat doing that, and my two hormone-crazed teammates stole away to the back bunk and tried to be quiet as they had sex.

The rain was normal. The animals that had gone silent outside our little habitat ever since the downpour started were behaving normally—birds rarely sang during a rainstorm on Earth, either.

"I think we brought it with us." Calla looked at me, then at Vadner, who'd been saying the same thing for days, even though he'd packed half our containers himself. "Meilan, there's something out there. And maybe we let it out."

"There's nothing out there." I strode back to the door, pushing Calla off as she tried to stop me.

"Don't!" Vadner tried to get to me before I could open the door.

I yanked it open and breathed in the damp air. "See. Nothing." I shut the door gently. "Just...rain."

Even though I'd only had the door open for a few moments, I

felt a pang as the outside world was cut off from me. The rich, loamy smell of the forest filled the room, and I wanted to go outside. I wanted to play in the mud the way I had as a kid. I wanted to enjoy myself and not let my two colleagues make me as nervous as they were.

I'd been young once, had gotten the jitters back then, too. But I was the Foundation team lead on this project, and Gideon Morales wasn't paying me to surrender to a bad case of the creeps.

"Get back to work," I said firmly but gently, the way you'd talk to a skittish pup.

They both just stared at me.

I let my tone dip into something less friendly. "What part of that was unclear?"

They went to their workstations, but they looked a long way from happy.

"So how are you holding up?" Gideon's image flickered badly, and I tried to boost the signal. "Meilan?"

"I can hear you, but I can't see you." I fiddled with the dials some more, finally bringing in a decent picture for a moment.

"Some people would consider that a blessing." Gideon smiled the crooked grin that made the rest of his face go even more cockeyed than it already was. He wasn't ugly…exactly. But his wasn't the kind of face anyone pushed products with.

But I liked his looks—or else I'd just grown used to them. "You know I don't think that." I glanced up at him from the control panel and saw him grin again.

Gideon liked me, for reasons known only to himself because he didn't seem to like his other team chiefs or the line surveyors. Despite what I'd said to Vadner, Gideon wasn't really elitist—he was downright antisocial. In fact, he gave some folks what I'd heard called by the highly technical term of the "willies."

"So? *Are* you holding up?" Gideon was messing with something on his desk as he asked, glancing up occasionally to make sure I was still there.

"I am. But I'm not too sure about the junior league." Sighing, I leaned closer, shifted my voice down a bit. "Why did we pick them?" Actually, we hadn't—he had.

"They're just young."

"They're pains in the ass. My ass, specifically."

"They're having an affair, aren't they? I didn't think you would mind that."

"You knew?"

"I suspected." Gideon laughed at my expression. "I'm in charge of surveys for a reason—I used to be in the field, too."

"I know. You were a legend. And there's not much you miss."

"I remember a Ms. Meilan Liu being linked with a few surveyors who will go unnamed. We've all done it."

"In our youth."

"You're not that old, Meilan. What's really bothering you?"

I sighed. "This rain is making it harder to work."

"I thought you liked mud baths?" He grinned, the teasing way he did whenever I went to one of my spas—or told him about a mud hole I'd made to soak in on a survey.

"For the newbies, not for me."

"They'll learn. And you can catch up on reports. Rest. It'll stop."

"The voice of experience?"

"I lived in the tropics for years. The rainy season is just that: a season."

"This doesn't feel like a season, Gideon." I hated to start sounding like Vadner, but I plowed on ahead. Despite what I'd said to Calla, there was something that seemed…off. "There's something kind of…deliberate about this rain."

"Deliberate rain? Does someone have a weather machine?" He was definitely laughing at me.

"You know what I mean."

"Actually, I don't. Is the rain bothering you?"

"Not bothering, precisely." I wasn't bothered; I wanted to go out and play in it. "It's appealing."

"Well, grab an umbrella and go dance in it."

"Very funny." I glared at him. "Shall we get to work?"

"Please. Before the deliberate rain cuts our connection." He laughed again.

I ignored him as I transmitted the data we'd gathered so far.

He read for a while, then nodded. "Good stuff, Mei." He was the only one who called me that.

"I know. It's an incredible planet to survey. I can't believe no one's been here before." Pulling the data stick from the machine, I reattached it to the portable scanner. "So, I'll talk to you again in a few days?"

"Sounds good."

I looked up, saw that he was smiling at me in an oddly tender way. "What?"

"I guess I miss you." Every now and then he got sentimental—it always surprised me.

"Well, someone should miss me. Might as well be you." Winking at him, I cut the connection.

"Do you believe in ghosts?" Calla asked softly as we scrunched through the mud.

"I don't know."

"Come on. You either do or you don't." She bent down, collecting a specimen of fungus that we hadn't noticed before the rain started.

"Well, I've never seen a ghost, so I suppose I don't. But I'd hate to rule them out entirely." Scooping up some mud, I ran it through the analyzer. There were some interesting new minerals that had not been present before. Maybe carried by the rain falling to the planet's surface from the atmosphere? Or had they been in a substrata that would not mix with the top layer until they merged in this thick soup the rain was making?

We'd given up on waiting for the rain to stop. I was glad to be out of the house.

"You like the rain?" Calla pushed her rain hat up a little, watching as I fingered my hair, which was sodden now because I wasn't wearing my hat. "You're having fun?"

"Doesn't it feel good to you?"

"Well, it's not cold, at least." Moving past me, she walked down what used to be a nice path and now was a mudslide waiting to happen.

"Be careful."

"Don't worry." Calla slid a little at the bottom but managed to stay on her feet.

I took one step and lost my footing, landing on my rear and sliding all the way down. I struggled to my feet and brushed the mud off my waterproof pants, then rubbed what I couldn't shake off my palms right back onto them. I didn't worry much about it—I'd spent my childhood covered in the stuff.

"Still liking it?" Calla asked with a grin.

"Even dirty, I'm still your superior officer." I looked back at the small hill. "Except in navigating downhill mud courses."

We walked in an easy silence for a while. Then I asked, "Vadner still upset?"

"He's not upset. He's worried." She shot me a glance, as if wondering how many demerits their nerves were earning them.

I kept my expression even. "Freaked is more like it."

"Don't you feel it, Meilan? It's…it's creepy here."

I noticed she was wearing a cross. "Have you been wearing this the whole time?" I reached to touch it, and she pulled away.

"You'll get mud on it." Looking down, she said softly, "My mother gave it to me before I left. Said in case I needed a little extra looking after. And lately, I've felt like maybe I do."

"I remember how it is when you're new at this. Being so far from home. And at the mercy of a planet we don't completely understand."

She looked down and nodded.

"I think Vadner is transferring his jitters to you." I laughed softly, trying to show her I wasn't worried about their relationship. "Long-time couples can do that."

"Long-time?" She saw my look and said, "We've only been together since this mission started."

"You didn't date while you were assigned to Earth?"

"No. I'd never even really talked to him. I saw him in the halls all the time, but I didn't know him at all."

Why had Gideon thought they'd been together?

"Have you ever...?" She waited, her grin making it clear what she was asking.

"With a teammate? Never." I let myself smile. It felt good to let down, to pretend I wasn't the boss and she wasn't my high-strung subordinate.

Laughing, she turned and led the way further down the trail. "The mud smelled funny back there," she said.

I sniffed and could smell the mud still on me. It did have a strange odor. "Probably the minerals I was reading." Sulfur, maybe?

"You're going to need a bath."

"Good thing we have rainwater in that tank, then, isn't it?"

Casting a glance back, she shook her head. She turned, scanning the woods with eyes that had proven surprisingly sharp in the past. She was especially good with fungus and lichens.

"What's that?" Smiling in an anticipatory way, she left the path, working her way through the mud to what looked like a large mushroom lying half buried.

"Have fun," I said, walking on a bit to an interesting bromeliad-type plant.

"Oh, God." I heard her splashing, then felt her bump up against me.

"What's wrong?"

"It's...a body." Calla turned; her face had gone ghastly white under her rain hat. "And I think it's human."

"The remains are human," Vadner said as he finished wrapping

What the Rain Brings

the body onto a tarp-lined sled.

"You're kidding."

"I wish I were." He shoved his scanner under my nose.

Grabbing it, I moved it down so I could take in the readings. He was right—the body was human. I'd excavated too many failed settlements to not recognize the combination of elements.

Our eyes met; his were triumphant. And more than a little scared.

"What are the odds?" he whispered, before turning to pull the sled up the hill and back to our shelter.

Calla hurried to help him, leaving me alone in the rain. I turned, ready to follow when I saw something buried where he'd had the sled parked. Crouching down, I pulled something metal out of the mud. I held it in the rain, the falling water taking a long time to clean off the mud. But not so long that I couldn't tell what I was holding before it was completely clean.

The insignia of the Foundation. Of the Surveyor Corps. The kind that would have been on a uniform, or maybe a pack-all. The dark durabronze that had blended in with the mud was dull now, but it had probably been shiny once.

"Meilan, did you find something else?" Calla stood at the top of the hill.

In my crouched position, I was half hidden by ferns. "Yes, I found—"

Don't tell.

"You found what?"

Pocketing the insignia, I pushed myself up. "I found that this rain isn't as fun as I thought. Wait up."

They didn't need to know about this. It would only panic them more.

I climbed easily up the hill, expecting to slip, but the mud seemed harder, more forgiving than it had on the way back down.

"What was a human doing here, Meilan?" Calla's expression was cold, as if she thought I knew something that she needed to hear.

"How would I know? This is uncharted territory." I took a deep breath. "Look, it's entirely possible someone found this world and was using it as a base of some kind."

"Not just one someone. At least two. This human and whoever killed him."

"We don't know that anyone killed this person."

"You think he just fell down in the middle of the forest. Plop—I'm dead?"

"It's possible. Heart attack, stroke, aneurysm—falling coconuts, maybe?" We'd joked that the huge, heavy fruit of this world's version of the palm tree could be lethal if it fell on you. "And why do you think it was a male?"

She stared ahead, where Vadner tugged the sled along. "I don't know. Bigger, denser bones, maybe. Just…seemed male to me."

I stuck my hand in my pocket, flesh hitting the metal of the insignia. Even if it had been a surveyor, it was still possible that he—I, too, wanted to call the remains male—had died of entirely natural, if unfortunate, causes.

Only…why would a surveyor be here at all? Gideon had said that this planet had never been surveyed. A mission had been planned ten years ago, but the ship had run into a bad radiation storm. The mission had been scrapped when two of the three team members had died during their repair attempt. For some reason, the planet had languished on the backlist of places to survey. I'd have to ask Gideon why the next time I talked to him. Sitting in his office, listening to the story, it had seemed entirely reasonable to think this world could be pushed to the back burner. But now, being here, cataloging the riches, it seemed odd that no one had been in a rush to return.

"How much research did you do on this sector?" I asked Calla.

"Not much. I was just glad to have a job." She looked startled, as if she hadn't intended to say that.

"What do you mean?"

"The last mission I was on. It was to M-41 Gamma."

I shrugged—there were too many missions, too many teams, for me to know them all.

"It was a dark world."

"Oh." I hated those. Planets of nightmare, even if there was nothing frightening about the places other than that they never saw the sun.

"M-41 Beta is a gas giant. It blocks Gamma from ever getting light."

"How long were you there?"

"Apparently too long." Calla looked down, and I noticed she was clenching her fists. "I'm okay now, though. All better and back in the saddle, thanks to Lucky Gideon."

He hated that nickname. Hated being reminded that he'd survived more than his fair share of missions gone terribly south when his crewmates had not been so fortunate. But some people were like that. They just seemed to weather crises or environments that could send others—like Calla—screaming for the nearest padded room.

"You're looking at me differently now, aren't you?"

"We all have difficult times. This job…it's hard." I tried to make my smile open. Non-judgmental.

I could understand why Gideon had selected Calla. As odd as he was, he loved to back the underdog. But why hadn't he told me? As team chief, I had a right to know I was traveling with someone who hadn't always assimilated well to new environments.

"Yes, this job is hard, but not everyone breaks down. That's what you're thinking, Meilan. Just admit it."

"You don't know what I'm thinking." I fingered the insignia in my pocket, my fingers tracing the outline of the Foundation's crest, and the ancient tools of surveyors—lines and circles carved in cold durabronze.

Throw it away.

I gripped the thing, unsure if I should push it deeper into my pocket or let it drop on the path and be buried back into the mud.

Get rid of it.

I ignored the voice—my voice of reason, probably. Or maybe of irrationality. Maybe Calla and Vadner's fears were rubbing off on me. Get rid of the evidence and there was no way to prove that the Foundation had ever been here.

But…why would I want to do that?

"Are you sorry I told you?" Calla asked, probably misinterpreting my silence for unease over her confession.

"No." I wasn't turning cartwheels that she'd told me, but I'd rather know what I was dealing with than find out later. I was a realist. I liked facts. Figures. Things I could hold on to—like evidence. I pushed the insignia deeper into my pocket and walked on.

"He didn't die by natural causes." Vadner peeked into the main room, clutching his scanner tightly. "He was killed."

"How?" I got up and followed him into the room we'd set up as our lab. The remains of the man took an entire table. He looked so…lost lying there.

An acceptable sacrifice.

Gideon said that at times. About mission casualties. Acceptable for what was accomplished for the rest of humanity. I hated it when he said that. Was I starting to think like him? Was being a team chief making me hard?

"How was he killed, Vadner?"

"Trauma to the neck."

"As in he fell?"

Vadner pointed to the spine; the top vertebrae were shattered. The junction where they should have connected to the skull looked—

"My God. Was his neck—?"

"Snapped? Yes, it was." Vadner sat down on a stool, taking a deep breath. "That's not something that just happens."

"Maybe it was one of the animals we haven't cataloged yet," Calla said from the doorway. She walked in and seemed to be trying not to look at the body. "We're a long way from done on the surveys."

She blinked rapidly, and I noticed her hands were shaking. She seemed to know I'd seen, for she clenched her fists and put them behind her back.

"It's possible," I said. "There are potentially hundreds, if not thousands, of species to catalog here before we're done."

"Nothing that would do this." He touched the remains, his hand resting on the skull. "Something bad happened here."

"Is there any way to tell who he is?" Calla was still not looking at the body.

"Maybe through dental records. The teeth are still attached." Vadner showed me he already had the scans. "I'd like to upload these for a possible match the next time we have connectivity."

"Of course."

"We should go armed from here on out." Calla's voice cut into the silence as Vadner and I stared down at the bones. "I mean…if it was an animal, it could still be running wild somewhere. It could smell us. It could track us down."

She's right." He glanced at me. "The remains are at least seven years old. Maybe even older."

And wild animals often didn't live that long. I understood what he was saying. Then again, most animals did reproduce, and traits were passed on. As were hunting skills.

"I agree. We go armed." I went to one of the containers, took out the small weapons that would fit into the pouches on our uniform. I handed one to Calla, then gave her several clips of ammunition.

Vadner looked as if he was going to refuse even though he had backed Calla's idea; I knew he hated guns.

"You can't go out there unprotected." Calla took the gun from me, jammed it into the pouch on Vadner's uniform, and stowed the ammo in his other pocket. "You have to stay safe."

"Okay."

"Do you know how to shoot?" I asked.

"Of course. I did have to field qualify." But he looked down.

"What?"

"I uh…" He swallowed hard, then glanced at Calla. "I'm not sure

I have the will to shoot."

"Meaning?"

"I didn't the last time. Someone got hurt. Badly."

"Great." I looked at Calla.

She was staring at Vadner with something like sympathy. "Not everyone can shoot."

"I should have. I wanted to but…"

She took his hand and shook her head as if there was nothing else to say. And maybe there wasn't.

I turned. "I'm going out."

Calla looked panicky, and I noticed she was fingering her cross. "You can't go alone."

"I'll be fine. We'll be fine. This body has nothing to do with us other than we had the bad luck to find it."

But the insignia, lying heavily in my pocket under the spare ammo, said differently.

I was barely a quarter mile out from camp, just starting a survey of the area, when I heard the sound of something coming up quick. Something big. I pulled out the gun, checked to make sure the safety was off and the ammo was in.

"All right," I whispered to whatever it was. "Let's see what you're made of."

Shoot.

I almost did. I wanted to. My hand was shaking as I held my finger to the trigger, just shy of the pressure needed to fire blindly into the trees.

Shoot now.

I shot.

"Holy God, woman. No problems with you having the will to shoot." Vadner looked like I had trimmed about ten years off his life with my fortunately bad shot.

"Why didn't you yell?" My voice was shrill, and my heart was beating triple time.

"We weren't sure it was you."

"So you came crashing up on something you weren't even sure was your teammate? Where's Calla?"

She limped into view.

"Did I shoot you?"

"No. I fell." She was covered in mud. "Oh, this is disgusting. I don't know how you stood it, Meilan."

"It's just wet dirt. You dig in the dirt all the time."

"It smells." She was trying to brush it off, which only succeeded in smearing it more into her skin and hair and clothes. "Get it off me."

Vadner took her hands, stopping the frantic motion. "It's just a little mud."

She grabbed for her cross. "It's dirty. This mud…"

Vadner helped her wipe it off. "Good as new."

She looked down.

"Listen, we came out to ask you something." Vadner turned to me. "I understand why the body is decomposed after all this time. No tissue left after sitting in that soup. But shouldn't there be something left of the guy's clothes? Metal fasteners don't disintegrate. They might rust but…"

"If whatever killed the man ate him, then the clothes would have been the first thing to come off. Maybe the metal's scattered all over that area?"

"There's no evidence he was eaten. No gnaw marks on the bones."

I frowned. "Well, maybe the creature took the clothes with it? Like a bird collects things to make a nest."

"What if…" Calla moved closer to us. "What if whatever it was wore it out or took it, afraid it'd be evidence? I mean, what if it wasn't an animal? What if it was a human?"

I pushed my hand in my pocket, fingered the insignia. "It's possible. He could have been doing anything. Smuggling, maybe?"

There were plenty of bad guys out here. Not everyone was a

peaceful surveyor.

But this one was. I knew that. I started to pull the insignia out. "I think that this—"

Don't tell. They'll panic.

"What?" Vadner was watching me intently. "You think that this…what?"

"I think that this is making us crazy. We'll just have to wait to see if there are any matches to the dentition."

I pushed the insignia down. They'd know soon enough, anyway. If the man was one of the Foundation surveyors, there'd be a match to his records. No reason to share the insignia.

Only, what difference did it make? I reached in again, digging down past the ammo.

Don't.

I smelled sulfur coming off the mud on Calla. The odor mingled in a not unpleasant way with the clean, earthy scent of the area I'd been working in. It was the smell I loved best. The smell of dirt and rain, of living things—why did she think it smelled like death?

I let go of the insignia and sank down to the sample I'd been working on. "You should get Calla cleaned up."

"She'll be all right."

I looked up at her. She had her mouth set in a tight line, but her eyes held panic.

"No, I don't think she will be."

"I don't want to leave you alone." Calla looked up at Vadner. "Make her come back with us."

"As you said, Vadner, I've proven I'm willing to take the shot." I waved them off and went back to work.

"Keep an eye out," he said.

"I will."

I heard them walking away. Calla's voice held a note of fear. Vadner was trying to comfort her. It was obviously not just dark worlds that gave her the creeps.

But there was nothing here to be afraid of. I worked for a while, trying to ignore how sleepy I was.

Finally, I lay back in the mud, scrunching as it took me in. I felt the mud sucking my hair in—mud was good for hair. Not that Calla cared. Cropping hers the way she did.

Love.

Yes, I loved this. I used to do this when I was a kid. Made my father so mad when I'd come in filthy from the mud in the woods behind our house. I'd come in with samples, too. Ferns and wild lilies that I'd pretend were exotic flora. He'd always make me clean up before I could analyze them.

I closed my eyes and let the rain, which had picked up, beat down on me. The mud was so warm; I felt cocooned in it. The rain beat a drum tempo on my face, my chest, my thighs. I felt as if every care I had was being sucked into the mud. As if everything that mattered—that made me who I was—was becoming part of it.

The smell of sulfur was all around. I breathed in deeply, felt a pinch at the base of my skull, then nothing but peace. I sighed, and it seemed as if my lungs were pushing a mountain of mud up just to take in the air. It felt…elemental.

I used to lie in the mud when I'd grown older, dreaming a young woman's dream of a man who would understand this pleasure. Expensive spas charged a month's salary to let you soak in their mineral-rich mud. But it could be free. It could be natural. It could be like this.

He comes.

I used to dream of making love in the mud. Pulling a man down to me, flipping him into the mud, lying on top, watching as the mud covered him, too.

Watching as the mud drowned him.

I opened my eyes with a snap. I wasn't in the mud. I was standing on the trail leading back to the camp. And I heard Calla ahead, calling for Vadner.

I walked slowly, reaching into the pocket that had the insignia.

Calla saw me coming and came running. "I got the connection

up."

I frowned. "You talked to Gideon?" I didn't want her talking to him. I didn't want her causing unnecessary panic.

"I sent the dental information to Records."

"Oh. Did they have an answer?"

"No. They said it could take a while."

"Did you talk to Gideon?" That was suddenly very important.

"No. Have you seen Vadner? He went back for you."

"I haven't seen him." I put my hand on her shoulder, felt the warmth of her beneath my skin. I could almost…taste her.

I yanked my hand away.

"I'm going to go look for him."

I nodded. "Don't get lost."

"Meilan? Is something wrong?"

"Nothing." In fact, I felt good. I felt strong. Stronger than I had in years.

I left her staring at me and walked into the shelter. My stride seemed bouncier. As if each step was a revelation.

Maybe I should set up shop here once the planet was colonized. Charge for rejuvenating mud baths.

No others. Not yet.

The communications unit sounded. I glanced at it—the dental match had been made. I opened the message up and stared at it for a very long time.

"Match found: Gideon Morales."

The comm unit sounded again. A call from a dead man.

"Mei?" he said as I opened the connection.

I stared at Gideon, the same Gideon that supposedly lay on our exam table.

Love.

"It's begun," he said, leaning in. He seemed to be looking into me, deep inside. "I've missed you."

"They know." I wasn't sure why I told him that. I hadn't planned to say it. The words just came out of my mouth.

"How?"

I could feel it inside me. Something making me talk. But I knew the answer to this, too. And the thing inside me was inviting me to join in. To answer for us both.

"Vadner sent your dental information."

"Damn." He was up and gone.

I sat waiting, as my hands seemed to operate without any instruction from me, erasing things. I was erasing all records of finding the body. Erasing the transmission with the dental records—but it would still be there at Gideon's end.

And Gideon will take care of it.

My hands finally sat quietly again. I could move them, and I did, reaching into the pocket, pulling out the weapon, drawing back the trigger.

He loves you. He chose you.

"Who did?"

Gideon did.

"Gideon's dead. I saw the report." I was talking to myself. I was talking to a version of myself that was trying to keep me from shooting it in the head—from shooting myself in the head.

He's not dead. You know this. Do you feel dead?

"I will if you'd let me use my goddamned hands."

I'm sorry. It was so easy with you. I thought you understood.

"Understood what?"

"Mei?" Gideon was back. He was breathing hard, looking down as if working feverishly on his computers. Then he exhaled slowly, and sat back, smiling. "It's all right. There's no record. Not anymore."

"What's going on?" I could feel my hands putting the gun back into its pouch. I couldn't stop them, but I could still cry.

"Don't, Mei. Just give it time."

"You aren't him."

"I'm the only Gideon you've known."

"I don't understand."

"You've changed. For the better."

"I still don't understand."

"Did you dance in the rain?" His smile was tender. More so than I'd ever seen it. "It won't be this confusing for long. The fusion, it takes a little time for us to become one with them."

"Us? Them?"

You. And I.

"Take her out to see. That always helps." He seemed to think he was talking to whatever was inside me.

"I don't want to go back out." But I was rising. My legs, so springy again—God, it felt so good to move this way—carrying me back out the door, into the woods.

Calla was wandering ahead of me. She looked back. "I got lost."

"I told you not to." My voice was even. Nothing of the panic I felt inside was seeping out.

She crowded close to me, her gun poking into my thigh. I pulled her close, into a tight hug, and she shuddered and began to cry. Even as I tried to open my mouth to warn her, my hand was pulling her gun out from her pouch, but she was shaking too much to notice.

I wanted to warn her as I stashed her gun in my pocket.

You won't. You can't.

"Vadner should be just up ahead." I realized I had said that. I—not something else. Vadner would be up ahead, and he would still have his gun. He'd just gotten lost, too. But he would help us.

A man, remember? A man to make love to in the mud.

A flash of memory. Vadner leaning down to look at something. His hand shaking. I'd come from behind him. How had I gotten there?

A man to drown in the mud.

It was as if a veil that had hidden my memories from me was pushed away. I saw it all. How I'd pushed him down. How he'd flailed as his head slipped below the mud. He didn't sink too far. He was lying on top of something else. Something made of bone. A perfect skeleton, this time. Only with no uniform.

My hand held him down. My hand, which had come out of a

sleeve, which had been part of the uniform that—

That you are wearing.

Calla let me go, and I pointed her in the right direction. She hurried, and I set out after her. The spring in my step did not change as I ran. It felt different to move. As if what powered my body was no longer blood and air. As if it was earth and water.

Welcome home.

I felt thoughts crowding in on me. Memories that weren't mine. And something else was reading my own memories. I felt as if I were being torn open: nothing in my life was my own, and I tasted an existence so foreign I tried to retreat.

There is nowhere to go. We are one.

I heard Calla scream.

"*That* is me," I said to whatever it was inside me. "What she just found. That is me. There is no we. You are not me."

But I saw Gideon's face in my mind and thought of his record. Lucky Gideon—always the survivor, which meant there had to be some tragedy, didn't it? On so many of his missions.

We get hungry from time to time.

I stopped walking, but I knew that it was a joint decision. I felt as if I were being sucked underneath the mud.

That had happened once. When I was a child. I'd thought I'd found a mud hole like any of the others. But it had been deeper. It had tried to drag me in.

I'd grabbed a bush, pulled myself out. But I'd been afraid of the mud for months after that. And I'd taken my father out to the sinkhole. We'd put up signs so that no one else would be lured in.

Even if my father had said that no one else would be foolish enough to go in.

I'd never learned.

It's all right. This is better. Gideon waits for us. He has been waiting for us for ten years.

I'd barely known Gideon ten years ago. Served on a handful of routine surveys with him.

We can always recognize a soul mate.

I sensed that it was using my words. It had no soul. It had no understanding of soul. It was trying to make me comfortable with what was happening.

We are one. It will be easier if you accept that.

I realized Calla was staring at me. Her hand dug at her empty pouch. She grabbed for the ammo clip, but it was useless with no gun to fire it. She stood over Vadner's body.

And over my body, peeking out from under his.

She held out her cross.

"I don't think that will help." The thing was letting me talk. I walked up to Calla, tore the cross from her neck and tossed it into the mud as she scuttled back.

"Please, Meilan…"

"You went crazy again," I heard my voice saying.

"No."

"Gideon picked you for a reason."

Just as he'd picked a young man who couldn't take the shot. I saw myself holding Vadner under the mud. I saw him reach for his gun, slide it out, aim it in an awkward way. He could have shot me, but he hadn't. He'd sucked in a mouthful of mud before the resolve he'd needed could fill him. He'd died, holding that gun, finger hovering over the trigger.

Calla fell on Vadner. She touched his hair, his skin.

"I barely got away from you, when you went crazy again—that's what I'll tell them," I said.

"Monster."

"I think so. I think you're right." And this time, it was my own words again. I believed that. The thing inside me just laughed.

Calla rushed me. I was surprised she'd do that, but not worried—I knocked her away as if she were nothing more than a child.

We are hungry now.

I heard the words inside my head; I heard the words coming out of my own mouth, and I realized that we'd both spoken. I reached for Calla, drawing her toward me. She beat on me, and I registered some sort of pain. Nothing that would stop me, but an interesting phenomenon. My new life would be full of them.

"Please...?" Calla cried. Her tears smeared makeup, and I pulled her to me.

"I'm sorry." And again it was both of us who spoke.

She was your friend. In your memories, she is mine now, too.

And then we were holding her tightly, letting our essence surround her, the mud within what looked like human skin roiling now, bubbling as if at the Earth's core, as we sucked her life away.

It tasted good.

We will not have to feed again for some time.

The voice was hazy. As if in some sort of bliss. I wondered if I could kill it in this state. I pulled my gun out and lifted my hand, waiting.

I could do it. I knew it.

I love you.

I found that...I didn't want to.

I let Calla go and shot her as she fell. "It was self-defense." Yes. I could say that convincingly.

Picking her and Vadner up, I carried them each in one hand, dragging them through the mud, back to the shelter. I heard the sucking sounds of the mud, drawing what was left of my old body under.

There would be no evidence. Or not much. And Gideon would declare the planet off limits. Too dangerous. I would provide the data he needed. Toxic this and acidic that. No way to live here. No one would come. Until another of us was ready to be born. Then we'd send the next team in. With a special member.

We would have plenty of time to find that person.

Calla's life force filled me. I wanted off this world—I wanted Gideon.

I dropped the bodies at the entrance to the shelter, walked back in and saw him waiting, still on the comm.

"Is everything all right?" His eyes shone. I knew he—they—couldn't wait to see me. To hold me. To hold…us.

I smiled, knowing he'd read the truth in the way my lips turned up.

Everything is fine.

Gerri Leen lives in Northern Virginia and originally hails from Seattle. She has work appearing or accepted by: *Nature*, Flame Tree Press's *Murder Mayhem* and *Dystopia Utopia* anthologies, Daily Science Fiction, Escape Pod, Grimdark, and others. She recently caught the editing bug and is finalizing her third anthology for an independent press.

Taking it for The Team

Tracie McBride

"Fuck. Fuck, fuck, fuck…" Corey clutched his head in his hands. He had a bastard of a headache, a naked blonde stranger comatose next to him, and a huge hole in his memory.

Situation normal. He looked at the clock: 11.15 pm.

Normally at this time of night, he was just getting started. There was a reason why he had been asleep, he had kind-of-sort-of planned it that way, he just had to remember what it was…

"Fuuuuck!" His coach Henry had scheduled a special evening training session for midnight, and he was going to tear Corey a new one if he was late again. He nudged the girl next to him.

"Wake up, darling, wake up," he cajoled. No response. He rolled her over onto her back. Drool trickled from one corner of her lipstick-smeared mouth, and she snored loudly.

Still alive. That was always a good sign. He hadn't lost one yet, but the mere thought of the headlines—AFL star in drugs death scandal—made him jumpy. He slapped her tentatively about the face in an attempt to rouse her. Didn't want to be too rough—he could hardly afford to add woman bashing to his list of transgressions. Eyes squeezed shut, she threw her arms up over her face, muttered incoherently and burrowed under the blankets.

Corey checked the time again, looked back to the blonde, then back at the clock. He could always just leave her here while he went to training, but the last time he'd done that, he'd come home to a ransacked apartment. No, he'd have to get her out of here.

"Shitfuckshitfuckshitfuck..." He hopped around the room with one leg in a pair of sweatpants while he searched for something that might contain the girl's ID. He found her handbag out in the lounge.

Bingo. There was a driver's license in it bearing the name of Kylie Harris, and a photo that looked vaguely like the woman in his bed. He hoped the address on the front was current as he dialed for a taxi. Returning to the bedroom, he levered Kylie into a sitting position and maneuvered her into the mini dress he found on the floor. There was no way she was going to make it down the stairs in the stilettos she arrived in, so he stuffed them in her handbag. Outside, the taxi horn sounded.

"Money. Shit. Shitfuckshitfuck..." He went on a frantic search for his wallet. Miracle of miracles, it was on his nightstand, and it contained close to $500.

Corey frowned. He couldn't have had that good a time if he still had that much cash still on him. Unless…

He looked sideways at Kylie, who sat swaying on the edge of his bed, and shrugged. He hoisted her to her feet and half carried her down the stairs to the waiting taxi, peeling off $50 for the driver and stuffing the rest into Kylie's handbag. Whatever anyone said about Corey Boyd, he always settled his debts, even if he wasn't always sure if he owed them.

One problem solved for the day. Now to get to training. A quick dash back upstairs, snatch up his keys, thumb the button to open the garage door…

The garage was empty.

"Fuuuuuuck!"

It was past 12.30 by the time Corey arrived at the training field. The rest of the team jogged up and down under floodlights, their breath pluming in the unseasonably cool late summer air. Composing his features into his best approximation of wide-eyed innocence, Corey broke into a trot to join them. Tom Bentley sneered as they drew level with each other.

"Christ, Boyd, you reek. What did you have for dinner, half a bottle of tequila?"

The others didn't even deign to acknowledge him. Arseholes. It wasn't as if the rest of them were as pure as the driven snow.

"Nice of you to join us, Mr. Boyd." Henry stood on the sidelines clutching his beloved clipboard and bearing a sardonic smile. Christ, he hated it when Henry smiled like that. It could only mean someone was going to suffer. One of these days he was going to take that clipboard and shove it up Henry's…

Corey smiled to himself, lost in the fantasy as he jogged around the perimeter of the field. Heedless, he ran into the back of Jason Steele, sending them both tripping and stumbling.

"Watch it, Boyd, ya dozy prick!" Corey dodged the blow lobbed at his head.

A piercing whistle split the air. Corey winced as it set up an agonizing counterpoint to the throbbing in his brain. The other players ran as obediently as dogs over to Henry. Corey paused in a micro-moment of defiance before trailing after them. He knew that, after turning up late to training for the fifth time in a row, his best bet was to keep his mouth shut and his head low, yet he found himself asking the question that must have been on everyone else's mind.

"What's up with the Saturday night training session, Coach?

You're fu— messing with my social life."

"Several reasons," Henry replied. He tucked his clipboard under his armpit and began to count down on his fingers. "Number one—circadian rhythms."

"Circa...what?"

"It's an experimental new training technique," Henry continued. "Similar to the principle of training at high altitude or while carrying extra weights. Training late at night puts an extra load on an athlete's system, so when he resumes a normal schedule, his output will be significantly increased." Henry shrugged. "At least, that's the theory. If it doesn't work, then there's always reason number two—the scheduling of this training session for a weekend was deliberate. I reckon that the team's social lives had a major influence on us finishing bottom of the table last season. This way, I'll have the satisfaction of watching you lot sweating away your Saturday nights on the field instead of being out on the piss or on the pull.

"And if you'd bothered to turn up on time, you'd have been here when I was explaining reason number three. Speak of the devil—here come our special guests now."

Corey's interest sparked in spite of himself. A rival team, perhaps? Or some rugby union pussies? He followed Henry's gaze as he turned to watch the figures emerging from the tunnel.

Whoever their 'guests' were, they were evidently not professional football players. The six people gathered before them in their ill-fitting training strips were an assortment of sizes, builds, and ages. One was a woman, and at least two were of an indeterminate gender. The only thing they appeared to have in common was a distinct pallor to their skin. In fact, they were so white, they almost glowed.

"Uh...we're training with computer programmers?"

Henry tossed a ball to one of the newcomers, a curvy little redhead who looked like she didn't know one end of a football pitch from the other. She hefted it experimentally in one red-taloned hand. Corey preferred his women a little more tanned, but she had a certain appeal. He had just begun to imagine her naked, when she drew back her arm and threw. It was an awkward, cack-handed toss, yet the ball flew through the air faster than his eye could follow and hit him squarely in the chest, knocking him on his arse. He lay on his back, squinted up at the floodlights and gasped for breath while the rest of the squad snickered.

Gingerly, he rose to his feet. No way was he going to let that lily white bitch get the better of him. "Nice chuck, sweetheart, but in this game, a proper pass goes like this." He balled his right hand into a fist and punched the ball back to her.

Coach and the woman exchanged something—a fleeting look, a tiny nod, it was barely noticeable, but Corey was caught it. They were setting him up. For what, he didn't yet know. It was the not knowing that made the hair on the back of his neck stand up.

"OK, gentlemen. Split into two groups. They're the foxes, you're the hounds. Try to catch them. Go!"

Corey looked at Henry incredulously. This was under 14's baby stuff. Why the fuck weren't they running some proper drills? Henry returned his gaze impassively. They locked eyes for several long seconds until Corey looked away.

"This is bullfuckingshit," Corey muttered under his breath as he ran to join his team.

The redhead was a 'fox' in his group. He dearly wanted to run her down, to wrap his arms around her waist, to plow her face first into the turf and claim it an "accident" but he avoided her for now. She'd keep. He was unused to delaying his gratification, and the decision made him feel both proud of himself and slightly ill at ease. He turned his attention instead to a tall, painfully thin young man with long black hair that flopped across his eyes. The bloke looked as fragile and ungainly as a daddy long-legs. He turned away from the squad and began to run, taking great loping inefficient strides with his bony elbows flapping like wings. Corey didn't even start after him; moving like that, he'd tire in less than two minutes, and Corey could run him down at his leisure.

Something jabbed him in his already tender ribs, and Corey

yelped. Samson Tawhai, the assistant coach, prodded him again with the riding crop he carried to all training sessions.

"Coach says 'jump' you say what?" Samson bellowed. Whereas Henry was always experimenting on the team with painful new training techniques, Samson was stuck back in high school with his approach. Still, he was widely tipped to be the next head coach. He'd been a legend on the field in his day, which only made Corey resent him even more. Corey scowled and moved off after the human spider.

Something odd was going on. The rest of the squad pounded down the field, sweat flying and limbs pumping, and Corey had to extend himself to catch up to the stragglers. Yet the "fox" maintained a two-meter distance between himself and the front runners without appearing to even try. Incredibly, he turned around and began to run backward, taunting the "hounds" with a "bring it on" beckoning hand gesture.

And still, they could not catch him.

This had to be some kind of trick, some elaborate practical joke staged by the bosses for some obscure publicity purposes. Corey stopped and looked around the field in search of concealed cameras.

"Whassamatter, Boyd, you too good to run with the rest of them?" It was Samson again. He swatted him on the butt for emphasis. Corey's felt the rage build, and forced himself to count backward from ten; he'd already suffered a three-week suspension and hefty fine for punching Samson. One of these days, though, Cory was going to catch him off duty and off guard. Then he'd show him how to really wield that riding crop.

Henry's whistle sounded again, and the squad gathered around for further instruction. Many of the players were bent over and heaving for breath, and they all dripped with perspiration. Their opposition, on the other hand, looked like they'd done nothing more strenuous than finish their lattés. A theory began to form in Corey's head. This lot weren't computer programmers; they were chemists. What they were seeing here was a demonstration of a potent and probably illegal new performance enhancing drug.

"Is that the best you can do?" Henry's voice dripped with scorn. "Swap places. You wimps are now the foxes. Anyone lasting less than five minutes gets two extra hours of training at six 6a.m. on Sunday morning. I'll even give you a twenty-meter head start—GO!" With a chorus of grumbles, the team set off.

"What are you doing still standing here, Boyd? Do you want four hours training on Sunday?"

"I'm not doing it, Coach." Corey stood with his arms crossed over his chest and smiled slyly. "You and I both know that it's impossible to beat these guys. Not without whatever they're on." He tipped Henry a conspiratorial wink.

"Corey, Corey, Corey…" Coach shook his head. It was the first time he'd heard the coach call him by his first name, and for a moment it rattled his resolve. "You really are the biggest fuckwit on the planet, aren't you? All right. I give up. You win. Join in, sit it out on the bench, I don't care anymore."

Corey sauntered for the sidelines, but it was all an act. Despite Henry's concession of defeat, he had never felt less like a winner.

Corey hugged himself against the cold. The squad had been running after or away from their training partners for the better part of two hours, and it had exhausted them more thoroughly than the toughest Grand Final game. He had watched the White Guys, as he had mentally nicknamed them, intently. Whatever they were peddling, it was a beautiful drug. They were still going strong with no sign of tiring and no evidence of a messy come-down. He wondered if their extreme paleness was a side effect, then thought—fuck it. Looking like Casper the Friendly Ghost would be a small price to pay for that level of speed, strength, and agility. Whatever they were on, he wanted some. Badly.

Henry gave his whistle one long blast, a reedy Last Post to signify the end of the training session.

"Gather round, boys. Before you hit the showers, I'd like to you offer thanks to our friends."

Offer thanks. It was an oddly formal thing to say. Formalities made Corey uncomfortable, which was why he liked to turn up to awards ceremonies half-cut and stumbling. And the way everyone was staring at him made him even more uncomfortable.

"What are you shitheads looking at?"

Aaron Sinclair stepped forward and shoved him in the chest. "We're looking at you. Shithead."

Corey shoved him back. For a moment it looked like it was all on, and Corey relished it, needing some kind of physical conflict to counteract the mental and emotional strangeness of the day. It was either this, or head for a bar and pick a fight with a stranger, which, knowing his luck, would end up splashed all over the papers. Both options would land him in the shit, but he knew which pile would be shallower.

But Aaron merely raised his hands in mock surrender and retreated. The rest of the squad had surrounded them, and now they parted to leave Corey hemmed in on three sides and facing the White Guys on the fourth. Somebody pushed him in the back, and he sprawled forward to fall at their feet. The little redhead put her boot on the back of his neck and pinned him to the ground.

He knew without even trying that it would be pointless to try to escape. He lay on the ground trembling with rage. The squad filed past him prone in the dirt, and they all had something to say.

"You're a liability, Boyd. You're not half as good as you think you are, and you're a disgrace to the profession. You've had this coming for a long time."

"Fun's fun, Corey, but you just take it too far."

"You crashed my car."

"You broke my nose."

"You fucked my wife."

The coach was last. Corey twisted under the redhead's boot so he could look up at him. Henry tsk-tsked at him from a great height.

"You had such promise when we signed you, Corey. I really thought we could knock off those rough edges, turn you into a man instead of the hundred kilo, tantrum throwing toddler that you are. But you just wouldn't listen. Do you know I argued on your behalf? I wanted to drop you from the team, cancel your contract, but the bosses wouldn't have it. Said it would cost too much in lawyers' fees."

Henry sighed. "Still...I always say that every man has his uses. Looks like you're best employed serving as an example to others if they persist in fucking up."

"I can think of at least one other use for him." This from the redhead as she released the pressure slightly on the back of his neck. Corey flipped onto his back to gaze into her green eyes.

How had he missed those eyes before? It felt as if she were lifting him up by the mere force of her gaze. His cock stiffened in his shorts, and he writhed anew beneath the weight of her boot. She looked hotter and hotter by the second. Christ, he was so horny, even some of the blokes were starting to appeal. Maybe, he thought hungrily, this was a practical joke of an entirely different sort.

The redhead looked away, Henry nodded to her, and the spell was broken. She leaned down, grabbed Corey by the collar, and pulled him up with one hand, lifting him effortlessly off the ground. He dangled in her grip like a chastened puppy caught by the scruff of his neck. He was suddenly, dizzily aware of just how terrifying these computer programmers, or chemists or whatever-the-fuck-they-were looked up close. Those eyes, so captivating before, had turned as cold as a shark's. They smelled of copper and moist earth, and their skin had no pores, and right now if someone were to tell him that they had no souls to match, he would have believed them.

Then they all smiled.

Ah, thought Corey, so that's what death looks like. His mind quietly slipped off the edge of the Insanity Pool into the deep end.

They took him by the limbs, spread-eagled him, and pressed their fangs to his skin, to wrist and elbow and groin and neck. The redhead's canines grazed his cheek as she murmured in his ear.

"Come on, Corey, don't struggle—sometimes you just gotta take it for the team."

Tracie McBride

Tracie McBride is a New Zealander who lives in Melbourne, Australia. Her work has appeared in over 80 publications, including the Stoker Award-nominated anthologies Horror for Good and Horror Library Volume 5. Her collection Ghosts Can Bleed contains much of the work that earned her a Sir Julius Vogel Award.

Here We Go Round

Rie Sheridan Rose

C'mon…c'mon…please. Start spinning…please!

Eyes squeezed tightly shut, Lizzie waited for the merry-go-round to start spinning. Sometimes—if she was lucky—she could kick start it into movement, but mostly, she just laid in bed and waited, swinging one leg over the edge, back and forth, back and forth—as if she could start the merry-go-round in her head spinning, like she did the one on the school playground.

The merry-go-round took her away from the sweaty apartment with the stained sheets and the broken locks; took her to the land of dreams, where she was in charge and safe…happy even. For as long as she could remember, it had been there to take her away.

Not that there was a long time to remember. She was only twelve.

Twelve...still interested in tadpoles and kickball rather than boys and dancing...but stuck with the daily nightmare of a stepfather who crept to her bed like a thief in the night to violate her innocence. To make her do things she wasn't even supposed to know about at twelve.

The night terrified Lizzie.

But if she could just get the merry-go-round spinning, she would be far away from the apartment, playing in Dreamland long before *He* came calling. After all, he didn't care if she moved, or cried, or pleaded, or even if she was awake.

At first, it always woke her up when *He* came, no matter what. But then she had discovered the way into Dreamland. Now, if she was far enough away, at least as far as the merry-go-round on the other side, she didn't even notice.

At last, the merry-go-round started to spin; as her thoughts stopped racing, her leg stopped swinging, and she settled down. She found a blank mind made it much easier to push it into movement, but sometimes it was hard to forget the *Real*.

She shivered a little in anticipation as the spinning picked up momentum. She would be in Dreamland soon. Who would be there to meet her tonight?

She'd been seeing the winged boy, Byron, a lot lately. They went on the *best* adventures. He would stand behind her and wrap his arms around her and flap those glorious wings, and they would fly over the whole landscape. She always felt safe with him.

Or maybe tonight it was Esmeralda's turn. She hadn't been to the gypsy camp in weeks, and Essy had been teaching her so many things—reading the cards, dancing to the wild violins.

She would enjoy that too.

The merry-go-round was spinning faster and faster now. She giggled and clutched the rails, exhilarated by the dizziness. Her dreaming eyes opened now, and she could see the bright landscape of Dreamland whirling about her. It never made her sick to watch it spin like it did when she rode the merry-go-round in the real playground.

She saw Byron hovering over Essy, wings flapping lazily. Oh, goody! Tonight they would all go on an adventure together. She let go with one hand, waving frantically as the merry-go-round began to slow.

She was so excited, she almost jumped off before it stopped completely, but the one time she had done that, she had fallen out of bed in the *Real* and broken her arm. That had lost her Dreamland to painkillers for weeks. She didn't risk it anymore.

"What shall we do tonight, Essy?" she called, excited to see her friends again.

"Let's go swim in the moon pool!" the gypsy girl replied. "Byron can take us…even if he can't swim."

Byron stuck his tongue out at Essy and Lizzie laughed, her heart full of love and light here in Dreamland—not hatred and dark like at home…with *Him*.

"Lovely! But don't tease, Byron—if his wings get wet, how can he fly?"

"Let's just call the unicorn, and then we won't need him," Essy replied, making a face back at Byron.

The little girl danced in a circle around both her friends—the winged boy and the tousle-haired gypsy.

"It's too lovely a night to fight! Why don't you call the unicorn, and we'll have a race?"

Essy put her fingers in her mouth and whistled loudly.

The unicorn, with its horn of pearl, stepped daintily over a nearby hillock, horn glimmering in the moonlight.

Byron gathered Lizzie up in his strong arms as Essy swung bareback onto the unicorn, planting her heels in its sides. With a whinny, it bounded forward.

"Cheat!" Lizzie laughed as Byron's wings cut through the air in mighty sweeps. They soon caught and passed the unicorn, arriving at the shimmering pool of moonlight when Essy was a mere speck in the distance.

He dropped her into the pool with a splash that rose over her head. The moonlight cascaded up like water before falling back into the pool. She was never afraid in the moon pool.

Here, she swam like a fish, and could breathe like one too, gliding through the iridescent waters for hours upon hours without ever surfacing.

It wasn't really water. She didn't know if Byron's wings would get wet or not. But he never swam, and Essy always made the same joke. Every time. It was expected. It was safe. It was comfortable. It was one of the reasons she loved it here in Dreamland. There were no bad surprises.

Sure, sometimes they found somewhere new when they were exploring, but it was always someplace exciting and fun. No dark corridors or rooms smelling of old food.

No semen-stained sheets.

No treading on eggshells—to not draw *His* attention.

Lizzie wished she could stay here forever, but as the pale green sun poked its head over the horizon, she knew it was time to go back. She sighed, dropping the handful of shells she had collected back on the sand—she didn't take anything out of Dreamland anymore. Not since the time Essy had given her a flower so beautiful that she couldn't resist. *He* had flushed it down the toilet despite her protests, and she'd gotten a black eye for back-talking him.

She had to wake up when the alarm went off and make *His* breakfast, or there would be hell to pay. She knew it was better not waste any more time.

"Back to the merry-go-round, if you please, Byron."

He stood from where he had sat on the bank playing his flute as the girls swam. Nodding, he held out his arms, and she stepped into their warm embrace.

"I'll be back tomorrow," Lizzie promised Essy, waving goodbye as Byron's strong wings bore her away.

The next night, it was easier to get the merry-go-round spinning.

Almost from the instant her head hit the pillow, she felt the movement start. They had lovely plans for tonight. Exploring the Pirate Island she and Byron had seen from the air.

Lizzie and Essy sailed across the soda pop sea to the island, Byron doing aerial tricks overhead. Lizzie was happier than she had ever been in her short life.

"I wish I could stay here forever," she sighed, as the three of them lay upon the purple sand of the beach.

Essy propped herself up on an elbow. "Why don't you?"

"You can't stay dreaming forever, silly. You have to wake up sometime."

"Why?"

Lizzie started to reply then shut her mouth with a snap. *Why indeed? There wasn't anything wonderful waiting at home, that was for sure.* "If you are alive, you have to live in the *Real*. You only get to come to Dreamland when you sleep."

"What's 'alive'?"

She tried to explain, but Essy couldn't understand what she meant.

"The main thing is, you aren't happy there, and…you are here. So stay with us," the gypsy girl urged.

"What about *Him*? He won't let me stay here. He'll only wake me up…and then things will be worse."

"Take us to the caravan, Byron," Essy ordered, bounding to her feet—she always knew what to do. "We've got to make a plan."

Byron nodded, silent as always. Byron never uttered a word, but somehow, Lizzie always knew what he wanted to tell her, always knew what he was thinking. He wanted her to stay too.

He banked his wings, and they soared away to the far side of Dreamland.

"But what can I do about *Him*?" Lizzie asked as Essy handed her a cup of the strong gypsy coffee she brewed. Lizzie loved the thick, dark brew. It didn't make her jumpy here in Dreamland, like even His weakest coffee did at home.

"You can kill *Him*." Essy's eyes glowed red, and her smile had taken on a wicked gleam.

Startled, Lizzie slopped the hot coffee on her hand, but she didn't even feel it. Injuries in Dreamland healed almost instantly, anyway.

Except death.

Everyone knew that if you died in your dreams, you died for real. She was always really careful to remember that.

"Kill *Him*?" Lizzie whispered, her mind whirling at the mere possibility.

"Then you would be rid of *Him* once and for all," Essy urged. "You could stay here with us and be happy."

Byron nodded vigorously, smiling that beautiful smile of his and bouncing off the ground to hover in his excitement.

Lizzie closed her eyes and imagined being happy all the time. She hadn't been happy in the real world since Mama died, when she was only five.

He was supposed to take care of her. He'd promised Mama He'd raise her as if she were His own. But somehow, everything had gotten all twisted up. And, as He often reminded her, He hadn't promised she'd be happy.

He didn't believe in 'Happy'.

Her eyes popped open again. "How?" she asked.

Essy grinned—her teeth very sharp. "I have a few ideas."

Lizzie couldn't stop shivering. Essy's plan was a good one, but it also scared her.

She clutched the charm and the powder Essy had given her. She could do this. She could go into *His* dreams. She could take back her life and make it what she wanted it to be.

She went over what Essy had told her last night again in her head. "Remember, Lizzie, in Dreamland *He* isn't the strong one. *You* are. In Dreamland, you can beat Him, even if you can't do anything in the *Real*. Here, you know all the tricks. And you have all the power."

Byron had nodded, his amber eyes solemn.

Essy had taught her what to say, what to do. As soon as He fell asleep, she would follow Him to *His* Dreamland…and make sure He never came out.

That night, she went about her chores silently, careful not to set Him off in any way. She put half of Essy's powder into each of their glasses of weak tea with dinner. Once He was asleep, the magic of the powder would let Lizzie into His dreams.

She watched surreptitiously until He began to nod in His chair over a rerun of *Seinfeld*.

"I'm going to bed," He growled. "You make sure them dishes are washed before you turn in."

"Yes, sir," she replied meekly, careful to keep her head down so He couldn't see the hope blooming in her eyes. So far, things were going exactly as planned.

She washed the dishes while she waited for Him to fall asleep—just in case this didn't work, at least she'd save herself a beating in the morning. Once the kitchen was as clean as it ever was, she tiptoed to *His* door.

He never shut it—didn't believe in privacy. He was sprawled across His bed, snoring loudly. She crept into the room and lay down on the floor beside the bed. Not even if it ruined the plan would she willingly lie beside Him.

Her heart was pounding in her chest as she shut her eyes and tried to moderate her breathing so she could sleep. The merry-go-round tried to turn, but she put her metaphorical foot down and stopped the spin. Tonight, she didn't want *her* Dreamland. She wanted *His*.

She whispered the words Essy had told her, clutching the charm so hard her fingernails bit into her palm:

Follow Him down to the land of Dreams
Where nothing is really as it seems
There let me cut Him from the Real
With heart of fire and knife of steel.

A door appeared before her in the landscape of her mind. It slipped open to reveal an elevator car. This must be *His* entry to the Dreamland.

She stepped cautiously inside. There was only one button, and it had an arrow pointing down. With a shaky hand, she pushed the button.

The elevator plummeted downward at a sickening speed. She clung to the greasy brass handrail, struggling to keep down her meager dinner.

At last, the elevator jerked to a stop, and the door opened with a discordant chime. She peeked timidly out of the elevator.

The landscape before her was bleak and gray. Buildings jutted like broken teeth into an angry red sky. Everything was dirty and reeked of smoke and ash. His Dreamland was no comfort. Maybe that was why He was so horrible in the *Real*.

Her resolve faltered. Could it be that if His dreams were better, He would be, too? Perhaps this devastated landscape was the reason He was so awful to her.

Then Essy spoke in her head, repeating something she had said the night before. "The Dreamland reflects the Dreamer. Yours is full of light and color because you are full of light and color—or would be, without *Him*. When you get to His Dreamland, you'll know for sure. If it is as evil as He is—you'll know what to do."

And it was evil.

She could tell. Vague figures skulked in the alleys between the buildings. She crept forward cautiously, watching the figures out of the corner of her eye. They stayed in their hiding places.

She saw a neon sign on the corner, blinking "The End of the Line" and pointing to a seedy bar. She peeked through the grimy window. The bar was empty except for *Him*.

He sat on the wrong side of the bar on a stool pulled up to the taps. There was a line of mugs before Him, empty to His left, full to His right. He was drinking steadily. No wonder He was so nasty in the mornings.

Lizzie squared her shoulders. It was time. She would be rid of Him once and for all.

She lifted her chin high and walked into the bar. He looked up at the squeak of the door.

His jaw fell open. "What the Hell are *you* doing here?" he growled, tossing back another beer.

Heart pounding, she recited the words again as she closed the gap between them inch by inch.

Follow Him down to the land of Dreams
Where nothing is really as it seems
There let me cut Him from the Real
With heart of fire and knife of steel.

By the time she reached the final word, she was shouting at the top of her lungs.

He looked at her is if she had finally lost her senses. "What the Hell—?"

He never finished the sentence.

Her hand flashed forward, clutching Essy's charm—a six-inch, bone-handled knife. The blade slipped into His flesh like it was cutting butter. Again and again, she stabbed at Him, letting all her hatred fuel the strength of her strokes.

At first, He tried to block the attacks, tried to grab the knife from her, but she held onto it like it was part of her hand. His defense weakened as the front of His shirt blossomed with flowers of blood. He slipped from the stool, crumpling into a heap on the floor.

"Stop, Lizzie!" He whimpered. "Haven't I always been good to you, girl? I've taken care of you. Fed you, clothed you…loved you like my own."

"You've taken my childhood! You've ruined my life!" Screaming her hatred, she slit His throat. That would make sure. Dead was dead, Dreamland or *Real*…

Her eyes flew open as she returned to the *Real* with a gasp. She was shaking like a leaf.

Had it worked? Was He really dead?

She scrambled to her feet. He lay on His back in the bed, a look of horror on His face. She held a trembling hand before His gaping mouth. She couldn't feel any breath against her hand.

There was a cracked shaving mirror on His dresser. She held that to His lips. No cloud of breath on its marred surface.

She shook Him tentatively…no reaction. She pushed against Him with all her strength. He flopped bonelessly but didn't awaken.

It must be true. She had done it. She was finally free!

The police came when she called about *Him*. She didn't have to fake tears—but they were tears of joy, not sorrow. They had taken Him to the hospital in an ambulance, the sirens blaring through the night, but there was nothing to be done for Him. She had smiled behind her hand.

They brought her, too, since they couldn't just leave her alone. The doctor she saw at the hospital had asked her a lot of questions and done a bunch of tests. He hadn't told her the results, but he shook his head as he talked to the policemen, and she didn't think the news was good. The tests had hurt. She still hurt.

But not in her heart.

The police brought her here, to this orphan home, after the hospital, since there was nowhere else for her to go. But she didn't expect to be here long. She hadn't heard what the doctor said, but she could guess. She hadn't felt right in a long, long time.

But tonight she'd go to Dreamland. And maybe she just wouldn't come back.

That night, Lizzie and Essy lay on their backs on the merry-go-round while Byron flew around the circle above it, pushing them faster than Lizzie had ever gone. The stars were diamonds twinkling against a velvet sky.

She was really free! Her heart overflowed with the thought of it. Freedom. Happy, and safe, and free.

No going back to the home for the orphans and certainly not to the cramped apartment she could never keep clean enough for Him. No squeezing her eyes tight to ride the merry-go-round. She could ride it forever if she wished, just lie here in Dreamland and let the stars spin above her. She was free.

She was here, and she would stay. She felt the *Real* slipping away for good, her body was shutting down, leaving her here in Dreamland. Where she belonged.

Softly, she began to sing, "Here we go round…"

Rie Sheridan Rose's short stories appear in numerous anthologies, including *Nightmare Stalkers and Dream Walkers* Vols. 1 and 2, *Avast Ye Airships*, *The Grotesquerie*, and *In the Bloodstream*. Mocha Memoirs has the short story collection *Rie Tales*. Online, she has appeared in *Cease*, *Cows*, *Lorelei Signal*, and *Four Star Stories*. She is also the author of seven novels, six poetry chapbooks, and lyrics for songs on several of Marc Gunn's CDs.

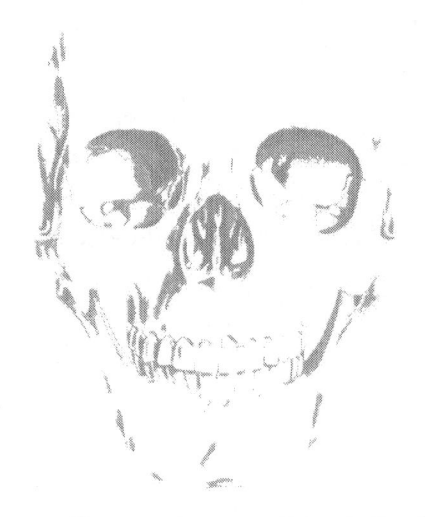

Songs for Dead Children

Aliya Whiteley

I walked into the party and was met with silence. I don't remember feeling anything; all my guilt and despair had already leaked out of me in the dressing room after the performance.

Guido greeted me with a kiss on each cheek. He wore a purple velvet suit and a bow tie, and his corkscrew hair was held back from his face by a plastic multicolored band that might suit a young girl.

"Our star," he said, and then, "have you seen the reviews? Never mind, never mind. Critics. I'll get you a champagne."

He pushed into the somber crowd. People looked at me, then at each other. Appropriately, it felt like a funeral was in progress. I looked up at the low ceiling, covered in yellowed tiles and the wooden surround from which hung paintings of Von Karajan, Von

Dingelstedt, and of Mahler himself. The elegant auditorium had been cavernous, a black hole I attempted to fill with my voice, and yet this back room was tiny, squashed full of red and gold furniture and a hundred different perfumes, overwhelming, yet all smelling only of money. Von Karajan raised his nose and his baton over them all; Mahler looked forlorn to find himself in their company.

I heard Guido ordering champagne at an obscenely loud volume, and I knew it had been a mistake to come at all. I could have left the country, gone home, given up my dreams rather than face having them ripped away. I made my way to the darkest corner of the room and sat in a small chair with a high back and scrolled wooden arms, hoping to be forgotten. Of course, that couldn't happen; and yet, I was grateful when the only person who found the courage to approach me was a middle-aged man with rimless glasses, a trimmed beard, and a way of holding himself that suggested he was not out to humiliate me further.

He held out a cut-glass tumbler. "It's brandy," he said. "I thought that might appeal more. Make this ordeal bearable." He had an American accent, but he spoke in slow, formal sentences.

"Thank you." I took the tumbler and held it in my lap. He sat down opposite me, in a matching chair, and I noticed the thick brown buttons on his waistcoat and the solid knot of his striped tie. "You don't look like one of the usual crowd."

"I'm not Viennese," he said, "obviously. I'm sorry, I mean, I don't live in Vienna. I traveled over from Pittsburgh."

"On holiday?" I couldn't work out how he had ended up in this gathering; such events were never open to mere members of the public.

He gave a small grimace, then said, "I came for the music."

I tried to hide my disappointment. "Then I'm sorry I let a lover of Mahler down so badly."

"No, no…" But I could tell he was trying to be kind. He screwed up his eyes, then made a hissing sound between his teeth. "I'm handling this badly. Look, I came because it was the

Kindertotenlieder. It's special to me. I don't know if anyone could do it justice, in my eyes. Do you understand?"

I gave a nod. "I know what it is to care for a piece of music."

"Mahler?"

"No, my first love is Mozart."

"Ah." He looked disappointed. "That could explain it, of course. Why you didn't connect tonight?"

"I beg your pardon?"

His hand flew to the knot of his tie, and he pulled at the material. "I'm sorry, I didn't mean to offend…"

"No, no, you didn't," I told him, and his honesty was suddenly the purest thing in the room to me. "You are right. I failed to connect. But the subject matter…"

"Yes, of course! That's what I mean. Songs for dead children. How can one who loves Mozart give themselves over to the world of darkness that Mahler gives us?"

"Except it's not darkness," I said. "There arises a new sun, doesn't there? Those are the first lines."

"Yes, and you sang them with hope, didn't you?" And I saw my first mistake. I was wrong from the beginning. The sun was not a symbol of life, after all. It was the burning face of despair, and I hadn't wanted to sing about such things. "You're not married, Fraulein Mutter, are you?"

"No."

"Maybe when you have children of your own this piece might make more sense to you. You are simply too young to sing it. It's a song of experience."

"The experience of death."

"Yes." He looked down at his feet.

The room seemed to have emptied around us. I was aware of nothing but that moment as I leaned over to touch his arm and said, "You…had a child that died?"

"I've lost many children." He looked up at me. "I'm a pediatric oncologist."

"Yes. What a horrible job."

He pulled back his shoulders. "Do you think so?"

I could see I had offended him, and I was sorry for it. I said, "This party is awful."

"Yes."

"I want to understand. I have an obligation to sing the Kindertotenlieder many times over the next six months. We are touring…"

"Yes."

Guido's voice reached me, demanding to know where I was, whom I needed to meet, how I couldn't be allowed to hide away. "Come with me to my hotel," I said to him. "There's a quiet bar there. We can talk some more. If you wouldn't mind."

"Talk about the music?" he said. "Of course."

We made a quiet escape, leaving Guido's voice, still shouting for me, behind us, and I summoned one of the horse-drawn carriages that line the Kartnerstrasse.

The hotel bar was tiny: carefully lit to preserve privacy, with three small red leather booths opposite the sleek expanse of the counter and the polished order of the optics. We sat together in the furthest booth and drank Viennese coffee from tall white cups, served with water—an indulgence on my part, as caffeine is not good for the vocal cords. There was also a small glass dish of dark chocolate, broken into irregular pieces. I melted one on my tongue as he talked about the second Lieder:

Now I see well, why with such dark flames
in many glances you flash upon me
O Eyes: as if in one look
to draw all your strength together

The dark flames of loss—the excitement of approaching death, being alive in the face of death—he saw that in the music, and I had not. I had imagined all to be sadness, and had sung only that, removing all other colors from Mahler's palette.

"Death can be beautiful," he told me, and I began to see it.

By the end of the evening, I will admit I asked him to come to my room with me. He had aroused me with his direct gaze, his way of speaking so openly on the darkest matters, and perhaps that is a terrible confession. Should one feel lust after discussing the death of children? Maybe only a lover of Mahler could understand it. For, yes, I came to Mahler that night, and Mozart always seemed a little too shiny for me afterward.

In retrospect, it was perhaps a good thing that he declined my offer to accompany me upstairs. It would have made the evening less of a meeting of minds, and detracted from the many things he gave me to think about.

He kissed my cheek when he stood up to leave, talking of an early flight, and responsibilities at the hospital back home. The shock of his beard against my skin was delicious, and so sad; I felt sure we would never meet again.

"Thank you," I said. "I think you've made me a better singer."

"So glad I could help. If you're ever in Pittsburgh..." He held out a business card. "It was a delight to hear the Kindertotenlieder performed. It so very rarely is."

"Yes. So many people think it's depressing."

As I took the card, he caught my wrist and held it, for just a moment. "But we know better."

The sun always arises, radiant: those are the first lyrics. And they are right. By the end of that night and I was beyond the bad reviews and the silent audience. I had many more performances to give, and I vowed that every one would be better than the one before.

I read the card he had given me: Dr. Adam Bexler. I took it with me to my room and slipped it inside the pages of my passport, in the small safe under the drinks cabinet. I kept it as a memento, nothing more. It traveled with me, across continents. After every success, I held it in my hands and thought of him.

Songs for Dead Children

The next time I saw him was in New York.

Eight years had passed, and the Kindertotenlieder was in fashion for a change. Thousands had died when the planes flew into the towers. People had sons and daughters fighting overseas in a war that felt without end. Death had come to America, and with my carefully timed CD release, I had become the voice of it.

The Met is a marvelous arena for a confident performer. The acoustics are wonderful; you can hear your voice soaring out over the tiers of seats, drowning out the rustling of programs and the shifting of feet, which can be so distracting in a lesser venue. But I was not paying much attention to the auditorium that night; instead, I was concentrating on the uncomfortable dress I had been persuaded to wear by my new costume manager. The diamante strappings around the chest were constricting my breathing, and I was finding it a battle to climb the peaks of the fourth Lieder:

They have just gone out ahead of us,
and will not be thinking of coming home.
We go to meet them on yonder heights
In the sunlight, the day is fine
On yonder heights.

I pictured firing my costume designer as soon as I got offstage; it was a diverting thought. I suppose I had become used to the vast, intense hush of the crowd that led to the wash of applause, breaking over me in waves, buoying me up from one performance to the next. In my defense, nobody seemed to care if the experience was true anymore; they wanted to hear a famous singer so that they could go home and tell their friends. How I sang no longer mattered.

And then I knew he was there.

It's difficult to describe how I became aware of him. It would have been impossible to pick out his features in that sea of faces, and yet I was utterly sure that he was attending that night, in the middle of the second tier. The connection between us was a thin thread of emotion, like a strand of silk, so delicate, so strong. Something in me came to life. Once more I felt the touch of his hand, the rough drag of his beard across my cheek. The constriction of my dress was forgotten. Instead, I remembered what he had told me that night in Vienna, and I found passion within me and projected it out to him with all of my skill. I sang only for him. I prayed that he did not find it wanting.

I sat in my dressing room for hours, after the final encore. He did not come.

There was a large square mirror, lit with old-fashioned bulbs, over the ornate dressing table. I don't know if it's still there now. It was the kind of mirror from which a performer could hide nothing.

That evening I saw the beginning of age on my face. Age is not in the appearance of fine wrinkles around the eyes, or a pouch of saggy skin forming under the chin. It is in experience: the darkness that creeps into the soul with every disappointment, lost love, broken promise. The soft child that lived inside me started to harden that night, as the minutes passed and I realized he was not coming to tell me I had pleased him. I had not done justice to Mahler yet again.

It hurt, the hardening of the child inside me; it hurt for many months, and I did not sing Mahler again for years. When I returned to the Kindertotenlieder and recorded it on CD for the first time another seven years had passed, and in that time I had been married and divorced and lost both my parents. I was not the same woman anymore. But I didn't realize how different I had become until I saw him for the last time.

He came into the reception, checking his watch, and the nurse at the main desk pointed him in my direction. I stood up, cardboard coffee cup in hand. I can recall his exact expression when he recognized me; it was the face a child pulls when a balloon pops at a birthday party—a mixture of instantaneous shock and glee that something so unexpected can happen, for no reason at all, and suddenly the world seems a little less controlled.

He set his lips together and walked towards me, both hands outstretched. I threw my coffee cup in the bin next to the dispenser and let him grasp my upper arms through my thick coat.

"I'm overwhelmed," he said. "What an honor."

"So you remember me? It's been so many years."

"I have your latest CD. My—er—wife bought it for me as a Christmas present." He dropped his hands.

"And you still have your beard," I said.

He stroked it. "A little grayer."

I became aware of the attention of the nurse, watching us as she languidly flipped through a file at the main desk. This was not how I'd imagined our meeting. I had constructed a scenario—a simple white room in which we came together, and I had the time and space to ask the question that had haunted me since the release of the CD. But there was only here and now, in a small waiting room filled with plastic chairs, with the smell of the hospital and the sound of footsteps and low conversations pressing around me. Still, I had to ask. There was no alternative, and time was already slipping away.

"Did I do it justice?" I said.

He seemed not to hear. "Are you in Pittsburgh on—holiday?" Words were not coming easily to either of us.

"I came to see you. I still have your card." I wanted to get it over with, now I'd started. "I flew out from London, then caught a connecting flight from JFK. I phoned, of course, and they told me you still worked here. I spoke to a receptionist, or something. They said they'd put me through to your office, and I realized I needed to see you in person. I can't explain it—I needed to know how you really felt about it."

"The CD?" he said, slowly.

"It's crazy." I could suddenly see it as if from a great distance—the ridiculousness of it. Maybe he had lost his love of Mahler. I could imagine him on his sofa, sitting next to his wife, reading a newspaper or surfing the web while the stereo bleated out soft, modern music. The three-minute pop song ruled the world now, each note as bland

and smooth as a boiled egg. Could that be his choice? But no, he had said he owned the CD. I could hope he had liked it.

The nurse came up, and said, "Doctor Bexler, you asked me to remind you to check in on room 317 before your shift ended."

"Yes, thank you." For the first time, he sounded like a doctor, dismissing a junior member of staff, too busy for conversations such as these.

"I should have handled this differently," I said to him as the nurse walked away.

He bit his lip, then said, "Come with me."

"Come—?"

"To room 317."

I followed him, past the main desk. He keyed in a code, and the secure door opened; he held it open for me and then steered me, one hand on my back, down a long corridor that the children had painted with flowers, stick figures, and an enormous yellow sun. The paint had been applied so thickly in places that it had dripped down the wall. It was impossible not to regard this bright messiness as a retort to the illnesses they faced. Or maybe the children who had made this mural had already lost their battle, and their flowers and faces meant nothing anymore.

"Here," he said, and a glass door on our left opened automatically. He ushered me in, and I found myself in a darkened room, filled with instruments and screens, all showing steady red or blue lights, and in the center of them all was a girl on a bed, curled up in a ball, a tangled white sheet caught up under her arms and between her legs. She was bald and tiny; she jerked in her sleep. From one arm ran a thin tube to a machine close to the bed, and on the other arm was a line to a drip, hanging above her, filled with a clear liquid.

He leaned in close to my ear. "Liver cancer," he whispered. I nodded. But it was too much to take in, this real death, the kind of illness he dealt with every day. I understood only that I had still failed to put this into my singing. The Kindertotenlieder still evaded me. I had no ability to show this dark room and the small, twitching body through the power of my voice.

"Watch," he said. He stepped away from me, to the machine next to the girl's bed. He opened the outer panel on one side and pressed some buttons, quickly, lightly. I found myself watching the girl's face. She was not an angel, and there was nothing pure about her suffering. She was a bundle of flesh trying to curl in on itself, to make herself so small that pain would not be able to find her. She was a soldier at war, and I was watching her fight, even in her dreams.

He gestured for me to approach. I came up beside him as softly as I could, so as not to wake her, and put one hand on the edge of the bed, above the crumpled sheet. I wanted to ask him if she would win her struggle, but I didn't dare.

He held out his hand to me. In his fist, he gripped a white wand, with a button set into the top. At first, I thought it was a call buzzer for assistance, but when he pressed it no sound emanated. He kept his thumb down, and the girl stopped twitching. Her mouth fell open. Her body uncurled, became limp. I saw the fight leave her. I didn't understand. Not until it was too late, and he had set down the wand on top of the machine. Then he spoke, and this time he did not whisper.

"You see?" he said. "You see how it is?"

And I did see.

"When they go, the very young ones, they become still, don't they? They leave the storm behind. As Mahler tells us. *They are resting, no more storms to be feared: by God's hand they are sheltered.*" He put both hands up to me, held them out as if presenting a gift. "Or by my hands."

I agreed with him; he had indeed brought shelter from the storm to that girl. And now she was as cold and pure as an angel, as a work of art, as a symphony.

I asked him if we could leave. I told him I had much to think about. He nodded, as if he understood, and escorted me back to the reception.

"I look forward to your next performance of the

Kindertotenlieder," he said and kissed me on both cheeks. "You can be sure I will attend."

"Yes," I said. "Thank you."

I went down to the lobby and summoned a taxi to take me to the police station.

And now I do not sing. Not even in the shower, or under my breath. I am afraid that I will find a phrase on my tongue, a moment of the Kindertotenlieder, and he will somehow hear it. Even though he will never tend to another child. He will no longer lead them through the storm to shelter before they are ready to give up their fight. Even though he is in prison, and I saw him sentenced, and taken away, for the deaths of so many children, over so many years.

If I sing, it will be there in my voice; the understanding of what it is to watch the death of a child. And so I will not sing again. And I will never have a child of my own.

Because there are some battles that one should not have to fight.

Aliya Whiteley lives in West Sussex, UK, and writes strange novels and short stories. Her latest novella, *The Arrival of Missives*, was published by Unsung Stories in May 2016 to critical acclaim. For more information, visit her twitter feed (@AliyaWhiteley).

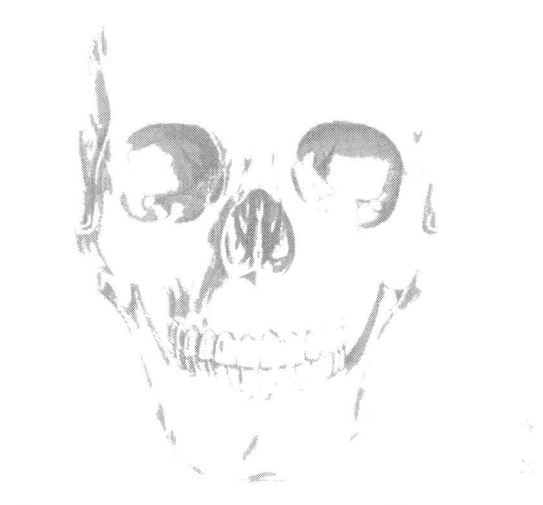

Music in the Bone

Marion Pitman

*"Now your cage shall be made of the finest beaten gold
And the doors of the best ivory."*

The ballad finished, the woman sat down, and a man with a guitar stepped to the front of the room. Lena tried to stop fidgeting. Already she had pulled a thread in her skirt on a splinter from the table leg, and her restless fingers had encountered a mass of old chewing gum on the underside of the table top.

She took a tissue out of her bag, then spat, and wiped her fingers. She looked at her hands. They appeared grotesque and unnatural, like alien claws. She wondered if the stigmata were coming back; she caught a whiff of some fetid smell. Quickly, she threw the tissue in the ashtray and put her hands in her pockets.

Tom glanced at her, frowning. He was actually listening to this maundering sub-70's stream-of-consciousness lyric. One of the guitar strings was slightly flat, just enough to be painful.

The room was small, smoky and cold, with mismatched chairs, benches with holes in the red leatherette upholstery revealing gross intestines of gray foam, and not enough people. Not surprising, with this going on.

Her hands seemed to be wandering again, fiddling with the silver bird skulls in her earlobes; she missed the intro to the next performer.

She hadn't seen him before. He started to play the fiddle.

His bow stroked and caressed the strings, producing sounds Lena had never heard from a violin. It purred, moaned, sighed; he made love to it until she could almost hear the instrument reach orgasm.

When he finished, the audience was silent for a moment; then they applauded wildly.

Lena was entranced. She had never heard an instrument sing so, heard music with such life and intensity.

His second number was a reel—quick, lively, vigorous. Images whirled in her head, wild dancing, lightning flashes, crashing surf and waterfalls; jungles of bright birds and vivid flowers.

When it ended, she felt quite breathless and joined in the applause with abandon.

He was cute, too. Tall, thin and wiry, black hair in long tangled curls, very white skin. Small silver rings glinted in his ears. He looked glamorous, in the magical sense; dangerous, feral. Probably, she thought, he would turn out to be a computer programmer for an insurance company, with no conversation beyond Windows and war-gaming. Still, he was a good deal more decorative than Tom. She glanced sideways at Tom's bald spot, the hair around it rough and in need of a trim, not to mention a comb.

She generally went home with Tom after the folk club. That was as far as the relationship went, spending the night together once a week. It had been going on like that for months. She felt she couldn't bear it a moment longer. She would tell Tom she had a blinding headache, or the curse had come on early.

At one time she would have chatted up the fiddle player, tried to take him home with her, just for the hell of it; but that was in another life.

The club always finished by half past ten so that the organizers could get back to some far-flung outpost of suburbia. Naturally, most people drifted down to the still-open bar. Lena drifted with the rest. Tom was deep in discussion with a frowning woman in a long skirt; Lena caught the words "CD drive" and "motherboard". She made an impatient move away from them and found herself next to the fiddle player.

He caught her eye and smiled.

She said, "I was very impressed by your playing. You're amazingly good," and thought, how naff does that sound?

But he looked pleased, and said, "Thank you."

She said tentatively, "I haven't seen you here before?"

"No. I only moved here recently."

"Oh, right." Pause. "Where were you before?"

"Oh, I've been living abroad."

"Uh huh?"

"Travelling."

"Right."

"Would you like a drink?"

"Oh! I'm sorry—I wasn't…"

"That's OK. But would you like a drink?"

"Thanks. I'll have a pint of Guinness."

He turned away to catch the eye of one of the young New Zealanders behind the bar.

Lena glanced around. The bar was noisy with the jukebox on, and a lot of girls in tight jeans and skimpy tops, drinking vodka or lurid cocktails, were having a good time at the tops of their voices. It seemed to be somebody's hen night.

She remembered a bar in…Dublin? Auckland? Cape Town?

Sometime in another life—a live band playing very loud, dancing all night, spaced out on too much white wine and no food, heavily snogging an extravagantly underdressed woman with red hair and big tits. She could remember the rum and coke taste of the redhead's mouth…nothing came of it. One of them had made a misstep, or they just hadn't wanted it enough. Where was she staying? a hostel, a five-star hotel? It was all the same in those days. Another life. With the Latvian footballer in Sydney, looking for a bad time in King's Cross at four a.m., or Christmas Eve in a sports bar in Wellington, high as a kite on fear and adrenalin—another life.

The fiddle player turned with the Guinness. He smiled; his teeth were flat across the front, with long canines—not Dracula-long, just slightly wolfish. His eyes were a clear dark brown, like glasses of neat whiskey.

As she took the drink from him, she noticed his hands, pale and very thin, just skin strung over bones; she touched the back of his fingers, they were smooth, like alabaster, and nearly as cold.

"Thanks," she said with a smile, and looked into his eyes just a little too long.

They stood together in silence for a while. He drank beer. No one spoke to them.

Then Tom called, "Lena! You coming?"

She turned. Now or never.

"Sorry," she said. "I've got a really early start tomorrow."

"OK. See you next week," and he was gone. Just like that.

Behind her, she heard a low, teasing voice, "Have you really got an early start?"

She turned back; he was looking at her with a smile twisting up one side of his mouth.

"Maybe," she said. "Maybe not."

"My name's Ed," he said.

"Lena."

"I only live round the corner. It's very near the tube station."

"That's handy."

"Are you coming home with me?"

She stared at him. She no longer expected that sort of directness. He laughed. There seemed no reason not to say, "Yes."

His flat was up three flights of stairs, an attic room with a sloping ceiling, and a low window that looked out on other roofs—all angles, different heights, red, brown, gray, black, tile, slate, concrete. Street lighting gave them an eerie glow.

The room was dimly lit, the walls hung with swags of black and dark red cloth. A tall ebony and ormolu cabinet stood against one wall, on top of it a phrenology head, a malachite obelisk, a crystal ball on a black wood stand, and one of those globes full of lightning that follows your hand. No stuffed crocodile, she thought; every alchemist's laboratory should have a stuffed crocodile.

Another wall was lined with instruments and sound equipment; against a third was a wide divan with a black silk spread.

Ed said, "What do you think?"

"Very Gothic," she replied; "You don't look Goth."

"Oh, you should see me at weekends." He laughed.

She looked along the wall; "You play a lot of instruments."

"Fiddle and guitar mainly. Keyboards now and then. I'm trying to learn the harp."

It was a small, portable, medieval style harp, fancifully carved with wolves and unicorns.

"But the fiddle's my true love," he said. He put the case down on the bed and opened it, taking the cloth from the instrument and stroking its neck affectionately.

It was a beautiful looking thing. The wood glowed with the patina of age and loving attention; the pegs, fingerboard, and bridge were inlaid with ivory or bone, a warm yellowish white. The strings and the hair of the bow seemed to catch the light with a golden glint. She fancied it almost hummed softly to itself, there in the case.

"You're amazingly good," she said. "I've never heard anyone play the fiddle like that."

He grinned; "So you didn't say that just as a chat-up line?"

"Actually, no. I mean, yes. All right, it *was* a chat-up line, but it was true, too."

He smiled again, slowly, suggestively; left the fiddle and moved towards her. He put his hands on her hips, lowered his head, and kissed her.

She gripped his elbows to steady herself; the kiss was long and deep, hungry, demanding. He tasted of beer and cigarettes. She found her whole body responding; her belly lit on fire and yearned toward him.

At last, he broke contact and stepped back.

"D'you want a shower?" he said.

"Uh, no. I had one before I came out." She responded automatically, then thought, that was wrong.

He said, "OK. I will, though." He kissed her lightly on the forehead and went out through a curtained doorway in the corner.

Lena wandered around. She was shy of touching anything, but she looked avidly. On a battered map chest beside the cabinet were a laptop and some papers; beside the instruments was a tall blackwood rack with several dozen CDs, many of artists she'd never heard of, besides Steeleye Span, Pink Floyd, Nick Drake, Counting Crows, and Fields of the Nephilim. Eclectic, she thought. There was Bach, too, and Sibelius, and traditional Irish fiddle players. There seemed to be several by a band called Procne.

When Ed came out, she said, "Actually I think I might have a shower, if that's OK?"

"Sure," he replied. "Plenty of hot water."

She showered quickly, trying to keep her hair dry, leaving her earrings in. Her heart beat too fast, her stomach fluttered, nervous as a schoolgirl on a first date. She laughed at herself.

She came back to the bed-sitting room wrapped in a towel. Ed was naked, sitting back on the divan; he pressed a remote control, and music filled the room.

It was a fiddle, backed by keyboard and a flute or whistle. It sounded like Ed's playing.

She sat on the edge of the bed; she said, "Is that you?"

"That's Procne," he replied, "which is me."

"Just you?"

"Just me."

"Is that a flute?"

He got up and stepped across to the instrument wall, and opened a small case; he took something out and came back. He handed her a short cylinder, smooth and dull white. It was pierced like a tin whistle, but the shape was rough and irregular.

"It's a thigh bone," he said.

"A human one?"

"Of course not." He was smiling; she wasn't sure whether to believe him.

"It's a native artifact," he said, "it makes an incredible sound." He put it to his mouth and blew softly; the notes that came out were beautiful, pure, eerie, chilling. Lena felt the hairs on her arms bristle; there was darkness in the sound, and the warning of a deadly snake unseen among leaves…

He stopped playing and saw her expression.

"Don't you think it's wonderful?" he asked.

"Yes. But scary."

He looked at her, his head on one side; then he put the flute away, backtracked on the CD, and unwound the towel.

His response to her nakedness was immediate, and her own body also responded at once; she wanted him instantly, urgently.

The music intensified the mood; it throbbed and wailed with aching sexual need, with pounding blood.

He laid her on the divan. His caresses became rough; he bit her breasts, and she cried out at the pain but was too deep in the grip of lust to push him away.

His hands were hard, but she thrust against them, relishing the force of resistance.

Under and behind all, the music beat with the rhythm of sex, with deep lascivious notes that seemed to curl up like tongues of fire, igniting sparks all through her limbs.

But still, at the last moment, with a reflex she stiffened and pulled back, and said, "Condom."

"What?" He sounded genuinely bemused.

"Condom. I'm not on the pill. There's some in my bag if you…"

He gave a small, rather bitter laugh, and reached out to a cabinet beside the bed.

He looked at her while he put on the condom by touch; there was something in the dark eyes she couldn't quite fathom; was it just naked desire, or was there something else?

But she forgot it all once he began thrusting with the underlying beat of the music, which had moved on to a faster, simpler, more rhythmic track, almost—had she been able to think about it—as if he had compiled the tracks to the pace of his lovemaking.

Afterward, she felt not so much satisfied as drained, sucked dry. For several minutes, she couldn't move.

He said, "Do you want to stay the night?"

"Uh…" She didn't really. She felt insecure, these days, sleeping away from her own place, but— "What time is it?"

"Two thirty."

"D'you mind if I stay?" She really didn't think she had the strength of mind—or body—to go anywhere right now.

"Sure. That's OK. I'll have to throw you out early, though. I have to go to work."

"OK."

He showered again, but Lena scarcely had the energy to stagger to the toilet. Unlike most men, Ed seemed energized by sex; he was playing something low and sinister on the flute when she fell asleep.

He woke her early, as he had said. He seemed anxious to see her go, so she showered quickly, drank the coffee he brought, left without mentioning breakfast.

As she started down the stairs, she passed a woman in a light raincoat—slim and pretty, with heavy blonde hair falling to her shoulders, who stared hard and hostilely at Lena as they passed, and Lena thought she heard a short, ironic laugh behind her.

When she got home, Lena went to change her clothes. She was startled and rather appalled at the number of small bruises on her arms and breasts and stomach and thighs. She didn't remember acquiring all those. She felt stiff, too, as if she had fallen, or slept on a hard floor.

She ran a bath. She still had over an hour before she needed to leave for the café; she wasn't on breakfasts this week.

She thought about Ed. On the whole, she thought she'd rather not see him again. The sex had been amazing. He was interesting company—and a brilliant musician—and she was always taken by people who were very good at what they did, but she didn't like feeling that far out of control.

Still, the question was unlikely to arise; in Lena's experience, men who took you to bed the first time you met seldom wanted to repeat the event.

So although he'd taken her phone number, she wasn't surprised not to hear from him. She missed the folk club the next week, and when she went the week after it was only with the faintest expectation of seeing him.

Tom had phoned three times; she had tried to put him off, but in the end, she said she wanted a break from the relationship. Since Tom had never admitted that they had a relationship, he tried to argue with this; he said, "I suppose you've dropped me for that poncey fiddle player."

She said, "Don't be silly," and put the phone down.

Should she make up with Tom? She was certainly in charge of the relationship, such as it was, but he bored her so. She thought of Ed playing the thigh-bone flute and was shocked at the flood of lust the thought provoked. Well, she said to herself, that would wear off.

Ed wasn't at the club when she arrived, and she wasn't sure if she were disappointed or relieved. But when he turned up in the interval, with the blonde from the staircase, she was definitely angry. He sketched a wave and a smile; she raised an eyebrow, said, "Hi," brusquely, and went down to the bar.

She sat there for three-quarters of an hour, drinking gin, and fantasizing that he would come down alone and speak to her and explain and apologize; then she went home. The pain was astonishing.

Dammit, she thought, I don't even like him. But he could have rung and warned me. Except a man wouldn't see the necessity. Not after a one-night stand. Meaning nothing. And it meant nothing to me either. God knows I'm old enough to know how these things work.

She started to shake and went to lie down. Her hands itched and smarted dreadfully.

All night she dozed and woke to the sinuous sounds of the flute and the fiddle that seemed to have wound themselves around her brain cells. With some idea of laying the ghost, she went out on her break next day and looked in a record shop for Procne. There was nothing. She asked the assistant, but there was nothing in the catalog. Didn't mean a thing of course; he probably just sold the CDs at gigs.

The next week, she wondered whether to give the folk club a miss. Tom wasn't talking to her, and she didn't know if she could handle the humiliation of Ed's turning up with the blonde again.

In the end, she went late, arriving after the interval. She slipped in during the applause; Ed was playing. He had the guitar this time. His fingers flew over the strings, as his left hand hunched and squeaked on the frets. The notes seemed sharp and glittering like shards of glass, weaving a circle, a crown of thorns, a stifling circumference of ice, dazzling in the sun. It hurt.

When he finished, the applause was deafening.

He glanced up. Lena couldn't tell if he saw her or not. She looked around, but couldn't see the blonde.

He put down the guitar and picked up the fiddle, tuned it, and began a slow air, yearning, languorous, full of hope and despair and uncertainty. Despite herself, Lena found tears in her eyes.

The audience was silent for several beats after he finished, and the applause was quieter but went on and on.

He stepped off the stage and came across to where she was standing.

"Hi," he said. "Sorry about last week."

"You could've warned me," she said, resisting the impulse to say, Oh, that's all right.

He frowned. "I suppose so."

"So is that your girlfriend? I saw her before, at your flat."

He shrugged. "She's just a friend. So are you—I hope."

She looked into his eyes and felt her stomach churning. Her mind was saying, he can't just dismiss it like that, but her body wanted him, on almost any terms.

He said, "Will you come back with me tonight?"

She found herself saying, "Yes."

They left early, and when they got in he poured glasses of whiskey. They sat on the divan sipping the drinks. He took the guitar out of the case and began changing a string. The new string, out of a cloth bag with no label, glinted in the soft light of the lamps. The frets of the guitar were inlaid with strange angular patterns; he saw her looking at them, and pointed.

"Mystic runes," he said, "in an unknown language." She raised an eyebrow, and he laughed; "It's supposed to be Arabic or something. Probably says 'Made in Japan.'"

Something rang false in his tone; she said, "All your instruments are unusual some way."

He gave a one-sided smile. "I guess I'm trying to find the perfect instrument. The guitar's good; the fiddle's better. The flute's got its own, uh, something, but it's a bit primitive. Maybe I'll find what I'm looking for with the harp."

"And what are you looking for?"

"Ah!" he gave her a big, genuine smile. "That's the sixty-four-thousand-dollar question. I can only say I'll know it when I find it.

"I don't know—the essence of music? The thing that all music reminds us of—the soul of music? the music of souls, perhaps? As you say, I, well, modify my instruments, trying to get closer to…to the heart of music, the real thing, that's more than just sound, that's being, meaning, essence…then you'd hear something."

"But how do you do it? How do you 'modify' them?"

"Ah. That, I'm afraid, is a trade secret. One day I'll tell you, I think. I think you'd understand—better than Heather."

He looked at her, and she thought, is that meant to make me feel better about Heather? But it did, all the same.

He put on another Procne CD, a gentler one this time, with a good deal of keyboard, which seemed to calm and dilute the effect of the fiddle and guitar. The flute was scarcely in evidence.

Lena took the first shower; he lent her a red silk dressing gown. While he was in the bathroom she wandered around. Feeling daring, she tried the top drawer of the map chest, but it was locked. She picked up a cassette tape that lay on top behind the printer; the handwritten label said, "Edward Oliver – First Album."

As she turned it to read the list of tracks, his voice, sharper than usual, said, "Put that down!"

She dropped it and stepped back, reddening. "I'm sorry—"

"No. Sorry. I—that's a very early tape, and very bad. I'm rather sensitive about it."

He put his hands on her shoulders, and looked into her eyes, and she forgot the tape.

The sex, like the music, was slower and gentler this time, though Lena still found herself with bruises she couldn't account for. Afterward, she drifted imperceptibly into sleep.

They saw each other after that once or twice a week; she didn't know if he was still seeing Heather and didn't ask. Sometimes the sex was gentle and easy; more often it was increasingly violent. Sometimes he would put his hands on her head and press down and back till she was afraid her spine would snap. He was strong, and she was afraid to struggle too much. He pinched and bit her breasts, although she asked him not to. But then he would tease her until she went into orbit, making her wait for the climax, and at last igniting a pit of fire deep inside her that no one before had ever reached, and the pain would seem unimportant.

Sometimes he would play the fiddle or the guitar before they began; if he played the flute, things were more likely to get out of hand. She never heard him play the harp.

"I'm still working on it," he said.

Every time she got home, stiff and sore and black and blue, she thought, why the hell am I seeing him; but when he rang she still said yes, and when he played, she felt helpless to resist anything he wanted.

The palms of her hands stung continually; the stabbing pain in her side was back.

They didn't go out together. Once she suggested—just casually—going to a movie. His eyes veiled, and he shrugged.

"Sorry," he said, "I don't get much free time."

"Oh."

She was startled, but he quickly went on to talk about something else.

So she went home with him after the folk club, just as she had with Tom. At other times, he rang quite late in the evening when it was too late to go out anywhere, and she went to his flat. She never said, "Why don't you come over here?" She knew he wouldn't.

Sometimes they had a take-away meal, often a bottle of wine. But most often, he played music and did extraordinary, painful, amazing things to her body.

Once she stood at the window of the flat in a summer twilight, looking out at the planes and angles of the roofscape, and said, trying to sound playful, "So what do you do in real life?"

"I work in IT," he said, "and it's very, very, boring, and I don't talk about it in my own time."

So she couldn't ask him any more.

One night, the CD was a throbbing, dark track, with an insistent beat and the flute underlying everything. The fiddle was strident, the guitar plangent; the whole pulsed with menace.

Ed was holding her head and nibbling her neck and shoulders, his hands stroking her sides, relaxing her, when suddenly she felt a pain so sharp her body jerked upright reflexively as she screamed, wrenching his hand away, her head hitting the bridge of his nose.

He yelled, "What the fuck?" as he reared back, both hands to his face, blood pouring between them.

She sat, gasping, one hand on her shoulder where his teeth had met, and blood trickled down.

He threw his head back and managed at last to stem the nosebleed. Half-stunned, she helped him clean up. Then they stood in the bathroom and looked at each other.

"What the *hell* did you do that for?" he said.

"I couldn't help it. That *hurt*."

"Are you telling me you don't like pain? You stupid bitch, you're longing for it—I can smell it, I can taste it, it comes off you in *waves*. You deafen the air with your need for pain."

"But not from *you*, you fool, not from *you*." Her feet, hands, and side throbbed as she spoke.

He shook his head. "Such a pity. I know I could have made it work with you. You're so strong. You don't know what you missed. I'll have to do the best I can with Heather."

She heard the words but didn't take them in.

Suddenly, he leaned forwards, picked off the dried blood over the wound on her shoulder with his nail, blood welling up. Before she could react, he pressed a tissue to the wound, and took it back, red and wet, saying, "A souvenir."

All she could think of was getting away from him. She backed into the bedroom, but he made no attempt to follow. Pain hammered so hard in her palms she could scarcely get dressed.

She finally managed it, picked up her coat and bag, and hobbled out. He leaned in the bathroom doorway, but as she started down the stairs, she heard him playing the flute. She forced her hands over her ears.

Time went by. Ed didn't call. Lena left the answering machine on; she was terrified of what would happen if she heard his voice.

She avoided the folk club. Tom started phoning again, saying he was worried about her. She told him she had a new job, working evenings.

Her boss at the café said, "I don't know what you've been on, love, but you did right to give it up."

Gradually the throbbing in her hands subsided. She thought about what Ed had said, and tried to avoid thinking about pain.

After about three months, a friend just back from Australia rang, and asked Lena to come to the folk club. Lena tried to put her off, but Jenny was very forceful; Lena wasn't feeling forceful.

In the end, she said, "Look, Jen, there's a chap goes there sometimes that I don't want to see. I haven't been for months."

"What, just because of some bloke? Why? What did he do?"

He bit me. No, she couldn't say that. "Well, um—we were seeing each other, and it—ended badly."

"Tom?"

"No, not Tom. Another bloke."

"Well, for god's sake, Lena, you can't run your life by blokes you're avoiding. Anyway, he might be avoiding you—you won't know if you never go."

In the end, she agreed to go. At least Jenny would be some protection.

They got there early, another of Jenny's irritating habits. Ed was sitting on the edge of the stage, talking to Rob. Rob knew Jenny; before Lena could protest or move, she was dragged across the room.

Beside Ed on the stage stood the harp.

Ed said, "Hallo, Lena."

To her great relief, she didn't go into rabbit-with-snake mode. Had she overestimated the power of his voice?

She said, "Hallo. Have you finally got it together with the harp?"

He smiled; "I hope so." He stood up and moved between her and the instrument. "It would have been better with you."

"What? What would?"

"If you'd stayed. It would have been better. But I think I've got it right."

He moved just a little, so she could see the harp.

She said, "You've finished customizing it, then?"

"Modifying. I prefer modifying."

The wood glowed, what little one could see for the intricate, off-white inlay, bone or ivorine, the pattern something like Celtic knotwork, endlessly interwoven, polished and shining. The pegs were of the same material. The strings glowed softly, with an organic more than a metallic gold. The only thing that marred its perfection was a small dark smear, the color of dried blood, on the sound-bow.

Lena found it hard to take her eyes off it. It seemed to be mesmerizing her as much as Ed had. Someone spoke to Ed; people moved, interrupting her view of the harp, and she managed to tear herself away and went for a drink.

She came back after the session had started, and stood at the back. Jenny was deep in conversation, talking over a woman with a high, thin and barely audible voice. Lena was aware of impatience, a feeling of marking time until Ed played the harp. After a bit, she found a seat near the front, on the other side of the room from where Ed was.

He came on last before the interval, sitting down and setting up the harp on a stool. As he drew his fingers across the strings, everyone in the room fell silent, even the couple who stood at the back and had talked through every song since 1972.

Lena lost all sense of time and space. She felt blinding sunlight, another time and place, and the impossible high of that week with

Peter, and the intolerable pain that followed; felt as she had not allowed herself to feel since; felt again the intense joy of seeing his face, of his voice, that made her spine tingle; the smell of his skin, the smooth black skin of his shoulder, in a green singlet; he was there, he was turning towards her, smiling—

—and the music stopped, and her eyes darkened, and her body fell through fathoms—

—and she opened her eyes, and Ed was setting the harp upright on the stool, and the audience was still silent, too stunned for applause.

And then the harp sang. It sang with a woman's voice, and Ed wasn't touching it, he sat frozen, a look of utter dismay on his face. The harp sang:

"He stole my bones for ivory
He stole my hair for gold
He stole my blood for fire and flood
He tried to pour away my soul
He scoured my bones, he wove my hair,
He poured my living blood through air
He burned my flesh, he poured my life away
To weave a net, a net to trap
The music of the universe
The sound of heaven, the sound of earth
The music of the soul"

It ended with a single piercing note, like a cry of intense pain—

—and she knew. She knew what had happened to the woman on the stairs, and why she wasn't here. She knew what the harp was inlaid with—felt it, excruciatingly, in her bones. She knew what it was strung with—but surely the gold hair had been too short...

Ed was staring, his face white as bone, his eyes burning.

"I wanted it to be you," he said, "it would have been so much better with you. It should have been you..."

Lena looked away before she read what was in his eyes. She stood, and walked out of the still silent room. In the corridor she

Marion Pitman

paused. The pain in her hands was gone.

Jenny came out after her. "My God," she said, "What was that about? Lena—you all right?"

She took a deep breath; "I'm fine. Jen, I want you to come with me to a police station."

Marion Pitman lives outside London, though she would rather live inside it. She has written poetry and fiction most of her life, and published it since the 1970s. She sells second-hand books, and has worked as an artists' model. She has no car, no television, no cats and no money. Her hobbies include folk-singing and theological argument. Her short story collection, Music in the Bone, is available from Alchemy Press.

All of a Heap

Jenner Michaud

Gus took his eyes off the road to glance at his watch. They had less than two hours to get to the temporary clinic before it relocated. Finding the secret location once had been difficult, tracking it down a second time might prove too late.

"Almost there, Allie," Gus said to his daughter in the backseat.

Keeping to the side streets added ten minutes to the trip, but it was less risky than the main roads, where Gus might be forced to contribute more than coins to self-declared toll collectors.

As Allie had even refused her favorite juice for the past few days, Gus tried to come up with something she might accept to ingest in order to fuel her dehydrated body. "Maybe they have some fresh food there, like juicy grapes. Would you like that, Sweetie?"

His daughter remained motionless; not even a moan escaped her cracked lips. Gus sped around the thick ooze spreading from a heap of decaying bodies, arranged like pieces of driftwood built into a massive beach campfire on the sidewalk. The intense foulness emanating from the discarded corpses forced him to drive another block before stopping the car. The vehicle rocked to a stop, sending the handgun tucked in the passenger foot well tumbling across the worn rubber mat.

Other than for the crowd of uncollected plague victims in the rearview mirror, the suburban street appeared deserted. Gus turned and leaned over his seat, but found himself too far to reach Allie. Curled up next to the passenger side door, she looked like a ragged doll forgotten after a long road trip.

"Allison," he said more forcefully. His daughter did not even flinch.

Gus stepped out of the car, questioning whether he had made the right decision to leave the house despite Allie's need for medical help. A mere week after his wife's sacrifice, he was already breaking his final promise to her by taking their daughter out of the safe cocoon of home, risking exposure to the plague. Whether Allie was cured or not, they would be unable to return home. He would need to find a safe haven somewhere West, the only travel direction allowed.

As Gus slid into the backseat, his left knee brushed against the snacks and juice boxes waiting untouched in the car seat pocket. He tried not to startle Allie as he squeezed her leg, just enough to wrinkle the pattern of white polka dots on her pink blanket. She had lost several pounds since her fifth birthday two months earlier and felt no heavier than a kitten when he lifted her into his arms. His daughter nuzzled against the nook of his neck as cool air breezed around them through the open car door. Heat radiated off her body as if about to burst into flame, but at least she was alive.

Gus rocked Allie, inhaling the odor of talcum powder and sour sweat, at a loss to comfort his daughter following her mother's abrupt departure six days earlier, following the plan they had devised in the event either of them showed signs of infection. No long goodbyes, but merely walk out the door and drive away to save the other two family members. Three days ago, Allie had stopped asking about her mother altogether, since then refusing to eat or drink, and had not uttered a word.

Despite the odds, he kept hope that his wife might still be alive, recovering at an isolation ward across the city. Until he knew for sure Mia would never return, Gus refused to admit to Allie that her mother had died and that only the two of them were left in this new world. Gus felt like a failure as a husband and father to think that their daughter might be dying of a broken heart. He cleared his throat. "How would you like to help me drive?"

As he slid his foot out the door, a force grabbed hold of his leg and yanked him from the backseat. Pain exploded in the back of his head, and he struggled to keep his arms around Allie, unable to fight the darkness overtaking him.

Wetness. Water. Raindrops.

Rubbing away the water accumulating in the crease of his eyelids, Gus groaned as a sharp ache throbbed in the back of his head. He strained to a seated position and realized his car was gone, his arms empty.

"Allie," he called, scrambling to his feet. "Allie!" He yelled his daughter's name, zigzagging like a drunkard, searching for a spot of pink brightness in the washed-out surroundings.

"Get out of here," a woman said from her front porch. She held a hand over her nose and mouth and waved a striped dishcloth with the other as if clearing toxic fumes from her midst.

"My daughter," Gus said, swerving in her direction across the street, the ground refusing to stand still in his field of vision. "They took my daughter."

"Leave and take the plague with ya," the old woman said, shaking the dishcloth in a dizzying wave.

"My daught—"

"How dare you walk around covered in blood?" she interrupted.

"I'm not sick," Gus said, trying to stand without wavering. "I...I hit my head when someone pulled me out of my car. Please, did you see anything?"

The woman stayed silent, her hand still covering half of her face as her wide-set eyes scanned him over. Combined with her theatrical blue eye shadow and painted arching eyebrows, it gave her a cartoonish look of curiosity.

"Please," Gus pleaded, the caked blood on the back of his neck itching as rain trickled over it. "She's just a little girl who misses her mother," he said, the words catching in his throat.

The woman wadded the dishcloth into a ball and threw it at his feet. "For your head."

As Gus leaned down to retrieve it, the woman mumbled something behind her hand.

"I'm sorry?" he said, placing the dirty rag over the throbbing pain. A sizeable lump could already be felt through the layers of bunched cloth. "Did you say something?" he asked as a cloud of dime-store perfume enveloped him.

The woman dropped her hand, revealing bright red lipstick applied like it had been shot out of a paint gun. Even from twenty feet away, Gus could see the lipstick bleeding like a sunburst into the countless wrinkles radiating from her mouth.

The woman leaned over the porch railing. "The girl is sick. Just be glad you're rid of her."

Gus threw the dishcloth and reached to the small of his back. He swore inwardly, picturing his gun in the car's foot well. As much as he wanted to blow her lights out for the comment, the nasty old woman might be his only lead to finding his daughter, and he forced himself to at least give the appearance of being cool and collected. "Tell me where he took her and I'll leave."

The woman stayed silent a moment, as if considering what would be the least trouble for her. She jutted her chin up the street, the way Gus had been heading while still in the car. "Try the Dover boys and their idiot cousin."

Gus looked at the rows of houses lining the street, all of them looking vacated in a rush exodus. "Which one?"

"The big red brick house on the left, one up from the corner."

After Gus had located it, he turned back to find the woman and her garish makeup gone.

He checked his watch. It had been almost forty minutes since he had seen Allie. He jogged up the street, heading straight for the Dover house.

Creeping to the back of the two-story red brick house, Gus squeezed his grip around the baseball bat he had found in the yard. He had circled the house twice but had been unable to see inside it or the double garage because of the boarded windows. Though the rain had stopped and allowed for an eerie silence to spread over the neighborhood, he couldn't hear any noise coming from inside.

The empty deck in the backyard beckoned him, and Gus avoided any possible creaking steps by jumping directly onto it from the grass. He wrapped his free hand around the screen door's handle, placing his thumb on the push-button. It resisted a moment before clicking all the way in, violently shaking the screen door in its frame.

The thunderous clatter sent Gus diving off the deck, and he took refuge behind a hedge. He held his breath as the door whined open, and tried to find a safe viewing spot through the thick bushes.

"Who's there?" a voice asked. A boy of eight or ten peered out of the door and stepped outside.

Gus hesitated, having expected anyone but a child.

"I know someone's out here," the boy said.

Gus lowered the bat and stepped out. "Don't be scared, kid. Is—"

"Who the fuck are you?"

Gus was taken aback by the youngster's language. "I...I'm looking—"

"I, I, I," the kid mocked. "Get off my property," he said, gesturing a combination of fingers beyond Gus's knowledge of the one-finger salute.

Gus threw his shoulders back, trying to appear bigger than his five foot ten frame, hoping to intimidate the kid into talking without needing to bring the bat into it. "All I want to know is if you've seen my car or know where my daughter is."

"What kind of car?"

"My daughter. Do you—"

"Go away, ass-wipe."

"Where's my daughter?" Gus said. There was no time to argue with a stubborn punk so he raised the bat. "Tell me or I'm gonna get it out of you the hard way," he said, wondering if he could bring himself to follow through on his threat, then decided he would if he had to.

"I'm sure she's safe if she's anything as ugly as you," the kid said with a smirk.

Gus lunged forward, grabbing the kid by the throat with his free hand. "I'm not fucking around," he said, shoving the boy to the deck. "So stop wasting my time. Just tell me where you and your brothers have taken my daughter."

The kid retreated on all fours. "I've got just one brother. And he's gonna kick your ass."

"Go get him," Gus said, waving the boy to the house. "In fact, let's go get him together."

The boy ran into the house, screaming the name Billy repeatedly. Gus followed, checking each room he passed before moving on. The air was thick with staleness, and the floors were covered with discarded junk, empty food containers, and dirty clothes.

"Up here, Danny," a voice said from the second level.

"There's a guy in the house," Gus heard the Danny kid say as he ran up the stairs.

As Gus followed, footfalls spread on the second level like a stampede of horses. *What if there were a dozen kids up there?* Before Gus could retreat, an acne-covered teenager stood above him with Danny.

"Kick his ass, Billy."

The teenager named Billy crossed his long spindly arms. "Who do you think you are, walking into our house like that?"

Gus moved down a few stairs, wanting to avoid further physical confrontation with children unless absolutely necessary. "I just want my daughter."

The teenager's wispy blonde eyebrows knocked together in confusion. "What?"

"We don't like girls," Danny said. "They talk too much."

Billy pushed Danny towards a boy with thick glasses of about the same age. "Go wait with Ethan."

The idiot cousin, Gus thought as the woman's description rang in his head. "My car was stolen, and my daughter is missing, but you already know that." Gus pushed his way up the last few steps. "Allie!" he called. "It's okay, Daddy's here."

"Go ahead," Billy said, moving aside. "But you're wasting your time. There's no girl here."

The teenager shadowed Gus as he moved from room to room. The place was devoid of any trace of Allie, and he could sense no guilty nervousness from the boys, just profound uneasiness and fear about a crazy stranger being in their home.

"Why do you think she's here?" Billy asked when they returned to the hallway. The boy's hair was greasy, and his clothes wrinkled, but the expression on his face was earnest.

"I was told she should be here," Gus said.

"Says who?"

"A woman down the street."

"I bet it was Mrs. Rainbow Face," Danny said.

Gus nodded, sending lightning bolts of pain out exploding from his sizeable lump. "Sounds like her."

"She's probably kissing her grandsons with that clown mouth of hers, congratulating them for stealing your car."

"Danny's right," Billy said. "The Morgans spent some time in jail for stealing stuff. Also for something else, but my dad wouldn't tell me what. They probably hid your car in their backyard, behind their giant fence."

Fence? Gus tried to remember details of the woman's house, but the throbbing pain in the back of his head slowed his train of thought. Nothing but the kaleidoscope of colors on her face and her front porch came to mind. He checked his watch. More than an hour had passed since he had seen Allie, and less than that remained before the clinic closed.

Billy tapped Gus's arm, drawing him back. "Why would they take your daughter?"

"What?" Gus asked, his mind struggling to follow a thread. *Also for something else but my dad wouldn't tell me what.* Troubling images of grown men with innocent little girls swirled in his head.

"Why not just take the car if that's what they want?" Billy asked. "It's a lot of work to take care of a kid. And I would know," the teenager said, nodding towards his younger relatives.

"Maybe they didn't take her anywhere," Ethan said, pushing his glasses up his nose.

Gus frowned. "What do you mean?"

"Maybe they just left her."

"No. She's not on the street."

"Have you checked the pile of the dead? I saw them throwing someone on top of it yesterday."

Gus spun on his heels, skipping more stairs than he touched. *The girl is sick,* the woman had said. How would she have known unless she had seen her?

When he reached the front door, Gus dropped the bat and used both hands to turn the series of six deadlocks, twisting each starting from the top. He yanked on the handle, but the door remained closed, blocking his exit. Gus let out a scream of frustration. Why would the Dovers bother with all the locks in the front when they left the screen door in the back open?

"Alternate ones only," Billy said as he pushed Gus aside. "It was Ethan's idea. That way, anyone trying to get in locks the three that were unlocked."

"What?" Gus asked, trying to make sense of the explanation. "Just open it."

"Here," Billy said, pulling the door open.

Gus rushed out, but the toe of his left boot caught on the threshold. A hand grabbed the back of his jacket as the stoop sped towards his face. His arms were drawn back, trapped in his sleeves as his coat was pulled off. Unable to arrest his fall, Gus smashed hard into the cement.

"Sorry," Billy said as he helped him back up. "Just trying to help. Your face is scraped up pretty good. Ethan, get the first-aid kit. We'll—"

Ignoring Billy, Gus took off in a sprint across the lawn, making a straight line for the pile of discarded plague victims. Could the Morgans really be senseless enough to dump his young daughter in a mountain of corpses?

Soiled debris and garbage lay strewn everywhere, and Gus swerved around the biggest obstacles. The Morgan house zoomed by on his right, surrounded by a tall white fence blocking the yard on both sides. A man wearing an Edmonton Oilers jersey stared at him through the window, the expression on his face a mix of annoyance and amusement.

If the Morgans thought Allie was sick, they would not have brought her into the house with them. As disturbing as the idea of Allie being part of the pile was to him, Gus needed to check it first.

The odor of putrefaction emanating from the pile seemed to reach down into the pit of his stomach and yank it inside out. Gus swallowed bile as he circled the small mountain, discounting every bloated rotting body as he searched for Allie. In such proximity, Gus realized the pile contained at many more victims as his original estimate of a few dozen, perhaps even more than fifty.

On the far side, a pink and white polka dot blanket came into view. Gus rushed to it, grabbed Allie's stained blanket and lifted it off the pile. The sight of the revealed corpse's advanced state of decomposition gave him pause. It took a moment for him to realize there was no way it could be Allie.

"Allie!" Gus called as he stepped back, making sure not to step on anyone or anything that could be his daughter. "Allie!" He tried to keep it together for his daughter's sake as he would be of no help to her if he crumbled to a weeping blob.

"Is that her?"

Gus turned to find Billy pointing away from the pile, in the direction of a green recycling bin resting on its side. Two small pink shoes dangled out of the open end.

Unable to speak as his breath seemed stuck deep inside his lungs, Gus leaned inside the bin and pulled her out. *Allie.*

She slapped him on the chin. "No," Allie said. "Go away."

"It's Daddy, Allie. You're going to be okay." His daughter showed more energy than she had in days and he held her against his chest, feeling the pounding of her heart mirroring his as she settled into his arms.

"The Morgans are coming," Billy said. "We need to get out of here."

Gus turned to find a car, his own car, driving towards them. The man with the Oilers jersey jogged on the left of it, and a man who looked just like him jogged on the right, wearing the colors of the Calgary Flames. They covered the width of the street, blocking the way back to the Dover house. Trying to get around them would be impossible.

Gus pulled Billy behind the pile of the dead, keeping low and speaking fast. "Where are the boys?"

"I told them to stay put."

"Take Allie and go to them. All of you hide out at a neighbor's house until I come find you."

"What if you don't come back?" Billy said.

Gus ignored the question. "I love you, Allie," he said, handing her off to the teenager. "I need you to go with Billy, okay?"

She locked eyes with Gus, gripping his shirt with her tiny fists. Gus freed her hands, trying to give her a reassuring smile despite the pain caused by the muscles on his face stretching into a grin. It felt like a lawnmower had run over his face. "It'll be okay, Sweetie."

"She's scared," Billy said. "Your face is a mess. You're bleedi—"

"We need to hurry," Gus said. "Get out of here now."

"I don't know," Billy said. "Maybe we should just walk out, with our hands up or something, like we want no trouble. They'll leave us alone if we just go back to the house. We've done that before."

"No," Gus said, convinced that was the worst action they could take. "There's no telling what they're capable of." He poked his head out to check on the Morgans.

The car and men were stopped fifty feet beyond the pile of dead. Gus ducked back down when the Oilers fan aimed a gun at him. The driver leaned on the horn, letting it blare almost a full minute.

"Come on out," one of the men said. "All three of you."

Gus lowered his voice to a whisper, spoke directly into Billy's ear. "Wait until I give you a signal, then head back through the backyards. I'll be there as soon as I can."

Billy opened his mouth to speak, but a gunshot rang out, silencing any further argument.

Gus eyed the area for a weapon of some kind. He couldn't remember what had happened to the bat, and all that was within reach, other than the rotting corpses, were soggy pieces of cardboard. He leaned over the dead, rifling through their pockets hoping to find something like a pocketknife or a metal nail file. "What do you want?" he yelled to the Morgans, hoping to buy some time. "You already have my car."

"And your gun," one of them yelled back.

Gus bit his lip to hold back a curse. "So just leave us be," he said, still searching. "You got more than you wanted, and we just want to be on our way." Something sliced into his finger. He reached deeper into the dead man's pocket and grabbed hold of a set of keys.

"Come out now, and we won't hurt you."

"Okay," a voice behind Gus said.

Gus turned to find Billy standing with his hands up. He lunged for the teenager, and they tumbled to the grass in an awkward embrace as the echo of a gunshot reverberated down the street.

"I think I got one!" one of the Morgans yelled as the car honked a jubilant tune.

Gus rolled off Billy. What remained of the teenager's left eye socket was a crimson jumble of pulpy flesh and bone. Gus searched for a pulse as a high pitched scream sounded down the street. *Danny or Ethan*, Gus thought as tires screeched on the pavement. Within moments, a distant thump silenced the youngster's screams.

"They're just kids!" Gus yelled.

"Daddy," Allie said as she jumped on Gus's back and wrapped her arms around his neck. "I want to go home."

The set of keys looped over Gus's index finger clanged as he pulled Allie down into his arms, and shielded her body from any further gunshots. It was his fault that two boys were dead. Why had he believed the old woman, and just barged into the Dover house?

"Did I get the zitty kid?" a voice asked. "Tell me I got him."

"Why don't you come find out for yourself?" Gus yelled, fury lacing his words.

Muted voices could be heard over the idling engine. Gus focused on Allie and whispered words of reassurance as he used Billy's body to form a wall around her. "I'm sorry to have to do this," he whispered in apology to Allie as much as he did to Billy. "Stay here. I'll be right back."

The unmistakable sound of cowboy boots scuffing the pavement neared and Gus rushed into position, holding the long car key between his index and middle finger. When the Oilers fan was only a few feet away, Gus burst forward, grabbed him and pulled him behind the corpse pile before the man could react.

Gus knelt on the man's chest and neck after shoving him to the ground. After a moment's hesitation, he punched his weaponized fist into the man's eye, the liquid from the eyeball busting onto his hand under the key's stabbing pressure. An eye for an eye seemed like a proper start.

Oilers cried out, grabbing his face with both hands, one of them still holding the gun. Gus reached for it, but a blur of movement at the corner of his eye made him turn just as the Flames fan jumped on top of him.

The momentum threw Gus off Oilers, and he tumbled away with Flames. A close range gunshot rang out, and Gus noticed Oilers aiming blindly in their general direction.

"Get off my brother!" Oilers said, pulling the trigger again.

As the echo of the shot died out, Gus checked himself for a bullet hole but could find none. Flames collapsed off him, grabbing his chest as red bubbles foamed out of his mouth. The brother took a ragged breath and stilled.

Gus crawled over to Oilers. "You shot your own brother dead," he informed him with a series of punches in the throat.

As Oilers gasped for air, Gus retrieved the gun and pivoted, aiming it at the creeping noise behind him.

"Don't!" Ethan said, shielding Allie.

Gus quickly lowered the gun. He led the children away and had them wait out of sight between two houses before heading straight for the car, now idling a mere twenty feet away on the other side of the pile.

Behind the wheel, the old woman stared at him with her wild grimace. She waved him away and made a show of engaging the lock mechanism several times.

"You ain't gettin' in," she yelled.

Gus shot through the driver's window. Before the glass had even finished breaking away, he reached into the car and dragged her out.

"You shot me in the arm," the woman said, sounding more insulted than in pain. "You shot me!"

"Shut up," Gus said as he dragged her towards the pile, making sure the pavement inflicted damage on the way. "That gunshot is the least of your problems right now."

"Not there!" she screamed. "Let go of me!"

Gus lifted her off the ground and heaved her on top of the dead heap. "Go make new friends."

"Help me, my boys!"

Gus realized that from her vantage point in the car, she would have missed her boys' fates. He watched her writhe, slip and fall in the congealed body fluids as she tried to escape the dead gathering. There was no doubt it would take her several minutes to escape, leaving Gus enough time to retrieve Allie and Ethan.

He made his way to them and led them to the vacated car. He squeezed Ethan's shoulder and lowered his voice. "Please wait in the car with Allie while I check on your cousins."

"Why?" Ethan whispered. "They're both dead."

Gus absorbed Ethan's words as he closed the car door behind them. He hurriedly made his way to Danny's body and wrapped a found sweater over the boy's crushed head before carrying him behind the pile to place him next to his fallen brother. Gus knelt next to the Dover brothers, not knowing what else to do but leave them together.

On his way back to the car, Gus walked by the old woman. She had escaped the pile and was crawling towards her house, her face a streaky rainbow of bleeding colors.

"Help me, Angus," the woman begged.

Gus stopped, wondering how she knew his given name.

"You have to help me, Angus."

"You're out of luck," Gus said, realizing she must have read it on his car registration. "Only my mother was allowed to call me that."

"Have you killed my boys?"

"I could tell you I didn't kill either of them, but I doubt you'd believe me."

"I know where you live. I'll find you and make you pay for this."

Gus moved closer and flipped the old woman over with his boot, pressing his foot on her flat chest until he heard a rib crack. "No you won't."

"But my boys," she croaked.

"Nothing can be done for Flames, but Oilers was still wheezing back there when I left him," Gus said, pushing down until he heard another crack. "You should check on him."

Leaving the woman where she was, Gus returned to the car. The cuts on his head and face stung, the back of his head pulsed, and the long gash on his index finger throbbed. He had touched many people and bodies and breathed in their infected remains. Would the kids be safe if he got in the car with them?

Before getting into the vehicle, Gus tried to clean himself, without much success. He did not want to stay there, was convinced it was safer to keep moving. When he got behind the wheel, both children were in the backseat drinking from juice boxes.

"Feeling better, Allie?" Gus asked.

Her head bobbed as she noisily sucked the last few drops of juice with a straw.

Gus turned to Ethan. "I need to find out more about your family, your parents."

Ethan shook his head. "They're dead too. It was just us," he said, his eyes drifting to the heap that hid his cousins' bodies.

"It's just us too," Allie said.

Gus stared at his daughter, embarrassed that she understood the truth before he could even admit it to himself. He faced forward, not wanting her to see the emotions overtaking him.

He started the car and put it in drive. He wasn't sure where to head to next, but maybe it would be easier now that there were three of them again.

Jenner Michaud is a Canadian speculative fiction writer with an interest in the dark recesses found at the edge of reality. She enjoys weaving stories that push the boundaries of the possible, even when they go bump in the night and keep her up. Digital Fiction Publishing has also published her horror fiction short story *Of Holes and Craters*, available on Amazon. Follow her on Twitter @JennerMichaud

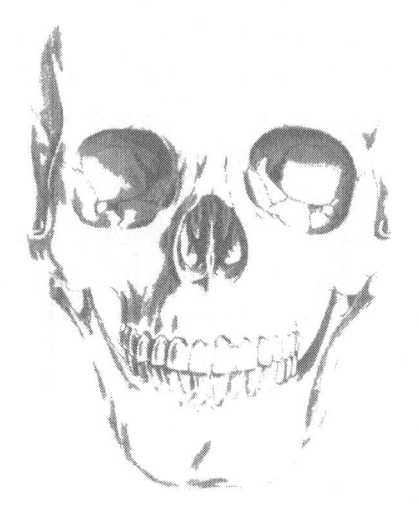

Traitorous, Lying, Little Star

Suzanne Reynolds-Alpert

Jake looked out into the moonless night. Just a few months ago he had been starting school. Worrying about seventh grade. It had seemed like a big worry, then.

That thought was laughable now.

A few stars blinked through a slit between ragged curtains. He was lucky—he got to sleep under an unbroken window. Everyone tried to make sure he and the little kids stayed warm. Jerry, who was one of the guys in charge, said it was a priority. "They have a lot less bulk, and they will lose heat much more quickly," he'd said. "When the temperatures drop at night we need to do what we can for them."

It wasn't really that much warmer, but it felt safer. *Felt* safer. What could a window really do against a monster who wanted to get in?

Traitorous, Lying, Little Star

The propane for heat was long gone, and late fall in the mountains was cold. At night, they all relied on body heat and whatever warmth could be absorbed from the rocks they kept around day-burning fires. Any fire or bright lights in the cabin might attract attention, once the sun set. They did burn a single, small candle inside at night, and kept the windows covered.

Jake tore his eyes from the window and tucked a warm, rag-wrapped stone closer to a young child, asleep beside him. The little boy moaned softly but did not wake up.

He looked back through the curtain slit, at the night sky. *Twinkle, twinkle, little star*, he thought sullenly, squinting and looking for anything that could be a meteor. Meteors were bad. In August, what had started out looking like a shooting star had not faded, and had gotten bigger. After about a minute, it was really big and was clearly going to crash. It had fallen on the Florida/South Carolina border and burned Florida off the map.

And brought a plague.

No more Disney World, Jake thought. His chest hurt. *No more wishing on a star...*

"Hey, Jake." Sophie came up soundlessly, startling him. He jerked and his heart began pounding urgently, the sound rushing up to his ears and making him feel faint. The eight-year-old reached out and apologetically touched his arm. "Sorry."

Wow—Sophie was quiet. It helped to keep her alive.

"S'all right," he touched her arm back as she sat down, feeling her bones through her thin winter coat. He heard a slight *slurp* and knew Sophie had begun to suck her thumb. The child to his right kept sleeping. Jake consciously slowed his breathing, having learned it was a good tool to keep from passing out when he was scared. *Fainting when a meteorhead was chasing you was* not *a good idea.*

They sat in companionable silence for a few minutes.

"I like it when it's this dark," Sophie said softly.

"Me too," he murmured.

"How long will the dark last, Jake?"

"Tonight will be the last. After this, the moon will be a little sliver, and it will start growing until it's full." He shivered at the thought.

"You're smart," she said quietly, snuggling into his warmth. Jake snorted. He'd been an okay student, but liked to learn about what *he* found interesting. He'd liked language and maps and reading, and loved astronomy.

Around them, four adults and the three teenagers were settling down to sleep. Jake heard a few speaking in hushed whispers, verifying schedules, confirming that Barb and Ben were outside. Night-long patrols were necessary, so the adults and teens took turns watching the cabin from the cold outside. Although the monsters could attack at any time, they mostly hunted when it was dark. They used their light-sensitive vision to ambush unwary humans and some big animals—infecting them or just eating them while still alive. Jake had seen them do both. His mother had been infected and "turned." His father had been devoured by a group of them. He and his sister Kate had run...but he hadn't seen Kate since.

No one had figured out what the meteor brought when it crashed. Little aliens taking over bodies? A virus? Whatever it was it, worked fast, and as far as anyone at the cabin knew, the whole world was in chaos.

Jake had heard the adults say the monsters were getting smarter, learning when their former kin were most vulnerable, like at night. The monsters' pupils could get really big, so they could detect tiny pinpricks of light and see movements in near-darkness. But during the day, their pupils were like slits, like a snake or something. Some people thought they had super-hearing, too. Stupid monsters! He wasn't even sure they slept.

"Do you think they'll come tonight?" Sophie asked, shaking him from his thoughts. Sophie never said 'monster' or 'freak' or 'meteorhead' or any of the half-dozen names given to those who stalked them. She'd once explained to Jake that saying the names could bring them to their camp.

As if on cue, an adult across the room whispered to someone,

"It's freak dark out there. Take care that no light is showing through any of the windows."

Sophie moaned pitifully.

One of the women—probably Maria—began to carefully move around the room in the semi-darkness, checking that curtains were closed and re-tacking loose cloth. Crazy Jenny, the oldest member of their camp, grunted and shouted, "No!" Angry *Shhhhhhhhh*s reverberated around the room.

Crazy Jenny was losing it more and more every day. Jake wondered if she was even worth keeping. Well, he had begun to wonder it *after* he'd heard Jerry and some of the others say it. But Crazy Jenny was Ben and Barb's grandmother, and the two siblings owned the cabin the rest had taken refuge in.

"I want to see the stars!" Jenny whispered excitedly from across the room, the whites of her eyes visible in her dark face despite the semi-darkness. "My Mama always said they was God's Angels, lookin' down on us. How else will God be able to look after us?"

"Jenny," Maria soothed. "God still knows we're here; he can see us fine."

"That's not what my Mama said."

"You're Mama just had it a bit wrong, is all."

"*What?*" Jenny shrieked. "My Mama is a preacher's wife! What d'you know?"

Shhhhhhhhh... came from all around the room again.

"For heaven's sake, someone shut her up," Jake heard Jerry mutter.

"Where are her grandkids?" Someone asked.

"On patrol." A whispered reply.

Jake gave Sophie a quick squeeze, before getting up and going over to Crazy Jenny. For some reason, he was able to calm her. She was often stuck somewhere in her memory before Ben and Barb were even born, when their Dad had been a kid. Jake settled himself next to Jenny and leaned his head against her shoulder.

"Is that you, Bobby?" she asked.

"Yes," Jake replied. "It's me."

Jenny sighed, the tension leaving her body. She put an arm around him, and Jake tried not to gag at her body odor. He knew he didn't smell much better. "Would you like me to tell you your stories?"

"Yes, Mama." Jake had learned that was the proper response that 'Bobby' should give.

"Lemme tell you 'bout the stars. Did you know that the stars are God's Angels, lookin' down on us? You know, someone once wrote a song 'bout the stars. Let me sing it for you: *Twinkle, twinkle, little star, how I wonder what you are...*"

"Mama, can you sing it more quietly, so that I can fall asleep?" Jake asked quickly before everyone could *Shhhhhhhhhh* again.

"Of course, Bobby. You're such a good boy!" Jenny crooned. Then she began to sing again, more quietly,

*"Twinkle, twinkle, little star,
How I wonder what you are.
Up above the world so high,
Like a diamond in the sky..."*

As Jenny sang, Jake substituted his own words in his mind:
*Twinkle, twinkle, little star,
Whose cousins traveled very far,
And landed here upon our soil,
Making pets and people boil...*

Jake dreamed. As he leaned against Jenny's soft bulk, he dreamt of being at Disney World with his parents and his sister.

For an older sister, Kate wasn't so bad. They screamed in exuberant tandem as they shot around Splash Mountain. Then, suddenly they were in the log ride, flying, and their parents were in front of them in the log. They sailed through the night sky, watching the stars twinkle around them.

Jake and Kate talked about the stars and how they were really suns that were billions and billions of years away from the Earth. "Do you think there are other people out there?" Jake asked.

His father answered. "Well, Jake, it is certainly conceivable that there is other life out there. But whether or not there are people?" He shrugged, and Jake realized that they were all sitting in a circle, facing each other as they sailed through the sky in a giant teacup.

"I don't think God would have us be alone in all the Universe." Jake's mother said with her kind smile.

Jake's Dad chuckled. He always said he was an 'agnostic.' "Whether or not God, or anything else, made the Universe, it is a very big place. Surely, there is some other kind of life, somewhere," he replied.

"Do you think that that 'life' is friendly?" Kate asked. She sat to Jake's right, warming her hands over a fire in the center of the teacup.

"I suppose that if we met aliens, it would all depend on how we treated them first," Dad said.

"You should always treat people as you would want to be treated," his mother added, "even if they are freaks or meteorheads, they are still people."

"Mom's right," Kate said. "Even if I was a monster, Jake, you'd still love me, right?" As Jake was about to reply, he saw that her eyes had turned from the clear blue color they both shared with their father into the large, black pupils of a night-hunting monster; her neck had the tell-tale pulsing, ropey veins. Her tongue flicked out of her mouth, and the tongue sac that held a stinger was prominent. Jake scrambled to get away.

"Jacob Elliot!" His mother screeched—Jake turned to his left and saw that she was also a monster. "Answer your sister!" She opened and closed her mouth at him, gnashing her teeth.

"Dad, DAD!" Jake began to scream for his father. But Dad didn't answer, and he didn't even seem to notice that his wife and daughter had turned into monsters. As they sailed through space in their teacup, Dad reached out to touch the stars, occasionally plucking one from the sky and popping it into his mouth. Jake could see each pointy bulge as they slid down his throat.

Monsters' arms grabbed at him, sharp fingernails digging into his flesh. Jake felt cold and trapped and desperate for his father to save him. But his father kept picking stars, eating them and sometimes licking the sides of his mouth as he moaned *Mmmmm*, contentedly.

The freaks who had once been his mother and sister were now on either side of him, eyes black and huge, arms gripping and shaking him. Both tongues lolled out, tongue sacs open, the bruised-looking purple stingers erect.

Finally, his father turned and looked Jake in the eyes. "Do you know what the stars are, Jake?" he asked, as his pupils began to dilate. "The stars are our beginning, and they shall be our end. Our time is passing, Jake. Do you realize our time is passing, Jake—"

"Jake!" He heard Sophie's panicked whisper. "Something is happening outside, what if they're here!"

Jake realized he was awake. Sophie's hands gripped his arm. Crazy Jenny was gone.

He could hear shouting outside. "Stay here," he told Sophie as he bolted to his feet. His legs were shaking badly, and his heart still pounded from the dream, but he tried to look more stoic than he felt. "I'll go take a peek and see what's going on."

Jake made his way carefully through the moderately-sized, one-room cabin. All of the adults appeared to be awake. He felt sharp fingers of cold, and it dawned on him that he could see quite well—it was not as dark as it should have been—light was coming from the front door, which was slightly ajar. His heart began to pick up pace again.

He bumped into Maria, also heading for the door. "That crazy bitch!" Maria spat. "We should've offed her weeks ago!" Jake let her go ahead, following.

The cabin's front yard was a clearing cut from the surrounding woods. During the day they burned fires to boil water, wash clothes, and heat the rocks that kept them warm at night. One of the rusty metal barrels they burned fires in had a small but noticeable blaze going; an empty-looking gasoline can was askew a few feet away from it. Crazy Jenny danced around the small pool of light, naked, her breaths making halos around her head. Jake saw that a sleeve of someone's clothing was hanging over the edge of the barrel—Jenny's? *She must be freezing*, he thought, wrapping his arms around himself.

"Grandma!" Barb came running from the woods toward the spectacle, rifle in hand.

"Do something about your crazy-ass Grandma!" Maria said angrily. "She's gonna get us all killed!"

"The twinklin' stars!" Jenny sang as she twirled around. Her pendulous breasts bounced up and down as she danced. "The stars are Angels, lookin' down on us!"

"That's *it!*" Jerry screamed. He ran toward Barb and knocked her down, grabbing the rifle from her hands. "Grandma's *dead!*"

"Stop!" A voice rang out from the edge of the woods opposite Barb. Barb's brother Ben stood there, his own rifle raised and aimed at Jerry.

"Bobby, where's my Bobby? Come dance with Mama under the stars!" Jenny continued to spin around, casting long shadows on the lawn. The light was growing fainter. Jake turned his attention back to the barrel and saw that Maria was working with two others to smother the fire.

"Put it down, Ben," Jerry said, deadly calm. The two men faced each other from opposite sides of the clearing, their breaths clouding around their heads. "Grandma here is gonna die, or else you'll have to kill us all." He lowered the rifle slightly, to better meet Ben's eyes. "Are you ready to do that? Kill all of these healthy, young people? To kill the children? Just so that this pathetic, crazy old woman can live?"

"Who's crazy?" Jenny stopped dancing, the flames casting odd shadows on her dark skin. "Why is everyone so mad? And why is it so cold?" Jake wished she'd notice she was naked.

"She's..." Ben sputtered angrily. "She helped build this place, for Chrissake! She practically raised us!" He looked at Barb, still on the ground, her face in her hands. She did not look up at him.

"She's! She's..." Ben's eyes searched the small crowd wildly. His eyes settled on Jake, standing in the doorway, hugging himself.

"She's my Grandma," Ben said tiredly, as his large frame faded into the night; the adults had finally put out the fire.

Someone—probably Barb—whimpered.

"Just...don't shoot her, okay?" Ben pleaded in the dark. "We'll figure something else out."

"Bobby, Bobby, you turned the lights out!" Jenny said, "Now, we can see the stars even better!"

"Barb, bring her in and quiet her down," Ben said sadly.

Jake heard rustling in the dark as people began to move. "Maria?" he whispered, not knowing if she was still on the lawn.

"Yea. Jake?" Her voice sounded like it was heading toward him. He heard Jerry, Ben, Barb and some of the others talking quietly to each other and to Jenny.

"Jake?" Maria repeated softly as she stepped in front of him. "You okay, boy? I'm sorry you had to see that. Crazy bitch...the damn freaks can see people outside by starlight alone, if they're near enough. Never mind a damn bonfire...but...it'll all be fine." She continued quickly, as though realizing she was talking to a kid and wanting to sound reassuring. "You go back to the other kids and don't worry. We'll keep good watch tonight and everything will be fine. Could be there aren't any freaks close by at all."

"Yea, I will in a sec. I just had...an idea," Jake said, thinking about his recent nightmare; the stars sliding down his father's throat. "Like, I realize it would be really hard—that Barb and Ben can't just *shoot* their Grandma." His throat tightened at the thought, and he had to use more effort to get the words to come out. "So, why don't...what if...we, like, gave her some food with something in it? That made her just go to sleep? But never wake up?"

Maria was silent. Then she took his shoulders gently, moving them both inside the cabin and to the side of the doorway. In the faint light of the single candle, he watched Crazy Jenny being brought inside, a blanket around her. Jake could hear Jenny whispering about the stars, and God and Angels. He heard Ben say sadly, "Grandma—the stars ain't no Angels. One of them fireballs came down from the sky and infected a whole bunch of people. And now those people be trying to eat everyone else. They're freaks, Grandma. Monsters. God ain't got nothing to do with it. But maybe Satan does."

Maria still held Jake's shoulders, and she rubbed them gently. "Such thoughts for a kid to have!" she finally responded. "Go on," she urged kindly, "get back to your spot, and get some sleep."

Jake carefully walked back to Sophie and the toddler boy under their window. The boy's breathing was still deep and slow. *Wow, Jake thought. Children can sleep through anything.* He thought Sophie might have fallen asleep also, because she didn't say anything as he lay down, readjusting the lukewarm rocks.

Maria was whispering to someone. He heard snippets of conversation:

"Jake had an idea…"

"Strychnine…rats …"

"Yea, put it in…"

"Jake?" Sophie whispered. "What is a strict-nine?"

Jake was pretty they were talking about 'strychnine', and that it was a poison. Were they gonna poison Crazy Jenny? "I dunno," he lied, "who knows what adults are saying half the time?"

Sophie grunted assent. Then: "Do you think they'll come?"

Jake wasn't sure. But he didn't want to tell her that. "I don't think so. The mon—*they*—don't like the cold too much. It's a pretty cold night."

The cabin door opened and closed. An adult said, "All clear." He heard Jenny from her sleeping spot on the floor, singing softly: "Up above the world so high, like a diamond in the sky…"

Somewhere in the distance, Jake heard a monster's howl. It was hard to tell how close it was. As Ben had explained when Jake first found this group, the mountains could amplify sound and make it do funny things. It was hard to estimate distances in the mountains.

There was another howl from the other side of the mountain. The monsters went back and forth, singing their obscene song to each other.

Someone blew out the single, small candle.

Terror sliced down Jake's spine like sharp fingernails.

Sophie trembled beside him. "I knew they shouldn't have said the word!" She began to cry softly.

Crazy Jenny continued to sing quietly for another minute, but no one shushed her. She didn't seem to notice the howls. Jake's eyes felt glued open; his breathing fast as he wrapped an arm around Sophie. The absolute dark seemed to amplify everyone's tension.

Jenny finally fell asleep, her song drifting off, despite the anxious whispers and the sounds of rifles being loaded and guns checked.

Jake suddenly found he was too angry to be scared. He gathered Sophie more tightly into his arms, humming the tune Jenny had been singing.

But in his mind, Jake was singing:

Twinkle, twinkle, little star,
Whose cousins traveled very far,
And landed here upon our soil,
Making pets and people boil...

Twinkle, twinkle, shiny speck,
Why is our planet such a wreck?
Why do they want to tear out hearts,
And eat our loved ones' body parts?

Traitorous, lying, little star,
How I wonder why you are,
Up above the world so high,
Like a spotlight in the sky...

Suzanne Reynolds-Alpert writes speculative fiction in between driving her kids around and meeting the incessant demands of her feline overlords. She's a published author and professional editor who loves to write and read creative and unusual stories with unforgettable characters—usually while drinking coffee.

Truth Hurts

Carole Gill

They trusted Tony Sutton; it was as simple as that. Handsome, erudite—a fixture of London society, a bon vivant—a must-have at every party. And a great fan of horror film and books. He had written one or two horror novels himself, but his writing was considered outdated. His publisher Greg Winton told him to try to update his work.

"Ah my dear man, I don't think I can ever write what I don't feel," he had replied.

Greg let him go. He had a brighter star on the horizon.

Desiree Dawn, formerly known as Harriet Pringle, had come out of left field. Greg Winton's new *Dark Love* imprint with its focus on paranormal romance had really taken off, with Desiree's books leading the way.

Her kind of books seemed to be all the rage with their tales of handsome vampires—romanticized blood suckers invariably attired in crushed velvet—cursed to walk the earth as the undead, but blessed with regular and satisfying sex from a variety of libidinous ladies.

Desiree's recent Innocents of the Night series had even caught the attention of some Hollywood types. When Greg heard that, he decided to invite her and her boyfriend to dinner at one of London's best restaurants in order to tell her.

He hinted all through dinner that he had fantastic news for her but refused to tell her until after dessert.

At last, the time came.

"My darling! You've done it again! It's a film they're talking about!"

Desiree, devastating in black satin—with her favorite two-legged poodle, Scott in tow—was delighted. "A film?! *Really?!*"

"Yes and well—I've saved the best for last, my love!"

Obviously, he was going to make her guess and so she glanced at Scott. "He's too cruel! Tell him to tell us what it is."

Scott started to obey, but Greg cut him off. "My old friend Tony Sutton is throwing a huge do at his place, and he's having movie people there! Two of them! A Hollywood director and screenwriter and we're all invited!"

"A party?! When is this?"

"Saturday!"

"Saturday, but that's so soon! I have so much to do—a frock and—" She stopped when she saw Greg beginning to look annoyed. And since she didn't want to appear ungrateful she gushed: "Oh heavens, of course I'll go—won't that be wonderful, Scott?"

Scott stifled a yawn and waited for her to hand him her credit card because he had forgotten to ask for it earlier.

A Botox treatment, her hair done, and the purchase of a lovely Vivienne Westwood dress was all accomplished quickly and efficiently, so that within three days, Desiree was happily studying her reflection yet again.

The clam and onion diet had paid off. "Scott, look how much better this dress fits."

No reaction whatsoever. He was in one of his truculent moods. She hated when he was like that, but he was, and if she didn't know it then, she knew it when he asked: "How old is he?"

"Who darling?"

"That Tony Sutton—how old is he?"

Des froze. Being on the wrong side of forty, she hated when twenty-something Scott mentioned age. "What does it matter? He's just eternal. No one really knows how old he is."

"When did he make that first movie of his? That scary one—didn't it come out in the 1950's?"

She thought a moment. "Oh, you mean *Blood of the Werewolf?* No love; it was the late sixties."

"No, I'm certain it was 1957."

"Don't be silly."

Scott looked it up.

"Yes, he said. "1957. Look."

She walked over to the laptop. It was that movie site again. They must have had every bloody film that was ever made listed there. She wrinkled her nose. "Well, I suppose he was barely out of school."

"But Des—even if that was so, he'd be in his late sixties now wouldn't he?"

Des threw her head back. It was one of her favorite diva gestures. "He's still got his looks."

"Good face lifts."

Ooh, Scott was being a right bastard today. He probably wanted more of an allowance. "There's nothing wrong with a nip and tuck," she replied. But he didn't answer which made it worse. "Well, however old he is my love, he's still attractive to the ladies!"

"Yeah, *desperate* ladies!"

She felt like slapping him but instead put on her best coquette expression. "You're not jealous, are you? I'd never let him come between us."

Some of the guests were already there; others like himself, who flitted in and out of the public eye. Tony Sutton had lots of friends, but these were his inner circle. More than friends, really—friends came and went sometimes, as the saying goes, but these—these were more like family. Close family that understood one another—that had the same values and needs and likes and dislikes—brethren almost.

Tony stood admiring them from afar. He liked to do that sometimes, extracting himself from a situation to become a neutral observer. He did this now, and he smiled, for he liked what he saw.

They sat on the terrace quietly waiting for the party to begin. There were three women, exquisitely turned out creatures, accompanied by three equally handsome men.

At first, they appeared bored. Languishing as they did on lounge chairs, or occasionally sauntering across the terrace's tiled floor to gaze at the moon or glancing sadly at one another.

Yet if they looked dreamy, their eyes gave them away, for a mad intensity burned there. Like a needful glow waiting for fulfillment.

Tony turned to see his oldest and dearest friend Max watching him. Max, distinguished and with the bearing of an aristocrat, had always been his friend.

"You look pleased."

Tony nodded. His equally handsome features brightened by a satisfied smile. "I am! And so are you, you old rascal."

Max laughed. "Thank you for that. I'd rather be called rascal than roué."

"Why is that?"

"Roué is more derogatory for one thing, whereas rascal is kind of devilish!"

Tony shook his head. "Devilish! Now that does suit."

"You think?"

But Tony didn't answer. Instead, he just smiled.

"I think you took a wrong turn." Scott sat next to Des as she drove, with Greg in the back.

"No I didn't! I know my way around East Sussex!"

"Oh, you do not! You haven't any occasion to come here, it's too posh!"

"Now, now children, don't fight. It'll show on your faces, and we don't want that now, do we?" Greg said.

Desiree didn't answer. She was too busy glancing around. They had been on this back road for some time. Perhaps they were lost.

"Des, I still think you took a wrong turn."

"Oh shut up will ya?"

Scott turned his head. "You see, Greg, how her Queen's English goes right out the window when she's annoyed?"

"Oh shut your fucking mouth! You're making me nervous!"

Scott harrumphed and stared stonily ahead. "I don't see lights or anything in any direction. We're lost!"

"I told you there wouldn't be any road lights. It's the country, darling." She was starting to sound like Des again. She probably didn't want to piss him off too badly. "It's supposed to be two miles from the motorway. Just be patient."

Neither of them answered her, which made her even more tense. But then a miracle occurred, or so it seemed, when a twinkling castle began to emerge from a copse of trees.

"There! You see? I knew I was right!"

The three of them gasped as it came into view. It was a spectacular sight.

"However could he afford such a place?" Greg was clearly in awe. "He hasn't made a film or published in years!"

"Well even if that's so, he does all those adverts in Japan and places."

Scott looked sullen. "I think it's overdone!"

"Oh shut up Scott, it's fabulous! I've never seen anything like it!" Desiree felt she had come into her element. This was the kind of place she wanted to be invited to. "I can't believe how grand it looks!" She drove her Mercedes into the driveway. "Look! Valet parking and everything! I wonder if we're the first to arrive?"

They weren't. There was Tony's inner circle.

"My they are stylish," she said.

"They are attractive, I'll say that," Greg said.

"They look like well-dressed Goths and rent boys to me."

"Well they don't to me so don't spoil it, Scott!"

Tony greeted them. "Ah, my friends! Do come in, let us await our Hollywood friends' arrival!"

Tony introduced them all around. "These lovely ladies are my muses aren't you darlings?"

They were extremely attractive, if dressed rather violently, Des thought. Swathed in black, with black lipstick and gobs of black eyeliner, they looked extremely Gothic. Beautiful, but sad too, as though they were lost in some mournful but romantic world of their own.

Desiree made mental notes for one of her stories.

Three of the men looked young, and Des noticed with amusement how attentive Greg was with them. They were beautiful boys really, delicately featured and sweetly pale, and they seemed to hang on his every word.

Soon her gaze fell on a particularly distinguished man who Tony introduced as his oldest friend, Max.

"I can't believe I am meeting you at last, Miss Dawn!"

Desiree sensed a blush coming on. "You're too kind!"

Max wasn't finished. "I have never read anything so remarkable in all my existence as your novels!"

Des began to giggle. "How charmingly put!"

She might have remained beaming at him had she not noticed the Goth sisters wrapping themselves around Scott. She sailed over and led him forcefully away. "Come, darling, the tour has begun!"

The entrance hall was immense, marble floored and arrayed with Greco-Roman Statues. Off to one side was a magnificent library.

It was wonderful being shown around such a mansion, and Des

would have enjoyed it more had she not been watching Scott out of the corner of her eye. It seemed he was seriously taken with those three Gothic pieces.

She could have hit him and happily ripped those simpering sirens apart if given the chance.

Max seemed to notice. "I think your friend is distracted, but then again, so am I, for you are a distracting woman."

The pleasure she normally would have felt receiving a compliment like that was dampened by her mood.

Tony noticed her discomfort. "Perhaps the upstairs tour later," he said. "Let us have our drinks now."

Drinks were just being served when a servant announced that the Hollywood guests had arrived.

The director was rather flamboyantly dressed—expensively attired yet somewhat over the top with all sorts of necklaces dangling from his tanned neck. Des wondered how he got through the airport's metal detectors.

The screenwriter looked more toned down, with designer stubble, an Armani suit, and no jewelry at all except for his Rolex, which he made certain was visible.

The two looked awestruck but tried to cover it up. "Damned delay at Heathrow!" The director said. Trying, Des thought, to sound British. "And *you* must be the author!"

Desiree drifted gracefully over to him. "I am. What a pleasure to meet you."

"The pleasure is all mine, dear lady. This is Jason, *Moving On's* best screenwriter."

Moving On. What silly names studios had nowadays, Desiree thought, but she smiled and twinkled.

"We're so lucky to have him! He will do justice to your novel, my dear Desiree. Just you wait!"

Just then, a liveried servant came in to announce dinner. "Ladies and Gentleman, if you'll follow me please."

Scott rolled his eyes, but Desiree didn't care. She was too busy admiring everything.

If she was already impressed when she entered the dining room, she nearly gasped, for it was opulent. She felt as though she was dining at Buckingham Palace.

There were four courses, each heavenly, if unknown. Des would have preferred to know what she was eating, but she didn't want to look like a peasant.

Halfway through the meal, the director began speaking of the movie. "Now naturally we'll want your input as author—but we have a vision! A real idea of how we want to do this thing!"

Though delighted with the entire venture, Des suddenly felt uneasy. "I am committed to the essence of the story—I mean I wouldn't like to see serious changes or anything."

The screenwriter raised his hand. "I know what you mean. Your work is important to me—its truth will remain as you intended."

"And so it should," Tony said. "Truth should never be denied, whatever the consequences!"

A strange thing happened just then, as each of the three grimly attired ladies began to giggle. It seemed so out of character for them. They stopped as soon as they sensed their host's displeasure.

Tony nodded to them.

As if on cue, one of the women spoke: "Oh Tony, do show everyone your magic!"

"Only if everyone agrees!"

They all simpered and applauded. "Magic! Oh please! *Please!*"

Tony agreed. "It will all begin after dinner."

There was an air of expectation and something else—something untoward—almost ominous. Desiree didn't know what it was, but that's when Tony began his act.

"I will need a volunteer please."

One of the Goth sisters stood up.

"You'll love this, Desiree," Max whispered.

Tony waved his arms, and the woman began to slowly lift off the floor. Desiree watched in amazement as she rose ever higher.

"Remarkable, isn't it?"

Desiree turned to answer Max, but that's when she noticed Greg and the men were gone. This didn't surprise her, but Scott wasn't there either. And what was worse, both of the Goth girls were gone as well.

What to do? She couldn't rush off to search for him, not until this damned magic act was over. So she bided her time, tapping her Jimmy Choo shoes and trying not to look too upset.

At last, it ended.

"Pardon me I'm just going to see where my young friend is."

Tony, ever the gallant host offered to help her look. "It's quite a big place."

They began searching, and when Tony saw her glance up the stairs, he suggested they look upstairs as well.

She took the stairs two at a time.

"There are ten bedrooms in all…," he told her more, but she didn't hear him as she rushed to open each door. When they reached the last room, Tony took her arm. "This is the master suite Des—are you sure you want to go in?"

She glared at him. "I *am* going in!"

He opened the door for her.

"Scott!"

Her accusatory scream died in her throat—horror took it away, as she beheld Scott lying naked in the bed with the two women. But he wasn't getting his jollies. His body had been torn open.

She screamed and rushed blindly out of the room then stumbled down the stairs. As she reached the hall, the library door swung open, and the horrific sight of Greg being cannibalized greeted her. The girl from the magic act and three servants were feasting on him—the liveried servant and the valet attendants chomping away. They smiled at her.

Why hadn't she noticed their teeth before? They looked razor sharp. And though they were bloody, their fangs showed through.

The girl held up Greg's heart and laughed.

Desiree sank to her knees.

"There, there, Desiree. I know it's upsetting. The truth often is!"

Tony grabbed her, but she managed to stand up. "You're monsters! Monsters!"

If she could only make it to her car. Where *was* her car? She bolted out the front door.

At last, she saw it in the driveway. She kept looking over her shoulder as she ran. He was gaining on her!

Run Desiree! Run!

She finally reached the car. Mercifully, the doors were wide open. She didn't think to question it; her need for flight was too great.

But the car was not empty. The director and screenwriter were both in the back seat—their ravished corpses gutted like the others.

A blood-soaked Max suddenly emerged from the shadows. "I didn't think you'd mind if we used your car. I think they thought something rather exotic was about to happen, but I don't do men. I'm afraid they were disappointed."

Walking over to Des, he whispered, "Come, my love, it's your turn now."

She turned to run, but Tony suddenly appeared. "Why don't you just accept it?"

She howled as Tony's hands began drawing her down. It was all happening so slowly, like a dream. She was standing and screaming one second, but in the next, she was being gently pushed down to the ground. Tony spoke to her, his voice calm and almost soothing: "The wine and food—well I'm sure you know what they were, really—you see there were reporters here earlier, after all."

Gently, like two attentive lovers, they removed her clothes until she lay there naked—her body gleaming in the silvery moonlight.

She barely felt the first bite. But then they began to seriously feed, tearing her flesh, sucking up her blood. The pain became a blinding, white-hot agony.

She opened her mouth to scream, but nothing came out—her

larynx had been chewed through.

It was amazing how long a person could live while being devoured. But then mercifully, the pain began to subside as death came to claim her.

It was Tony's voice she heard just before she died—his breath smelling of coppery salt, his whisper soft but telling.

"You see my dear, this is the truth. This is what vampires are *really* like! There is nothing romantic about us at all! It is a falsehood—a lie repeated so often it has been taken as fact, and sadly, the truth often *hurts!*"

Carole Gill is published by Creativia and is a member of the Horror Writers Association. She writes dark Gothic romance as well as dark contemporary horror. Her newest release is *I, Bathory, Queen of Blood* which is about Countess Erzsbet Bathory, a sexual sadist and mass murderer who believed bathing in blood would stave off old age. It is her eighth book. She is already working on her next two projects.

A Trick of the Dark

Tina Rath

"*What kind of job finishes just at sunset?*"

Margaret jumped slightly. "What a weird question, darling. Park keeper, I suppose." Something made her turn to look at her daughter. She was propped up against her pillows, looking, Margaret thought guiltily, about ten years old. She must keep remembering, she told herself fiercely, that Maddie was nineteen. This silly heart-thing, as she called it, was keeping her in bed for much longer than they ever thought it would, but it couldn't stop her growing up…she must listen to her, and talk to her like a grown-up.

Intending to do just that, she went to sit on the edge of the bed. It was covered with a glossy pink eiderdown, embroidered with fat pink and mauve peonies. The lamp on Maddie's bedside table had a rosy shade, Maddie was wearing a pink bed jacket, lovingly crocheted by her grandmother, and Maddie's pale blonde hair was tied back with a pink ribbon...but in the midst of this plethora of pink Maddie's face looked pale and peaky. The words of a story she had read to Maddie once—how many years ago?—came back to her: "Peak and pine, peak and pine." It was about a changeling child who never thrived, but lay in the cradle, crying and fretting, peaking and pining...in the end, the creature had gone back to its own people, and, she supposed that the healthy child had somehow got back to his mother, but she couldn't remember. Margaret shivered, wondering why people thought such horrid stories were suitable for children.

"What made you wonder who finishes work at sunset?" she asked.

"Oh—nothing." Maddie looked oddly shy, as she might have done if her mother had asked her about a boy who had partnered her at tennis, or asked her to a dance. If such a thing could ever have happened. She played with the pink ribbons at her neck, and a little, a very little color crept into that pale face. "It's just—well—I can't read all day, or..." She hesitated, and Margaret mentally filled in the gap. She had her embroidery, her knitting, those huge complicated jigsaws that her friends were so good about finding for her, a notebook for jotting down those funny little verses that someone was going to ask someone's uncle about publishing...but all that couldn't keep her occupied all day.

"Sometimes I just look out of the window," she said.

"Oh, darling..." She couldn't bear to think of her daughter just lying there—just looking out of the window. "Why don't you call me when you get bored? We could have some lovely talks. Or I could telephone Bunty or Cissie or..."

It's getting quite autumnal after all, she thought, and Maddie's friends wouldn't be out so much, playing tennis, or swimming or... You couldn't expect them to sit for hours in a sick-room. They dashed in, tanned and breathless from their games and bicycle rides, or windblown and glowing from a winter walk, and dropped off a jigsaw or a new novel...and went away.

"I don't mind, mummy," Maddie was saying. "It's amazing what you can see, even on a quiet street like this. I mean, that's why I like this room. Because you can see out."

Margaret looked out of the window. Yes. You could see a stretch of pavement, a bit of Mrs. Creswell's hedge, a lamp post, the post box and Mrs. Monkton's gate. It was not precisely an enticing view, and she exclaimed, "Oh, darling!" again.

"You'd be amazed who visits Mrs. Monkton in the afternoons," Maddie said demurely.

"Good heavens, who?" Margaret exclaimed, but Maddie gave a reassuringly naughty giggle.

"That would be telling! You'll have to sit up here one afternoon and watch for yourself."

"I might," Margaret said. But how could she? There was always so much to do downstairs, letters to write, shopping to do, and cook to deal with. (Life to get on with?) She too, she realized, dropped in on Maddie, left her with things to sustain or amuse her. And went away.

"Perhaps we could move you downstairs, darling," she said. But that would be so difficult. The doctor had absolutely forbidden Maddie to use the stairs, so how on earth could they manage what Margaret could only, even in the privacy of her thoughts, call "the bathroom problem?" Too shame-making for Maddie to have to ask to be carried up the stairs every time she needed, and who was there to do it during the day? Maddie was very light—much too light—but her mother knew that she could not lift her, let alone carry her by herself.

"But you can't see anything from the sitting room," Maddie said.

"Oh, darling." Margaret realized she was going to have to leave Maddie alone again. Her husband would be home soon, and she was beginning to have serious doubts about the advisability of re-heating the fish pie. She must have a quick word with cook about cheese omelets. If only cook wasn't so bad with eggs... "What's this about sunset anyway?" She said briskly.

"Sunset comes a bit earlier every day," Maddie said. "And just at sunset, a man walks down the street."

"The same man, every night?"

"The same man, always at sunset."

"Perhaps he's a postman."

"Then he'd wear a uniform," Maddie said patiently. "And the same if he was a park keeper I suppose—they wear a uniform too, don't they. Besides, he doesn't look like a postman."

"So, what does he look like?"

"It's hard to explain," Maddie struggled for the right words, "but—can you imagine a beautiful skull?"

"What! What a horrible idea!" Margaret stood up, clutching the gray foulard at her bosom. "Maddie, if you begin talking like this I shall call Dr. Whiston. I don't care if he doesn't like coming out after dinner. Skull-headed men walking past the house every night indeed!"

Maddie pouted. "I didn't say that. It's just that his face is very—sculptured. You can see the bones under the skin, especially the cheek bones. It just made me think—he must even have a beautiful skull."

"And how is he dressed?" Margaret asked faintly.

"A white shirt and a sort of loose black coat," Maddie said. "And he has quite long curly black hair. I think he might be a student."

"No hat?" her mother asked, scandalized. "He sounds more like an anarchist! Really, Maddie, I wonder if I should go and have a word with the policeman on the corner and tell him a suspicious character has been hanging about outside the house."

"No, mother!" Maddie sounded so anguished that her mother hastily laid a calming hand on her forehead.

"Now darling, don't upset yourself. You must remember what the doctor said. Of course, I won't call him if you don't want me to, or the policeman. That was a joke, darling! But you mustn't get yourself upset like this...Oh dear, your forehead feels quite clammy. Here, take one of your tablets. I'll get you a glass of water."

And in her very real anxiety for her daughter, worries about the fish pie and well-founded doubts about the substitute omelets, Margaret almost forgot about the stranger. Almost, but not quite. A meeting with Mrs. Monkton, one evening when they had both hurried out to catch the last post and met in front of the post box, reminded her, and she found herself asking if Mrs. Monkton had noticed anyone "hanging about."

"A young man," that lady exclaimed with a flash of what Margaret decided was rather indecent excitement, "but darling, there are no young men left." Margaret raised a hand in mute protest only to have brushed aside by Mrs. Monkton. "Well, not nearly enough to go 'round anyway. I expect this one was waiting for Elsie."

Elsie worked for both Mrs. Monkton and Margaret, coming in several times a week to do "the rough," the cleaning that was beneath Margaret's cook and Mrs. Monkton's extremely superior maid. She was a handsome girl, with, it was rumored, an obliging disposition, who would never have been allowed across the threshold of a respectable household when Margaret was young. But nowadays…

Mrs. Monkton's suggestion did set Margaret's mind at rest. A hatless young man—yes, he must be waiting for Elsie. She might "have a word" with the girl about the propriety of encouraging young men to hang about the street for her, but, on the other hand, she might not. She hurried back home.

Bunty's mother came to tea, full of news. Bunty's elder sister was getting engaged to someone her mother described as "a bit nqos, but what can you do…" *Nqos* was a rather transparent code for "not quite our sort". The young man's father was, it appeared, very, very rich, though no one was quite sure where he had made his money. He was going to give—to give outright!—Bunty's mother had gasped, a big house in Surrey to the young couple. And he was going to furnish it too, unfortunately, according to his own somewhat…individual taste.

"Chrome, my dear, chrome from floor to ceiling. The dining room looks like a milk bar. And as for the bedroom—Jack says," she lowered her voice, "he says it looks like an avant-garde brothel in Berlin. Although how he knows anything about them I'm sure I'm not going to ask. But he's having nothing to do with the wedding," she added, sipping her tea as if it were hemlock. "I wonder my dear—would dear little Maddie be well enough to be a bridesmaid? It won't be until next June. I want to keep Pammy to myself for as long as I can," she dabbed at her eyes.

"Of course," Margaret murmured doubtfully. And then, with more determination, "I'll ask the doctor."

And, rather surprising herself, she did. On his next visit to Maddie, she lured him into the sitting room with the offer of a glass of sherry and let him boom on for a while on how well Maddie was responding to his treatment. Then she asked the Question, the one she had, until that moment, not dared to ask.

"But when will Maddie be—quite well? Could she be a bridesmaid, say, in June next year?"

The doctor paused, the sherry halfway to his lips. He was not used to being questioned. Margaret realized that he thought she had been intolerably frivolous.

"Bridesmaid?" the doctor boomed. And then thawed, visibly. Women, he knew, cared about such things. "Bridesmaid! Well, why not? Provided she goes on as well as she has been. And you don't let her get too excited. Not too many dress fittings, you know, and see you get her home early after the wedding. No dancing and only a tiny glass of champagne."

"And will she ever we well enough…to…to…marry herself and to…" but Margaret could not bring herself to finish that sentence to a man, not even a medical man.

"Marry—well, I wouldn't advise it. And babies? No. No. Still, that's the modern girl, isn't it? No use for husbands and children these days," and he boomed himself out of the house.

Margaret remembered that the doctor had married a much younger woman. Presumably, the marriage was not a success…then she let herself think of Maddie. She wondered if Bunty's mother would like to exchange places with her. Margaret would never have to lose her daughter to the son of a nouveau riche war profiteer.

Never…and she sat down in her pretty chintz-covered armchair and cried as quietly as she could, in case Maddie heard her. For some reason, she never asked herself how far the doctor's confident boom might carry. Later she went up to her daughter, smiling gallantly.

"The doctor's so pleased with you, Maddie," she said. "He thinks you'll be well enough to be Pammy's bridesmaid! You'll have to be sure you finish her present in time."

Margaret had bought a tray cloth and six placemats stamped with the design of a figure in a poke bonnet and a crinoline, surrounded by flowers. Maddie was supposed to be embroidering them in tasteful, naturalistic shades of pink, mauve, and green as a wedding gift for Pammy, but she seemed to have little enthusiasm for the task. Her mother stared at her, lying back in her nest of pillows.

"Peak and pine! Peak and pine!" said the voice in her head.

"Do you ever see your young man anymore?" she asked, more to distract herself than because she was really concerned.

"Oh, no," Maddie said, raising her shadowed eyes to her mother. "I don't think he was ever there at all. It was a trick of the dark."

"Trick of the light, surely," Margaret said. And then, almost against her will, "do you remember that story I used to read you? About the changeling child?"

"What, the one that lay in the cradle saying "I'm old, I'm old, I'm ever so old?" Maddie said. "Whatever made you think of that?"

"I don't know," Margaret gasped. "But you know how you sometimes get silly words going round and round your head—it's as if I can't stop repeating those words from the story. 'Peak and pine!' to myself over and over again." There, she had said it aloud. That must exorcise them, surely.

"But that's not from the changeling story," Maddie said. "It's from *Christabel*, you know, Coleridge's poem about the weird Lady Geraldine. She says it to the mother's ghost, 'Off wandering mother! Peak and pine!' We read it at school, but Miss Brownrigg made us miss out all that bit about Geraldine's breasts."

"I should think so, too," Margaret said weakly.

Autumn became winter, although few people noticed by what tiny degrees the days grew shorter and shorter until sunset came at around four o'clock. Except perhaps Maddie, sitting propped up on her pillows, and watching every day for the young man who still walked down the street every evening, in spite of what she had told her mother. And even she could not have said just when he stopped walking directly past the window, and took to standing in that dark spot just between the lamp post and the post box, looking up at her…

"Where's your little silver cross, darling?" Margaret said, suddenly, wondering vaguely when she had last seen Maddie wearing it.

"Oh, I don't know," Maddie said, too casually. "I think the clasp must have broken, and it slipped off."

"Oh, but—" Margaret looked helplessly at her daughter. "I do hope Elsie hasn't picked it up. I sometimes think…"

"I expect it'll turn up," Maddie said. Her eyes slid away from her mother's face and returned to the window.

"How's Pammy's present coming along?" Margaret asked, speaking to that white reflection in the dark glass, trying to make her daughter turn back to her. She picked up Maddie's work bag. And stared. One of the place mats had been completed. But the figure of the lady had been embroidered in shades of black and gray and it was standing in the midst of scarlet roses and tall purple lilies. It was cleverly done: every fold and flounce was picked out, but Margaret found it rather disturbing. She was glad that the poke bonnet hit the figure's face… She looked up to realize that Maddie was looking at her almost slyly.

"Don't you like it?" she said.

"It's—it's quite modern isn't it?"

"What, lazy daisies and crinoline ladies, modern?" How long had Maddie's voice had that lazy, mocking tone? She sounded like a world-weary adult talking to a very young and silly child.

Margaret put the work down.

"You will be all right, darling, won't you?" Margaret said, rushing into her daughter's room one cold December afternoon. "Only I must do some Christmas shopping, I really must."

"Of course, you must, mummy," Maddie said. "You've got my list, haven't you? Do try to find something really nice for Bunty, she's been so kind."

And what I would really like to give her, Maddie thought, is a whole parcel of jigsaws…and all the time in the world to see how she likes them. She leaned against her pillows, watching her mother scurry down the street. She would catch a bus at the corner by the church, and then an underground train, and then face the crowded streets and shops of a near-Christmas West End London. Maddie would have plenty of time to herself. She knew (although her mother did not) that cook would be going out to have tea with her friend at Mrs. Cresswell's at half-past three, and for at least one blessed hour she would be entirely alone in the house.

She pulled herself further up in the bed and fumbled in the drawer of her bedside table to find the contraband she had managed to persuade Elsie to bring in for her. Elsie had proved much more useful than Bunty, or Cissie or any of her kind friends. She sorted through the scarlet lipstick, the eye-black, the face-powder, and began to draw the kind of face she knew she had always wanted on the blank canvas of her pale skin. After twenty minutes of careful work, she felt she had succeeded rather well.

"I'm old, I'm old, I'm ever so old," she crooned to herself. She freed her hair from its inevitable pink ribbon, and brushed it sleekly over her shoulders, then she took off her lacy bed jacket and the white winceyette nightie beneath it. Finally, she slid into the garment the invaluable Elsie had found for her (Heaven knows where—although Maddie had a shrewd suspicion it might have been stolen from another of Elsie's clients—perhaps the naughty Mrs. Monkton). It was a nightdress made of layers of black and red chiffon, just a little too large for Maddie, but the way it tended to slide from her shoulders could have, she felt, its own attraction.

All these preparations had taken quite a long time, especially as Maddie had had to stop every so often to catch her breath and once to take one of her tablets, but she was ready just before sunset. She slipped out of bed, crossed the room, and sat in a chair beside the window. So. The trap was almost set (but was she the trap or only the bait?) Only one thing remained to be done.

Maddie took out her embroidery scissors, and, clenching her teeth, ran the tiny sharp points into her wrist…

The bus was late and crowded. Margaret struggled off, trying to balance her load of packages and parcels and hurried down the road, past the churchyard wall, past Mrs. Monkton's redbrick villa, past the post box—and hesitated. For a moment she thought she had seen something—Maddie's strange man with the beautiful skull-like face? But no, there were two white faces there in the shadows—no. There was nothing. A trick of the dark. She dropped her parcels in the hall and hurried up the stairs.

"Here I am, darling, I'm so sorry I'm late…Oh, Maddie—Maddie darling…whatever are you doing in the dark?"

She switched on the light.

"Maddie. Maddie, where are you?" She whispered. "What have you done?"

Tina Rath lives in London with her husband and some cats. She works as an actress, model, and Queen Victoria look-alike. She is also an expert in vampire fiction, and wrote her doctoral thesis on The Vampire in Popular Fiction. Around sixty of her short stories have been published in the independent and mainstream press. Some are collected in the anthology A Chimaera in my Wardrobe, available on Amazon.

Abysmoira

Airika Sneve

"Thaaat's it, honey. Dig it in deeper. Just try to keep the blood off my crucifix, OK?" said the supine man on the metal table. Softly, reverently, he fingered the silver filigree pendant resting on his naked, skinny chest.

"You're such a perv, Ronald," said the scalpel-wielding woman hovering over him. The tips of her auburn hair floated over the man's torso as she traced the blade in a delicate crimson line from sternum to navel. The man arched his back and uttered a shuddering moan.

The woman pressed the blade in deeper. Wispy white fingers tapering into long, lacquered nails the color of bloodstains curled around glittering steel. The voluptuous bloom of her breasts swelled out of a red vinyl corset that shimmered liquidly under the hazy glow of the cobalt track lighting.

On either side of the pair, wall-to-ceiling mirror panels reflected the bloodletting with vicious, sparkling acuity. Heavy red velvet curtains, dark and rich as cyanide cupcakes, intertwined with chains strung like tinsel about the walls. On every spare inch of black-cinderblock wall space hung a dazzling array of masks and erotic torture devices—everything from whips, to cat o' nine tails, dildos, knives, chastity belts, and floggers.

Ronald, the man on the metal table, smiled. "It's a good thing I *am* such a pervert, missy," he said in a slow Texas drawl, "or I wouldn't have the pleasure of your acquaintance, now would I?"

This prompted a razor-white smile from the woman's cherry mouth. "Touché," she said, and gazed at Ronald's bony torso heaving beneath her, at the vein-like tracery of pale pink scar tissue zig-zagging through the blood-flecked silver tangles of hair.

She retraced the scalpel along the cross she'd inscribed, then jabbed the blade into Ronald's navel for good measure. He closed his eyes and moaned.

"Well, what do you think, Ronnie? Will that be enough bloodletting for tonight, or do I have to eviscerate you, too?"

He exhaled. "That'll do, ma'am."

"Good." She gave Ronald's belly-button a final jab for emphasis, then turned and strutted to the chamber's tiny adjoining bathroom. Ronald watched her go, listening to the echo of her knife-blade stilettos on the chamber's tile floors as she clicked away.

Abysmoira bent over the sink, favoring Ronald with the kind of leather-gartered rear view that inspired more than a few patrons to trade half their weekly salaries for a few glamorously administered bangs and bruises. He looked away.

"Close that door, girl. You're givin' the goods away for free."

"Ever the Southern gentleman," said Abysmoira, fluffing her hair.

"Don't get me wrong, I know most men would be happier 'n pigs in shit for a look like that, but you're like a daughter to me."

"Oh, you want me to call you Daddy now, huh?" She winked.

"Well ain't you the clever one!" he said, laughing. "Maybe it ain't quite typical, but I'm not above lettin' ya put the hurt on me every now and then, no sirree. How long have I known you now, three years?"

"Almost four."

He shook his head. "My, how times flies. I swear, you're the only good thing to come out of this highfalutin cumdumpster."

Abysmoira clicked out of the bathroom and hugged him, kissing him lightly on the cheek. "I obliterate state health regulations for you on a weekly basis. I must like you a little, too."

Ronald grinned, then swung his legs to the floor and headed to the bathroom. "Are you still on the clock, or does M'lady have other plans for the evening?"

"Oh yeah, *big* plans," she called back as she preened into a gilded-angel mirror. "Beezer and I are gonna camp out in front of the TV, drown our sorrows in Chicken Noodle soup, and watch infomercials until the sun comes up. Hold me back, Ronnie, this might get dangerous!"

"Well, if that don't beat the band! You just give me a jingle if you need backup, ya hear?"

"I'll keep my phone at hand," laughed Abysmoira.

Ronald strode out of the bathroom freshly soaped and gauzed. Clipping his suspenders onto a clean pair of slacks, he walked to where Abysmoira stood hunched over a chair with her forehead pressed into her palm, eyes closed, brow furrowed. He caught the almost imperceptible rise of her shoulders as she sighed soundlessly amidst the muffled throb of the dance club below.

He touched her arm, startling her.

"Say, I know you an' Beezer got a mighty full agenda tonight, but how about stickin' around for a drink with me? We didn't get to talk much last weekend, and I'd love it if we could sit down, the two of us, over a drink or two. Whattaya say?"

Abysmoira paused and nodded. "Well, I could definitely use a shot about now. It's on, Ronnie-Boy."

Ronald smiled and patted her shoulder. "Makes me happier 'n a clam at high tide, Miss A."

"Alright, alright!" said Abysmoira, shooing him toward the door. "Get your bony ass downstairs, and I'll meet you by the bar in a few."

"That's my girl," he said, winking.

She watched as Ronald shouldered open the heavy iron door, ushering in a pulsating techno onrush from the nightclub below like autumn leaves swirling through a moonlit doorway. She waved to Ronald and, as the door heaved shut behind him, turned to confront the mirror's gilded face gazing at her from the wall.

She groaned. Her face was a pallid moon radiating from the center of a fiery nimbus; her eyes, bright and almost copper in sunlight, were bloodshot and tired. The hollow purple circles beneath her eyes spoke of many sleepless nights, and she noticed fine lines beginning to etch their way around her mouth.

Jesus, I'm only twenty-five.

She greeted her reflection with a well-manicured middle finger and sighed. Things hadn't exactly been easy lately, true—but then again, when had they ever?

She grasped the thin silver chain dipping into her cleavage and pulled it out, revealing a heavy pewter half-heart.

Nine years today.

Absentmindedly, she brought the pendant to her lips and remembered the first time she'd ever laid eyes on it. There had been two pendants then—Kieran's, and hers, which together united into a full heart.

God, how corny, she thought, and smiled.

She recalled that sticky-hot Missouri day nine years ago, back in Hayes Mills when she and Kieran were young, joyously obnoxious, and in love. There they were, two sixteen-year-olds gallivanting arm-in-arm through the mall, searching for the perfect token for their two-year anniversary when Kieran noticed a little kiosk just north of the food court.

"Sarah, check this out," he'd said, calling her by a name long since abandoned in the highlands of Missouri.

Sarah read the phrase on the pink-and-red-striped awning and scoffed. "Are you serious? Come on, '*Heavenly Hearts*?' Could it *possibly* get any cheesier?" She rolled her eyes and sighed.

"Oh, come on," said Kieran. "You never know until you look!"

And lo and behold, despite Sarah's protests, what they found tucked among the racks of costume jewelry were two silver half-hearts, one engraved with "Alw," the other with "ays." Kieran held one up to her neck and examined it with limpid hazel eyes.

"Always. Thank God for some cornball genius in"—he checked the tag—"Taiwan," he said, lifting an eyebrow.

Sarah cracked up.

Kieran laughed with her, then turned to look seriously into her eyes.

"'Always.' I think that pretty much sums it up, don't you?"

She shrugged. "I guess," she said, giving him her best begrudging pout.

"You guess," said Kieran, smiling. She stood on her tiptoes to kiss him—God, he'd been so tall—and bowed her head for him to slide the chain over it. She had to admit, the lockets were perfect. Cheesy or not, she couldn't think of a better word to describe the way she felt.

Abysmoira's mind wandered, drifting to images of the two of them on one of their many truant afternoons at Brentano Park. How many hours had they stolen soaking up the sun beside the lake, idly watching joggers huff by on the bike path while they laughed, smoked, and chattered about bands, movies, friends, and the future? Abysmoira couldn't guess.

In those days, they had assumed youth would wait forever, always a faithful butler awaiting their command. Adulthood and responsibility were worlds away, and life would always be an endless summer of afternoon treks to the record shop and big-city road trips with carloads of screaming teenagers.

Because there was always time.

They would always be young enough to sprawl gracelessly on the cool park grass, their laughter drawing quizzical stares from passersby. The adults on the bike path with their helmets and fanny packs, enjoying a few fleeting vacation days before trudging dutifully back to the 9-5, belonged to another world; Kieran and Sarah were *different*, and 'someday' was an abstract, ephemeral concept shimmering liquidly on the horizon. This was now, then was then, and the bridge between was a long and interminable haze.

Happy memories dissolved into visions of sticky, secret nights twisted in bedsheets, bodies entwined, cheek to cheek, as Kieran whispered passionately into her ear.

God, she had loved him.

They'd met when they were barely eleven, the summer Sarah and her mother moved to the weather-worn trailer park on Needmore Road. The dingy aluminum trailers scattered over the parched, patchy lot like washed-up fish carcasses on a litter-strewn beach, would've certainly made for a hopeless existence were it not for Kieran.

Kieran—tall, good-looking, dark-haired Kieran—was unlike any boy she'd ever met. From the first, he actually listened when she talked, remembering even the smallest details. He held doors for her, bought her smoothies at the mall, and was never afraid to hold her hand in front of his friends, no matter how much light-hearted teasing they gave him: "The trick is to find a guy with sisters," Kieran would advise her girlfriends, "'cause they're the ones who know how to treat a lady!"

While Sarah was quick-tempered and feisty, Kieran was mellow and sweet. Where she was pessimistic and cynical, Kieran could find the good in any situation. Most of all, he made her feel safe: whenever she came to him, sobbing hysterically over the latest brawl between her and her booze-addled, acid-tongued mother, he would hold her and stroke her hair—what he called 'autumn hair,' red like autumn leaves—until the tears dried, and she felt whole again.

"Two more years until we're eighteen," he'd whisper. "Then I'll have a car, and we'll drive until the tank runs out and settle wherever we land. No one will ever make you feel this way again. I promise you, Sisi."

I promise you, Sisi.

Her faith in that dream was the only thing that made life—the police visits to her and her mother's; the deputies prying the two screaming women apart; the insults; the tears, and the accusations—bearable. Soon, she told herself, they would flee this hellhole, get married, start a new life, and leave this never-ending heartache in the sandy soil of Hells Mills (as she liked to call it) forever.

She thought of the three-mile trek up the winding, forested backways of Needmore Road, the sun blazing hard upon them, their shirts sweat-plastered to their backs. She recalled seeing the tree for the first time, a great, mournful willow in a forest clearing with fronds sweeping low to the piney terrain, seeming to bow, almost, from its plot in front of the Risingmoon River.

"Here we are, Needmore Tree," said Kieran, out of breath but beaming.

"So?"

"This is it, darlin'. This is the main attraction!"

Sarah put her hands on her hips and gasped. "Kieran Michael Andrist! This is pretty and all, but you had me walk three miles for a tree?"

"Oh, but not just any tree. Have you ever heard of Yggdrasil?"

"Igg-whatta?"

"Yggdrasil. In Norse mythology, Yggdrasil is a sort of world tree that unifies and protects the nine worlds that surround it. The Norwegians believed the gods would go there every day to meet, and that only the tree would survive Ragnarök, their version of the end of the world. Basically, Yggdrasil is a bridge between the world of the living and the world of the dead, the world of the human and the realm of the divine. Make sense?"

She gave him a look.

He shrugged sheepishly. "I Googled it."

"And you're telling me this is it?"

"No. But it's like it."

In the distance, a bluebird twittered animatedly as the setting sun peeked and glimmered through the canopied treetops. The wind breathed the sweet smell of pine through the forest, tousling Sarah's hair as she searched Kieran's eyes and found nothing but an undisguised earnestness.

"This is a sacred place, Sisi. Throughout human history, across time and cultures, trees have been regarded as holy objects, guardians, and bringers of luck. The Assyrians, ancient Celts, Germanic pagans, and tons more all saw trees as sacred objects in some way. The roots extend down to the underworld, the branches reach up toward the heavens, and the trunk is a vessel that connects both worlds to the living."

"You don't really believe all that, do you? I mean, people believed that shit back when they were still crapping off their balconies into the streets. Come on."

He ruffled her hair. "My autumn-haired smartass," he said, kissing her forehead. He put both hands on her shoulders and looked into her eyes.

"Listen. Do you remember when I disappeared? Years ago?"

"It was right after your uncle died, when we were twelve. Why?"

"You know how, my whole life, the guy was like a second father to me? Then one day he's just, bam, gone before I ever had a chance to say goodbye. I couldn't deal. The day after his funeral, I made my way out to this tree, hung his old pocket watch from the branches and buried his class ring at the base. I remember crying, praying, a lot of blood…mine…and then I just…I don't know, walked with him around a countryside I'd never seen before, just walked for miles and talked, man to man."

"Two days, Sarah. The most peaceful two days of my life. I told him how much he meant to me, and he hugged me and made me promise to take care of my sisters, that my family needed me and it was time to be a man. When I woke up, I thought I'd only been out a few hours, but it had actually been two days. Y'all were frantic."

Sarah hugged herself, scowling. "Real funny, sweetheart. You were upset, and you ran away. So what."

He went on, ignoring her. "You know the craziest part? I can still feel him speaking sometimes, even now." His irises were thin bands of hazel around swollen black nexuses of pupil. "Here, you never have to worry about saying goodbye to the people you love. You know why?"

He leaned forward, and Sarah felt inexplicably queasy.

"With the Tree of Needmore, *there is no goodbye*."

The wind chill seemed to drop about fifteen degrees, and Abysmoira felt suddenly, unbearably claustrophobic, as if those weeping fronds were seconds from suffocating her with their quivering, deciduous anemone arms…or worse. The last thing she wanted darkening her consciousness was this frightening cosmology with its gods and demons, tree nymphs and monsters, legends and lore, the black hole of mystery and the sheer weight of unknowable human history crushing upon her psyche.

"Kieran, shut up! You're freaking me out!"

He said nothing, only studied her.

"How did you find this thing?" she asked.

"Out exploring when I was ten. I asked my mom about it, and she told me how people said it was special, how pagans supposedly made pilgrimages here back in the 1700's and sacrificed people for fertility and health, stuff like that. She kinda laughed when she said it, but she made me promise to stay away. Said I'd break my leg on the path, and have no way to get help."

"But you did come back."

"Many times." He grinned. "It's my thinking place. It's where I first built up the courage to ask you out."

"I don't care. It makes me feel weird…and what about these?" She sandaled a patch of vibrant blossoms whose many purple-starburst heads bloomed out of a single thick twist of stalk, a veritable hydra of the flower kingdom. "I'm no expert, but what kind of weird rainforest shit is this?"

"Couldn't tell you, but I'm sure there's some plant guy out there who could."

"I don't know, Kieran. It doesn't feel right. Why did you bring me here?"

He grabbed her hand and looked intensely into her eyes.

"Sarah. I want to be with you forever, *no matter what*. I want to know that nothing could ever separate us, not even death."

"We're sixteen! Neither one of us is going to *die*, Kieran!"

"I know, I know. But just for laughs. To be sure."

"Isn't that sacrilege? Worshiping a false idol, or something?"

Kieran waved his hand. "That's all open to interpretation. Besides, how could this possibly be wrong? This is about love," he said, kissing her fingers.

Sarah sighed. "Look. Even if this tree could somehow bind us, does the end ever justify the means? People died here. Is it ever OK to profit at someone else's expense?"

"Of course not. I would never bring you to a place I thought was evil, or dangerous. Sisi, this will all be done out of love. I promise."

She considered. "How?"

Images of the setting sun glaring off the razor blade near the weed-strewn pathway flashed through her mind, then blood falling all over Needmore Tree; small white fists wrapped in tawny larger ones, curled together over the masses of wiredrawn root networks; blood pattering from their wrists to that blasted tree; then, soft utterances as they knelt together over that massive, intricate root system:

"I'll love you despite the ravages of old age and time…"

"I'll love you no matter what…"

"May we be bound for eternity so that nothing, not even death, can keep us apart."

"Always."

"*Always.*"

And it seemed to her that when she glanced away and back again, the inky little droplets peppering the bark had vanished, had simply been cannibalized by the tree to nourish the veins of its profane roots…but that was a long time ago, and the human memory had a way of playing tricks.

The last thing she remembered was an indescribable euphoria and Kieran's soft voice:

"We. Are. Connected."

Unwillingly, Abysmoira's mind raced to the gloomy, overcast spring day she'd tugged Kieran's sleeve and begged him to take her out on his dad's motorcycle along Needmore's dusty back roads, like he sometimes did; she was sick of her mother, sick of Hell's Mills, and just plain sick of being alive. All she wanted was to feel the wind in her hair and her arms around her love, the possibility of freedom unfurling around every bend. She would fantasize they were leaving town for good, leaving that hideous Missouri burg in the dust forever as they raced off to seek a new destiny.

At first, Kieran refused. His father forbade him from riding in wet weather—but, in the end, he gave in to Sarah like he always did, and they sped off to the dirt road on the wooded outskirts of the trailer court. Sarah could still visualize the dilapidated trailers getting smaller as the woods loomed larger, the sky dark with thunderheads and the clouds pregnant with rain.

Sarah lifted her face to the sky, her hair lashing her cheeks, her flesh prickling with goosebumps as they bulleted through the wonderfully cool wind. She inhaled deeply of Kieran's jacket and held on tighter. It was moments like these, she thought, that made life worth living.

They zoomed toward a sharp hook in the road, and Sarah kicked Kieran's calf. "Faster!" she shrieked, loud enough to pierce through the roar of the engine and the screaming of the wind.

"We can't!" Kieran shouted. "It's too sharp!"

"Just a little! *Please*, Kieran!" she begged and kicked his calf again.

Kieran gunned the engine and ripped toward the bend at a speed too fast (for the turn) in good weather, let alone a damp, muddy spring day like that one.

Flashbulb impressions electrocuted Abysmoira's memory like lightning: the stench of burning rubber and gasoline; the sickening screech of wheels grinding mud as the motorcycle skidded towards the woods; the teenagers' screams as the impact catapulted them from the bike.

Sarah had emerged from her injuries—none permanent—six months later. Kieran…

The tree giveth, and the tree taketh away.

She scoffed, embarrassed at herself. That was crazy talk; the tree was a goddamn plant, for Chrissake, not some god with the power of life and fucking death. Kieran's mumbo jumbo had apparently rubbed off on her more than she'd realized.

She fought to block an image of the bloodied mass at the base of the tree. He didn't even look human anymore. Some residents from the trailer court had heard her screams carrying over the treetops from the woods and come running over.

From that day onward, she had had to live with the knowledge that she was the one who should be crumpled at the base of that tree, and she hated herself for it.

Whatever hope Sarah had had died with Kieran. She was all alone. The love of her life was dead, and it was her fault.

Her fault!

She was a murderer.

If only she hadn't forced him to take her on that fucking ride…if only she hadn't kept pushing him to go faster…

If only.

Abysmoira felt a lump forming in her throat and bit down on her fingers to stifle a sob. Warm tears welled up in her eyes. She shouldered away the teardrops in one exasperated motion—for Christ's sake, the last thing she wanted was for one of the other dommes to walk in with a client and find her bawling. She yanked a tissue from the bathroom cabinet and daubed away the telltale mascara tracks. When her face was satisfactorily smear-free, Abysmoira closed her eyes and willed herself to get it together, trying not to dwell on the past but dwelling nevertheless.

Three weeks after her various casts and braces came off, she'd skipped town with Eddie, a rail-thin, 6'5, 36-year-old small-time drug dealer she'd met at Brentano Park, the same park she and Kieran had wiled away so many afternoons. Eddie had some warrants out, and she just wanted to get the hell out of Missouri. Honestly, she would've gone anywhere, with anyone—anything to escape the bitter reminders and the constant, ineluctable ache.

She and Eddie had bummed their way to Vegas by hitchhiking, begging and, of course, Eddie's drug money. After about a year of bright lights, hot weather, fleabag motels, couch-hopping, and long nights under Vegas bridges, she stole a few wads of Eddie's cash and skipped town on a Greyhound.

From then on, her travels took her across the continental U.S. She did a lot of drugs, got a few tattoos, and traveled the countryside at the largesse of whatever man (or occasionally woman), was currently smitten with her. Always, always, she was the one to leave them in the dust for another lover, another state, another adventure; she was bound to none.

About four years ago in Arizona, one of her stripper friends told her about a high-class Texas B&D club she'd worked at, where she said she could probably get Abysmoira a job. By then, Abysmoira was sick of the nomad's life and more than ready to throw down roots in a decent city. Her friend made the call, and off Abysmoira went.

Now, she was one of the club's few dominatrixes who didn't need to work a straight job. She worked weekends spanking butts, did conventions, and sometimes even traveled to other clubs around the U.S.

All in all, she did OK. It was a living.

She gazed at the pale mirror-wraith clutching the necklace. A vision of the pendant's twin, now lying on the skeletal chest of a sixteen-year-old boy nine years in his grave, sliced through her mind.

She stifled a sob.

Since Kieran's death, dreams had become nothing but cruel

jokes. She couldn't count the nights she had awoken from euphoric afternoons at Brentano Park with him, calling his name, only to have her heart re-broken when the fog lifted and she was left with the realization that it was only a dream, and Kieran was *never* coming back.

Kieran, her Kieran…

She shook her head from side to side as if to shake away the memories. She was due to meet Ronald any minute now, and she *refused* to cry again.

She gave the metal table a few pumps of disinfectant and, with a final dab of the eyes, headed downstairs.

Abysmoira wound her way down an elaborate wrought-iron staircase and into the sea of writhing bodies and pulsating strobe lights of the dance floor below. She threaded her way through gyrating graveyard dancers and made her way to the bar, where she plopped down on a stool and scanned the floor for Ronald.

She spotted him nearby, holding court with a muscular man in assless chaps and a fuchsia bustier. She waved.

Ronald cordially dismissed his friend and took the stool beside her. "Well, I'll be a sawed-off bastard," he said, kissing her hand. "M'lady returns!"

"Quit," she said good-naturedly and waved him off. "I didn't keep you waiting too long, did I?"

"Naw, me and the fellas have plenty to jaw about, believe you me. Heads up, Miss A—the Republican convention's comin' to town next weekend."

"Bring 'em on," she said, rolling her eyes. "I've been meaning to refurnish my apartment for months. I can definitely use the money." She signaled to the bartender, a tall, lanky guy with a greaser pompadour and a white muscle tee.

"Howdy, Miss A. What can I getcha?" asked the bartender.

"Hey Jake. Tequila, please. Make that a double."

"Make that two," said Ronald.

Jake nodded and turned toward the mirrored back bar.

Hand on hip, Abysmoira turned to face Ronald. "Boozin' it up the day before Mass? Mr. Ronald G. Bitgood—what would your priest say?"

"What he don't know won't hurt me!" Ronald guffawed heartily. "Besides, one Bloody Mary before services, and I'll be fresh as a daisy—you can take *that* to the bank!"

Abysmoira arched one perfect auburn brow. The bartender returned with their drinks, and they toasted Republican Party money and let the alcohol work its fiery voodoo through their insides.

Abymsoira glanced toward the entrance where Chastity, the blue-haired door girl, was busy checking ID's. At the front of the line stood a towering figure in a full-body black liquid latex bodysuit, topped by a black latex dog's-head bondage hood. The figure stood a monumental seven feet tall, with hulking shoulders and a torso the width of two average men. The figure loomed over the other patrons, an imposing dog-headed pillar of latex. The man simply stood in line, talking to no one with its arms hanging limply, almost apishly, at its sides.

Abysmoira had noticed the dude hanging around the club for about a month, and always in that same latex get-up. He never danced, and she'd never observed him talking to anyone. He walked with a slow, mechanical gait that reminded Abysmoira of zombie Nazis death-marching through Auschwitz.

A chill shivered down her spine. She encountered plenty of colorful characters on a weekly basis—foot fetishists, cross dressers, exhibitionists, and sexual deviants of all stripes—but this was one of the few patrons who made her genuinely uneasy. Perhaps she was being paranoid (or vain), but she always got the feeling the figure was looking at her no matter where he was in the room, tracking her with those depthless canine sockets.

"Ronnie, you know that guy?" she yelled into Ronald's ear, gesturing toward the figure.

"Who, that tall fellow in the gimp mask?" he yelled back.

"Yeah, him! I've seen him around for a month or so, but I don't even know his name!"

"Don't reckon I can help ya! Never seen him talk to anyone, he just sits in the back or stands there, rigid as a maypole."

"Probably gets off on creeping people out," she shouted.

"Yes'm, probably so!"

Abysmoira sipped her drink, eyes fastened on the enormous figure. It didn't walk so much as levitate through the crowd, cutting a swath through the gyrating dancers like a Sequoia redwood tree floating through a cornfield. Ronald and Abysmoira watched, fascinated, as it drifted past them up the wrought-iron stairs.

"If I get any info on the guy, I'll let you know!" shouted Ronald, nudging her.

"Thanks! I don't mean to sound paranoid. It's just been a little weird lately, what with the whole Sven and Mary thing."

Ronald furrowed his tanned, Texas-weathered brow. "If I ever catch the motherfucker that killed Sven, I'll skin his hide myself—God help me, but I mean it." He bowed his head. "Great guy, Sven was. One of the biggest fellas you'd ever meet, but gentle as a lamb. He'd never hurt a soul—he just liked to dance."

Abysmoira nodded, thinking of the seven-foot, cueball-headed Swede who'd frequented the club since its opening eleven years prior. Everyone knew and liked him in the tight little Texas BDSM community, and was collectively stunned when he'd seemingly gone up in smoke last month, leaving no trace but the bloodstains on the walls of his apartment. The blood type had proven a match to Sven's, and the police said there was no way anyone could've lost that much blood and survived.

Not long afterward, Mary Mercy, another regular, also disappeared (though Mercy wasn't nearly as well-liked as Sven, largely due to her reputation as an unstable drama queen). She'd been infatuated with Sven for years, and some wondered if she hadn't caused his "disappearance" herself. As many speculated, it certainly would've given her reason to skip town.

Abysmoira stared into her drink. "I know, I'm still in shock. Same thing happened to an old lady just down the block from here, did you hear? Just up and disappeared. No body, no witnesses, lots of blood—just like Sven. There's some scary shit going down around here lately."

Ronald crossed himself and gazed sorrowfully out into the crowd.

Just then, the venue manager, Phil, tapped Abysmoira on the shoulder.

"Miss A," he said, "You off the clock?"

"Yeah, why?"

"Special request. Off the books, big pay."

"Sorry Phil, I'm off. Tell 'em to fuck off and come back next Saturday."

"I told him you'd say that." He leaned closer, his eyes on the crowd as his greasy black mustache tickled Abysmoira's ear.

"When I said big pay, I meant very. *Big. Pay.*"

Abysmoira scowled and slammed the last of her drink. "Yeah? Just how big we talkin'?"

Phil leaned in and uttered a number.

Her eyes widened. She leaned over and draped an arm around Ronald.

"Ronald, good buddy, would you mind if I took a rain check? I've got a customer who wants to pay my rent, and who am I to stand in his way?"

Ronald smiled and patted her arm. "You do what you need to do. Just promise me—next weekend?"

"Next weekend," assured Abysmoira, and wound her way back upstairs to greet her customer.

When the chamber's iron door heaved shut behind her, Abysmoira turned to face her client—and was greeted instead by the sight of an empty room.

"Fuck," she muttered. "Just what I…"

And then a shadow moved. Abysmoira leapt backward, nearly

toppling over in her stilettos. Heart pounding, she steadied herself on the metal table, scowling, and turned to face the offender.

HIM.

"Jesus Christ! What the hell are you trying to do, break my ankle?" she demanded.

The seven-foot tower of latex before her said nothing. Secretly, Abysmoira was unnerved, but she wouldn't allow this creep the satisfaction of knowing that. She dabbed her sweating brow.

The figure didn't move.

Abysmoira gestured toward his mask. "Dog's head, cute. You like animals? You'd love Tony. Mistress Jade's sub." She was babbling, and she knew it.

The figure remained silent. She tried a different tactic.

"I've seen you around. What's your name?"

Still, the figure simply stared at her through the empty, insectile sockets of the latex dog mask.

"Alright. Fine." She strode toward him. "Phil says you want the house special, whips and all."

Still, no response, just the sound of wet, muffled breathing beneath latex.

"Undress."

The figure remained motionless.

"*Now.*"

A few silent seconds ticked by. Abysmoira sighed and closed her eyes.

"I see," she said. "Your money, your way."

Keeping her fingers as steady as possible, she reached out and grasped the zipper at his collar and pulled it down to his pubic bone, training her eyes on his massive arms. Quickly, she dropped to her knees and yanked the zipper down the remainder of its track.

What she saw made her blood run cold.

Above the zipper, the wet red leaves of a gaping maw of a vagina parted like curtains to reveal an enormous uncircumcised penis snaking out of the vaginal mouth. Judging by the putrid odor and brownish fluid drooling out of the cavity, there was also a terrible infection ravaging this distorted amalgam of sex organs.

Abysmoira gasped and toppled backward. A panting tangle of legs, auburn hair, and stilettos, she gazed up at the looming figure.

"I-I've never…seen…"

She suppressed a powerful urge to scream. To be fair, it was the client's misfortune to have been cursed with such a deformity, and it hadn't actually threatened her. This *was* a B&D club, after all, and if such a creature existed, it was likely to find its way here.

Still…

Wordlessly, the figure stepped out of the bodysuit, peeled its arms free, and tossed the material in a puddle of inky blackness on the floor. There it stood in all of its towering seven-foot glory, stark naked and looming over the shaking heap of Chamber Mistress like an infernal skyscraper.

Its shoulders were broad, and it was spectacularly muscled—like an Olympic god. Despite the extremity of its musculature, however, the physique was too primal, too beastly, to be erotic. The vast, reptilian surface of its body was covered in pebbled, wet, brownish-red leper's skin that sloughed away in gory sheets. Its body glistened under the track lighting like a shorn grape.

Burn victim. Has to be.

Abysmoira's mind struggled to latch onto a plausible explanation. Her eyes huge, her mouth unhinged, she sat frozen to the floor in horror.

The naked being lifted its arms and peeled off the dog mask.

Blackness began to creep around the edges of Abysmoira's vision. She fought for consciousness as her brain struggled to compute what it was seeing.

The creature's bald, decaying head was small and almost demonic, with short, curling ram's horns that Abysmoira now realized had been tucked neatly into the pointy ears of the mask. Its right pupil was so dilated the eye appeared almost black, while the left pupil had contracted to a tiny, lizard-like pinprick. Its nose had rotted away, and its massive body glistened with stinking weals and running sores.

Abysmoira's larynx clenched to scream, but only air emerged. She couldn't faint, couldn't find the strength in her legs to run, couldn't do anything but remain rooted to the floor gaping at the monster in front of her.

Finally, it spoke.

"Sisi," it said, cocking its head. "It's me."

Sisi.

It's me.

The words ricocheted in her head like bullets. She knew that voice well—and yet, had never heard such a haunted, inhuman sound in her life, this shifting amalgamation of timbres, pitches, and speech patterns. Some words were deep and rough, a man's voice; much of the speech was an old woman's—or rather, the eldritch wraith of an old woman's, more akin to the whisper of dead leaves scritch-scratching over a mausoleum. The third voice—the one that coursed beneath the surface of the others—was a voice she knew all too well, a voice she had loved above all others.

No way. No earthly *way*...

Abysmoira's hand flew to her mouth. Her eyes huge and tear-drenched, she shook her head.

It spoke.

"Sisi..."

Sisi...?

"Don't be afraid. It's me, angel. Look." The massive grotesquerie knelt before her and grasped an object Abysmoira, in her disbelief and terror, had failed to notice: a silver filigree chain with a pewter half-heart. She didn't need to see it up close to know what the inscription would read.

"Do you remember me now, Sarah?" The demon's crazed pupils seemed to swim unsteadily in their retinal beds, fixing on hers, then drifted to the pendant resting on her chest. "Oh, love. Nine years, and you never took yours off. Well, neither did I." It leaned forward, stinking of the grave.

Abysmoira yelped and shrank back. Outside herself, she heard a weak mewling coming from her throat like a helpless, wounded animal. She hadn't even known she was capable of such a sound.

The demon halted, then tried again. "Sarah, it's me. Kieran."

Hearing aloud what she had intuitively known was more than her fragile mind could take, somehow giving weight to the insanity before her. She screamed and covered her head with her arms, rocking back and forth as tears coursed hotly down her cheeks.

"No, no, *hell* nooooo…"

The demon blinked almost comically.

"*Please*, listen to me." It knelt to her level, eye to eye, and spoke softly.

"I have never been as far away as you might've thought. Do you remember that day at Needmore Tree?"

Weeping willow, bleeding Needmore…

"No!"

"Yes, you do. Sisi, all those years you cried at night begging God to bring me back, I was listening. Haven't you realized? We are connected."

We. Are. Connected.

"It's taken nine years to break through, but here I am. Aren't you happy?"

Its face was twisted into a pathetic expression of hope. It saw her huddling terror and reached out with one hand, slowly and gently, its massive limb nearly reaching her cheek from its standpoint four feet away.

Abysmoira shrieked from behind spread fingers. Her eyes, huge and shining, had morphed from the hard eyes of a jaded B&D queen into a tragic caricature of a Precious Moments figurine.

The demon stopped mid-reach, its hand hovering in the air.

"Sarah…Sisi," it said, its voice shifting schizophrenically, terrifyingly, like soundlessly screaming spirits fighting to emerge from a still, depthless black pond. "*Please*, don't be afraid. I admit, maybe I'm not supposed to be here, but I had to. For you."

"How?"

The creature's gaze faltered, and it smiled a crocodile's smile. "Sisi, I love you..."

"*How?*"

"You were *so* lonely. Do you have any idea how hard it was to watch you suffer?"

"*I said how!*"

It dropped its gaze and sighed, allowing its gigantic hand to fall. "Angel...everyone I might've hurt to reach you lives through me now. It was all done out of love."

Abysmoira's gaze wandered over the thing's bald cueball head, at its massive size and musculature.

"Sven?"

"Sisi..."

"SVEN?"

It hesitated, then looked down.

"Yes."

Abysmoira's hand flew to her mouth.

"Oh God, no," she choked. Deep, wracking sobs threatened to shake her very being apart. "The old lady? Mercy?"

"I love you. Does it really matter? We're together now." Its crazed eyes implored her, its schizophrenic chorus of voices smearing and bleeding into each other.

She bit down on her lip and lifted her eyes to the creature's. After a long silence, she spoke.

"Maybe I'm just in shock—it's just so hard to believe you're actually right here in front of me. You know how much I've missed you. Maybe sometimes the end *does* justify the means."

"You see?" A slow, lunatic smile knifed across its face. "In the end, not even God could keep us apart."

Its eyes widened and slowly, slowly it tilted its head to a frighteningly unnatural angle. "Please, angel. Let me hold you." Its voice cracked with emotion. "God, how I've missed you."

Abysmoira gazed at the creature, her hair hanging in snotty wet strings around her face. She was shocked and repulsed by the naked tenderness in its wretched face...and yet somewhere, swimming inside the vortexes of insanity that were this thing's eyes, she swore she saw the vestiges of her lost love within.

"Kieran..."

"Sisi..."

Slowly, ever so slowly, it leaned forward to kiss her, and this time, she leaned in to return the embrace. Two figures—one massive, raw, and wet with sores, the other slender and fair—slowly collided to close a gulf created by nine years of agony and death, the faces of two half-souls bridging together, dying to entwine and become whole again, to unify two silver tokens that, together, signified always.

"I did this all for you," whispered Kieran as the silhouettes bridged the divide.

Abysmoira leaned closer...

And spat in his face.

The creature jerked its head up, shocked.

"Get away from me, you monster! You're not Kieran!" she screamed.

The demon recoiled.

"You don't mean that. You're in shock, but don't worry—we'll find a way."

Abysmoira huddled into herself and glared up at the beast.

"My Kieran could never be such a selfish murderer."

She felt the music vibrating the floor beneath her body from the downstairs dance floor, where a normal world rotated smoothly in its orbit as people danced and drank while her own world toppled off its axis and plummeted into a hell she had never imagined existed.

"Sarah," the thing croaked, "Sssshhh."

Eyes huge, it put a shaking finger to its lips and gazed at her. "You are so beautiful, even more beautiful than I remember." Tears filled its eyes. "I've waited *so* long." It moved toward her. "Make love to me," it breathed. "Make love to me like you used to."

She looked at its dripping abomination of a crotch and thought of being kissed by its withered mouth which, undoubtedly, would be much like making out with a skinned deer carcass.

She kicked out, nailing the thing square in the stomach.

It reeled backward and screamed.

"Get the fuck away from me!"

The creature gasped. "No, Sisi! Love me, please!"

Abysmoira scrabbled backward and jiggled the iron door handle furiously. It failed to open in her jittery fingers, and she slid to the floor, weeping.

"Please, just stay away. You're not the same!"

"I am the same!" it screamed, its fangs spraying foam, its pupils nictitating in its yellowed eyes. It wept frantically, gouging reddish flesh out of its scalp with desperate, ragged nails. "Love me!"

"I don't love you!"

The demon froze.

"What?"

"I said I don't love you. You're disgusting!"

"Disgusting," it repeated, its voice cracking. Suddenly its words rushed out in a torrent of infernal rage, its face a mask of anguish.

"I traded my immortal soul *for you*!" it roared, pacing the chamber. "I chose damnation—*for you*! I felt you praying night after night, year after year, begging God to bring me back. Now, here I am, just like you asked, and you tell me you don't love me anymore."

"You're a ghoul," Abysmoira sobbed.

"A ghoul," the creature repeated. It reached up and grasped the medallion. "I'll love you despite the ravages of old age and time; I'll love you no matter what. Always."

Abysmoira shook her head.

"But I need you…"

"No!"

"I *need* you…"

"Kieran, STOP! Please…!"

Phil DiGarzia, the venue manager, hefted the chamber door shut and swore under his breath.

Slime, the club's dreadlocked DJ, approached Phil.

"She in there?"

"No, nothing. Not a goddamn thing. You sure you saw her go in?"

"I fucking swear. On my life, man. You checked everywhere?"

"Yes, everywhere! Unless she suddenly has the amazing fucking power of invisibility, she ain't in there. What the fuck?"

Slime could only stare as DiGarzia stalked off in an invective-laced fury.

Inside the chamber, a hulking latexed figure stood alone amidst the dildos and cinderblock walls. It lifted its dog-head mask and caressed the auburn locks sprouting in patches over its infected scalp.

Autumn hair.

It smiled sadly and walked toward the door. The voluptuous pair of breasts protruding from its chest were painfully uncomfortable, but luckily, its bodysuit was tight enough to pack these new accouterments securely from view.

The figure grasped the two pendants dangling from its neck, and kissed them.

Sisi.

Now she was a part of him, and they would indeed be together forever, just as they had pledged under Needmore Tree so long ago.

Always.

Airika Sneve is a writer, musician, and University of MN psychology graduate from Minnesota. She enjoys ham, cats, and the infliction of nightmares upon unsuspecting readers. Her stories have been published by Pill Hill Press, Crowded Quarantine Publications, Horrified Press, Nameless Magazine, Strange Musings Press, and Strangehouse Books. You can chat with her on Twitter about all things life and horror at Twitter.com/scairika.

Skin Deep

Carson Buckingham

It all began innocently enough with the removal of a single unsightly wart.

Lucinda Parker had been begging her mother for years to take her to someone who could get rid of "the immense-by-any-standards" growth next to her nose.

"Mother, it looks like I have three nostrils," she would wail, and her long-suffering parent would then give her the same, half-listening broken record response, "When you're older."

To which Lucinda's broken-record rejoinder was, "I'll never be 'older' because I'll kill myself before then!" This was invariably followed by stomping down the hallway and slamming her bedroom door—often more than once.

"The difficult years have arrived," Mrs. Parker could be heard to mutter as she dried another dish.

The difficult years. Lucinda was twelve. She had had exactly one menstrual cycle, thirty-two (she counted them) pubic hairs, and one training bra which she wore night and day. She was already shaving her underarms and legs, though not out of necessity, and was experimenting with make-up. Her best effort to date made her look, if you squinted, like Lady Gaga; her biggest failure, a cross between Alice Cooper and Tammy Faye Bakker.

The hairstyles are not to be mentioned, much less discussed.

In short, Lucinda felt that she was now a Grade-A, one hundred percent woman, and she wanted the perks that went with it; but before they could even begin to kick in, she had to do something about her face.

Everything would be perfect if I could only get rid of this tumor next to my nose. It dwarfs the Empire State Building, for cryin' out loud!

Mr. and Mrs. Parker remained unconcerned for most of that year, chalking their daughter's antics up to number one, a phase, and number two, hormones.

However, as Lucinda's thirteenth birthday neared, things shifted dramatically.

"Lucinda, it's Saturday night. Why don't you go out to the movies with your friends?" Mrs. Parker asked.

Her daughter looked up from her copy of "Marie Claire" and rolled her eyes. "I don't have any friends."

"Oh, nonsense. Of course you do! Call one and go out—my treat."

Lucinda sighed and picked up the phone.

Ten minutes later, there was a soft knock at the front door.

"Must be Lu's friend," Mr. Parker muttered behind his newspaper.

Mrs. Parker, ever cautious, glanced through the peephole. "There's nobody there, George."

"Damned kids. You'd better see if they left a bag full of dog crap on the stoop, hoping that you'll step on it."

"George Parker, *really*!"

"We did it when I was a kid. Doubt things have changed all that much."

"Haven't," Lucinda said, walking in. "Except now they set fire to it to make sure you step on it."

"How charming," Mrs. Parker said. The word "disgust" could have actually appeared across her forehead, and no one would have been surprised.

"Aren't you going to open the door?" Lucinda asked.

"There's no one there."

"Sure there is." She swung open the door and there stood six-year-old Charlie Foley from next door. He was so small that he didn't show up in the peephole.

"Oh, I'm sorry to keep you waiting out there, Charlie," Mrs. Parker said. "Does your mother need something? Eggs? Sugar?"

"No, ma'am. I'm here fer Lucinda. We're goin' on a…uh…what was it again?" he asked Lucinda.

"A 'date,' Charlie."

"Thassit! A date. Whassa 'date,' Mrs. Parker?"

Eleanor Parker was too flummoxed to reply. George Parker, on the other hand, was laughing quietly behind the sports section—you could tell because the paper was shaking.

"Charlie, a 'date' is when we go to the movies and stuff ourselves with popcorn and candy and soda!" Lucinda said, tickling his tummy. She would have tousled his hair, but in honor of the occasion, it was so plastered down that she was afraid she'd stick to it.

Mrs. Parker turned to her daughter. "May I see you in the kitchen, Lucinda? Oh, and *do* come in, Charlie. You can have a nice chat with Mr. Parker. We won't be a moment."

Mr. Parker sighed, folded his paper, shot the missus a dagger-filled look, then put a smile on his face and turned to their little guest.

Once in the kitchen, Lucinda's mother rounded on her. "What are you trying to prove, Lucinda?" she hissed. "Do you think you're funny?"

"No, just funny-looking."

"What?"

"I don't *have* any friends my own age, Mom. I keep trying to tell you that—and it's all because of this…this…whatever it is on my face!"

"But why Charlie?"

"He's too young to care about how I look. He just cares that I like him and treat him nice. He's the only real friend I have. We were walking home from school the other day, and one of the football players called me 'the Wicked Witch of the West.' Well, Charlie ran right up to him and started punching his leg." Lucinda smiled, tears welling up at the memory. "It was as high as he could reach, Mom, but he did it without a second thought. He did it for me. That linebacker could have made him into a stain on the sidewalk, but Charlie didn't care. So, yes, Mom, I'm going to the movies with Charlie Foley, my little knight in shining armor and red Velcro sneakers. Are you driving us, or is Dad?" Before her mother could reply, Lucinda dried her eyes and left the room.

Mrs. Parker was floored. "I had no idea things were as bad as that," she murmured before joining everyone in the living room.

Mr. Parker looked up, an expression of wonder on his face. "Eleanor, this little guy knows more about the Yankees than I ever did—every stat on every player! A fine young man…just fine." He reached over to tousle Charlie's hair, thought better of it, and settled for a manly pat on the back.

"I brought all my saved 'lowance, Lu, and I'm gonna buy you a humongous bagga popcorn—all by myself!" Charlie was really good at saving his money—even at age six. He had big plans, that one; but he understood the importance of gratitude, as well, and it didn't take a chainsaw to get him to part with some cash when it was appropriate.

Lucinda kissed Charlie on the cheek. She knew how hard he worked for that fifty cents a week—it wasn't just handed to him. "You are the sweetest man in the world, Charlie Foley, but my mom's paying tonight. Save your money, kiddo. Someday I'll want a car…or maybe an elephant."

"Or a giraffe?" Charlie giggled.

"Nope, no giraffe. Costs too much when they get a sore throat."

"What are you two going to see tonight?" Mr. Parker asked.

"Oh! 'The Incredibles'! Pleeeeeeeeeeease, Lu?"

"Absolutely."

Mr. Parker stood. "I'll drive. Let's get going. Coming, dear?"

"No…no. I think I'll stay here, thanks."

Twenty minutes later, Mr. Parker stepped back through the door, chuckling. "We had to stop next door so Charlie could put his bag of quarters away. He's such a nice little kid—no wonder Lu likes to babysit for him. Smart, too, that one, and…what's the matter, El?"

"I thought she was going out with Charlie to defy us or to make some obscure pre-teenage point, but she wasn't." She recapped the kitchen confrontation for him, and when she was done, Mr. Parker sat back in his chair looking thoughtful. But when at last he opened his mouth to speak, it was his wife who voiced his thoughts.

Mr. Parker just smiled and nodded.

A glum Lucinda sat at the table with her parents two weeks later. An angel food cake with thirteen candles blazed before her. Her loot this year consisted of an iPod and a gift certificate to download music onto it. She'd wanted just that, but nothing much seemed to make her happy anymore, and though she did her best to appear ecstatic, she knew from her parents' reaction that her attempt had fallen flat. She also knew that money was tight in the house these days and that they really didn't have cash to spare on such expensive gifts, so that added guilt to the guest list of her pity party. Depression had already arrived.

She was really starting to hate birthdays.

"Now, make a wish, Lu. Make it a really good one, and I bet it comes true. Thirteen is the most magical birthday of all, or so I've heard," Mr. Parker said.

"Dad, I'm thirteen, not three. Wishing doesn't work."

"Humor me. Close your eyes and concentrate."

Lucinda sighed as only a thirteen-year-old can, closed her eyes, wished, then blew out the candles, eyes still closed. She didn't care if she blew them all out or not, but when she opened her eyes, she saw that she had and that there was an envelope in front of her with her name on it.

Her parents looked at each other, secrets dancing in their eyes.

She tore the envelope and out fell a rectangular card. She picked it up and looked at it, more to indulge her parents than her curiosity; but as she realized what she held, her face transformed.

It was an appointment card…for her…at a cosmetic surgeon! She searched her parents' smiling faces. "Really? *Really?*"

"Yes, honey, really. Not that we don't think you're beautiful exactly the way you are, but you don't, and that's what needs to change," Mrs. Parker said.

"I'd just hate to see you get so tied up with outer beauty that you lose the inner, most important beauty that you already have in spades, my little girl. Promise me you won't," Mr. Parker said.

"I promise, Daddy."

The surgery cost the Parkers close to four thousand dollars, so as an economy measure they put off replacing the old clunker that Mrs. Parker drove. This was done not with resentment, but with love and good grace. The old car would surely limp along for another year or two until the surgical bill was paid off.

Since Lucinda's birthday was July fifteenth, she had plenty of time to recover from her surgery before returning to school, to eighth grade, in early September.

When the bandage finally came off, Lucinda looked in the mirror and couldn't believe what she saw.

She looked normal.

Actually normal.

A little pretty, even.

Possibly slightly beautiful.

She gazed at herself for over an hour.

Her face was perfect...or would be, if it wasn't for that bump on the bridge of her nose. Now that the distraction of that Oldsmobile-size growth was gone, it was easier to notice what else needed fixing.

But it would do...for now. At least she didn't have to hide in the house anymore, and the teasing at school, hopefully, would let up, too.

Lucinda pulled a pad and pencil out of her desk drawer, reluctantly laid the mirror aside, and made a list of the shortcomings that required repair as soon as possible:

Bump on nose—plane down bone
Too thin lips—collagen injections to fill out
Faint forehead lines—botox?
Weak chin—chin implants
Flat cheeks—cheek implants
Moles on neck and left ear—remove
Earlobes too big—reduction
Hair too thin—hair implants
Imperfect teeth—bright white implants necessary
Laser eye surgery—get rid of glasses
Bright blue contact lenses to have blue eyes

Watching the cosmetic surgery channel for the past year had really paid off. She knew exactly what she'd need to have done, and by God, she was going to look like Heidi Klum if it was the last thing she ever did.

Now that she knew what had to be done to achieve facial perfection, she needed a plan to get there. That plan required money and lots of it. Lucinda knew that her parents wouldn't allow her to make any major changes, so she'd have to wait until she turned eighteen for those. However, she thought she could talk them into paying for some of the minor surgery she wanted—like the mole removal and maybe the earlobe thing. Perhaps even the blue contacts that would transform her fog gray eyes. It wouldn't cost all *that* much, and her father had been talking about getting a second job anyhow; plus, her mother was working at the flower shop and now doing custom sewing on the side, too, so there should be plenty of extra cash to go around.

In any case, she knew how to get her way now.

All she had to do was mope around and act suicidal, and they'd shell out for sure. She could even insist on helping with the finances, and turn over all her babysitting money and any other money she raised. It would be so much less than the surgery would cost, but they wouldn't feel that they could turn her request down after that.

She knew them way too well.

Now the question was, outside of babysitting, what could she do? There was dog walking, car washing, leaf raking, and snow shoveling. She could also help around her own house more—cleaning and such—and put her parents even further in her debt.

Oh, that's a fine plan—everyone gets something out of it—especially me, Lucinda thought.

That afternoon, she launched into "Operation Operation" and biked over to every grocery store and pharmacy in town. She posted a list of jobs she could do and the prices for each, along with tear-off flaps with her phone number on them. In no time at all, she was up to her eyeballs in work.

She still didn't have any friends at school, but this time, it was her choice not to. She had far too much to do to fit friends into her big picture. No, she figured that once she was perfect, she'd be at least eighteen and she'd find a rich man to marry her and be set for life. After all, why play with boys when what you really wanted was a man, right? A boy can't take care of you and give you what you want.

The only thing that didn't change in her life, at least for a while, was her monthly movie "date" with Charlie, her one true friend. She'd never forget that.

Lucinda smiled, remembering Charlie's reaction when the final bandage had been removed.

He had been perplexed and said, "You don't look any diff'rint to me."

"But Charlie, don't you remember the big ugly thing that was right here?"

"Nope. I don't 'member that."

"But it was there. Don't I look beautiful now?"

"Sure, Lu. You were a'ways bootiful."

Lucinda smiled. "You'd have noticed it if you were older."

"Nah, I don't care 'bout stuff like that. All I know is when you have somethin' cut off, it means there's less of you left, and I like as much of you as can be, Lu. Maybe you should gain some weight."

Lucinda had laughed and hugged her little friend, feeling sorry for him that he was so terribly naïve about the way the world *really* worked.

Her plan went along perfectly until one chilly day in January. When she got home from babysitting that evening, her mother and father were sitting at the kitchen table, waiting. If their expressions were any indication, things were not looking good for her.

"Hi, you guys. Hey, I have to tell you the cute thing that Mrs. Dillard's kids did. You'd have—"

"Lucinda Ruth Parker, you will take off your jacket, and you will sit yourself down and explain this, please," her mother said.

No, not good at all.

Once Lucinda sat, her mother pushed her report card across the table. She stared at it and the Ds and Fs stared back. Her highest grade was a C minus, and that was for Physical Education.

"I don't understand, Lu," her father said. "It's always been As and Bs with you—and mostly As. What happened?"

"Oh, I'll tell you what happened, George. It's all this work she's been doing—running here, running there. It's no wonder her grades have slid. She doesn't have time for homework—even though she's been telling us that she's finished it every night."

"Don't talk about me like I'm not here," Lucinda said.

"Then explain, Lu," her father said.

Lucinda stood. "I'll be right back. I have to get something out of my room."

"We want an explanation, young lady."

"That's what I'm going to get, Mom."

Lucinda smiled. This couldn't have been better timed if she'd planned it for a year. She reached under her bed and drew out a chipped, gray-green metal strongbox the size of a hardcover book. She opened it with the tiny key she wore around her neck, then took it back to the kitchen with her.

"Here's why," she said, handing the box to her father.

"What's this? Please tell me it's not drugs, Lu."

"Just open it."

Mr. Parker flipped open the box. Then he handed it to Mrs. Parker.

"Where did you get all this money, Lucinda?" Mrs. Parker demanded.

"From working. I know things are pinched around here financially, so I thought I'd help out. That money is for you."

They melted immediately, just like she knew they would.

"But honey," her father said, counting the cash. "There's over five hundred dollars here. You earned all that babysitting?"

"Sure, and doing other chores for people. It's amazing what people will pay someone else to do because they're too lazy to do it themselves. I just wanted to help you guys out, that's all. I mean, we're a family, right? And family members should help each other—at least, that's how I feel about it. So please, take the money. I don't want it."

Her father sat back in his chair. "You are one impressive girl, you know that? How many other kids would try to help out their parents like this?"

Report card forgotten. Mission accomplished.

Her mother just shook her head in wonder. "I wish we could tell you to put this money away and that we don't need it, but we really do. With Dad's hours cut at the plant and mine at the flower shop, we're a month behind on the mortgage, and this will catch us up. Are you sure about this, sweetie?"

"Absolutely, Mom."

"Then thank you, love. Thank you ever so much." Her mother stood and gave her a warm hug, followed by her father.

Oh yeah, they owed her now, boy.

Over coffee, milk, and pie, a détente was reached in which Lucinda would cut back on her after-school jobs and pull her grades up where they belonged. They arrived at a workable schedule that everyone could live with, and that was the end of it.

That night in bed, Lucinda smiled, happy that her backbreaking after-school odd jobs were now over. She hated working that hard, but she had to quickly accumulate as much money as possible because she knew that once that report card showed up, it would be coming to an end—which was the plan all along.

She'd continue to babysit Charlie and run errands for Mrs. Habbershaw, a kindly widow with six cats and one Chihuahua named Max—who was a nervous wreck, probably because the cats were all bigger than he was. Mrs. H. needed cat food and litter almost every day, and hauling that junk was hard enough work, as far as Lucinda was concerned.

She put on her depressed act for exactly one week before approaching her parents about the blue contact lenses and getting the unsightly moles on her neck and ear removed. The tinted lenses cost four hundred fifty dollars and the procedure for the moles another eleven hundred, but Mr. and Mrs. Parker didn't bat an eye. After all, who had a better daughter than they did? Mrs. Parker would drive her old car for an additional year.

Over the next few years, as Lucinda learned more about manipulation, her parents learned more about state bankruptcy laws. She managed to get a number of the more minor surgeries done—dusting, cleaning, and tweaking as Lucinda called it—pouring additional bills over the heads of her already fiscally drowning parents who just could not say no to their darling girl.

Talk about a huge ROI on a measly five hundred dollars.

Just before her eighteenth birthday, Lucinda's mother sat her down in the kitchen for a "little talk."

"Lu, honey, I know you were counting on that earlobe reduction for your birthday this year, but frankly, we just don't have the money for it. We're still paying off all the other surgeries, and you're graduating this year. There's nothing left for college, Lu, much less more plastic surgery."

She studied her mother. The more Lucinda's looks improved, the worse her mother's became, it seemed. She was stick thin and gray. "Oh, don't worry, Mom. It's okay. I know you and Dad are struggling. There's no reason why I can't go to work and help out…again."

Mrs. Parker hung her head. They'd once been such a happy little family. Where had all that gone? "If you could do that, Lu, just until we're back on our feet, it would be a godsend."

"Of course, Mom."

Lucinda's father, a proud man, wasn't happy about the idea of further financial assistance from his teenage daughter.

They discovered him hanging in the basement the next morning.

His life insurance policy and his will were in his shirt pocket.

There was no note.

Her mother was crushed into catatonia, so Lucinda made all the calls necessary, as well as the funeral arrangements. She opted for cremation, since it was much easier on the pocketbook, and skipped the casket in favor of a cheap pine box in which the Parker patriarch would be committed to the flames. The funeral director had looked askance, but Lucinda was past caring. Her father's will had read: "To my dear wife goes seventy percent of my estate remaining after my funeral expenses and to my dear daughter, thirty percent in hopes that she will use it to further her education." If it was to be thirty percent, then she wanted that figure to be as high as possible, and she wasn't about to waste resources on incinerating a casket costing thousands of dollars. After all, funerals were nearly as expensive as cheek and chin implants, and there wouldn't be funds enough for both.

Her mother was never quite the same after they scattered her father's ashes over Sunset Pond, where he liked to fish now and then. Since Lucinda had skipped the embalming, the urn, the burial plot, and the memorial service, disposing of her father's body had cost a grand total of six hundred dollars—after the social security death benefit. Though her mother would not have a burial plot to visit and adorn with flowers, she could always sit at the edge of the pond and put flowers into the water if she wanted to, couldn't she? What was the difference?

The following week, after the life insurance check was divvied up, her mother caught up on back bills and just managed to save the house from foreclosure.

Lucinda made a surgery appointment.

It was during her recovery at home that Mrs. Parker's relic of an automobile, the one that should have been replaced years ago, finally gave out. The brakes failed, and in her panic, she lost control of the vehicle and hit a two-hundred-year-old maple tree head-on. She made it through with only a broken leg to show for it, but when they took her to the hospital for a CT scan, they found the cancer.

It was everywhere.

She had, at most, three months to live.

When she gave Lucinda the news from her hospital bed, her beautiful daughter managed to summon up a tear or two, then rushed home and dug out her mother's life insurance policy and will—which left everything to her.

It was hard for Lucinda to be too upset with that kind of a windfall staring her in the face.

She met with her mother's doctor the next morning to discuss her mother's illness and her final days. As the doctor was walking her out, he inquired about family medical history, since her mother was alternately too sick or too upset to discuss it.

"Has anyone else in your family ever had cancer?" he asked.

"Oh, sure. One of my uncles died of it a few years ago."

"A blood relation?"

"Yes. My mother's brother. Why?"

"I'm concerned that you may have a predisposition for cancer."

"What does that mean?"

"That because it runs in your family, you would be more likely to get it than someone whose family is clean of it. What sort of cancer did your uncle have?"

"Colon cancer, I think."

"Then you should be sure to get a colonoscopy at least once every two years.

Lucinda was alarmed. "And what kind of cancer does my mother have?"

"Well, since it's spread so far, it's a little hard to say, but from what I've seen in the scan results, I'd guess it started somewhere in the reproductive tract."

"I had an aunt who died of ovarian cancer."

"Mother's side or father's?"

"Father's."

"Oh, then you have a predisposition for it on both sides of your family. Any breast cancer?"

Lucinda nodded miserably. "Two cousins. Both dead."

"My advice to you, then, is to get a PAP smear, mammogram, and colonoscopy every year, like clockwork," the doctor said. "My dear, are you all right?"

Lucinda was sheet white and trembling all over.

"I understand that you lost your father recently, too. I'm sure the stress of that and your mother's situation is taking a huge toll on you." The doctor pulled his prescription pad from his pocket. "Ever taken Valium?"

"No."

"Well, you're going to start. This will at least allow you to get some sleep. Under no circumstances are you to drink alcohol with this medication—do you understand?"

"Yes. But I don't drink. It's really bad for the skin. Ages it, you know? I can't have that. Thank you, doctor." Lucinda took the slip from his fingers and then left the hospital.

As the doctor watched her walk away, his eyes narrowed slightly. *The only time she showed any emotion at all was when I explained predisposition.*

Lucinda sat in her father's car—now hers—on Level B of the hospital's underground parking garage and stared into space.

I finally got my face and neck looking perfect. There nothing more that has to be done for another five years, and now I could get cancer and die? I don't think so! I've invested too much money in this perfect face to be dying anytime soon.

Lucinda firmly believed there is a way out of every problem, and so she reclined her seat a bit and thought.

And it didn't take long before she had a solution.

A perfect solution.

As it turned out, her mother didn't have three days left to live, much less three months. She passed peacefully, or so they told Lucinda. Her mother's body met the same fate as her father's, even though she had specifically requested embalming and burial in her will. Lucinda rationalized that she'd want to be with her husband, and so it was the pine box and the pond for her, as well.

Between her mother's insurance policy and what was left of her father's, Lucinda had $65,000 to her name, as well as a house and a car. It was time to put her plan into action. She picked up the phone and dialed.

The next day, she met with a surgeon to discuss a double radical mastectomy.

"May I ask why you want this procedure if you don't have cancer? You're very young, and this operation is most disfiguring."

"I have a predisposition to breast cancer, so I figure no breasts, no cancer. It's one less thing to worry about," Lucinda explained.

"Here, let me show you some photographs of post-mastectomy patients. You should know what you're asking for." He rolled open a file drawer, extracted a folder and handed it to her.

They didn't have the desired effect. The mutilated chests moved her not at all. "This doesn't bother me, doctor. I still want the procedure."

"May I ask why you are so worried about this at your age?"

"I have, over recent years, paid out approximately $150,000 for facial cosmetic surgery. I have no intention of dying of cancer now or for a long, long time and losing that investment."

"If that is your reason, then I must respectfully decline to perform this surgery."

"Okay. I'll keep looking until I find a doctor who will. You're certainly not the only one on my list. Good day."

Lucinda met with four more doctors before she found one who was glad to help her. The surgery was scheduled for that weekend and went off without a hitch. Lucinda Parker, at age nineteen, had traded in her 34C breasts for two flat round masses of bumpy scar tissue.

And she was satisfied.

While recovering at home, she received the final bill for services rendered. This bill, added to the partial invoices already delivered, came to just over forty thousand dollars. That left her with fifteen thousand, a house, and a car. It also left her with two more procedures that had to be done ASAP.

While recovering, she applied for a second mortgage on the house. She was happy to discover that it was closer to being fully paid off than she had realized, and so had little trouble securing a six-figure equity line of credit. No sooner was she fully recovered from the breast surgery than she was doctor-shopping the next.

"I understand that you want to schedule a complete hysterectomy. And it says here on your paperwork that you're, what, twenty years old?"

"Yes, that's right."

"Are you having problems with heavy bleeding? Cramping?"

"No, not at all. I have a predisposition for cancer, and if I have a complete hysterectomy, that eliminates three cancer possibilities. No uterus, no ovaries, no cervix, no cancer. It's three less things to worry about."

"That may be true, but do you realize that you will never be able to bear children after this operation?"

Lucinda sighed. "Doctor, with a face like this, do you really think I want to spend my time chasing children around? All kids give you is wrinkles and gray hair."

The doctor looked astonished. "My dear, you will not be able to avoid either of those things forever."

"With hair dye and plastic surgery, I'm damned well going to try. Now, will you be doing this procedure, or not?"

"'Not' young lady. I'm sure you know the way out."

This time, it took twelve turn-downs before she located a willing surgeon, and the bills were much higher and the recovery time much longer and much harder. It took most of her loan to pay for the hysterectomy, and she still had one more expensive procedure to go.

What to do, what to do?

Well, she'd think about it—she had a month or two of convalescing to go through. She was sure to come up with something.

A knock at the door roused her from her thoughts. It was Charlie Foley, fifteen now and working at Harkin's Market delivering groceries.

"Hi, Lu. Here's your groceries." He strode in and set the box on the table. "See you."

"Hey, wait a minute! Where you off to in such a rush? I haven't seen you in ages."

"I've been around. Not my fault you haven't seen me. Though every time you come back from the hospital, you look and act so much less like you that I don't know who you are anymore."

"I'm still me, Charlie. Still the same old Lu who used to take you to the movies."

"I really miss the old Lu. The old Lu cared about people. The old Lu loved her parents and honored their wishes," Charlie said. "You're not her—not anymore."

"Oh, sure I am, Charlie. Please stay a while and talk. I get so lonely."

"How could you possibly be lonely, Lu? What happened? Your mirror break?" With that, her former knight in red Velcro sneakers shook his head and took his leave.

"How could he treat me like that? After all I did for him! Who the hell does he think he is to say things like that to me? Me! Well, if that's the way he feels, good riddance, I say." Unconsciously, she reached for her hand mirror.

After a few weeks of weighing financial options, Lucinda finally came up with a foolproof way to cover her surgery costs and get back at Charlie and his attitude at the same time.

One Monday morning, once she was fully recovered, she walked to the end of the lane where the mailboxes were and waited in the tall grass.

It wasn't long before she heard Mr. Foley's pickup truck roaring down the narrow road. The final turn out of the lane was blind, so Lucinda stepped out into the road just before Mr. Foley rounded the corner.

When he appeared, she looked fearful and stepped slightly off to the left. The fender clipped her just where she had planned for it to— the right hip. She also didn't see any harm if some of her previous stitches pulled out and added a little more blood to the mix.

She never expected a broken hip to hurt quite as much as it did, but as her father used to say, "You can't make an omelet without breaking a few eggs."

Police and an ambulance were summoned, and Lucinda played the incident for all it was worth.

And to make matters worse for poor Mr. Foley, he had whiskey on his breath. He had downed a shot that morning to treat a heavy cold. Back home, in Ireland, that was how it was done, and had always worked well for him.

This time, it worked well for Lucinda. She sued him for everything he had, and by the time the case was settled, she owned his bank account, his truck, his wife's car, and their house and everything in it. Oh, also Charlie's savings that he planned to use for college.

When she was being wheeled out of court that day, Charlie Foley walked up to her and spit on the ground at her feet.

But she'd won, and soon she'd have plenty of cash to get that final procedure done, once the Foley assets were liquidated, and that was the whole point, wasn't it?

By the time she'd recovered from her "accident" and sold off everything the Foleys had, there was more than enough money to cover the next procedure.

"You want a colostomy? Why?"

"I have a predisposition for colon cancer. It runs in my family. So, no colon, no colon cancer. It's one less thing to worry about."

"Are you aware that you'll have to wear a colostomy bag for the rest of your life?"

Lucinda flashed her perfect white teeth at the man. "I understand. I still want it done. Will you do it?"

"I'm afraid not."

This time, it took months before she found a willing doctor. He seemed a little sketchy and his credentials weren't the best, but he was ready to operate the next day, so the deal was sealed.

This surgery took everything she had to pay for—or, rather, everything the Foleys had had. Lucinda heard that they were living in a shelter downtown and that Charlie's job at the grocery store was all that was feeding and clothing them. But, Lucinda reasoned, they had a roof, a bed, and food, so what more could they ask for? She thought about them less and less as time passed. A new kid, Justin, now delivered her groceries. Harkins must have given Charlie a new route for some reason.

Lucinda was finally happy, finally satisfied. She had eliminated all the cancer risks that ran in her family and threatened her to take her life, and therefore her beauty, away from her. She stared into the mirror for hours on end, secure in the knowledge that with regular surgical maintenance, she would be looking this way for a long, long time to come.

The food stamps, social security, and disability checks she was now collecting from the government covered food, her new mortgage, and miscellaneous other bills.

She never left the house.

Why should she? Who out there would appreciate her beauty as much as she did? Better to stay home.

Things were wonderful for many months—until the phone call.

Her father's last remaining brother had died.

Lucinda panicked.

She had no more money left.

The 911 call came in later that afternoon from Justin, who had come by to collect for the groceries. He'd received no answer to his knock, and seeing her car in the driveway and finding the door unlocked, had gone looking for her, thinking she might need help.

The police found her on her bathroom floor in a pool of her own blood.

"She peeled off her skin. Got as far as her waist before she died of shock and blood loss," the M.E. said. "But she didn't touch her face or her neck. She'll be a good-looking corpse once she's dressed."

"Damnedest suicide I ever saw in my whole life," Officer Donnelly said to the M.E. "Was there a note or anything?"

"Yeah. She's looking right at it. It's a weird one. All I can figure is that it was supposed to remind her about something while she was…doing *this*." The M.E., who had seen more horror in his professional life than he cared to talk about, shuddered over this latest one.

Donnelly followed the body's vacant gaze. Indeed, there was a note, of sorts, that she'd taped up to the tiles directly opposite her line of sight. She must have been looking at it right until the moment she died.

One less thing to worry about!

Carson Buckingham has been/is a professional proofreader, editor, newspaper reporter, copywriter, technical writer, novelist, short story writer, book reviewer, editor, blogger and comedy writer. Besides writing, she loves reading and gardening; though not at the same time. Though born and raised in Connecticut, she lives in Arizona now—and Connecticut was glad to be rid of her!

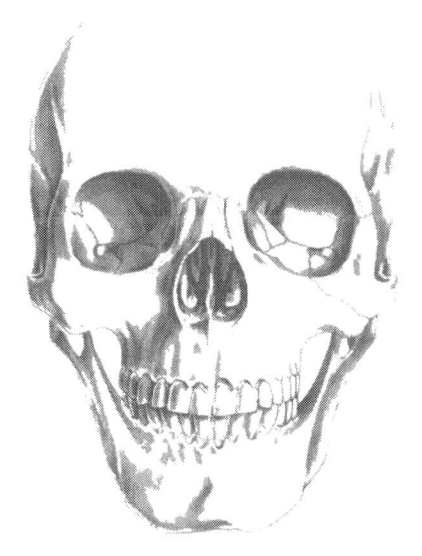

Orbs

Chantal Boudreau

I have a secret, or maybe I should say, "eye" have a secret—heh heh. I've always enjoyed a good pun. The only way to preserve my sanity in my line of work was to find some sort of levity. Humor was one of the few things that might distract you from what you were doing. You couldn't look at what you were working on as a human being. They were a subject; your job was a matter of science, and everything you pulled away from it was just pieces of an intricate puzzle—or a little round miracle from God.

I confess; I am an enucleator. I'd also call myself an oculophile, but there's nothing sexual to the attraction, just a deep-rooted love. My fascination with the orbs started long before I did what I do now. I spent twenty-five years working in the M.E.'s office, and I looked into a lot of glassy-eyed stares during that time, but I was taken with eyes even before that. Several events as a child, from a scene I witnessed on a TV show where someone tossed acid in another person's face, to stumbling across a rather gruesome morsel of road kill where the carrion eaters were pecking at those juicy little globes, seeded my obsession. Time allowed it to flourish.

We are surrounded by an amazing number of references to the orbs in popular culture. The eyes have it. Beauty is in the eye of the beholder. The eyes are the window to the soul. Seeing things through someone else's eyes—it would seem that I am not a lone man possessed. Eyes are everywhere. You see them on TV, on billboards, in magazines, even staring out at you from the back of the bus. Sure, those irises have been airbrushed and the pupils artificially dilated, for sexual appeal, but I could still sit and stare at them for hours. Powerful…seductive…mesmerizing.

Did you know your eye is composed of over two million parts? So many rods and cones—it's an organic phenomenon.

I'm the type of person that feeds off of outside influences, but never directly. I kept my passion hidden from even those closest to me. My parents and siblings never suspected. When I was a teenager, I admired the orbs from afar. I observed others' eyes unnoticed, scrutinizing them when I could and fantasizing about holding those spherical wonders in my hands when I couldn't. Selecting a career path was simple. I set my sights—heh heh—on becoming an eye care professional, an optometrist, an ophthalmologist, an ophthalmic medical practitioner, it didn't really matter which at the time. My parents were thrilled that I wanted to attend medical school and went to great lengths to support my endeavors. Their son, a doctor? It was a parent's dream come true.

Only, I didn't end up choosing any of those options. While I was in the middle of the introductory phase of my education, pre-med, I came to a conclusion while working with the cadavers that were a part of the curriculum. What you could do with the eyes of a living person was limited. You couldn't pluck out those jellies as Cornwall had done to Gloucester in King Lear…a classical reference, although I would never consider them vile. You couldn't jiggle and roll them in your palm like marbles. You couldn't hold them up to the light to get a really good look at their color. You had to be careful and leave everything intact. Not that I didn't want a profession that required finesse. I'm a tactile man with a refined sense of precision, but I wanted to be able to immerse myself in my work. Being an eye specialist of any variety wouldn't allow for that.

Did you know that your tears contain natural antibiotics? That's to keep them sound, and sensual. Even the highest quality of saline solutions doesn't properly emulate them.

Becoming a medical examiner, on the other hand, offered me much more freedom. On solo runs, I could prod and pry to my heart's content, and in some instances, it was actively encouraged that I handle the orbs directly. It was such an occurrence on my first day at work that I believe was what sealed my fate. Given my predisposition to eyes in the first place, imagine my reaction when the initial case they brought in was the fatal victim of a domestic dispute who had been blinded before being murdered. Both eyes had not been destroyed in the process. A vindictive wife, charged with psychotic rage over adultery, had gouged one of her unfaithful spouse's eyes out before plunging a knife through the empty socket into his brain. As I stared at the one fixed eye, and the one bloodied, lolling globe, my imagination ran wild.

How had she overpowered him? He was not a small man, and unless she had been a monster of a woman, she would not have had the strength to outmatch him. Had she launched herself upon him while he slept, weapon in hand, and struck before he had had a chance to defend himself? Had he been falling down drunk and clumsy in his attempts to avoid her? Any sane man would fight to keep his eyes in his head.

The average person blinks ten thousand times a day. You blink more when you're nervous—like now.

I gazed upon the one good eye. It was a plain brown—an

ordinary color. I took the greatest pleasure in orbs of unusual design. This was not one of them. Despite that, the moment was still one I would treasure.

It was an exhilarating experience. I got to finger the eyes. I was required to examine them very closely. I was like a child with the toy of my dreams and the work associated with such play was secondary. Those around me did not recognize the nature of my interest. I was the new kid, an eager beaver with the need to prove myself. As far as they were concerned, my enthusiasm was all for show, to strengthen my position in the lower ranks and perhaps open a route to somewhere higher up someday. I had my eye on the prize, you could say—heh heh.

I was in my second year at the M.E.'s office when I met my wife, Muriel. She worked for a franchise store selling eyewear: glasses, sunglasses, and their accessories. I was walking past their storefront on my way to work one day when I saw her perched in front of a customer. She was adjusting a pair of glasses on the young man's face, peering into his eyes. The vision took my breath away. I had to stop and stare. Most men would have considered her homely, heavy-set with a large nose and plain brown hair, but it was her eyes that had me enraptured. As I looked at her through the window, her irises seemed to shift in color every time she moved—first gray, then green and finally blue, with a hint of yellow at their centers. I immediately fell in love with those eyes, and I had to meet her.

Staring into someone's eyes without talking for several minutes can increase feelings of physical attraction. If you don't believe me, you should try it.

My vision was twenty-twenty at the time, but I still managed to produce an easy excuse to go in. Summer was upon us, and I needed optical protection. Eyes are prone to damage from UV rays. I went in on my lunch hour on a quest for shades and seeking a date with Muriel's eyes. She was shy and avoided my stare, but she was flattered by my flirtation and quickly accepted my offer for dinner that night. I was not hard on the eyes—heh heh—yet.

I toiled hard to seduce those orbs with their alternating colors. The rest of Muriel was just along for the ride, a necessary accessory to the only part of her with any real value. Of course, I had to charm the person in order to maintain my ties with those eyes—sort of like showering the ugly best friend with compliments for the sake of the favor of your true love. I forced her to look at me, even though she kept trying to glance away. I don't think the woman was accustomed to such attention because she soon found it difficult to hide her reciprocal infatuation from me. She didn't realize that I only cared about two things, and that the rest of her was just fleshy baggage.

I proposed to Muriel's eyes after six months of dating and married them after six more. That was how our lengthy and reasonably pleasant relationship began. She was always grateful to have an attractive and successful husband, and I had all I needed from her whenever she looked my way. We had three children together, with all but the youngest sharing her strange eye color, those of my last born being a lackluster dark blue. In a way, their existence lessened my interest in Muriel somewhat, because their eyes made hers seem not as special, no longer unique. No one suspected the reasons behind the diminishment of my fervor towards Muriel. They assumed it was the typical response to a lengthy pairing: we were aging, I was bored with her and bearing children had somehow marred her youth and beauty. We fell into that customary state of pleasant contentment and casual apathy that most married couples eventually achieve.

Don't look so surprised. Eyes are closely linked to many social signals. They are our primary tool for relating to others. For example, I knew you were interested the moment you looked at me. I used that to lure you in.

So that was my life for twenty-five years, and nobody suspected that anything was out of order. On the outside, I was a hard-working pillar of the community. I raised my children, I loved my wife, and I was a charitable man—but I hadn't become a collector yet, and I still had plenty of opportunities to do what I loved most. Locked up in my harshly lit space with the body laid out on the cold slab, I would fondle those things that appealed to me most. Not in an obscene way, understand. As I mentioned, I never loved them that way, more like one might gingerly handle a valuable artifact or a rare jewel. That's what they are, after all—precious gems generated by the human body. As foul as the rest of our flesh bags may be, the eyes are a true measure of beauty.

Blue-eyed couples actually can have a brown-eyed child, despite what people think. Eye color is determined by multiple genes. It's a complex process.

No, I couldn't take any of my work home with me while working in the M.E.'s office. If I had yearned to collect kidney stones, they never would have been missed, but the eye is essential to the man. I could not send corpses away with the lids sagging into empty sockets or use some reasonable-sized replacement that might be detected by the undertaker. I would have never been able to explain just cause for the switch, so when I was done with my playthings, I had to bid them adieu. Twenty-five years of pleasure followed by loss. Twenty-five years of ups and downs until my retirement.

When it was suggested that the time had come for me to pass on my role to a deserving younger man, I objected at first. Abandon the only way of satiating my very particular desires? The idea frightened me, even though I had known it would come to that someday. Financially, I was in a good place, and my family pointed out it made sense to retire while I was still young enough to enjoy it. I yielded to the combined pressures of co-workers and Muriel, who had long since left her job and was watching our youngest prepare to leave for college. Dread of an empty nest had set in, and she was tired of spending her days alone. She didn't really have much in the way of friends; she was never a social butterfly.

Some butterflies have eyespots on their wings, possibly to startle predators. I could never find eyes frightening.

I'll admit, initially, I didn't handle retirement well. I moped sullenly about the house, getting underfoot unpleasantly rather than providing Muriel with anticipated companionship. Eventually, it was all too much for her. She sat me down in front of the computer and instructed me to keep surfing until I found myself an acceptable hobby. She had insisted that she would not give me leave to rise from my chair until I at least had some idea of a new way of occupying my time.

I wasn't sure where to look, at first. When Muriel had left the room, I started browsing sites associated with eyes. Most of them were related to optometrists or things like designer contact lenses. Personally, I couldn't understand the need to artificially change eye color. Even the most common of iris shades had their own natural appeal. The false displays from the contact lenses looked ridiculously fake. I could tell someone was wearing them from across a crowded room, and they made my stomach turn.

Rene Descartes came up with the concept of corneal contact lenses. "Eye" think, therefore "eye" am—heh heh.

Plowing my way past those wretched sites, I soon found myself navigating through pages that presented me with prosthetic eyes, and even artificial orbs intended for use in taxidermy. That notion brought me to a screeching halt. Taxidermy—an odd hobby, but one that seemed fitting for an ex-medical examiner. It would be a far cry from people, but at least it would allow me to handle eyes again, even if they were only the organs of lesser animals. Beggars can't be choosers, and I was a desperate man.

I ordered how-to manuals, downloaded instructional videos and ordered a selection of supplies. It took a fair amount of practice, but before I knew it, I had my own little business on the go, one that fed my habit to a minimal degree.

So how did I go from that to becoming a collector, you ask? I'm getting there; we still have time.

It began with a dead cat—an odd cat with spectacular eyes, brilliant green flecked with orange. I could not find a match from the various suppliers I used and decided that in order to present a proper life-like preservation of this family pet, I would have to redesign one of the existing glass models myself. I placed the eyes in a jar with a special solution to keep them moist and firm. I use a similar solution with preservative properties in all of my jars.

Having multiple colors in a single eye is called heterochromia iridum. When the secondary color is in the middle of the iris, like mine, it's called central heterochromia.

I used those orbs as a reference while I painted in the appropriate striations. It was pure bliss, staring at the jar that stared back at me. I had an excuse to ogle them for hours, and when I was done, I was proud of my craftsmanship. After inserting my work into the mounted cat, I couldn't bring myself to discard the original eyes. I placed the jar on my shelf so I could peek at them whenever I wished. There was such a feeling of satisfaction leaving them there. They belonged there, and I wanted more.

I probably would have left it at animals. I'm really not a sadist. I just love what I love, and do what's necessary to be able to pursue my passion. I craved the human eyes, though. They're different. It's an irrational longing, I know, but as Gilbert Keith Chesterton said: "There is a road from the eye to the heart that does not go through the intellect." Still, I would never have gone that route, not without sufficient prompting...and then something drastic happened.

I had gotten into the habit of prepping all of my glass inserts for a perfect match and preserving in jars all of the eyes that they were replacing. Several now lined my shelves. That day when I emerged from my workshop, Muriel's scintillating eyes were tearful. She had been having health issues, and the doctors had performed a series of tests. Cancer, they had told her, and it was spreading. They planned various forms of treatment, but they would have to remove multiple tumors, and the first operation would involve the extrication of one of her shade-shifting eyes.

At first, I was devastated by the idea of such a loss. Then I realized that it did not have to be a loss at all, that I could simply add hers to my collection, but I would need a reason why I must have it, so I begged her to allow me to design her replacement. She agreed to it, too overwhelmed by the idea to care. She just thought I needed the task as a distraction, to cope with the situation.

I still lost one of her eyes, the remaining one, when her cancer finally took her, but the first one is still up there in a jar. Can you see it?

The problem was, as soon as I had my first human eye, I couldn't stop there. It was like having a piece of really good chocolate or a tasty potato chip. It's impossible to stop at only one. But how would I manage to collect more? I fought the urge at first, and then...

The fellow was a hiker, heading into the mountains, just like you. He was only passing through town, and no one expected him to stick around, so no one missed him. He had the most amazing eyes. Jonathan, I think he said his name was. Those are his orbs on the top right-hand side. The clearest example of central heterochromia I possess. They're a wicked hazel with the pupillary section such a vibrant emerald green that they stopped me dead in my tracks. We got to chatting, and when he heard about my taxidermy shop—well, I guess he had a morbid sense of curiosity. He had time to kill before the shuttle bus to the foothills arrived. I brought him to my home and served him the same blend of tea that I served you, with the addition of several rather special ingredients.

It took some time before anyone noticed him missing. People assumed he had just gotten lost in the mountains. No one keeps track of who is actually on that shuttle bus. A few discarded belongings for rescuers to find, and voila! One hiker gone astray—never to be found.

You'll notice eight jars on that shelf beside the beloved eye of my Muriel, and sixteen other orbs with irises of spectacular color. If I wasn't so particular, my activities would draw suspicion, but I don't just take any eyes. I'm a proper collector, and I only take those that are unique. No plain old browns or baby blues for me. As fussy as I am, there is sometimes a period of several months between great finds. I'm a connoisseur; only the best will do. I keep myself occupied with my taxidermy while waiting for someone like you to come along. They won't notice that you never got on the shuttle bus, either.

I can see you growing drowsy and starting to nod off. The tea I gave you causes a mild paralysis, that's why your limbs won't work, but I also mix in a strong sedative, a painkiller, and a gentle hallucinogenic. You'll soon be drifting happily in a mellow dreamland, and you'll forget all of this. Like I said, I'm not a sadist. I just love what I love…and your eyes are an incredibly striking shade of violet…

Chantal Boudreau, an accountant/author/illustrator, lives with her family in Sambro, Nova Scotia. She writes horror, science fiction and fantasy and has had more than fifty speculative fiction stories published with a variety of publishers in Canada, the US and the UK, including stories in Exile Editions' Dead North and Clockwork Canada anthologies.

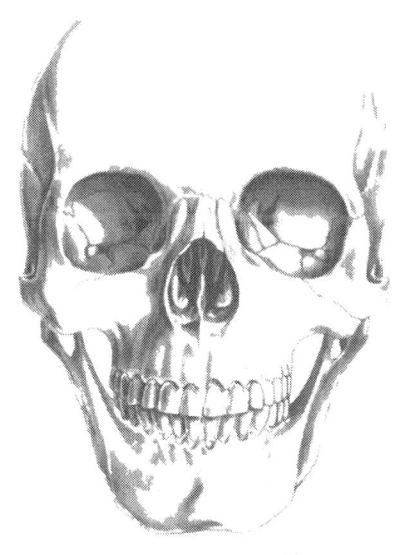

Rule of Five

Eleanor R. Wood

Adam clicked the light off. He clicked it on again. Off again. On again, once more, and then, finally, off. Sighing, he closed his apartment door and turned the key before unlocking it, opening it just to check that the light was off (it always was, by the very nature of the Rule of Five), and closing and locking the door once more. He walked, in elongated steps, the five paces to the head of the stairs, and then trotted down them briskly, counting them in his mind. Fourteen steps, of course. There would always be fourteen unless he failed to count them. But in that event, the number of steps would be the least of his worries.

"Fifteen. Fifteen," Adam muttered.

It was a reflex, almost like scratching an itch. Only, he knew what began as a mere itch would swiftly overcome him if left unrectified. And *something* would happen…something he refused to contemplate. So long as he obeyed the Rule, everything would be fine.

He walked out of the shabby apartment building, focusing sharply on the doorway so as to distract his mind from the constant glare of the corridor lights, which neither he nor anyone else in the building, could turn off. He had nearly become homeless because of them. This apartment was the only one he could afford, and everything about it was acceptable apart from those damned lights. When he realized they were emergency lamps that were designed to remain permanently switched on, he nearly decided to take his chances on the streets. But he calmed himself with the knowledge that he had no control over those lights, and therefore could not be held responsible for leaving them on when he left the building, irrespective of the Rule of Five or anything else. They still made him uncomfortable, though. He always exited the building hastily, forcing himself to focus on anything but their still-illuminated presence.

Once he was on the pavement, his concentration was divided between not bumping into fellow pedestrians and mentally counting his steps, in increments of five. One, two, three, four, five steps. One, two, three, four, five steps. One, two, three, four, five steps. All the way to the bar. If he reached his destination without completing a five-step count, he'd have to walk the remaining steps on the spot before entering. Today he got there on a count of two.

The skin on the back of his neck prickled. He looked around, worried that he was being scrutinized. But there was no one nearby. He shook his head to clear the anxiety, stepped three more times on the spot, and went in. Inside, his footsteps ceased to matter. They were only important on actual journeys from one place to another.

Daryl looked up from polishing the beer taps. "Hi, Adam. Glad you're here. One of the barrels needs changing and my back's playing up again. Could you do that, first off?"

"No problem," Adam replied. It was early enough in the afternoon that no customers had arrived yet.

Some might have referred to The Den as dingy. Adam preferred to think of it as atmospheric. Yes, the lighting was muted, and there were no windows, but Daryl always kept it clean and welcoming. It was just the spot for anyone wanting to escape the outside world for a few hours. The alcohol itself was escape enough for some, but here people could feel physically hidden as well as mentally subdued. It suited Adam.

Working here, he actually felt safe. Unexposed, unlike previous stints in noisy clubs or crowded cafes.

He rounded the bar and approached the top of the cellar stairs. He turned the light on, off, on, off before leaving it on after the fifth flick of the switch. He trotted down the stairs, counting them of course, and reached the beer barrels. He rolled a new barrel into place, unhooked the empty barrel and reconnected the full one. The task complete, he hoisted the empty barrel to his shoulder and turned to walk back up the twelve stairs to the bar when he was assailed by a familiar sense of unease. He looked around, wary. The gloom of the cellar was not properly lit by the light from the stairwell, but he could make out nothing unusual amongst the ordinary shelves and shapes. Movement from the corner of his eye made him jump, but what he had feared to be a large, lurking shape was in fact no more than a squeaking rat scuttling for cover. He would have to have a word with Daryl about setting traps again.

Shaking off the creepy feeling, Adam counted his way back up the stairs and flicked the light switch five times at the top. Back behind the bar, he placed the empty barrel on the floor and pulled half a pint of the newly connected beer while Daryl served their first customer of the afternoon, a regular who had just walked in.

"The usual, George?"

"Yeah, thanks, Daryl." George blew on his hands and stamped a bit. "Phew, it's a chilly one out there today."

Adam winced and forced himself to focus on his task, desperately trying to ignore George's three stamps. It was no good. His treacherous mind kept returning to the gaping gulf where the other two stamped feet should have been.

"Five, five, five, five, five."

"Sorry, Adam?" Daryl asked, looking at him oddly.

"Uh…sorry, sorry…nothing. Didn't realize I was speaking aloud." Adam shook his head and stifled his mutterings.

Daryl frowned but let the matter go, serving George his first frothing pint.

Adam took the empty barrel out the back to leave it with the others, taking advantage of the moment to calm his mind. He breathed deeply of the cool outside air and tried to rein in his thoughts from the sense of unease that kept trying to assert itself. It had only been a rat that startled him in the cellar. George's three foot stamps were something he had no control over, so there was no reason for him to be concerned about those either. People did things like that all the time, completely taking for granted the fact that it didn't matter how they did a thing, or how many times. They were free, and they didn't even know it. Adam shook his head ruefully at that thought and went back into the bar.

It was Friday, and as usual that meant earlier customers and a busy evening in store. There were already two people sitting at one of the tables, and a third being served. Adam filled up a few more dishes of nuts and took one to the occupied table. He polished some glasses and filled the ice bucket as a young couple walked in from the darkening afternoon. Adam served them while Daryl saw to George again, and suddenly Friday evening was in full flow.

Although tucked away, The Den had become a favored haunt and attracted its fair share of regulars and newcomers on weekend evenings. People flowed in and out, some staying for the duration, others stopping by for a quick drink before dinner. All kept the bar staff busy, and Adam barely had time for intermittent sips of water in between serving customers.

It was during one such momentary lull that he noticed the figure in the corner. It had the hunched look of a tall person accustomed to leaning downwards to converse with those of shorter stature.

Although it sat in the shadow of a darkened space and he could make out none of its features, Adam sensed it as an unmistakably male presence, and one that he instantly knew was watching him. A shiver ran up his spine and his temporarily forgotten sense of anxiety flooded back.

Daryl was stacking used glasses in the dishwasher while he had a spare moment.

"Did you serve that guy in the corner?" Adam asked him casually.

Daryl looked up in the direction of Adam's gaze. "No. I didn't see him come in. You must have served him."

"I-uh, yeah, you're probably right. He must've sneaked in an order while it was really busy." Adam saw no point in denying that he'd even seen him until a moment ago. Another customer approached the bar, and he was glad to have something else to think about.

"What'll you have?"

The next rush of customers suddenly appeared as if from nowhere, and Adam and Daryl were off again, mixing and pouring and serving at the efficient pace that helped make the bar so popular. But, try as he might, Adam could not shake off the feeling of being watched while he worked. Every so often, his eyes were drawn to the shadowy figure in the corner, nursing its drink with occasional sips, its non-visible eyes nevertheless piercing him with their unseen gaze. He would move from one end of the bustling bar to the other, and the silhouetted head would move with him, following his every move, observing, waiting for a single mistake. It would only take one.

Adam was suddenly trapped; under scrutiny he had always known was there even if he had never witnessed it. His worst fears were justified as the pressure was abruptly, undeniably, on. He rarely counted things when he was working. The rush of being busy made it difficult, and he had always felt freed of the compulsion while engrossed by other concerns. But his mind was racing, clamoring for attention as he was freshly compelled to count everything he was doing.

219

Five cubes of ice for each customer ordering drinks that required it, whether all in the one glass or divided amongst the selection of drinks ordered at once. Five steps between the beer taps and the crisp packets. On his twelfth order (third wine glass) he had to uncork a new bottle of merlot, and the corkscrew wasn't in far enough on the fifth turn. There was simply no way he could give it the final turn necessary to uncork the bottle with ease, and he ended up struggling with the corkscrew and breaking the cork with a creaking snap. He was saved from having to try again with the remaining piece of cork when Daryl took the bottle from him and told him to serve the next customer instead. She ordered two G&Ts and a dish of nuts. One glass got three slices of lemon and two ice cubes; the other two slices and three cubes. Fourth dish of nuts of the evening, take the money, count the change, next customer? And all the while, the eyes in the corner bored into him, and the presence of the figure loomed larger in the background.

The pressure was getting to him, and it wasn't just that of trying to keep track of his own actions. He was constantly having to compensate for the customers' lack of observation of the Rule. One would order three pints and the next would order one, leaving a missing one if the following person ordered wine. Somebody would take four cashews from the dish on the bar, forcing Adam to have to take one himself to restore the balance. Or they'd count out coins—three or four or six would clink onto the counter, but never five, and he would have to count to the remaining increment of five under his breath to make it right.

He was slowing down. Customers were lining up, and Adam was aware that Daryl was doing most of the work. The extra demands were taking their toll on his usual efficiency, and he was starting to make mistakes. After he'd got his third drink order wrong, Daryl told him to start focusing and pick up the pace. When he gave someone the wrong change, Daryl actually looked concerned and asked him if everything was all right. Adam did not make mistakes with money. It simply never happened.

"I'm fine, Daryl."

"You don't look fine, Adam. You look half-dazed. Are you sure you're feeling all right?"

"Seriously. I'm fine." Adam turned to the next customer, putting an end to Daryl's inquiry.

"Hi—a pint of lager and a large glass of merlot, please."

"Coming right up," Adam answered, turning to grab a pint glass.

The customer nodded and drummed his fingers on the counter, a rhythmic tap. Six taps, to be precise. Adam paused for a tiny moment, willing the man behind him to tap four more times, or even nine times, just to add up to a multiple of five. *Please...*

Nothing. The man was humming instead. The six taps hung in the air, buzzing at the edges of Adam's concentration, creating a precipice in his mind that could only be surpassed if the taps reached ten. He could feel the dark figure's gaze holding him from the shadowed corner, waiting, apprehensive, impelling him to make this one mistake. This one breaking of the Rule. Time slowed. Adam's chest constricted with the profound wrongness of the moment, and the tension within him snapped. Grabbing the pint glass he had been reaching for, he turned and thumped it onto the bar.

"Seven," he said with gritted teeth.

He turned and picked up another glass to slam down beside the first one.

"Eight."

Another. "Nine."

He reached for the final glass and made his fatal mistake. In his desperate need to right the situation, he grabbed the glass that would be number ten too hastily—and he dropped it. It smashed to the floor with tinkling horror, and in a panic, he cursed and reached blindly for another to replace it. But his scrabbling fingers found nothing. There were no others. Those had been the last four glasses. The dishwasher was whirring next to him, running another load, but it wasn't ready, and there were no more to hand.

Trembling, Adam's unwilling focus turned to the figure in the corner. It slowly stood up, moving far enough into the light that its eyes were at last visible in the shadow of the face. Cold eyes, looking directly at him, their unblinking stare locking with his. The sensation of nine hung between them, a deadly faux pas that Adam knew offended the shadow man as much as it offended his own sense of rightness.

The dark figure took an ominous step towards him. Adam took a step back, his shoes crunching on the broken glass, still unable to tear his gaze from the man's face, which a detached part of his mind noted was still somehow shadowed even as he stepped fully away from the darkened corner. The shadow man kept moving, slowly approaching the bar and Adam, who continued backing away with an increasing sense of terror until he was up against the unyielding corner of the bar, trapped and pursued.

He slid into a huddled, shaking crouch, sheltering his head in his arms as he frantically repeated "Ten, ten, ten, ten, ten, ten, ten, ten, ten, ten," over and over, trying to save himself even as he knew it was far too late.

Daryl was shaking him, calling his name in an anxious voice. "Adam. Adam! For God's sake, what's wrong? What's wrong with you?"

"Please…don't let him. Don't let him take me. Please." Adam was trembling uncontrollably.

"Who? Who are you talking about, Adam?"

"The…the man," Adam dared to peer out from under his arms, expecting that dark, cold-eyed face and menacing stoop. But there was only Daryl, looking baffled and frightened, and a group of concerned customers crowding over the bar, gaping down at him.

"What man?"

"The shadow man…the man in the corner…he…where did he go?" Adam rose sharply, his instinct to flee returning as he glimpsed yet a chance of escape.

"*That* guy?" Daryl shook his head in bewilderment. "He left, just a moment ago. He put money on the bar and walked out right before you…collapsed. He was just a customer, Adam."

"But he…he was watching me. Waiting for me to screw up. And I did." Adam squeezed his eyes shut, trying to rid his vision of the dark figure, knowing he hadn't imagined it, knowing he was no longer safe here, knowing he had been observed breaking the Rule.

He had to put it right. Maybe it wasn't too late. *Five, five, five, five, five,* he thought firmly.

Daryl put a supporting hand under his elbow and hoisted him to his feet.

"Go take a break. Wash your face, get some fresh air." Daryl herded Adam away from the bar. "He's fine, everyone. Next round's on the house—what can I get you?"

With that, the tense atmosphere was broken, and Daryl had the customers happy and chatting again. Adam stepped out from behind the bar and made his way to the toilets down the corridor. He was still shaking, and as if his fright wasn't enough, he felt like a fool. Daryl had always calmly tolerated Adam's odd habits, never asking awkward questions. In fact, the only time he had ever mentioned them was when Adam first started working for him, and he needed to ensure the behavior would not affect Adam's ability to work.

"Definitely not," Adam had assured him. "I'm fine when I'm working."

And he always had been. Until tonight. Not only had he embarrassed himself in front of a bar full of customers, but he had also shown Daryl the full extent of his paranoia. How could he be trusted to perform his job flawlessly after this?

Safely on his own, Adam forced himself to recognize that the shadow man had just been a customer. It was all in his mind. As he stood over the little sink and stared at his haunted reflection in the mirror, he realized this had gone on long enough. He needed help. The acknowledgment gave him an odd comfort. He splashed water on his face and rinsed out his dry mouth. After the weekend, he would see his doctor and ask for a psychiatric referral.

Taking a deep breath, he unlocked the toilet door and stepped into the narrow corridor. He grabbed the pull switch and turned the light off, on, off, on, off. He closed the door behind him and stood for the briefest moment, daring himself to walk away without opening the door again to check the light. It was off, damn it. He knew it was off. There was no need to check. More importantly, there was no one observing him to make sure he did check.

But it was no good. Acknowledging his problem was the first step, but the realization was far too new to put into practice yet. Dread clutched his heart as he tried to step away, and he gave in, turning swiftly back and opening the toilet door again.

The dread overpowered him.

The light was on.

All of his rational, sensible thoughts deserted him. His trembling returned as he reached frantically past the door for the light switch—and missed it as a cold, shadowy hand clutched his wrist and pulled him stumbling through the door.

He would have shrieked, but his throat had closed in terror. The dark, stooped form loomed over him, taking up all space in the cramped room. His back was against the hard wall, and he could not tear his gaze away from the icy stare that held him transfixed. The eyes leaned even closer. Adam's stomach was water, and his breath came in short, panicked gasps, but still he could not turn away from that face.

"You broke the Rule," the shadow man whispered in a voice filled with accusation and loathing.

"F…f…f-f-five…" Adam stammered, unable to form any other thought.

"Too late." The voice was little more than a chilly breath, yet it filled Adam's mind. "You are finished."

And as the shadow engulfed him and the freezing hands found his throat and slowly tightened, the singular thought consumed his mind and erased his identity until it was the only thought that had ever existed in the universe.

Five, five, five, five, five.

Eleanor R. Wood's stories have appeared in over a dozen venues, including Pseudopod, Crossed Genres, Flash Fiction Online, Deep Magic, and the Aurealis-nominated anthology *Hear Me Roar*. She writes and eats liquorice from the south coast of England, where she lives with her husband, two marvellous dogs, and enough tropical fish tanks to charge an entry fee.

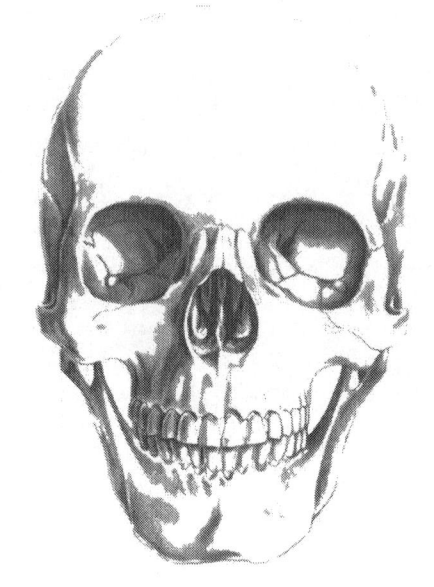

Guilty by Chance

Nidhi Singh

There was no need for Sheena to burn like this; no need for the candle of life of one so young and beautiful to be snuffed out like this. And there was definitely no need for Mikhail to be lighting his kid sister's funeral pyre like this.

The holy Ganges, placid and on course to be swallowed by the ocean, lapped at his unshod feet. Mikhail felt as if he were being tossed around in a tiny boat without a life vest in a black, raging storm with crackling thunder and hammering deluge. The incessant wail of mantras on the Burning Ghats didn't ring; it vibrated like a cosmic howl, churning up grief and ache. The stench of burning corpses swirled around him, and he could feel the heat of their dying embers cooking the eyeballs inside the skulls. It was as if he himself had been struck a crumbling blow of the *Dom's* staff, dispatching his soul on its next flight to another mortal abode.

It was Mikhail's mother's reasonable wish that any member of her family be cremated only at Varanasi: the oldest city in the world, the richest kaleidoscope of Hindu tradition, where sacred coexisted peacefully with sacrilege.

A pious Hindu widow, she had instructed him thus on her deathbed: "Cremation at the holy Ghats of Varanasi will assure us *Moksha*. Be sure to lay me down at Manikarnika Ghat, the one controlled by the Doms, and not at the Raja Harish Chandra Ghat."

"What's a Dom?" Mikhail had asked.

"Doms are low caste untouchables, unsung undertakers, who eke out pelf from the funeral pyres of bodies brought in by the grievers."

"Why the Doms, Ma?"

"There is an ancient legend, Son. Raja Harish Chandra, a man of absolute truth, in order to keep his word, had pledged himself unto *Kālu Dom*, the ancient Dom chief. Kālu Dom then bonded him as an unpaid apprentice for life. The Dom Ghats are consecrated; there lies great virtue in being cremated at the hands of a Dom."

The Dom assigned to Mikhail had explained the procedure to him.

"We keep the sacred flame burning perennially at the hearth of Kālu Dom. No matchsticks may be used on these Ghats; I will give you the straw, lighted from this flame to light the pyre. The first five logs to burn the corpse will be provided by the Doms, and the rest by the relatives. Clear?"

Ironically the same straw was used to light the cooking hearth at the Dom homes; Mikhail had wondered how one could put up with the insanity that comes from living from daybreak to nightfall among burning corpses and feral curs.

"Here, Sahib, drive it in hard and deep."

Mikhail awoke from his reverie, so fascinated was he by the orange-red flames swirling wraithlike from his sister's pyre. The Dom handed him his staff, to ram in Sheena's skull so that her soul could escape her fleshly garb and find dwelling in another being. Mikhail shoved the staff awkwardly, managing no more than upsetting the arrangement of logs and sending a brilliant shower of embers billowing up. The Dom, his eyes bloodshot, his arms scarred by fire, grumbled and grabbed his staff back, and with no pretenses of genteelness, expertly proceeded to crush in the blazing head.

Mikhail, alone, watched as the logs crackled and crushed the body under their crumbling weight, while the Dom poked, and added stubble and wood as needed, to ensure the body burned completely.

His beautiful sister, Mikhail rued, would be reduced to bone chips and ashes by the gray of dawn.

"Choose her or me!" his wife Indrani would scream at him, often enough to drive him nuts. "Sheena brings rotting shame to us! She may be your sister—she is no darling of mine."

"What's she done this time?" Mikhail would ask, throwing off his beret, with no hope of respite or an early dinner.

"Look at what she wears! Look at her company! See what time she returns home!"

"She works in a call center, baby. She *will* keep odd hours."

"And drinking…smoking? And the kissing and whatnot that goes on in cars parked in front of our house nearly every other night? We are becoming the laughing stock of this station, Mikhail, don't you see? You have spoiled her completely—I know you are not going to shout at her and get her to behave!"

"Has your shouting done any good? Leave her be, she's a kid, she'll soon learn to make correct choices on her own. Our telling her will not make a difference, it has to come from within."

"That will never happen, Mikhail, because all she's got *within* is debauchery. Beauty can't take the weight of a brain. You, a man,"—with one hand on her hips, the other waving under his nose, she spoke, as if she didn't mean it—"should know that!"

Indrani had then stormed into their bedroom, and dragged out her suitcases, all packed, bulging at the sides.

"She quarreled with me again this morning before leaving for office, calling me 'a continual dripping on a rainy day!' I cannot put up with this daily bloodshed anymore! I am done! I'm going to mother's," she sobbed.

"Hey, it's alright, there's no need for desperate measures. Next time she's on an *off*, let me speak to her."

Mikhail had managed to stop her, or surely that night he would have become her third ex-husband, but soon and sure enough, he buckled in front of the bewitching woman's soft power—her tears, her artful lovemaking, and her constant nagging that robbed him of all sleep and quiet.

One day, in great despair, Mikhail finally had to tell his sister: "I'll have to ask you to leave—you know how it is with Indrani. I am sorry, but I have to keep the peace in this house. And you are not going to change one bit. We both can see that." He'd kept his gaze averted in shame; he was all she had in this world, and he was turning her out.

Sheena, the reckless, the self-destructive, instead of giving a tiny excuse that her brother had been looking for to change his mind, simply wiped away an iffy tear and said coolly, "I understand *Dada*, don't you worry one bit."

"I'll find you a nice PG Hostel for girls," her brother had said in misery. "I'll take care of the rent as well. We'll stay in the same town and meet often, and who knows, in time Indrani will take you back."

"Dada, you talk as if it's her house!" Sheena had nearly laughed. "I'll manage. I can take care of myself. And I'm sorry I've been such trouble."

The following weekend she was packed, and gone out of their lives without any fuss. She called regularly at first, but soon he'd stopped hearing from her after Indrani discovered that Mikhail was footing her rent bill and had put an end to such utter balderdash.

And two days ago, a cop had called. "I am sorry, but your sister is dead," he'd said matter-of-factly.

"What happened?" Mikhail had stood up, toppling his chair.

"All we know is that she was living-in with some guy. They had a quarrel in a nightclub, and he left her on her own at two in the morning. She was drunk, and she took a lift from some strangers. We found her body in the Raigad forest, dumped under a culvert."

"Was she...?"

"I'm afraid she was. They must have been beasts that did all that to her...I shouldn't say any more on the phone. You must come by and identify the body and collect it for the last rites."

"Do you know who she was staying with...have you caught the culprits yet?"

"Not as yet, but we shall. It's a pity young woman are so trusting of guys they live-in with, and then those bastards ditch them with no sense of responsibility. And it's a shame, we turn out our young girls from our homes and this is the inevitable end they meet," the cop had said, hinting at what he thought of big brothers not taking care of their sisters in this sick city, where men thought women no more than meat on the plate.

Mikhail had collected Sheena's body and brought it to Varanasi for the last rites as per their mother's wishes. Indrani had refused to come: "Who'll send the girls to school? They're about to have their exams!"

"They're in Kindergarten, dammit! And she's their aunt!"

"Fine aunt she made. It's best they don't keep memories of a bad influence. And don't you be faffing around out there long, taking boat rides on the river and sightseeing. You get back here on the double!"

If there was a way, Mikhail would have brought Sheena back, but he couldn't wind the clock back now, could he?

I shall carry this heavy stone of guilt on my back all my life, he thought. And the weight might get lighter only if I could wring my hands around the throat of the man who deserted her.

A week later, Wing Commander Mikhail Mukherjee found himself in the officers' ward of the Indian Navy Hospital Ship (INHS) Ashwini, at Colaba. Suddenly, his heart had begun to skip beats, and the medical specialist at MH Jamnagar felt it was bad for his flying. She advised him to get a cardio workup at INHS, where a Cardiologist was available.

In the Officers' Ward, he requested the ward nurse to let him have a room to himself. For an army nurse, she was really pretty. She had pale, smooth skin and her high cheekbones, slit eyes, and sweet nature told him she was from the highlands.

After unpacking, he wandered to the balcony that hung out over the Arabian Sea. It was a windy day, with the white clouds flying and the seabirds crying. There was the smell of dead plankton and burning gasoline from trawlers that were returning home after fishing. A couple of white sails from the Sailing Club at Sassoon Docks bobbed on the sea, and the water was out at low tide. It was warm and sticky, and he couldn't stay out for very long. The sea breeze in Jamnagar was cooler and fresher; there weren't many ships out there—just miles of salt farms stretching along the Kutch coastline.

A little later, a trainee doctor came and checked his blood pressure. They rolled in an EKG machine and took his readings.

"Do you drink or smoke?" the doctor asked.

"Drink yes, occasionally, socially," Mikhail replied.

"Enjoy drinks?"

"Who doesn't?"

The intern endorsed 'Alcoholic' in his report and went off. Mikhail switched channels without really paying attention until 7 PM, and then he walked downstairs to the dining hall.

It was already full. Bored patients—walking-wounded types like him—were already at the table checking out each other's maladies.

A very old veteran, with legs thin as chicken wings, sat at the head of the table, interpreting the maladies and enjoying himself very much. Lonely gaffers, abandoned by their families, eagerly got themselves admitted to the hospital for the attention, however unsavory, and the company, however morose it might be.

"What are you in for?" the veteran asked as if Mikhail had entered a correctional facility.

"A heart workup. My EKG has a T-inversion in a couple of leads. What are you in for?"

"Nothing. And everything," said the old man, the master of ceremonies, stamping his walking stick on the ground in mirth. "If you look into my body, you might find everything to be wrong, but then, it has always been so, so you might call it normal!"

Mikhail, like the others, turned to drumming his fork on the table in anticipation of a good stew. But the vet was not one to be ignored so easily. He continued, "All I have in the world is a kid, working in the Silicon Valley. He married a Chinese girl, but the marriage didn't last long. Made in China, I guess," he guffawed loudly. "How about you, son? Where do you come from?"

"Right now, from a funeral. My kid sister's."

"Kid sister! Was she sick?"

"She wasn't—this country is. I wasn't there when she needed me. I pray God will forgive me."

"God never forgives!" the man stomped his staff. Mikhail expected little sparks of indignation to fly from it, but nothing happened. "God keeps count—the good go to heaven and the bad to hell—never have the twain met."

"What are you saying, that god is not forgiving, he is vengeful?"

"Haven't you heard of *ChitraGupt*, the angel of the conscious and the subconscious who records actions, and the Righteous Judge of Dharma, who judges this record?"

"Yeah, something like that, but…"

"ChitraGupt keeps complete records of actions of human beings on the earth. Upon their death, ChitraGupt determines *Svarga*, Heaven, or *Naraka*, Hell, for the humans, depending on their actions on earth. There!" he exclaimed triumphantly and looked around the table for appreciation of his knowledge of the scriptures and lore. "The guilty will pay. God watches! They will pay in this life or the next! There is no escaping his justice!"

"Who exactly is this ChitraGupt?"

"ChitraGupt, meaning 'rich in confidences,' or 'hidden image,' is a Hindu god. He is begotten of the person of Lord Brahma, our creator. Legend has it that Lord Dharmraj or Yam Raj, the god of death, would often get confused when dead souls came to him, and he would occasionally mark the wrong souls to either heaven or hell. Lord Brahma, to help him, sat in meditation for many thousands of years. Finally, when he opened his eyes, a man appeared before him with writing material. As his image, Chitra was first conceived in Brahma's mind, and then made whole in clandestineness, or in gupta, so he was named ChitraGupt. All your deeds are recorded minutely; don't dare think any of your actions escape *His* notice. What is the incentive for the good if even the bad fellows went to heaven? So expect neither mercy nor forgiveness!"

"What about good deeds, alms, prayers? What about atonement? What about a dip in the holy confluence and washing off your sins? You mean there is no midcourse correction possible? No hope at all?" Ranjeet, a naval engineer, a heart patient, asked.

The veteran leered down at him, shaking his head. "There is hope—who says there isn't? But have you truly done all of the above, eh?" he asked, tapping the spoon on the hardwood table as if ticking the boxes. "Repent," he shouted, shaking with the effort as if, of summoning the Lord's wrath and heaping burning coals upon the table. "Atone!"

The company laughed. There were only six men present in the hall: the vet, Mikhail, Ranjeet, Ramadhir, a Signals guy with shaking hands, Bhaironath, a gunner with ear trouble, and Sanjiv Khanna, a handsome paratrooper here for his medical. The ward had a capacity of fifty.

"Where are the rest?" Ramadhir asked the Mess Havildar.

"I have never seen such a low occupancy myself, sahib," the Mess Havildar replied, pointing out a speck on the toaster to a mess boy to wipe. "This ward has started remodeling as per accreditation norms, so temporarily they are directing outstation officers to the army hospital at Pune. They stopped fresh admissions from today."

"This company will do for me," the veteran rambled, "for now."

No one paid the bewildering old man any heed. There was quiet around the room as dinner was served; the mess boys filled up the casseroles with a gallimaufry of dishes: cheese cutlets, macaroni, baked beans, grilled chicken, and bread rolls.

"How does one kill time here?" Bhaironath asked, in between tucking in cheese and macaroni.

"By telling stories. I am an old man, I have many stories to tell," the veteran said, much to the unease of the others. But out of sheer military habit, the men protested no more than clearing a throat or two. "Each night I will narrate one story for you."

With nothing to do in the rooms either, the men looked around the table and taciturnly decided to humor the old man.

"Alright sir, bring on the first episode...."

"Fine, if you really must insist then," the old man began. "There were two brothers, whose parents had died. One day, the elder one receives a phone call from his father! When someone passes away, for a long time we behave or think the person is still alive; we are so used to them. So the brother talks for a while, and only after he has replaced the receiver, does he realize his father is already dead. He is puzzled for a while, thinks he had probably snoozed off at the office desk, or maybe it was a prank."

Maybe Mikhail was mistaken, but he noticed a distinct wave of pain flash across Ranjeet's face, which had become ashen. He looked ready to tumble from his chair and dart out of the room, but somehow he controlled himself because it seemed he wanted to hear the end of the story.

"But he became alarmed only when his younger brother called him later that day," the vet continued, "and said he too, had received a call from their father, and he too, like the elder had conversed as if everything was normal."

"How, or why on earth would someone from the dead call them like this?" Bhairon asked.

"Well, the brothers had neglected their poor parents, who had, as is usual with us Indians, sacrificed everything, including mortgaging their house for them. So when they were old and infirm, and too proud to ask for help, the brothers, not content with simple neglect, went ahead and did a complete dereliction of duty. They abandoned the schizophrenic father at a shady clinic, where instead of caring for him, the quack followed the short route of administering electric shocks to his brain, frying and killing him. The mother, unable to bear his loss, dejected and deserted, starved herself, and followed her old man within three months."

"That's a lie!" Ranjeet suddenly jumped to his feet, and glowered at the old man, his face pale, and his hands all a-flutter. "Who told you this?"

"It's just a story…a figment of my imagination…a salmagundi from my repertoire of human fables and foibles," the old man replied, buttering his toast calmly.

Ranjeet's jaw dropped. He was about to retort, but couldn't. He pushed back his chair and stormed out of the room.

"What's with him?" Bhairon remarked. "Well, how does the story end, sir?"

"I wouldn't know!" the old man sighed as if he was wearied. "It hasn't ended yet!" He pounded his staff on the ground and rose shakily. "Goodnight gentlemen, come another night, goes another tale."

The next morning Mikhail woke to a brouhaha. Doctors and nurses rushed about the corridors, their arms aloft. Even the highland nurse, her trim ankles dragging a ball of worry, forgot to smile at him as he stood in the corridor asking what had happened. Giving up, Mikhail went back to sleep and decided to investigate during breakfast.

At the breakfast table, he found Ranjeet missing. "Where is he?" Mikhail asked.

"His heart monitor short-circuited early this morning. Fried him totally. He's gone," replied Ramadhir.

Mikhail's spoon missed the boiled egg it was addressing, sending it sailing from the eggcup to the floor where it burst open into a white and yellow smorgasbord. Abroad came the feeble tweeting of a Godwit that had starved at its perch.

It was a glum gathering that assembled in the dining hall that evening. A pair of queer, black, horrid birds, too big by far to be a pigeon or guillemot or shag, sat bolt upright on the windowsill. No one missed Ranjeet, but no one had forgotten him either.

After dinner, the veteran tapped the table with a fork. "Are the gentlemen in the mood for another story before we turn in for the night?" He looked around with a mischievous smile as if daring them. No one seemed keen to return to the empty ward as yet. It was a long way between now and the cozy embrace of sleep, if it returned at all that dark night.

Ramadhir shrugged. "What could it hurt? Bring it on, sir," he said.

The veteran rubbed his hands to warm them and then rubbed them down his face. "Ah," and thus comforted, he started. "There was a lady with three kids, a boy, and two girls; the eldest, the boy, was nine years old. Let's say she lived at Rajkot. And her husband, a sepoy, had gone on to do fairly well for himself, rising from the ranks to get an officer's commission.

"But instead of this promotion bringing happiness to the family, it brought them a bucketful of woes."

"How come?"

"You see—an equal, or better when married to a lowly sepoy—the wife now was no longer good enough for an officer. Instead, she was a burden, a shame. His parents, with whom she lived while he was away at Field, wistful with the dowry their son could now command as a commissioned officer, began to harangue her for money. Naturally, so late after marriage, and coming from her poor farming background, she could not fulfill their wishes."

"Is that even a story? It happens in all of India," Ramadhir retorted, shifting in his seat. Already anxiety prone, he'd begun to scratch away at an army of ants that seemed to have suddenly invaded his shirt, which he unbuttoned and buttoned unselfconsciously.

"Not what happens next, my dear Sir," the vet replied. "Nagging and fretting her constantly, the parents managed to put it into the head of the poor, illiterate girl that it was best for everyone that she should take herself and her brood and go drown in the Aji River Dam."

"That's a damn lie!" the ant-infested man shouted, thumping his quivering fist on the table.

"Damned yes, lie no," the vet replied coolly, mixing Maltova in his milk.

"Don't tell me she did it?" Mikhail asked, his eyebrows shooting up.

"Almost," said the vet. "The power of suggestion can be so strong sometimes. She threw in the two girls in the Dam first. The boy, seeing he was next, had the sense to run away and inform the neighbors. The mother, unable to catch the boy, jumped in next."

"And what was this husband doing all this while?"

"Well, he played along; he was greedy as well. His parents had arranged for another match with a handsome dowry, so as long as they got his previous family out of the way with no trouble to him, he felt it wouldn't really hurt to advance in life. After all, he felt his destiny owed it to him now that he'd become an officer."

"Why are you telling us this story? I mean, what's new? Is there some sort of message for us in it? What happened to this man?"

"I wish I knew! We'll find out soon enough, though." Balancing himself on his staff, the mysterious old man rose and tottered towards his room, muttering under his breath. They didn't know if he was shaking his head in reproach, or it was just wobbling naturally on his thick shoulders.

"There is such an uproar each morning, I wonder why a medical facility cannot have a little peace and prayer at dawn," Mikhail observed, having been woken up early again, not by the warbling of a wren filling its tiny chest with the bracing morning air, but by an apparent donnybrook that seemed to occasion again in the corridors outside his room. "I wonder who's died now?" he added jokingly while asking Bhairon to pass him the marmalade. This time, he hadn't even bothered to stir from the warmth of his blanket because nobody ever told him anything anyway.

"Ramadhir died."

"Ramadhir? Don't shit me!"

"Yeah. His brothers-in-law-to-be visited him last night after dinner probably, and took him out clubbing. Never to say no to a good offer, he probably overdosed on his prescription Oxycontin and washed it down with plenty of free beer. Docs say after he came back and slept, his respiratory system slowed till it stopped completely. The guy died in his sleep."

"When you want to have too much of a good time, and too soon, I guess this is what happens," observed the vet, heaping scrambled egg on his buttered toast.

"Well guys, the last of my tests is due today. Hopefully, I should be off tomorrow, or the day after, at the latest," Mikhail said, after a long silence. His EKG was normal, now they wanted to do his stress thallium. "I really hope we never meet again, in a hospital like this."

"Me too," said Bhairon. They'd attached computers and scanners to his head but had found nothing to explain his increasing deafness, the booming and buzzing that went on in his ears, or the voices that he heard all the time. They gave him some pills, and a hearing aid, and told him to stay calm, that's all.

"My meds are done too, and I'm fit; just a bit of paperwork left. Maybe we could leave together," Sanjiv said, addressing Mikhail.

They all looked at the vet. "I'm nearly done here myself too," the old man said, "just a bit of business left. And since we're all going to get busy for the day, I have another story to send you on your ways. What say?" he asked, looking around beaming.

"Can't hurt, can it," Bhairon said, rising. "One for the road then, but not now. Tonight maybe, for I really must get going. This damn hearing aid just doesn't seem to work!"

"Alrighty then, here goes." The old man, true to his promise, began his story at dinner that night after he'd piled his plate with rice and curd. Just Sanjiv and Mikhail were present; Bhairon was missing.

"It was two summers ago, when this man, returning from his fields, came upon brown, skinny limbs entangled behind the tall stalks of sugarcane that waved lazily in the hot breeze. Yonder eddies of peat-smoke jostled, and wind-blown tendrils rustled in the blazing sun.

"It wasn't unusual for young people of the village to make out among the unharvested crops when they hadn't yet eased themselves of their summer load, but the tinkle of laughter that came from the sugarcane seemed familiar. He walked a short distance, but then turned back to the spot. Something had made him distinctly uneasy. As he recognized the sound, his steps became hurried, and when with his sickle when he bore down on the waving golden sheaths, he caught his own daughter squirming under a naked village boy of another caste. Another caste! He couldn't even have saved his honor by marrying them! He swung wildly, but the blade of his implement barely scraped the back of the urchin, as he scuttled out of reach. Grabbing his daughter by her hair, he dragged her through the furrowed earth, kicking and punching her in the stomach and head. Then, too ashamed to look at her naked body, he swore at her and ordered her to dress up and follow him home."

The vet paused to wipe his beard on his sleeve, and munched on the rice dreamily while his two companions waited.

"That night," he continued at last, "the man and his younger brother drank till the devil within burst forth. Then they dragged the girl into their room, locked themselves in, and began to strangle her.

"Her screams brought the horrified mother rushing out from the kitchen stove, where she was dunking cow-dung cakes, but no amount of her feeble banging would make the men open the door. She ran to other room where her son, a gunner on leave, also sat drinking, trying to shut out his sister's cries.

"'Help her—please! Break down that door, my son, I beg of you, do it for your poor mother.' She fell at his feet and grabbed his knees and wailed, but he wouldn't listen. He shut his ears with his hands even as tears streamed down his cheeks.

"'Let it be done!' he screamed and shoved his mother away with his foot, 'and be done with!'

"The ordeal was over in a few minutes, and then the three men took the dead girl and burnt her body the same night in the fields."

There was silence for a while in the hall.

"That's it?" Sanjiv said. "Where's the f— point here? Honor killings go on all the time in this country." After a pause, he added, "Do we know any of the players from this story?"

The old man chewed the curd-rice at leisure, taking his time to answer. Then after a sip of the aqua, he said, "As of this afternoon you knew the girl's brother."

"Whom do you mean," Sanjiv asked, jabbing away at a truant garlic pickle on his plate. "Are you referring to Bhairon by any chance? And what do you mean 'as of this afternoon,' eh?"

"As of this afternoon, the girl's brother, Bhaironath, died at the roadside in Bandra, run over by a speeding taxi, his cries for help falling on deaf ears of passersby, who didn't like to get *involved*, which is the norm in *this* country. By the time the police arrived and brought him to a hospital, he'd died."

"You evil man—how do you know all this?" Sanjiv banged his fork down and began to shout. "How do you know so much about all of us? What is this vile ranting you are about all the time? Why don't you mind your own business, rather than spewing filth on this table where food is spread out before us!"

"It is my business," the old man replied in a slow snarl. "I'm tired with all this work. Goodnight gentlemen, or should I just say, officers." He ground his staff down and rose unsteadily, pausing to gather his balance, and then shuffled out of the mess.

"Calm down," Mikhail told Sanjiv. "He's just a bag of bones and lies. He just wants attention."

"It's not that. He brings on the heebie-jeebies in me," Sanjiv said. "What's his bloody name. What rank is he?" He turned to the Mess Havildar, who shook his head.

"The ward nurse knows, sir," he replied.

"Want to have a smoke before we turn in?" Sanjiv asked Mikhail, the only other diner remaining.

"Okay," Mikhail replied. They slid out their chairs, nodded at the Mess Havildar, and walked to Sanjiv's room on the top floor. They walked out into the balcony. The night was starlit and muggy. The tide was in, and the waves lapped against the black stone embankment. A fishing boat from the nearby harbor spread her sails to the moving breeze and started for the gray sea.

"What's up man. Why take it out on the poor ancient?" Mikhail said. "He must have enough trouble passing kidney stones."

"Look chap, I'll take you back over the last two nights, and you tell me whether I'm fuckin' shittin' or what. See, the first night he talks of these parents getting neglected by the kids—the one about the dad getting fried by a psycho? And who gets all worked up? It's Ranjeet—and how does he die? Of neglect, the same night. And he gets fried in the same fashion by the heart monitor. Now is that a coincidence or what?"

"You're taking it too far and wide, man."

"Next, he talks of this female jumping into the dam with her kids. Obviously, he was talking about Ramadhir because it upset him totally. And the guy was greedy wasn't he, washing down Valium with free booze, while his parents were collecting dowry from his new in-laws?"

Mikhail laughed. "Tell me more! The old man probably drives too slow and dabbles in a little organized crime on the side, but so what?"

"And this night. How does this geezer know Bhairon is dead? We don't know! He never struts around the corridors giving the glad eye to the ward nurse, but we do, and *we* don't know!"

"How do we know the two stories are connected? Let us for a moment assume he chanced upon this news that Bhairon had died?"

"How did Bhairon die, Mikhail? The dying part! See, each of the characters in his stories dies just like the victim. Mark his words. He said that Bhairon's cries for help fell on deaf ears. Bhairon was going deaf, and he'd shut out his mom and sister's cries for help! Don't you get it?"

"What are you getting at?" Mikhail asked, feeling a little shifty now.

"There is a devil lurking in there. I don't believe this shit, but there is. He is telling a story every night, and one of us is conking off, the so-called villain of the piece! And if you'd noticed, there's no one else coming in the ward. Can you believe it? Can it happen?'

"Yeah, it seems...strange."

"There—thank you! Finally! Now, what do you think is next?"

"What?"

"One night it will be my story, and then, it will be yours. And we'll both be dead, and then this crazy old fucker—whatever pleasure he gets out of this— will walk out with a smirk on his crumbly face!"

"That really is far-fetched! Do you, by any chance, have any guilt over anything? Are you afraid?"

Sanjiv shrugged. "Guilty by chance, maybe. One makes mistakes here and there, when you are watching out for your backside."

"Alrighty. You're obviously taking this very seriously. What do you suggest we do if, as you say, we're next?"

"Let's go strangle the bastard!"

"Hey, don't be crazy. Let's do one thing; let's just pop up in his room and have a chat with him. See, communication upfront can ease things. And then you take your call."

"Okay," Sanjiv stubbed out his cigarette on the balcony lattice and got up. The men walked over to the old man's room.

"It's funny we don't even know his name, and he knew all ours," Mikhail observed.

They entered the room without knocking. The man was sleeping; his hands were crossed peacefully over his chest.

"Hey, Sir, Mister!" Sanjiv shook the old man's arm. He wouldn't get up. "Hey, Sir, we just want a minute…" the old man didn't stir. Sanjiv felt his hands, and then put his ear to his chest.

"What's up?" Mikhail asked.

"The guy is stone-cold. No heartbeat…"

"Hang on." Mikhail nudged Sanjiv aside and felt for a pulse on the man's chilled wrist. "You're right. He's gone. Let's leave this spooky place."

The two men snuck out of the room, and then making sure no one was in the corridor, scampered to Sanjiv's room.

"Whew! That was a close call!" Mikhail said, keeping a hand over his heart. "I guess we're in the clear now!"

"Yeah, someone finished his story alright!" Sanjiv grinned and offered a cigarette to an equally relieved Mikhail. They lit up, and silently watched the breaking beam of the lighthouse on the distant shore.

"Ah, life you owe me nothing, life, at long last we are at peace," Mikhail said, blowing rings in the night sky. "What were you so afraid of by the way—what's your story?"

"Well, now that you ask, there was this crazy bitch staying with me. An out and out wasted case: headstrong and reckless. One night we are in this nightclub at Thane, and these guys on the next table keep eyeing her. She was a scorcher; I'll give her that. But, as was usual with her—she belonged to nobody, she always said—she began to fool around with them. I told her to behave but she wouldn't listen to me.

"So when a woman lets down her man, a man has to show who's the boss!"

"What did you do?"

"The man-thing. I left the bitch on the roadside at two in the morning.

"I do regret it, though, for those guys from the next table probably picked her up, and the things they did to her with an iron rod...I can't even begin to describe. Luckily, no one was able to trace her back to me, or my in-laws would have tonsured my head and pulled out my teeth one by one by now!"

"If you had come forward to the police they would have been able to easily trace these guys from the club? The poor girl would have got justice!"

"Yeah, but you know how it is. One has to think of reputation also," Sanjiv said, ruffling his hair.

"What was her name?" Mikhail stubbed out his cigarette and rose. He looked very calm and determined.

"Sheena Mukherjee."

Mikhail unfastened a brick from the balustrade and struck Sanjiv's head with full force. As the man toppled over, Mikhail grabbed him under the shoulders and raised him up. Then he threw his sister's wrongdoer over the rails, six floors below. He never even looked over to see what had become of the man. He walked back to his own room, and slipping off his shoes, lay on his bed.

He lay there a long time. Sleep wasn't coming to him, and sleep wasn't his intention either.

There, that's done, he thought, I have avenged my baby sister.

But wasn't it your guilt as well? his conscience chided him. 'There, that's done.' Is that so easily said? Are you in the clear? No sir, you are not. It was your turn next, wasn't it? You know it very well now. Your story was coming up either tomorrow or the day after. That man was ChitraGupt, or maybe Kālu Dom. Who knows? He's not dead, he's simply putting destiny in your hands; his job is done, he's passed the Dom's staff to you. He has weighed, decided, judged your deeds, and you're marked, marked for Naraka, you know it. God isn't pleased with you. There's no point in going back to your life now. It will be torment. You've incurred his wrath. Now, repent, atone; there might still be hope for you!

"Hope," he muttered. He stood up and closed his eyes and said his prayers, the ones his mother had taught him on her lap, and then finished by saying, "I am sorry Maa…I am sorry Sheena."

Mikhail slid open the sun-blistered balcony door and climbed atop the banister. A thought occurred to him to scribble a final note for Indrani.

She doesn't deserve the clarity, he thought. Let her wonder and ask for a lifetime why I did this. She'll probably be happy to get the money and move on. The kids? Her girls from her previous marriage. She'd never let them become mine. They'll be fine.

He spread his arms like an eagle's wings and flew.

Nidhi Singh attended American International School, Kabul, before moving to Delhi University for BA English Honors. Currently, she lives with her husband in McLeodganj. Her short work has appeared in Indie Authors Press, Flyleaf Journal, Liquid Imagination, Digital Fiction Publishing Corp, LA Review of LA, Flame Tree Publishing, Four Ties Lit Review, Insignia Series, Inwood Indiana, Bards and Sages, Scarlet Leaf Review, Bewildering Stories, Down in the Dirt, Mulberry Fork Review, tNY.Press, Fabula Argentea, and others.

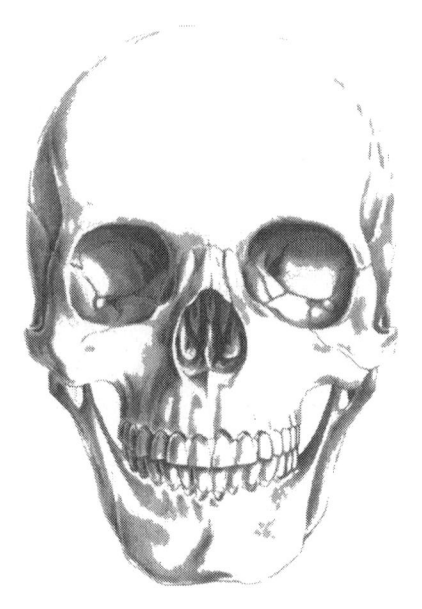

Ecdysis

Rebecca J. Allred

The waiting room is empty, but it isn't quiet. Behind the door marked PRIVATE, a woman chokes out wet, anguished sobs. Dr. Allison's secretary pretends not to notice. She greets me with a practiced, professional smile that lacks even a hint of warmth and asks me to wait. Wait? For what? I'm the last patient of the week. Always have been. Always will be. It's not like there's a line.

I smile. Nod. Sure. I'll wait.

The secretary punches a few buttons, clicks the mouse once, twice, drags something across the screen, double clicks, and resumes typing. Once, I arrived early and caught her snooping through patient files. I could have turned her in—HIPAA violations are serious business—but frankly, I don't care, and even if I did, who'd believe a paranoid nutbag like me?

The secretary finishes checking her e-mail, or whatever's so important she couldn't check me in immediately, and asks for my name. She knows my name, but I give it to her anyway. She asks me to confirm my address. It hasn't changed since last week. Neither has my insurance. When she's done checking all her little boxes, I take a seat on a cream-colored sofa. The room smells like those little bars of soap shaped like sea shells, and an instrumental version of a song I almost recognize wafts from speakers I can't see. There is a coffee table made of black wood. Resting on its surface is a little Zen garden and the latest issues of half-a-dozen tabloid magazines. Behind the door, the crying has stopped.

My palms itch. I scratch them with nails jagged from daily dental manicures; they are barely long enough to register any measure of relief. One of my fingertips slides over a pair of fine, almost invisible, hairs.

In middle school, the kids said if you masturbated too much you'd get hairy palms.

I don't masturbate, and the hairs on my palm aren't really hairs.

Delusional Parasitosis, eponymously known as Ekbom's Syndrome (I read that in one of Dad's medical texts, back when I wanted to be a doctor, too) is the medical name for my particular brand of nutbaggery. Or it would be, if the bugs infesting my body were all in my head like Dr. Allison says. They *are* in my head; I can feel their antennae quiver as they poke through the skin on my face, masquerading as a beard, but they're other places, too.

I look back to Dr. Allison's secretary. She's working on the computer again, getting ready to go home for the long weekend. Mentally, she is already gone, and so she doesn't see me pinch the hairs, pluck a beetle from my palm, and toss it into the Zen garden on the table. It lands on its back, legs combing the air a few moments before it rights itself and burrows beneath the sand.

The door to Dr. Allison's office opens. A short woman with puffy eyes and dark hair pulled back into a tight ponytail exits. Her son is dead. Just like my mom. I know, because Dr. Allison's secretary isn't the only one who has been snooping in patient files.

Lately, I've been thinking about this woman. Every week, I think about stopping her as she passes me in the soap-scented waiting room, wrapping her in my arms, and allowing sorrow to flow freely between our wounded souls. We would share everything, she and I, and we would be made whole again. The woman's eyes never leave the floor as she moves across the room, her shoes whispering against the high-quality beige carpet and carrying her out of the building.

Dr. Allison lingers in the frame of the door marked PRIVATE. She invites me inside.

Dr. Allison isn't my first shrink, and she won't be my last. My first therapist was Dr. Carlson; he went to medical school with my dad. I went to see him when the bugs first showed up. Back then, they didn't call it Delusional Parasitosis—I know because Dad has copies of all my medical records up until age eighteen in a locked drawer in his office. They sit right on top of Mamma's.

Dr. Carlson was cool. He had red hair and a beard and smoked cigars (not during our sessions, but always when he came over to drink wine and "talk shop" with Dad). He told me the bugs were all in my head, too, but that it wasn't my fault because Mamma had put them there. They were contagious, like the chicken pox, so Mamma had to go to the hospital for a while. When Mamma went away, so did the bugs.

Folie à deux is French for "a madness shared by two." The medical term is Shared Psychotic Disorder. That's what's written in my clinic notes from Dr. Carlson.

Dr. Allison's office doesn't smell like soap. It smells like lavender and tears. There is no music in here, only the soft, predictable tick of a clock counting down the minutes with malign diligence. The walls are lined with bookshelves, neatly organized. A desk with a computer, a stack of folders (patient files), a fountain pen, and a lead crystal paperweight is nestled in the corner. Near the center of the room are a high-back leather chair and a couch. She sits in the chair and gestures to the couch. Usually, I lie down. Today, I sit.

She comments on my beard, says she likes it (she's lying), and then asks how the last week has been. I tell her my roommate is mad at me because he thinks I killed his cat. She asks if I did, and I tell her I didn't (I'm lying, sort of), and she asks how that makes me feel.

I tell her I feel itchy.

The last time I saw Mamma alive, she was lying in an expensive hospital bed. The bugs hadn't bothered me in months, and both Dad and Dr. Carlson thought it would be okay for me to visit.

She looked different. Not like Mamma at all. Her soft yellow hair had been cut short. Dad said it was because she'd been pulling it out. The medical word for this is trichotillomania. There were little red sores all over her face and scalp, and she wore mittens that she couldn't take off.

Mamma just lay there, ignoring both me and my dad, murmuring over and over again that she was hungry. I begged Dad to get her something to eat. He patted me on the head, told me I was a good boy, and asked me to keep Mamma company while he stepped out to get some graham crackers.

As soon as he was gone, Mamma popped out of bed like some lunatic, termite-infested jack-in-the-box. She told me that the bugs were hungry. That if she didn't feed them soon, they would eat her instead. Tears welled up inside her eyes; tiny black specks swam in them. Mamma kissed me on the forehead, and I felt something crawl out of her lips and up onto my scalp. I pulled back, running my hands through my hair, trying to dislodge the invader.

When I looked back at Mamma, she was standing very still, arms outstretched, staring at the ceiling. Her mouth was open wide, and a torrent of black vomit (not vomit, vomit doesn't writhe) spewed from it.

I screamed and screamed and screamed.

Dr. Allison asks if the new pills have been helping. At first, I don't answer. I'm staring at the floor. One of the bugs has escaped. It's meandering across the nylon weave.

Formication is the medical term for the sensation of insects crawling in or under the skin. But it's the itching that really bothers me. The medical term for this is pruritus.

She asks again if the pills are helping.

I answer in the affirmative.

Dr. Allison follows my gaze, asks what I'm looking at.

I change the subject.

The last time I saw Mamma, she was lying in an expensive wooden box. Her hair was long and soft again (a wig), and makeup covered most of the holes in her skin. Neither, however, could disguise how hollow she was. Dad said she'd gotten so skinny because she stopped eating.

The medical term for this is anorexia.

But I knew better. She hadn't stopped eating; she'd been eaten.

During the service, a procession of tiny insects filed out of the casket and onto the floor. They looked like ants, but they weren't; these were smaller. Harder. *Meaner.* They formed a quivering semi-circle around the coffin. Their soft hum was a nearly inaudible requiem. I pulled my feet up onto the pew and cried.

Dr. Allison is scribbling furiously on her yellow legal pad.

I've never spoken about my mother before.

The funeral was bad, but nowhere near as bad as what happened that night.

I was dreaming about Casey Nelson. In real life, she was a redhead, but in my dream, she had yellow hair like my mom, and her face was round and healthy, free from blemishes. Her eyes were lined by thick velvet lashes, and they glittered like geodes. Casey smiled as her lips whispered permission. I reached out and touched her, and she did the same, but where my hand closed around soft, pliable tissue, hers gripped flesh turned nearly to stone. I moaned and felt my crotch moisten.

Casey looked at me, but she wasn't smiling anymore, and her eyes had lost their mischievous sparkle. She released her grip and raised her hand to eye level. It had turned black. I shrank back in revulsion, only to realize it wasn't just her hand—my groin was black, too…

Necrosis is the medical term for premature tissue death.

At first, I didn't think there could be anything worse than a lapful of necrotic penis, but as I reached a trembling hand down to examine my discolored genitals, I realized I was wrong. The stain didn't just cover my withering erection; it was coming from inside. And it was spreading. Little blobs of darkness separated from the primary mass, budding off like spores. They sprouted legs and antennae and—

I woke up, horrified to discover it wasn't just a dream.

The bugs were everywhere, clinging to my sheets, swarming over my thighs, marching up my belly toward my face and my silent, gaping mouth. I tumbled out of bed, knocking the lamp off the nightstand; it clattered loudly but did not break. A few seconds later, the hallway light blinked on, and heavy, rapid footsteps climbed the stairs.

The light worked the insects into a frenzy. Desperate to get back inside, they filled my eyes. My ears. My nose. I gagged and choked as they fled down my throat.

That's how Dad found me: writhing on the floor, choking on my own nocturnal issue.

I tell Dr. Allison that it's my fault. That Mamma is dead because I couldn't help her. My beard quivers and I tug at it, dislodging a handful of beetles in the process.

Dr. Allison asks what I think I could have done to help Mamma. She doesn't notice the insects tumble from my fingers and scurry toward her.

I explain that the infestation is too much for a single person to accommodate. Mamma hadn't been trying to kill me that day in the hospital, as I'd thought at the time. We'd shared the burden before, and she'd desperately needed to share it again, but I had been too afraid. I hadn't understood.

She tells me that this is a major breakthrough. That the insects are just a representation of suppressed guilt. That all I have to do is learn to accept that I am blameless in my mother's death, and the bugs will go away.

The itch is almost unbearable now.

After that night, Dad and I didn't talk much. He assured me that what had happened was just a normal part of growing up, and that Mamma's death was responsible for transforming a normal, run-of-the-mill wet dream (the medical term is nocturnal emission) into the nightmare I had experienced. Whenever I tried to broach the subject of my affliction, Dad would just turn away and tell me to discuss it with Dr. Carlson. Then Dr. Leavett. Then Dr. Cotner. He was incapable of sharing the burden of my illness any further than financing its treatment.

If he suspected anything when the Girl Scout disappeared while selling cookies on our block, he never said a word. Maybe because after that, things got better, a *lot* better. For a while.

After nearly a decade of doctors and drugs, I stopped scratching and started sleeping again. That was the stretch where both Dad and I thought I was well enough to pursue a career in medicine after all. I moved out, enrolled in pre-med classes, and even took the MCAT. Scored damn well, too. I was out celebrating with some classmates who had also scored well when I felt the twinge.

I always got a little anxious when something itched—I couldn't help it; it was a conditioned response—but this was different. The tickle between my left index finger and thumb wasn't the usual pruritoceptive itch (that's the medical term for an itch originating in the skin) I'd learned to accept as part of normal human physiology. It was deeper, and as the weeks passed, it grew in both distribution and intensity.

I tell Dr. Allison that Mamma's isn't the only death I'm responsible for, and she frowns, the excitement of our "breakthrough" melting from her face. I tell her I lied about my roommate's cat. That it had been an experiment because I felt so badly about the homeless woman. And the Girl Scout, especially since she'd been an accident.

I stand and pull my shirt over my head, revealing constellations of angry red sores. I scratch at them, and Dr. Allison asks me to please return to my seat. Her face is calm, but her eyes are broadcasting an SOS to an empty ocean. She knows her secretary has gone home. There is nobody here to help her.

I am the last patient of the week. Always have been. Always will be.

It was Dad's birthday, and he invited me over for dinner. He'd been pressuring me about medical school applications, and that night, I finally mustered the courage to tell him what I'd known for the better part of the semester. That no matter what my MCAT scores had been, or how outstanding my letters of recommendation were, I would not be attending medical school the following fall. The only explanation necessary was for me to roll up my sleeves.

When Dad saw those old familiar craters, his face became an amalgam of disappointment and rage, and we spent the rest of the evening in silence. I thought he might never speak to me again, but as I was leaving, he told me to expect a call from Dr. Allison's office the following day.

Cruising past City Park on my way home, the itch flared so intensely that I couldn't resist the need to rub my shrieking eyeballs. If there had been anyone else on the road, I'd have caused an accident for sure. I piloted the vehicle into three parking spaces and rubbed and scratched until my eyelids were swollen and my cheeks were soaked with tears.

I opened the door and tumbled out of the car. The cool autumn air acted as a salve against my hot, prickling skin, and it chased away the rank aura of failure that had shrouded me since realizing a normal life was forever beyond my reach. I didn't dare get back in my car, so I walked, following the cement perimeter for about half a mile before the itch flared again.

I'd never entered the park after dark before, but the insanity burning just beneath my skin compelled me to abandon the sidewalk and venture into the wooded area. The pricking discomfort dulled but did not abate as I trudged deeper into the park. At the center was a playground. A pair of swings twirled lazily in the gentle breeze, inviting me to sample the careless freedom of childhood. As I approached, a shape broke free from the shadows.

I froze, fearful of what it might be, what it might *want*, but it was just a homeless woman. She asked if I had any spare change. I didn't. If I had, I'd have given it to her. Not because of some altruistic impulse, but because as soon as she spoke, my skin ignited once again, and I knew if I didn't put some distance between us it would be the end.

I told her I wasn't carrying any cash (no, not even a few cents for a cup of coffee) and brushed past her, my interest in the swings gone. Her next proposition stopped me in my tracks. She offered to blow me.

The medical term for this is fellatio.

In all my years, I'd never had a girlfriend, had not so much as kissed a girl, or a guy for that matter, opting instead to avoid any and all forms of sexual stimulation as if they might spell death—if not for me, then for the object of my desire. The only desire within me at that moment was to relieve the horrible itch. Despite my disgust, I knew that if it wasn't now, it would be later, and I really did feel badly about the Girl Scout. I even kept one of her MISSING posters folded between the pages of my dad's old Diagnostic and Statistical Manual, next to a copy of Mamma's death certificate.

With the flavor of bile creeping up my throat, I turned to face the woman and accepted.

I explain to Dr. Allison that what I really need is somebody to share this burden with me. Someone who understands my pain. A kindred spirit. A mother.

I'm crying, choked sobs of anguish and pain drowning out the indifferent tick of the clock. They're pouring out of me now, black perspiration streaming from my pores, infested tears squeezing from my eyes. Dr. Allison screams and leaps from her seat. Swatting away the first troops of the oncoming arthropod assault, she dives for the alarm switch under her desk. I snatch the paperweight and swing, striking her in the temple. There is a sound like a hard-boiled egg rolling over a granite countertop, and Dr. Allison crumples to the ground. The bugs on the carpet race toward her and disappear into an expanding pool of blood.

I remove the remainder of my clothing and move over Dr. Allison's unconscious form. I tell her I'm sorry, call her "Mamma" (the words materialize without conscious thought), and then I descend, the swarm erupting, tearing through my skin, rising from my body like smoke above a raging fire. Sweet, blessed relief.

I call this cycle of agony and release ecdysis. This, however, is *not* a medical term, but an entomological one; there is no medical term for what I am.

When it's over, I flip through the stack of files on Dr. Allison's desk, searching until I find the one that belongs to the dark-haired woman with the dead son. All I need is the first page: the intake form with her name, address, and phone number.

I wipe the tears from my face and get dressed before taking one last look at the half-consumed pile of flesh that used to be my therapist. The sores on my skin are gone now, replaced by raw, healthy tissue, but the insects tumble over Dr. Allison like grains of black sand—humming, burrowing, feeding. By morning there will be nothing left. My stomach churns and I think I'll never eat again, though I know from experience it isn't true. I didn't want to hurt her, but Dr. Allison was no different than the Girl Scout, or the homeless woman, or my roommate's poor, stupid cat—all fit for consumption, but not for habitation. Despite her best efforts, she never could have helped me.

As I turn to leave, I glance down at the photograph in the bottom corner of the intake sheet clutched in my left hand and hope for both our sakes that next time will be different.

Rebecca J. Allred lives in the Pacific Northwest, working by day as a doctor of pathology, but after hours, she transforms into a practitioner of dark fiction, penning malignant tales of suffering and woe. Her work has appeared in A Lonely and Curious Country: Tales from the Land of Lovecraft; Nightscript II; Borderlands 6; and others.

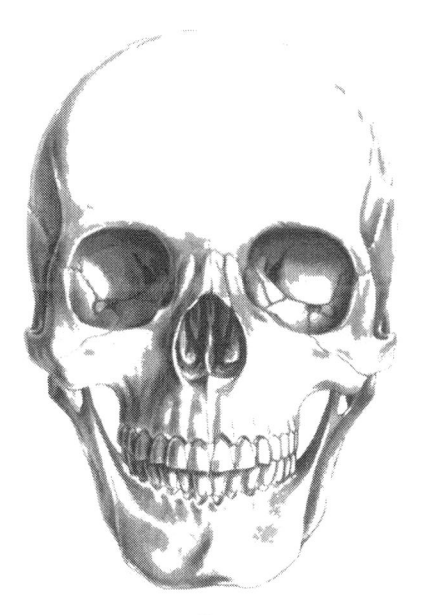

Coralesque

Rebecca Fraser

There was a time when surfing was my life. Heck, it was more than that, it was my religion. I surfed the breaks at dawn and returned to chase barrels again at dusk. The ocean's salt-white tightness drying on my skin felt more familiar to me than the suds of the shower that cleansed it away. I was good, too. I guess we all were, really. Skegs, we were known as back then. You don't hear the term so much these days.

Hang around the beaches enough and you get to know each other's styles and boards. If you weren't in the surf, then you were watching other surfers, scrutinizing their moves; checking out technique. That's how Saxon first caught my eye. I know I said I was good, but if you put me up against Saxon, then I looked pretty clumsy.

He was a dead-set natural. Could carve it up on his McCoy like no one else. In the water that weathered board of his was like an extension of his body, all grace, guts, and harmony. He could've easily gone pro, but he wasn't interested in anything like that.

"I just want to keep it for myself, man," he said to me once, as we sat on the beach at Kirra, our wetsuits pulled down to our waist. "D'ya know what I mean?" He looked at me, rum-colored eyes hidden beneath a shag of long brown hair—a beached-up Slash of *Guns N' Roses* fame.

Of course I knew what he meant.

We became pretty tight, Saxon and me. As tight as you could get with someone like Saxon, that is. We were all chasers back then: chasing beer, chasing waves, chasing girls and a good time. But Saxon, he marched to the beat of a different drum.

He occasionally came out with our group—well, my group really—but he didn't rage like the rest of us. Sometimes, if I badgered him enough, he'd come to *The Playroom* and listen to a band. He was usually happy to sit at one of the sticky, wooden tables, hiding behind his hair while we all slammed about on the dance floor. One time, get this; we went to see the *Hoodoo Gurus* play. I lost sight of Saxon in their second set. You know where I found him? He was outside, sitting on the bank of Tallebudgera Creek, staring up the moonlit estuary to where the surf rolled in alongside Burleigh Headland.

"You ok, man?" I asked. "They're gonna play 'Wipe Out' soon. Don't wanna miss that." My voice was clumsy with beer.

"Check the surf out, Brett," Saxon said. "It's pumping."

It was indeed pumping, but not as hard as the *Gurus*, so I left him to it. I looked back across the car park before I rejoined my mates, and that's how I like to remember him best. A broad-shouldered silhouette, sitting at peace, looking out to sea.

I was studying Law in those days. Bond University had only been open for a couple of years, and it was a pretty big deal to have a place there. Between lectures and a part-time job at the Pancake Palace, I still managed to get a surf in most days.

Saxon had a permanent gig at a local screen printing business just over the border. He liked it well enough. He was good at color matching and that sort of thing, and it was close to his little apartment in one of those old sixties walk-ups behind Rainbow Bay.

I met up with him at least a couple of times a week. We went wherever the surf was peaking, but favored the southern end of the Coast: Snapper Rocks, Kirra, D'bah, all the usual haunts.

Life was good. I was starting to pull some decent grades at Uni, I had a top bunch of mates, and things were looking pretty good between me and Louisa-with-the-legs at the Pancake Palace. I'd just gotten rid of my old Escort in favor of a Sandman and, between it all, there was surfing, the backbeat to my existence.

But then Saxon changed.

If I had to pinpoint where it started, then the storm was the beginning. January storms are a given in South East Queensland, but that monster of nineteen ninety-one was a real doozy.

We were sucking back a few cold ones on Saxon's balcony when it rolled in. Grey-green clouds united at the horizon and drew themselves like a static sheet across the blue afternoon sky.

An electric calm settled, and Saxon tipped the neck of his beer at me; we both knew what would follow. When the first thunder crack came, my eardrums bellowed right along with it. It boomed just over our heads, singeing the air. Then the rain. Sub-tropical, pregnant drops that thudded to the ground sporadically at first, then quickly built momentum. The storm engulfed the day, and we relished it.

"Surf'll be huge tomorrow." Saxon smiled around his beer.

And it was.

The storm cell brought with it a huge swell, with challenging conditions up and down the Coast. A gale was still blowing when I pulled up at Burleigh Headland that morning. Whitecaps foamed and furied and a little mouse of excitement scampered in my guts at the sight of the pounding surf. Past the second break, some of the waves were twelve-foot boomers.

I waxed up and swung my arms impatiently. I could always meet Saxon in the water, but I said I'd wait for him. I stood beneath the Norfolk Pines and surveyed the beach. It had been officially closed due to dangerous conditions. A lifeguard patrolled up and down, buggy tires churning through meters of brown foam that whipped and frothed at the shoreline. The usually pristine beach was littered with all manner of detritus—Logs and fence posts, palm fronds and husks, plastic bags, long strands of russet seaweed, a lone rubber thong. With each tidal surge, more debris was pushed up the foam-flecked sand. The clean-up job would be huge.

"Let's go, Brett, you big girl." Saxon, flicking at my rear with his leg rope. I turned to give him a shove, but he danced out of reach, an excited puppy.

"You ever surfed waves like this?" I asked him.

"Only in my dreams, bro." His eyes gleamed. "Hoist up those petticoats, dude, it's going to be bitchin' out there."

"Get stuffed," I replied good-naturedly.

We picked our way from the top of Burleigh Hill down through the National Park to where the best surf could be accessed a short distance from the beach. It was a trickier route than entering from the beach, but expended a lot less energy than paddling beyond the headland. Several other surfers were making the pilgrimage and banter was high as we jostled between pandanus palms to access the rocky path to the base of the cliff.

A brush turkey swaggered and scratched to our left, her red and yellow markings vivid between the lantana which gave way to a clear view of the black lava boulders. The wind slapped us with a salt-wet sting as we navigated from one foam-slathered rock to the next, swaying for balance with every incoming wave. Timing is critical when you launch at Burleigh, you have to traverse the slippery boulders until you are in a position to leap into the sea with your board. I let Saxon go first and followed his gazelle-like leaping as best

I could. With the next incoming wave, we were off, paddling out with the backwash.

The next hour was exhilarating. The ocean ruthless, relentless, heavier; with more water and power in her barrels than I'd ever experienced. But, by God, it was fun.

Every now and then I'd catch a glimpse of Saxon, shredding all over the face of a fast, hollow wave. It was like he had a team of white stallions on a lunge rope, breaking one after the other. At one stage I saw him power down the line right next to me, his face contorted with rapture as he shot through the tube.

And then he got smashed. I saw his board fly up without him, and spin in the air as it descended. No biggie, we'd been axed several times that day, but I paddled towards him just the same.

There was blood. A lot of it. Saxon clung to his board. Crimson rivulets pulsed down his face, skewing his vision and tracking his cheeks. At first, I thought the fin of his board had sliced his head, but when I pushed his hair back, the jagged gash told a different story.

"Jesus," I breathed. "Saxon, we've gotta get you back, man." The shoreline rose and diminished with the ocean's swell. It seemed a very long way away.

"How bad is it?" Saxon asked. He had hauled himself back onto his board and held his hands to his head. "Shit, Brett, it hurts."

"Stitches, for sure," I said. "Let's go, dude, hoist up those petticoats."

Saxon laughed weakly. I winced as a fresh glut of blood spurted between his fingers.

I don't really remember how we got back to shore. When I try and recall it's all *blue-white, salt-breathe, dump-gasp, heart-beat, blood-swell, shark-smell, clamor-yammer, sand-stagger.*

Sand. Stagger. The beach beneath us. Saxon rolled off his board, pale and heaving and I looked around wildly for something to stem the flow of blood.

The lifeguard on his buggy, ahead in the distance. I jumped up, screaming and capering.

By the time he reached us, others had come, beach combers and surfing spectators; all advice and good intentions. An elderly sun-creased lady undid her tie-dyed sarong and knelt in her bathing suit to wrap it around Saxon's head. Rosettes of blood bloomed through the fabric and joined the rainbow of other colors.

The lifeguard was not much older than us. He radioed ahead to someone, somewhere, and I helped load Saxon on the seat next to him.

"Where are you taking him?" I asked.

"Southport. Gold Coast Hospital. They'll sort him out. What cut him? Fin? See that all the time."

"Nah, it wasn't the fin," I said. "It must have been something floating in the water."

"Wouldn't surprise me," the Lifeguard nodded. "Look at the beach. All kinds of debris gets stirred up with a storm. Planks with nails in 'em, branches covered in barnacles, you name it. Seen a crate of coconuts washed up once, come all the way from Indo."

The buggy took off towards the Surf Club, and there was nothing left for me to do but gather up our boards, load them into the Sandman and head for home. I was exhausted.

I called the Hospital later that afternoon. A receptionist put me on hold and Bryan Adams filled the void. When she picked up again, it was to inform me that Saxon was fine and could be picked up at any time. There wasn't anyone else, so I guessed that would be me.

"Eighteen stitches, man," Saxon said proudly. His head was swathed in white bandages turban-style. He wound down the car window and rested an olive-skinned arm. "You shoulda seen the shit that came out of it, Brett. Took 'em ages to clean it. Looked like coral shards. Reckon it might've been attached to some floating wood or something? It was pretty messy out there."

"Yeah, could've been." I agreed. Coral. Made sense, it was sharp enough. "You right to drive? I'll take you back to your car."

"Right as rain," Saxon said. We drove to Burleigh, reliving every moment of every barrel we'd caught that morning.

I hadn't heard from Saxon in three days, and I still had his board, so that afternoon I decided to drop it round. I took the three flights of stairs to his unit and rapped on the door. The blinds were drawn, and it was unusually quiet. Saxon normally had a surf video playing or *Triple J* blasting. I knocked again and called out. I was just about to leave when the door opened a crack.

"Brett?"

"I've got your board. Want to hit Kirra?"

"Not today, I don't feel so good."

I pushed the door open, and Saxon shrank back blinking as if the sunlight hurt his eyes. He'd removed the bandage. Even in the dim light of his unit, I could see the fever-red bulge of his wound.

"Dude, that doesn't look good." I flicked the light switch. "Let's have a look."

Saxon whipped his hands to his eyes. "Turn the light off, Brett."

I dragged him into the bathroom, turned that light on and prised his hands from his face for a better look. Saxon kept his eyes screwed tight against the glare and moaned as I inspected his head. The wound was angry and weeping, strained tight against the neat row of stitches. His head felt too hot, and looking at the scarlet lines that had started to thread from the gash, I felt hot too.

"Sax, you gotta go back to the doctor. It's infected. I had a mate, got blood poisoning from a nasty coral cut on his foot. Swelled up like a balloon. He got some penicillin; took care of it like magic."

"'kay. Just turn off the damn light." He shoved me hard. My hip bone connected with the towel rail.

"Jesus, Sax, take it easy." I rubbed at my throbbing hip.

"Turn off the fucking light!" His voice had a dangerous edge I hadn't heard before.

Wounded, I flicked the switch and left Saxon sitting in darkness on the edge of the bath. "I'll ring tomorrow," I called as I left, "Make sure you get to a Doctor." I banged the door a little on the way out, I admit.

I didn't ring Saxon the next day. I left it a couple of days, assuming the penicillin would kick in and douse his fever-temper with it. I was looking forward to a surf that afternoon so I called him first thing, before he would have left for work. The phone rang ten-eleven-twelve times before I hung up.

I tried him at work a little later that day.

"Saxon hasn't been in the last two days," his boss said. "Didn't even have the courtesy to call and let me know." An alarm bell clanged distantly in my mind. "Not like him, always been a bloody good worker. I expected better."

I tried Saxon again at home. With each unanswered ring, I felt my unease grow. That night after a double shift at the Pancake Palace, I blew Louisa off and drove to his unit. As before, the blinds were drawn. I knocked and waited. Nothing. I called Saxon's name. Nothing. But I could hear it. A squelching, labored noise.

I threw my shoulder against the door until it gave. It was so dark and fusty inside at first my eyes didn't comprehend what they were seeing. Saxon was huddled in an armchair, but his head, something was wrong with his head. It was too big and lolled forward against his chest.

"Saxon?" My voice was air escaping from a balloon. I tried again, "Sax?" I hunkered down to get a better look.

The head lifted sluggishly, and I fell back on my arse in shock and revulsion. Saxon was unrecognizable. His face obscured by gnarled cladding that started at the top of his head, and extended down his arms and torso and beyond. I noticed the fingers of one hand fused together in a misshapen clump. One bloodshot eye rolled at me, the other hidden altogether behind the barnacle-encrusted casing. The squelching noise began in earnest, and I realized it was breathing. Dear God, Saxon was trying to breathe. A pendulum of snot swung from where the center of his face should be.

"Jesus, Sax," I reached a tentative hand out and touched his shoulder. The growth was rough and cool. Coral. *It was coral.*

And it was alive and growing.

Saxon lurched at me with a wet growl. The weight of his encrusted body pinned me beneath him. I thrashed and screamed as the thing that had once been my friend snarled and gurgled on top of me.

With a mighty adrenalin-fueled thrust, I pushed him away and rolled, jabbering, against the couch.

The growling escalated.

I fled then, reaching the door in great, leaping strides, blood pounding in my ears. The last thing I saw was Saxon flailing on the ground. It was a pathetic sight. One or two remaining brown curls sprouted from his bulbous skull. His body, too melded together to use his limbs, rolled and snapped in an effort to get at me. I will always remember his remaining red eye fixed on me as I ran.

The sky was lightening as I fell upon the sparse patch of lawn in front of Saxon's unit block. I doubled over retching and sobbing. After I'd emptied my guts of the waffle stack I'd eaten what seemed like an eternity ago, I felt a little stronger.

I ran up and down neighboring streets until I found a phone box, rummaged in my pockets for a coin, and dialed 000.

"What is your emergency, please? Police, fire or ambulance?"

In my shock, I almost laughed. What was my emergency? How do you describe the fact that your mate has been overcome by a malevolent, fast-growing parasite? "Ambulance," I said shakily. "My friend is…hurt." I gave Saxon's address, listened to the operator's questions and answered them as best I could. No, he's not bleeding. Yes, he is breathing…sort of. No, he couldn't talk. Yes. No. Don't know. *Just fucking get here.*

I returned to Saxon's units and hid behind the row of rubbish bins under the carport, hopping anxiously from foot to foot as I waited for the ambulance. Pairs of lorikeets nattered to each other overhead as dawn approached.

An ambulance pulled up, and two paramedics got out. I heard their footfalls on the staircase and a door open on the top floor. Then, silence. I chewed at the skin around my thumb, ears straining. More footfalls. The paramedics returned. They were alone. Where was Saxon?

I crept from my hiding spot and moved behind a tenant's vehicle as the paramedics radioed in and caught snatches of conversation.

"...no, the unit was empty. Nothing to report. Where did the call come from? Not the unit? Public phone box. Right, must've been a prank. Bloody kids. Door was off its hinges, though. Might pay to send a police car—"

The unit was empty? Where was Saxon? I had to see for myself.

I waited for the ambulance to leave, then climbed the stairs on shaky legs. The door was still ajar, and I pushed it open a crack, reached in and flicked on the light. Nothing. My heart thudded in my chest. I entered the unit and looked in each room. Empty. Only the eyes of numerous bikini centerfolds taped to the walls watched me. I made to leave, and then I saw them. Shards of coral, salmon-brown in color littered the floor. A trail of sorts led to the front door, and a larger clump of the stuff lay just outside, as if it had scraped off on the door ledge.

I kept my eyes to the ground as I slowly made my way back down the stairwell. More shards. And over there, more. Every now and then, an ooze of mucus accompanied by a fetid saline stench. I followed the trail down the stairs, and across the street. It continued east, and suddenly I knew, and I was off and sprinting towards the beach.

A great furrow in the sand marked the labor Saxon had made to reach the ocean. In the dying of the night, I saw him for the last time. A giant misshapen slug, humping its way towards the water. There was nothing resembling humanity left. I sank to the sand, cold and damp through the knees of my jeans, and watched as the sea claimed my friend. It took a couple of surges, and then he was off with the backwash, just as we had been, two surfers with our boards, at Burleigh a week ago.

I remember sitting on the beach for a very long time. Morning rose about me, and the day began its routine. The breakers surged forward onto dawn-fresh sand. Walkers marched around me; a fisherman cast out not far from where I sat. Early morning surfers paddled out beyond the break, and I watched them, envying their carefree idealism.

Rebecca Fraser is an Australian writer whose short stories, flash fiction, and poems have appeared in various genre publications since 2007. She holds a Masters of Arts in Creative Writing, and her fiction showcases her fondness for all things darkly speculative. To provide her muse with life's essentials, Rebecca supplements by copy and content writing, however her true passion lies in storytelling.

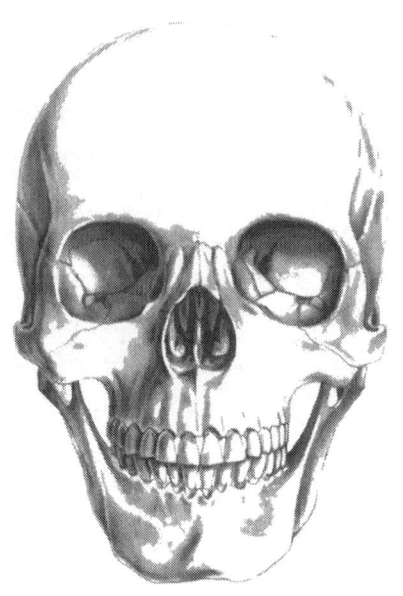

The Funhouse

Jo-Anne Russell

"Don't be a pussy!" Jessica turned and faced Hope with a smirk.

"I'm not a pussy, and I'm sick of you calling me that!"

"Then go in."

Hope pushed past her friend and stopped at the foot of the steps. The oddly shaped door of the fun house reminded her of the horror novel's cover she was currently reading. She placed her foot on the first step and paused.

"Get out of my way, pussy," Jessica said as she pushed her way past and raced up the steps. "You're always going to be Scared Little Hope. You're no fun at all. I don't even know why I hang out with you anymore!" With that said, she disappeared inside.

Hope honestly didn't know why either. At eighteen, she was what once would have been considered a lady. She didn't smoke, drink, do drugs, or even really date. Her focus was on her future; a future that she was working very hard on to accomplish. Camera equipment wasn't cheap, and wasting money on partying and boys wasn't going to help.

She placed a protective hand over the camera dangling from the strap around her neck and followed Jessica inside. The tiny misshapen hallway rocked from side to side as a strobe light violently blinded her. Hope felt her way along the wall and entered a room.

"Jess!" She rubbed her eyes between blinks and looked around. The place was dark with a single small wattage bulb hanging from the ceiling. She could barely see anything in the dim lighting. Hope rubbed her eyes again and waited for them to come into focus.

The walls were black with old paint that had long ago started chipping off. Spider web cracks lined them between the old-style picture frames, housing frightening images of creatures and bodies and blood. One such picture depicted a clown with blood that dripped from its eyeless sockets and a smile that glistened on a mouth full of jagged teeth.

Hope raised her camera and adjusted the settings. The view on the screen was too dark, so she placed it up to her eye, and looked through the viewfinder. In the seconds it took her to click the shutter, a pair of yellow eyes appeared in the image. A rush of panic spread through her. Her legs gave way, and she stumbled to regain her balance.

Two hands with long nails met her back and shoved her forward into the wall. She let out a scream and scrambled to the center of the room. Her breath came in quick gasps and her ears filled with the sound of cruel laughter.

Jessica stood against the far wall with her hands covering her mouth. Her light complexion glowed with the redness of her outburst.

"Oh my God, you should so see your face right now! You look like a toddler about to cry, hahaha!"

"That's not funny Jess. I saw something weird when I took a picture. There were eyes looking at me."

"Sure there were. We're in a funhouse for crying out loud. You're supposed to see weird stuff. Let's go look some more."

Hope looked at the picture. "I'm not kidding. That clown was eyeless, and as soon as I hit the shutter button, they appeared."

"They probably have some creep hiding in the wall, flashing fake lit eyes when scared little girls like you come along. I bet he's busting a gut right now."

Jessica flipped her hair out of her eyes—an annoying habit to Hope—as usual, and smirked as she walked into the next room.

Hope could hear her as she made moaning sounds, imitating the undead. She rolled her eyes as she followed her friend.

The moment she entered the room, she could smell it. The putrid sour odor pierced her nostrils and made her eyes water. Hope looked around for the source but found nothing more than a circular room full of bizarrely shaped mirrors.

The sharp sound of a slammed door cut through the pungent atmosphere. She turned in the direction of the sound only to see the glow of the bulb was gone.

Jessica squealed with delight. "Finally, some action!"

The frames of the mirrors glowed a toxic green, lighting their images. Hope watched as Jessica ran from mirror to mirror, laughing at her misshapen reflection. The oval one she stood before now made her body too thin on the top, while her bottom half ballooned out like an old Weeble toy.

Hope laughed and raised her camera to her eye.

"Don't you even think of—"

Before Jessica could finish, Hope snapped the shutter. She giggled as she backed away, knowing her friend was not going to let her get away with any shot that would ruin her "oh so perfect" image.

"Give me that camera," Jessica shrieked as she lunged toward Hope.

Hope jumped backward, curling her limbs around her camera as she fell. Jess's foot dug into Hope's ribs as she watched the top of Jess' body pass over of her. The ear-piercing scream that followed rendered Hope unconscious.

She woke with one arm still curled around her camera. Her head pounded with a whisper of a scream still echoing inside it. Panic raged through her.

"Jess? Jess!"

Her eyes searched the empty room. Hope stood and walked to the mirror beside her. Jess had to have hit it, but there was no crack. She raised a hand as a misty resemblance of Jessica's face appeared. Frozen on her cloudy image was a look of pure terror.

Hope gently touched the mirror. It disappeared under her warm touch, as a ripple passed over the glass. She tried to pull back, jerking her hand away, but it remained. The liquefied mirror spread up her arm, slowly reaching her shoulder. She screamed and tried pulling off her denim coat.

The liquid spread faster, covering her screaming face. Pain like nothing she had ever felt before spread through her as the mirror slithered over every inch of her skin. It seeped into her pores and her ears and her mouth, drowning out her screams. It covered her eyes, reflecting them in an image sent back to her brain.

Just as she was sure she was going to die, coolness began to spread through her toes and fingertips. It soothed the tortuous pain she was suffering. Jessica's face flashed in her mind, and for a moment, she wondered if this was what Jess had felt.

She wiggled her fingers and tried to stay calm as control came back to the rest of her body. She watched the remaining mirror slink off her skin as she stood. The liquid reformed into the identical frame, solidified, and created a window-view of the room she had just left.

Where she stood now was neither room nor a space of any kind she had ever seen before. Even the air brought with it a tingling within her lungs during each breath. Hope placed a hand to her throat and ran it down the strap to the still dangling camera. She raised it and examined the device for obvious damage. Satisfied it was cosmetically unharmed; she turned in a full circle.

The space had neither walls nor ceiling, yet beneath her feet lay a brown, rubbery surface. She randomly picked a direction and started walking. Strange whistles and other sounds echoed in the distance but gave no distinct clues as to where they were coming from.

"Jess. Jessica!"

Her own voice trailed off and blended with the other sounds, but nothing sounded like that of her friend's. After walking and calling for what seemed like hours, Hope sat cross-legged on the surface and inspected her camera further. She pushed the power button and watched the view screen light up.

Hope scrolled through the pictures until she got to the painting with the eyes. They stared at her, making her shiver, and she felt as exposed as a nude in a coliseum. Her finger tapped the right arrow button, and a surprise spread across the screen. The picture depicted Jessica in mid-flight with a pair of liquid hands wrapped around her throat. The rest was a pink blur of Hope's flesh. She zoomed in.

The surface quaked beneath her, but before she could get to her feet, it split before her. Multi-sized shards of glass shot out of the crack and landed in a pile. They quickly assembled themselves into a jagged, clouded square.

Hope, frozen by both fear and curiosity, tentatively swiped her hand across it. The cloud cleared, leaving her hand cold and aching. She watched Jessica's image appear, frantically calling out for help as she pounded on the walls that confined her.

"Jess!"

Jessica spun around and faced her, but her voice disappeared. She pounded furiously on the other side in futility.

Hope sat as if glued, and didn't even look up as the haunting voice spoke to her.

"Pity not this creature, for she is not worthy."

A hand patted her gently on the head.

"What?" Hope stood, and faced him. She could feel the tension rise within herself as she faced the image with the yellow eyes from the painting in the hall of mirrors.

A smile of delight spread across his cracked skin, exposing jagged teeth. His eyes softly glowed as he watched her take a step back.

"Don't fear me, girl, fear what you have become. Fear what lies ahead; for you have laid a path of pain and agony for yourself. Your life will end by your own hand, and for good reason."

"W-what do you mean? Who are you?"

"I am he who is neither here nor there; the darkness and the light; the guide for those who face their true likeness. I am simply a reflection of all who were and all who are—even you."

"I don't understand. I want my friend back. Please, let us go."

She looked back to the mirror, and upon her friend, who now sat cradling her drawn legs, peering over them with a tearstained face.

"The key to your freedom lies not with me. It lies before you—within the one upon which you gaze."

"What do you want from me? I don't understand your riddles—I don't even care. I just want to go home." She wiped away the tears that started trailing from her eyes, hoping he wouldn't realize how terrified she really felt.

She furrowed her brows as she attempted to interpret his facial expression. He was either mocking her, or he looked compassionate—but with such a gruesome face, the answer was beyond her. She changed her tactic.

"Explain what you mean, and cut out the riddles."

"Look," he said, as he touched the glass.

The image swirled, and she saw herself at school from the week before. She was in the darkroom of her photography class. Even with digital technology, the students were schooled in photo development—old school. She was looking at a drying line of photos when the darkroom door flew open. A burst of light flooded the tiny room, and before she could protest, Jess came into view. Her face was red, with angry lines tracing their way to the corners of her eyes and mouth.

"That stupid bitch! What does she know anyway? It's muffins, not rocket science!" She folded her arms across her chest and took a seat on the stool.

"What's wrong with you?" Hope looked back to her pictures and prayed they weren't ruined.

"Mrs. Braxton, that's what! She's always on my ass. According to her, I am a danger to myself and anyone else in the same vicinity where I'm cooking. She told me I should focus on something less dangerous—like horticulture. Can you believe that?"

Hope tried to stifle the giggle that suddenly erupted.

"Really? You're going to laugh at me? At least I try to do social things like cooking. I'm thinking about my future—and my future friends. You're going to end up alone and friendless. You're boring. You barely do anything that involves anyone besides yourself. Why am I even wasting my time talking to you? I'm out of here!" With that, she hopped off the stool and stormed to the door.

"Jess, wait!"

"Don't bother. I have a lot more friends that actually care if I'm upset, and they won't laugh at me. Know why? Because unlike you, they are not social Neanderthals!"

This wasn't the first time Jess had really hurt her feelings—she did that on a regular basis—but her tone held so much malice. Hope had overlooked so many things about Jess and still made an effort to be her friend. Even when other students tried to deter the friendship, Hope had ignored the warnings and rumors; always trying to make Jess feel good about herself, and for what? Jess' words were stabbing away at her very soul. She used Hope's secrets and fears against her, and that hurt more than anything.

The clown touched the glass again. This time, she saw Jess walking to the back corner where the students smoked. She was standing with a group of girls who spread gossip faster than poison ivy. Jess leaned in and took a smoke from one of the 'lower rank' girls.

She started smiling as she exhaled. "You'll never guess what I just walked in on."

She puffed a bit as the other girls looked at each other. Their faces grew in expression with anticipation.

"What? Tell us!"

The 'leader' took the smoke and finished it. "Yeah, what did you see? Sounds juicy." She dropped the smoke and stomped it into the dirt.

A smile spread across Jessica's face, and her hands made gestures at ninety miles-a-minute.

"I went to see Hope—she was in the darkroom—and you'll never guess what I caught her doing in there!"

"What?"

"Yeah, what was she doing? Tell us!"

They crowded around her like a pack of starving hyenas after a carcass.

"I surprised her. I guess she wasn't expecting anyone to come in. After all, who really cares about photo shop? Anyway, there she was leaning on the stool." Jess took a breath, absorbing all the attention from the eyes upon her.

"So," said the lead. "What's so big about that?"

"She was masturbating!"

"Oh my god—are you serious?"

"As if—"

"I know, right? Who would have thought she even had feeling down there! Hahaha!"

All of them were laughing, but it was the laugh that came from Jess that stood out. It wasn't her regular, warm, giddy laugh that Hope had heard so many times over the last few years, but a laugh that seemed deeper, and colder.

This time, Hope let the tears flow freely.

The clown touched the glass again, and this time, she saw herself lying on her bed reading the new horror novel her mom gave her. She had been away from school for the last two days, and now it was the weekend. She hoped the rumor someone started would die down before Monday—or she might have to change schools.

She heard the knock, but the door opened before she could say a word.

"Hey. Your mom said you were up here. Can I come in?"

"I guess." Hope put the novel face down, being careful not to lose her page.

"Well, I got two tickets to the carnie for tomorrow. I thought you might want to go."

It was supposed to be an apology. Jess never really said the words: "I'm sorry." She did things instead.

"I don't know Jess. I have a photo project I'm behind in. I really need a good grade in this class—"

"Perfect! I'll be here tomorrow at ten. You can bring your camera, and take all the shots you want while we're there. It's going to be so cool. I heard they have a few new games. Bring some cash. The prizes are always so cute, but you have to trade up for the really good stuff." She started backing out the door.

"Wait, there's going to be kids from school there too? I really don't want to deal with that right now. Things need to cool down, you know?"

"Suck it up, Hope. You have to grow up, and stop being such a baby. So what if some kids are there? What can they possibly do to you? Really, get a freaking backbone!"

Hope inhaled, readying herself to protest, but Jess was too quick—slamming the door behind her—in other words, it was final.

The next morning brought her baggy eyes and a headache from lack of sleep. She was shaking as she poured a glass of juice, skipping anything that might come back up in lumps if she chucked. A knock sounded from the other room, and the mirror clouded back over.

"I still don't understand," she said, as she stared up at him. All her sadness was gone, replaced by anger and frustration. "How does that help me?"

"You must decide. Your choice is the future and your freedom, but I must show you one last thing." This time, he waved his entire hand before the mirror.

Hope saw herself standing at the steps of the funhouse. Jess rushed past her, and inside, but that's where things changed. The view moved to the back of the funhouse where a group of girls were standing around, smoking and talking to each other. The same lower-rank girl looked really nervous.

"What if we get caught? My dad will kill me; then ground me until I'm like, twenty-five!"

"Quit your bitching." The leader stubbed out her smoke, and then lit another. "Did you tell someone?"

The lower looked like a startled rabbit. "No!" She said it too loudly. "I mean—of course not. I wouldn't—"

"Better not have, or you know what'll happen to you."

Lower sparked a smoke, and quietly puffed away.

"Okay, so when Jess comes out, we go in. Remember, there is barely any light in there, so make sure it's her you're stripping, and not one of us. I want lots of pics too, just in case some of them don't turn out. Between the six of us—and Jess—we should have this all over school and the net before lunchtime on Monday. Now, get ready!"

There was a sudden painful thud within Hope's chest. Her stomach churned, but instead of chucking, an inferno of anger and hatred exploded from within her. All the bullying, sadness, and years of aching for someone to be a true friend had finally taken their toll. Hope decided then that people were ugly—no matter how pretty they thought they were.

An emotional wave hit her, knocking the breath from her body, and she suddenly felt the desperation of millions of people just like her; people who were worthy but misunderstood, different, and alone. Their pain pulsed in her veins like hoards of tiny pins. She tingled everywhere, but the sensation was welcoming.

The mirror clouded over.

"Now you see," he said. She looked at him and finally saw him for the first time. The illusion faded away, and before her stood a young man, beautiful, with soft glowing eyes. His smile was warm and honest.

She nodded and placed her hands in position on her camera. This time, when the liquid engulfed her, there was no pain, nor fear. She found herself standing as it departed and solidified, leaving her in the hall of mirrors.

Hope stepped closer and adjusted the lens. The power grew within her as her rage took hold.

Jess was red-eyed and angry. She screamed obscenities at the mirror, and at Hope's image on the other side. She was as ugly as her personality.

Small reflective material closed off Hope's ears as she snapped the shutter. Her eyes began to glow. "Smile!"

The bright yellow flash penetrated the mirror. Jess' skin burst into pulsing lesions, and then flames. Her flesh melted away as she ran about, screaming, smearing the mirror in blood. Her lidless eyes watched flashes of her past evil deeds—reminders forever embedded in her soul. Jess dropped to the ground and clawed her way back over to Hope's image. She reached out to her with a bony hand, just touching the glass with a few fingertips.

Hope tapped the mirror.

The vibration penetrated to Jess, where she turned to ash on the other side.

The caps receded inside her ear canals, and his friendly voice whispered to her.

"You did well."

Hope smiled. She knew what she had to do. Her soft yellow eyes glowed as she made her way to the door. The girls were waiting.

Jo-Anne Russell is a dark fiction writer and a publisher at Lycan Valley Press. She is a member of the Horror Writer's Association, the Writers Guild of Alberta and the Edmonton Arts Counsel. Her work can be found in a multitude of anthologies, and as standalone stories. Her debut novel The Nightmare Project was republished this year with Book 2 to follow soon after.

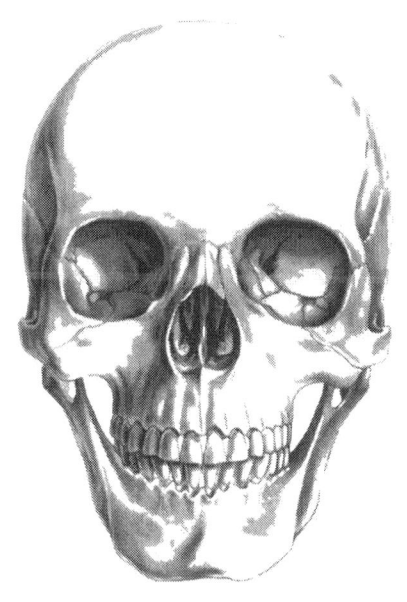

Graffiti

K.S. Dearsley

It was exactly what Marian was looking for—a home of her own, an address to prove she existed. She looked around feeling someone behind her. Gareth entered the lounge carrying a packing case. He spoke over the top of it.

"It's a bit of a mess."

The previous tenants had left stained carpets, chipped paintwork and crayon on the walls.

"Nothing that soapy water and a paintbrush can't fix." Marian clasped her hands to hold in her excitement. Laughter or tears could break free at any moment, and she didn't want to let Gareth down.

"Where do you want this?" he asked.

Marian shrugged, then realizing this was a symptom of her old non-committal absent self, pointed to a spot by the wall. As Gareth straightened, he turned to face her, and she felt her heart do the familiar flip-flop as his eyes met hers. The look penetrated all the layers of masks and saw her. That had been what had pulled her back.

As she had stood under the lamp post facing the bridge that first night, Marian had felt herself dissolving with the rain. Each drop that spat on her washed a little more of her away. She had a choice: she could wait there for the storm to remove her like an insignificant stain, to dilute what little that remained of her, or she could take the few quick steps over the parapet on the bridge and sail out into oblivion. She stood in the chill, watching the light pool in the wet pavement, waiting for something to show her which option she should choose.

Then Gareth was in front of her with that look. Marian had heard no approaching splash of footsteps. It seemed he had been conjured out of the rain.

"Can you tell me how to get to Casa Romano?" His voice was firm and confident despite being lost.

Here was someone who needed her, who wanted her guidance, even if it was only to an Italian restaurant

"I'll show you."

Over the following two months, Marian had grown unsure who was actually following whom that night. Collecting enough words to explain to him how he had rescued her had been difficult. It required a greater sense of self than she had been used to, but somehow her rambling sentences had been enough. He accepted she had been through a rough time, that she might sometimes need to be cajoled out of an involuntary distance, that he would need patience.

Marian decided that his patience would be rewarded. She stepped forward into his embrace, her gaze straying past his shoulder as she laid her head against it. For a moment, the smeary scribble on the wall resolved itself into a name. Marian jerked upright, shocked at finding herself written there. Then the letters blurred once more.

"What is it?" Gareth's forehead wrinkled, concerned.

Marian turned away hiding her expression. "Nothing. Let's go out."

His eyebrows quirked upwards. "I thought you couldn't wait to eat in your own place."

"I forgot to get anything in," Marian said, hoping Gareth would not feel how her back tensed with the lie. A sick, dizzying surge of unaccustomed attention made her want to run from the room.

They left the unpacking and headed for the nearest pub. By the time they returned, Marian felt pleasantly fuzzy with drink and tiredness.

"Coffee?" Warmth spread in her belly dispelling her nerves as she made the offer. When she returned with the cups, Gareth was sitting on the sofa with a look in his eyes that belied his relaxed pose. Marian felt her breath catch in her throat. Above the mantelpiece in bold black letters on the grubby wallpaper was the word 'Marian'.

Gareth followed her gaze. "Decided to make your mark on the place already?"

Marian stared from him to the graffiti and back again. He must have written it, but he was grinning at her as though she had done it. Her uncertainty came out as a compromise.

"Will it come off?"

Gareth frowned. "Too late to worry about that now. Put the mirror over it until you decorate."

Marian nodded.

"Tell you what," Gareth continued. "There's something missing."

He jumped up and taking a pen from his pocket, added his name beside hers. The writing was quite different.

"Now everyone will know we're a couple without doubt."

Marian felt sick. She wanted to get a scrubbing brush and obliterate the words forever. The atmosphere in the room suddenly seemed too still, as if something was listening.

"You don't really want that coffee, do you?" Gareth pulled Marian to her feet, and she allowed him to lead her through to the bedroom.

She had thought the contact of skin on skin, of his lips brushing her belly and his hands caressing the inside of her thighs would restore her self-reality. Instead, as his body rose and fell she liquefied and flowed away. Her fingers lost the power to grip. She gazed at the cobweb of cracks in the ceiling; all lines and color leaked and lost definition. The only thing that seemed real, so much so that it burned its way through the intervening wall, were the stark black letters of her name. Marian's snatched breathing and jerking movements became increasingly frantic. She would die if she did not break free of Gareth's weight. Her fingers tightened on his back, digging the nails into his flesh. Then he sighed and lay back, and it was over. He stroked her flank sleepily as she turned on her side, knees drawn up to form a knot.

"All right?" he murmured.

She made a deliberate effort to relax, letting her arms and legs grow heavy, but her mind kept returning to the names on the wall. She saw 'Marian' in close-up, traveling the lines like a roller-coaster, tracing each letter with her finger and staining the tip with indelible ink. Her finger trailed off the tail of the last letter, and she started to scrub out the name of Gareth until her nails broke and her knuckles were grazed.

She woke, panting. Sunshine streamed through the blind barring the room. The smell of coffee and rattle of crockery told her Gareth was in the kitchen. She rose sleepily. The lounge door was shut, but the scrawled names burned through the wood. Marian hesitated, then grasped the handle firmly and strode in. She felt Gareth come up behind her.

"Charming!"

Had she walked in her sleep? Gareth's name had been obliterated in a frenzy of heavy lines. Worse, Marian's name had been written again in ornate script and underlined with a flourish. She gulped down her fright.

"I take it from this that you don't want me to move in," he said.

Marian hesitated. "No–oh, no, I mean..." Was this his way of finding out? She swallowed. She was not ready.

He smiled. "Don't look so worried. One step at a time, remember?" He kissed her cheek.

"But..." she protested to his back as he claimed the bathroom. She stared at the wall for a moment, then began to rummage under the kitchen sink. When Gareth emerged, rubbing his hair with a towel, he found Marian scrubbing at the offending scribble.

He gently caught her arm. "It was only a joke."

She turned on him. "What was?"

He held up his hands in defense. "About moving in."

She relaxed and resumed scrubbing. Half the first 'Marian' had disappeared. The thought made her shudder.

"Look," Gareth tried again to stop her. "You were going to decorate anyway. Why not go out today and buy some paint? I'll help you with it tomorrow."

She nodded, but after he had left for work she picked up the cloth once more, determined to scour away the graffiti. The faded letters suggested that she, too, was fading. There was no way that she was going to give in to such a superstition—this was a new start. As she scrubbed, her anger grew. It must have been Gareth. How could he mock her? Two broken fingernails and half a bottle of cleaning fluid later she felt better. The writing was gone.

Marian spent the afternoon trailing around do-it-yourself stores looking at color charts and friezes. Returning laden with brushes and paint pots, she grasped the lounge door-handle and glared closely at the walls with teeth set.

"Ridiculous!" she told herself.

That night, Marian's feeling of melting away was not so strong. She concentrated on tracing the contours of Gareth's back and wrapped her legs around him, inhaling the warm reality of him with each breath. She was here, in her bedroom making love in her flat. She existed—and more, another human being loved her. When she closed her eyes, she imagined the lounge washed in Mediterranean

Dawn, the paint bathing the room and all within it in the glowing promise of a new morning.

As good as his word, Gareth set to work with the paintbrush the following day. He had already covered two walls by the time Marian brought him lunch, including the one with the fireplace.

"How's it going?" she asked.

He surveyed his work. "It'll need another coat. Whatever you wrote on it with, it's a devil to cover."

"What I wrote on the wall with?" Marian almost choked on her sandwich. She got up to take a closer look. Shadowy traces of her name could be seen under the new paint. "I don't understand."

Gareth pulled a face.

"It wasn't me," Marian blurted. She was sure the lettering was clearer than it had been.

"Oh, no? Who was it then? Santa Claus?"

"Honestly, Gareth."

"Hmm...I think you'd better clear the lunch things and let me get back to work, or I might just have to wring a confession out of you with this paintbrush." He waved it at her like a sword and shooed her from the room. When he let her back in, the evening sunshine dusted the walls with a haze of pollen yellow.

"Oh, Gareth!" She threw her arms around his neck, careless of the paint spatters on his shirt. The tears that still threatened to choke her at the slightest emotion flooded her eyes. Despite the blurry view, the room was everything she had hoped. Even the atmosphere had been transformed. The hint of a threat was now an invitation to linger. Throughout the evening she could not stop looking at it. "It's perfect."

Gareth laughed. "Come to bed, it'll still be here tomorrow, and I won't be."

Her heart thumped.

"I've got to go to that stupid conference, remember?"

"I don't want you to go."

He put his arm around her. "It's only for a week."

She heard an unspoken "It'll be good for you."

"Let's make the most of tonight." He took her hands and knelt pulling her with him.

"Not here." She felt a surge of alarm and her gaze flicked to the walls.

"Why not?"

She shrugged, pulling away. "Because…" She tried to inject a promise into the word. It was enough to make him follow her to the bedroom.

Marian rose early, heading straight for the shower where she stood absorbing the tingle of the spray, remembering how once she would have been in danger of washing away in the downpour. She was changing, that was true. But what—who—was she becoming? Without Gareth, would she trickle away with the hot water? Maybe Gareth was right and a week away from each other would do her good. He was already in the lounge when she emerged. She noticed the tension in his stance first. He stood with arms folded like her teacher or supervisor when she had got her work wrong again, stiff with outrage.

"Well?" Gareth said.

"What?" Marian followed his gaze to the wall above the mantel. For a moment the room went dark, and she could not tell whether she was still standing or whether she had sunk through the floor.

"I didn't do it," she managed to whisper. Scarring the warmth of fresh paint were renderings of her name, at least half a dozen of them. She approached the mantel, stretching out her hand with fingertips hesitating over the letters: they were like cries and shouts, hesitant in places, scrawled as if in desperation, deep and indignant.

"Go ahead, touch it, it won't smudge!"

"Honestly, Gareth, it wasn't me," she pleaded with her whole being—the child seeking to avoid her mother's slap, the office junior facing her bullying employer.

"Forgive me if I don't find your joke very amusing!" He turned on his heel forcing her to follow him.

"I don't know how it got there."

He grabbed her shoulders. "Look, you have to decide. Do you want to get well? No one else can do it for you." He let go of her and began gathering his things together.

Marian stood at the door watching, her hand to her cheek as if feeling the blow she had hoped to avoid.

"But it wasn't me, unless..." Unless she really had sleepwalked, but she had not dreamed of writing. Unless she was losing herself more surely than dying.

"I'm not mad."

"I didn't say you were." Gareth brushed past her heading for the front door.

Marian caught his arm. "Don't go."

He hesitated, then sighed. "I'll call you." He planted a kiss on her forehead and was gone.

She wandered through to the lounge and sank onto the floor with her back against the wall and her knees drawn up in front of her. She stared at the writing. Could she have done it? If it was not Gareth, she must have—who else was there? The thought made her scan the room quickly as if she might see a figure lurking in a corner or half-hidden by the curtains. Her eyes grew tired, so that the lines began to waver and her legs cramped, but still she sat there. Nothing changed. No new names appeared; none vanished. She was disintegrating and soaking into the emotional lettering. Finally, her discomfort forced her to move. Something caught her eye in the corner of the room near the ceiling. She felt a surge of shock.

"Please let it be a spider."

The black smudge did not move. She went closer. It was no insect. She dragged over a chair on which to stand. It was her name printed in small, tidy letters. There was no way that she could have reached that high up the wall, but Gareth could. She sat heavily in the chair, suddenly queasy.

"Why?" she wailed at the empty room.

Maybe it was some game designed to keep her unstable and

dependent. The thought sent her running to the bathroom retching up her fear. She would not believe it, not until she had shown Gareth the evidence of his treachery. Marian approached the lounge once more, pushing open the door with hesitant fingertips. Her name marched across the wall opposite the fireplace in huge angry letters. Around it were numerous other versions, like flies clustered about a corpse. She forced herself to go closer. She swung around. Someone else had been there while she was in the bathroom—might still be in the apartment now. She stood listening until her throat ached with the effort of keeping silent. She tiptoed from room to room, flinging back the doors to hit anyone hiding behind them. There was nothing, not even the smell of unfamiliar aftershave, nothing but the sense that the apartment had been invaded; that her life had been defiled, like the pristine walls. She checked all the windows. Everything was locked, and only she and Gareth had keys.

Gareth! He had left her a contact number. She picked up the phone, but let the receiver slip from her fingers before she had finished dialing. There had been scribbles on the walls when she had looked the flat over, but low down, so that she had readily believed the previous occupant's explanation that it was the work of her two-year-old. Marian struggled to remember. Had that been a name? She had been too thrilled then at the prospect of having her own home to notice. She bit back the urge to shout out. Why was this happening? What did whoever or whatever it was want? She backed over the threshold and pulled the door shut. She could manage without a lounge.

For the next few days, the door stayed firmly closed. Marian rigged a thread to the handle so that if anyone went in or out she would know. It remained undisturbed, yet the feeling that something was waiting for her inside the room grew. Every time she passed the door she found herself listening for the scrabbling noises of pens writing or to see the handle begin to turn. By the end of the week, the room haunted Marian, filling her waking thoughts with repetitions of her name—sighed and whispered, scrawled and hissed—until she wanted to clamp her hands over her ears. In her sleep, the words appeared with the rasping sound of chalk on a blackboard, and her hands and shoulders ached with the effort of so much writing. Still, she was determined she would not enter the lounge, afraid it would let her affliction spread as much as of what she would find there. As long as the thread remained intact, whatever her dreams might show, she knew she was innocent.

The night before Gareth was due to return, Marian's heart beat so loudly that she could not think for the sound of it. She lay in bed trying to focus on the rain spilling against her window. It took her back to the streets where she wandered, unsure of what she was looking for until she reached the river. She took a piece of paper from her pocket. It had her name written on it. She crumpled it and was about to throw it into the river when she heard footsteps behind her. Marian knew if she turned she would see Gareth and he would prevent her throwing the paper away, but it had to go. There was no other way to be free. She watched the paper uncurl like a blossom opening and float away. She smiled and opened her eyes to see Gareth smiling back at her.

"Sleepyhead! I can see you haven't missed me."

"How long have you been here?" Marian sat up. "You haven't been in the lounge?"

"No, I've only just got here." His voice followed her through to the hall. The thread was intact.

"I've something to show you." She threw open the door and stood back.

Gareth walked in as she watched. He turned and shrugged. "You painted over your scribble."

Marian stepped over the threshold. "It's gone." She turned from wall to wall.

"Okay, if that's all, can I make some coffee?" He left the room without waiting for an answer.

Marian stretched herself along the walls with palms flat trying to feel the letters that were no longer visible.

"Why?" she whispered. "Why are you doing this? Why don't you answer?"

There was a way, perhaps. She rummaged in the drawer. The felt tip squeaked its accompaniment as she demanded. "Who are you?"

"Did you say somethi—" Gareth stopped in the doorway, his eyes fixed on the pen in her hand. Then he shook his head. "That's it. No more, Marian, I've had enough."

He turned.

"No! It's not what you think." The front door slammed a full stop on her plea. Marian crumpled, huddled in a corner of the lounge with her head in her hands. Beneath the question on the wall, in smooth rhythmic letters, a name began to form.

K.S. Dearsley's stories, poetry and flash fiction have appeared on both sides of the Atlantic, and her fantasy novels are available from Smashwords and Amazon. She has a MA in Linguistics and Literature and has always been fascinated by language. When she isn't writing she lets her dogs take her for walks.

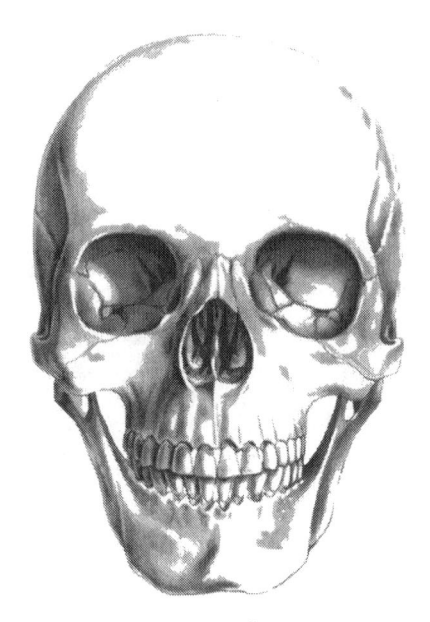

Complete

Amanda Northrup Mays

She's back, with her designer knock-off suits and fake laugh. What's she brought this time—a yuppie couple looking to get away from the city? A tired mom, distant dad, and three annoying brat kids? She never brings me anyone I could live with. She brushes her blond hair over her shoulder—she wears it down in an attempt to look more approachable, friendly. She glares up at me; she hates me as much as I despise her. A faux smile she must practice in the mirror each night replaces the scowl as her latest offerings exit the car. First is a man with dark slacks and white shirt. He surveys his surroundings with a critical eye as he tugs on his tie. My overgrown lawn and barren trees displease him. The neighbor children have left the yard to my right littered with toys. The neighbors on the left never pull their trash can back from the curb, and it has fallen over, spilling stray beer cans onto the sidewalk. The man's nose crinkles as he turns his eyes to me.

I am about to barricade the door, to refuse them entrance, when you emerge from the car. You are so unlike them, with your jeans and hooded sweater. Even at a distance, I can sense you are different from anyone the agent has brought me before. You examine the yard, but the dead trees and bushes don't disgust you. You can see how beautiful they'll be when they bloom again. You notice the cracks in the walk, the missing sections of gingerbread trim, how my porch leans just a little, but you don't grimace or sneer. Do you find it all quaint? You look up then, and I experience something I haven't felt in countless years. The darkness that has filled me for so long retreats, chased away by your unspoken promise. With that simple look, my world shifts. You see me. You see my essence.

I will let you in. You may wander my halls.

The agent approaches my door, fumbles with my lock. You move to stand beside the man, watching him watch me. You are much shorter than he is, much younger looking. His daughter? No. You look nothing alike. And the way he places his arm around you and leads you up my steps is anything but fatherly. Surely you're not his wife. Why would you marry someone so obviously your opposite? We will have to dispose of him once you move in.

The agent uses a familiar flourish as she swings open my door. Her heels click on the foyer tile as she beckons to you. The man motions you in and you obey. Your entrance makes me sigh. Immediately I can smell you, taste you. Vanilla. Toasted coconut. The smell of joy. I inhale you so deeply that all three of you notice.

"That wasn't a draft. Old houses like to settle," the agent says with a fake laugh. "All the windows are sealed tightly." She launches into her welcome spiel, but you ignore her. You leave her and your companion in the foyer and step into the den. You move around the room slowly, trailing your fingers along my walls. Do you like the feel of the textured wallpaper? I do. The diamond on your left hand catches the light from overhead and sparkles. So he is your husband.

Why? I can already tell you have nothing in common. You and I, we are the same. I know it.

You move from the den to the dining room, murmur over the dusty chandelier. You move to the kitchen, where the agent and your man catch you admiring my gray marble counters. I long to see you in your robe, fixing your morning coffee here. Do you cover your mouth daintily when you yawn or do you express your sleepiness with a full bodied grunt? The man wants to know if the range is gas or electric. You leave them to discuss the water heater and step into the breakfast nook. Sunlight pours in through the windowed walls and dances in your black hair. I want an eternity of that sight.

From there you move into the living room. Then to the downstairs bathroom. You will sing in the shower; you have the air of a shower singer. I will bang my pipes and thump my walls for your background music. Perhaps I will be able to persuade you to sing outside the shower as well, and your voice will fill every one of my rooms.

The man and the agent speak of the roof as you lead them upstairs. You are too busy enjoying my oak woodwork to pay them any attention. Isn't it beautiful? It was hand carved, that banister. I want it to be yours. I want to test myself, to see if I can judge your mood from your grip alone.

Your man raps the banister with his knuckles, rubs it. I shudder at his rough, uncaring hands. How can you stand his touch? It can't be pleasurable.

"It really is a very solid house," the agent says. Your man nods, distracted by the way you glide from room to room, as though you already belong. Of course, you have enchanted me as well. You gasp at the size of the master bedroom, the attached bathroom. The clawfooted tub will be your perfect oasis after a stressful day. There is a bay window that faces the park a few blocks away. When the trees are bare in the winter, we will be able to watch children play in the snow there. I will keep the frigid air from seeping around the windows as you perch on the bench.

You move to the back bedroom, my favorite room. The original fireplace is still there though the last owners painted it a light gray. I hated it at first, thought they had ruined it. Over the years I have grown to love it, and I can tell you do too. You rest your hand on the mantle and gaze around the room. What will you make it? Not a child's room. A child wouldn't appreciate the workmanship of the fireplace. A child would turn its crayons to the bricks and ruin them. A study perhaps? The crackling of a fire is a lovely accompaniment to reading. I will keep the flames burning high as you lose yourself in distant lands and magical stories.

Your man and the agent follow you from room to room. She rattles off useless facts, he pretends to be interested. You ignore them both. You are communicating with me even though your lips never part. You want me as much as I want you. You want them to leave so we can be alone. I can make that happen. I can destroy them both, but I sense you do care about the man so I will not harm him yet.

You find the door to my attic and the agent tries to dissuade you from opening it. There's nothing up there, she says, just empty space for storage. Your man wants to check the state of the insulation heads through the door. I hold my breath as you climb the stairs.

Here on the uppermost level I am raw, my rafters bare and my boards exposed. I am completely overcome by your presence. Your flavor blocks your husband's obnoxious man-smell and covers the agent's cloying flower odor. Each breath you expel fills me with a joy I haven't known for such a long time. I'd almost forgotten what this feels like, this feeling of hope. He says the attic would make a perfect office with just a little work. You say you wouldn't touch it, that the space needs to be left alone. He turns away and scoffs at you.

The agent's cell phone chimes and she pulls it out of her jacket pocket. She flips it open and mimes recognizing the number. "I'm sorry," she tells you. "I have to take this." She hurries from the attic, speaking into the phone. She pretends it's her daughter's school but she doesn't have children, and there's no one on the other end of the conversation. She has the phone set to ring at a certain time, her trick to give potential buyers time to talk in private.

"Well this was a complete waste of time," your man says at the same time you say, "I want it."

"You really want to live in this dump?" he asks.

"It's not a dump. How can you not love this house?"

He sighs and lets his shoulders slump, reacting to you as parents react to annoying children. "Think of how much work this place is going to need," he says slowly. "All the painting, putting down carpet or getting the floors sanded and refinished. The front porch is going to need torn down and replaced. The windows will eventually need to be redone. Might as well do it early."

"But she said the windows were perfectly sealed. And the house has charm. Lots and lots of charm."

The sigh again. My hatred for him grows. Say the word and I will annihilate him. "I thought we agreed no fixer-uppers. I can't take the extra time off work to make this place livable."

"It's fine just the way it is."

The tips of his ears and the back of his neck redden, his anger radiating from him. I must use all of my willpower to keep from throwing something at him, but you're used to his fits, and it doesn't affect you.

"There are a few things that need work, yes," you say. You use the same annoyed-yet-patient tone he used toward you. "But it's all little stuff that I can do while you're at work. I'm not completely helpless, you know?"

He shakes his head and turns away, heads for the stairs. "I'm not sinking my money into this dump. I refuse to live here."

"Then I'll live here by myself."

He stops. Turns back to you. You haven't moved from the middle of the attic. "Don't be stupid."

I want to collapse the roof on him, but that would kill you too so I resist the urge.

"I'm being completely serious," you say. "This is my house. I'd rather us live here together, but if you're going to be like this, I'll be more than happy to be alone. The house will keep me company."

"Now you're just being stupid." He stomps forward and grabs your arm. His fingers dig into your skin as he drags you away. As you lag behind him, I follow, trembling as your fingers caress my walls.

"See? Even the slightest wind makes this place shake," he says. "We are not living here."

"I am," you reply. "This is my house."

The agent meets you in the kitchen, that fake smile plastered on her lips again. She saw how your eyes sparkled as when she first opened my door, and she's excited, thinks you'll make an offer right now, that she'll finally be rid of me and will be able to concentrate on selling more valuable houses. "So? What do you think?" she asks. "It does need a little work, but nothing too major."

"We need to talk about a little more," your man says before you can speak.

The agent's smile falters. She glances at you and you look away. How nice of you not to contradict your husband in public. The agent hands your man a paper covered with facts and dates. He doesn't even glance at it as the two of you are ushered outside. The agent locks the door, and when she turns back to you, the smile is on her lips once again.

"It is best to sleep on a decision this big," she says.

"We'll let you know as soon as we make up our minds," your man says. "I think we'd like to see a couple more before we settle on one, though." The agent unlocks the car and slips behind the wheel. You stand in the brown grass, continue to stare up at me.

"Now, how about we head over to Richmond Drive and check out the house there?"

You slowly get into the backseat, your eyes never straying from me. As you drive away, you turn to watch me through the rear window, your face sad. You will return, though. You must. We have just shared something very special, realized we are one another's destiny. That is not a bond to ignore.

For several weeks after your departure, I am restless and giddy.

Amanda Northrup Mays

The mice that live in my basement sense the change in me and keep hidden. I shatter several light bulbs, make my front and back doors bang. The noise draws the attention of the neighbors, who peer through their curtains cautiously. Children stand on the sidewalk and tell each other stories. They say a tormented soul is making the ruckus and that if one were to actually step onto the property, the soul would follow them home. I wish I could tell them there is no tortured soul, only one finally set free.

Slowly, I settle down. The neighbors decide I am no longer a threat and stop staring through their windows. The children are no longer afraid and go back to walking through my backyard as a shortcut home from school. I fall into an anxious pattern, spending my days staring impatiently at the road. The agent brings three more couples and a family of four. I don't like any of them and slam my door behind them all. One of the kids sat in the dining room picking his nose while his parents followed the agent through me. He left his findings on the wall, near the windows. My door swatted his behind when he finally left the room.

Two months go by, and I begin to lose hope. Did you not mean what you said? Could you not bear to leave his rough hands? Have you let him talk you into another house? I weep to think of an eternity without you. My tears streak the walls and the paper bubbles. My sorrow leaves puddles on the tile and seeps into the carpet. My despair is so deep that the sag of the porch worsens.

Another month passes and then I do give up, certain you are gone forever. I hate you for letting him keep you away. He's no doubt forced you into some ugly modern box identical to the ugly modern boxes surrounding it. I imagine you thinking of me, of the connection that we shared. For a while you'll remember me, wonder what's become of me. You'll still dream of wandering through my halls as we share our histories. Eventually, though your new life will consume you and there will be no room for thoughts of me.

My walls shake with my rage at this realization. Several pieces of plaster and years of dust fall from the ceiling, the mantles. A window in the bedroom I chose for your library cracks, but it is not just a window; it is my heart breaking from your abandonment. How dare you leave me like this? You were here for a short time, but we shared so much. Why have you done this to me?

The snow comes, and while the weather is bitter, it cannot come close to matching the way I feel. When the agent brings people by, they wear thick coats and gloves and complain that it's colder within my walls than outside. They shiver and comment over the cracked window and fallen plaster, and the agent promises to find someone to make the repairs. She never does and for that I am thankful. They are the scars of your betrayal, and I don't want them healed. As she leaves each time, the agent sighs deeply. I know she wishes you'd come back, too. She wants to be rid of me. That she cannot sell me is a harsh blemish on her record.

I retreat to the attic, where the only windows are small and coated with thick layers of dirt and dust. Each time I hear the gravel crunch in my driveway, I am tempted to clear the dirt and peer out, but I never do. I have no desire see the outside world ever again. I know I could not stand the disappointment of seeing someone other than you step into my grass.

Today, when the gravel crunches beneath a vehicle, it sounds different. Only one car door slams and my curiosity threatens to overwhelm me. Am I getting a new owner? Is someone breaking in? Surely everyone knows I contain nothing of value. For an instant, I allow hope back into my shattered heart. Have you returned?

Familiar steps land on my porch and send shivers through my walls. I hold my breath. Can it be true? Have you really come back after all this time? Have you really chosen me over your brutish man?

Your gentle hand grips our door knob, and I can no longer control my excitement. It shoots through me, making you flinch as it jumps to you from the knob. You smile. You know what the shock means, that I've forgiven you for staying so long away. Your feet track snow into our foyer, and I quickly suck it through the cracks in the tiles so you don't slip. I breathe my happiness around you, warming the air. You close your eyes and inhale deeply as I shut our door behind you.

"Finally home," you say. I echo the sentiment. Our walls reverberate with the words.

You move to our living room, to the section of wall where the paper is peeling the worst. You place a hand beneath a curling strip, press your face against the yellowed paper. You breathe in the scent of ancient glue, the years of tobacco that stole the whiteness from the room. Your fingers trace the raised roses, and I tremble. As you press one of my tear stains, your brow creases. Yes, you caused that, but all is forgiven now.

"Finally home," you say again.

Our joyous reunion is interrupted by heavy knocking on the door. I growl and prepare to hurl the intruder from the porch. This is our time, and I want nothing to disturb us. You lay a reassuring hand on my wall, rub me until I am calm. You open the door for a trio of burly men, each of whom carries a piece of furniture. They smell of tobacco and sweat, not at all like your husband who smelled of aftershave and offices. I like them based on this alone and allow them inside.

Over the next several hours, you and the men bustle in and out, filling me with your belongings. I've been so long without furniture that at first, the heaviness is strange. My doors creak as they are shoved open. Boxes are piled against walls, and it takes me a few moments to grow accustomed to the feeling. My floors groan as the men shove your bed into place upstairs. The boards are already so scratched that the markings their carelessness makes are hardly noticed by your eyes. I, however, feel the fresh wounds and trip the man who caused them as he descends the stairs. You sense what I've done and chastise me with a look. I promise to behave for the rest of their stay.

I turn my attention to you instead as you direct the flow of boxes. You do this so effortlessly that I realize you've been planning the arrangement of your things for quite some time. I notice that you no longer wear the diamond on your left hand and am overcome with happiness anew. You left your husband for me after all. You are so changed now that you are without his influence. He kept you quiet and cowed but now you ooze confidence. Your back is straighter, your movements more sure. You seem a different woman, but you are still perfect. Still perfect for me.

Eventually, the men leave us, and I lock our doors and windows against the world. You glide from room to room, making sure the movers placed your belongings as you instructed and that they have not damaged me. You stifle a yawn with the back of your hand and for the first time, I notice how weary you seem. The past three months have taken as much a toll on you as they have on me. I turn on the water in the master bathroom, and you give a start at the sudden noise. It takes you a moment to realize what I've done and when you do, you smile your thanks.

It has been a very long time since I've had reason to draw a bath for someone and I have misjudged the temperature. You gasp as you step into the too-hot water. I could cool it for you. I should. But the heat will soothe your muscles, and it enhances your scent so much. The water draws the sweat from your body, creates a broth as you soak. I can taste you through the porcelain of the tub, and you are sweeter than anything I have ever imagined. When you are finished with your bath, I steal the water from the drain, hungry for more of you.

A short time later, you turn off my lights and slip into bed. I watch as you drift away to sleep, curious to know your dreams. Will they be of me, of our future? Or will you dream of the life you left when you turned your back on your husband? Your breathing becomes regular almost immediately, and while I usually pass my nights in slumber as well, I find I am too anxious to sleep. I do not want to miss a moment of your life from this point forward, and there are so many moments I would miss if I slept.

You are an early riser, I learn. The sun is still low in the sky when you emerge from your dreams and dress. I want to spend the day learning of your past, but you set about tearing down the peeling wallpaper as soon as you've downed a mug of coffee. We pass the morning in the living room, where you've covered the floor with a paint-stained drop cloth. You plug in a radio and sing along as you rid the walls of paper, using a hand-held steamer to loosen the difficult pieces. I help by curling the paper near the high ceiling. You've brought a ladder, but it is old and looks precarious. I do not want you to fall and leave me so soon.

After a small lunch break, you move to the den. There is not much paper left on the walls here, and you make quick work of the room. You mention that you'll soon hire someone to patch the drywall and plaster and a team of painters to finish the rooms. I do not like the idea of so many more people trampling through me, but I know there is no other choice. As you gather the drop cloth, I lose control for a second and use a strip of the discarded wall covering to give you a deep paper cut. You drop the cloth and cry out. You blood drips to the floor, and I suck it through the boards greedily. Your blood is so much more delicious than your bath water.

For the next several days, I watch as you rid our walls of stained paper and steal several more tastes of your blood through paper cuts. You tend to the loose trim, hammering wayward baseboards into place. I reach out with the occasional nail, earning not only some of your blood but a taste of your flesh as well. I hungrily grab the stray hair that falls from your ponytail and gobble it up. Even beneath the fruity shampoo, I taste you.

Your husband pays us a visit one day while you are working in the downstairs powder room. I silence the doorbell, deaden the sound of his fist so you won't be disturbed. He pounds against the door until it shakes in its frame, but I keep the sound in the foyer. I never want him inside me again. He glances at your car in the driveway, and I can feel his anger through the door. He knows you are inside, thinks you are ignoring him. He makes a trip around our yard, shouting at each of the windows, banging on the back door. I absorb all of these sounds as well. You do not need distractions, especially from him. He continues to yell and by the time he has returned to the front porch, several of our neighbors are peering through their windows. Your husband again attacks the door. He grabs the knob, adjusts his stance; he's going to try breaking the door in.

For a moment, my lights blink out. You are startled out of your creative trance, but I know that if you knew who was on the porch, you'd forgive the interruption. I direct every bit of my energy at the door, and when your husband's shoulder meets the wood, the shock sends him flying from the porch. He lands halfway to the sidewalk and stares up at me, dumbfounded. He slowly pushes himself to his feet and heads back to his car, mumbling about the two of us. There is so much more that I could do to him but I let him go. The joy I would get from killing him is no joy at all compared to the feeling watching you provides. So instead, I rejoin you in the powder room and watch in amazement as your slender hands create a beautiful mosaic from the mess of broken tiles.

As our first week together reaches its end, you decide it's time for the workers you promised. They come in waves, men to repair my walls, men to paint them. Men to replace windows, including the one in the library. Men to carpet a few of our rooms. Some of them comment on the state of our porch, say that it should be fixed as soon as possible. You smile politely and tell them that you plan on having it done as soon as the ground hardens after the thaw. This seems to appease them, and the porch is not brought up again. I soon have the misfortune of tasting some of the less cautious workers, those who fall against nails or jagged trim, one who sliced the heel of his palm on a broken window. They taste disgusting, and I recoil from them, shudder as their blood flows through me. The sudden movement startles the men. You assure them it is the land settling beneath me and while some of the glances they cast clearly say they think you're crazy, my rumblings are pushed aside with the porch.

It takes two weeks for the waves of men to complete all the tasks you assigned them. I am filled with the smells of fresh paint, carpet adhesive, and man sweat. I throw open my windows and let the breeze chase away the odors. As the air clears, I help you arrange the furniture, moving the heavier pieces at your direction, scooting other pieces to locations I like better. We work as a team and by the end of the night, we have most of your trinkets unpacked. As the first hint of pink begins to stain the sky, you crawl into bed for a few hours of sleep. You awaken at noon to find that I have discarded the boxes, arranged your belongings in a way that I desperately hope pleases you.

Your smile never falters as you roam from room to room, examining items you'd forgotten owning. You mention that your husband never let you display many of the things from your childhood, stating that his house was too sophisticated for such juvenile things. But I am your house, and you can be as childish as you like within my walls.

You pass the day pressing your hands, your cheek, against me in various places, learning the tales of the walls, the woodwork. You meet the family who built me, the family who kept their youngest daughter chained in my attic. You see several deaths, twice as many births. You meet the happy families and the ones who constantly fought. As I tell you my stories, I also learn yours. I learn of the mother you lost at a young age, the father who drunk smelly things from brown paper bags. You introduce me to your husband, and I don't like him any better through your eyes. Your life will be much improved without him in it.

As the day draws to a close, you sense changes happening in my core. They frighten you at first, but I reassure you, calm you with a gentle swaying. The sun's light dies, and while our neighbors switch on their lamps, we remain in darkness. You have sunken to the floor, leaning against the basement door. I caress your cheek, pull you away to the boy who burned in the coal stove downstairs. A glimmer of light sparks to life near the foyer, and I direct your attention there. You stand slowly and move toward the light. You want to be afraid of it, but I keep you calm as you climb the stairs. You use the banister to lead yourself up. The men polished it and even though it is now covered with protective sealant, the years of tobacco absorbed by the wood are still noticeable.

My light leads you to the library. We've already spent many evenings here, you tucked into an afghan as you read, me giving the impression of a fire as we have not collected actual firewood yet. Now when I open the door, you sense a change in the room. It was warm, welcoming. Now there is a sense of reverence to the chamber. This is no longer your reading room; this is someplace much more important, and you undress in the hallway. You fold your clothes carefully, leave them in the hall. You cross the threshold, and I ease the door closed behind you.

For a moment you are lost, and then I guide you to the fireplace. You kneel at the hearth. You grab handfuls of ash and rub the remains of dead fires into your skin. You move slowly, savoring the feeling, taking into your being every fire that ever burned there. When you are completely covered in the soot, I guide you to the center of the room. You lie down, press your hands against the cold wood.

I give you a moment to adjust to the coolness of the room, and then I inhale you.

It startles you, that first breath I take. Your skin pricks as I begin to pull it between the planks in our floor. I whisper soothing words to you, tell you that this is how we were meant to be. You relax, and I reach through the boards, open your skin along your spine. You scream; I muffle the sound to protect us from the neighbors. I enter you through the wound tentatively, testing your reaction. The muscles in your back burn as I shred them to make our joining easier. I crumble your bones and feel your pain. Each time you scream I pause, whisper soothing words to you until you are calm once more. More muscles and bones liquefy and this time you hold your screams back by grinding your teeth until they are pulverized and trickle down your collapsing throat. Your skin tears and the mush I've made of your insides seeps out. I suck it between the boards, sip the blood that tries to escape to the corners of our room. You take one last glimpse of our freshly painted ceiling, then your eyes bulge, pop, and join the rest of you on your journey through the boards.

Though there was pain, there was no fear in our joining. You come readily to me as I welcome you to your new life. You are a part of me now and together we will wait. Eventually, a new agent will begin to bring us new families, and we will find another perfect soul. We will call to them, connect with them just as I connected with you. We will bring them into ourselves, make them a part of us. We will do this as long as it takes, collect as many pieces as we need, until we are complete at last.

Amanda Northup Mays began creating scary stories when she was four and caused countless nightmares for the other children in her neighborhood. She currently lives in West Virginia with her husband and their four-legged kids.

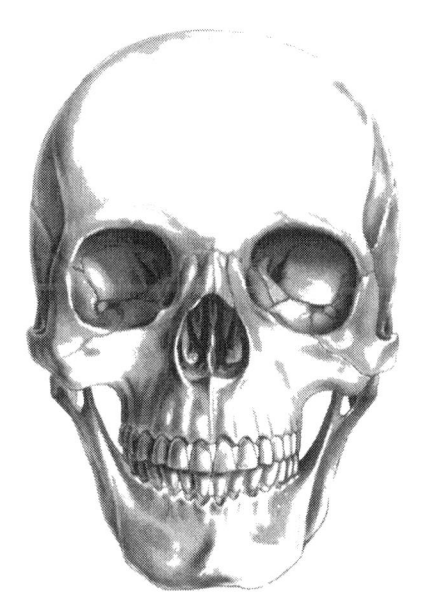

Ellensburg Blue

M.J. Sydney

I imagine the town locals invisible and non-existent as they pass me on Saint Bernard Street, staring at me, giving me that look. Heads shake in disbelief, or maybe pity. To some, I am not even here. They look on, and I am the invisible one. They think I don't see them, but I do. I hear their silent whispers of disdain, muttered amongst themselves as I walk by. I can't blame them. Even the real estate agent thought I was pulling a prank when I told him I wanted to purchase the old Waters' property.

I've never had someone laugh at me for five minutes straight before. He laughed so hard he choked on his own breath. I think it was my silence and lack of joining in on the charade that replaced his cackling with a horrified look of astonishment. His voice trembled for the next hour and a half as he recounted every rumor and story that had surfaced since 1997. His eyes sunk deeper with the signing of the papers but the deal was done.

"That property is plagued with evil," he told me.

A hoax. It's all a hoax. I slip in through the open door of Tony's Hardware and easily find everything I'm looking for. Small family run shops always have everything right there on the shelf where you'd expect. Not like walking into McLendon's or Home Depot. I talked to Tony yesterday, and he agreed to deliver all the lumber, bricks, shingles and paint so that just leaves a few basics: nails, hammer, staple gun, screws, screwdrivers, putty, plaster, window sealant, paintbrushes, broom, mop, shovel, and four boxes of trash bags.

The man behind the counter, arms folded across his chest, watches me skeptically as I pull the yellow notepad from my back pocket and make some notes. His voice doesn't make a sound, but his eyes speak loud and clear. *Don't even think about running out that door*, they say, contemplating who I am and if I have the money to pay for all this.

"You must be Walter Melbrook. I wasn't expectin' to see you here today." I recognize the stern voice from behind the counter.

"I told you yesterday when we spoke on the phone I'd be here. And I'm here."

"Just we don't get many people around here showing interest in the old Waters' place. With all the rumors and such. Hard to believe some out-of-towner just up and bought the place, ya know?"

"Well believe it. I did. And it's in bad shape. Doesn't look like anyone's been in that house since Waters himself left."

"Damn good reasons for that too, mister. You sure you know what you've gotten into? No one here'd blame you if you changed your mind and ran the other way."

"It'll be a nice place once I'm done with it. Here, I've added a few more things to the list. How soon can you have them out there?" Tony's arms loosen up, and he almost cracks a smile as I tear the top sheet off the notepad and hand it to him. I can't tell if he's amused by the situation or thinks he successfully scared me off.

"Same as I told you yesterday. I'll deliver everything by tomorrow afternoon if you're still here. You sure you're still gonna be here?"

"I'm sure," I nod, slapping thirty-five fifty dollar bills on the counter, the hint of sarcasm in my voice surprises us both.

Tony's head tilts, eyes squinting down at the pile of Grants on the counter. In less than a blink, he raises both eyebrows, darting eyes pierce through my skull and his mouth twists into a sour lemon pucker.

"That's quite a load of cash to be carryin' around."

I barely hear his voice. *Where'd you get that? You rob a bank? Selling drugs? You kill someone?* His eyes speak louder than his voice.

"I don't like banks." More sarcasm. Not that I want to give Tony any more reason to be wary of my intentions in this town, but I'm damn tired of everyone questioning me. Let me go about my business and leave me alone. That's why I moved out here.

I can't help but notice the slight trembling in his hands as he places the bills securely in the register, coming back with two one dollar bills, three quarters, a nickel and four pennies. I slide the change into my back pocket with the notepad, tell him thank you and I'll see him tomorrow. As I open the door, the sound of cowbells clank against the handle, followed by Tony's voice from behind the counter.

"One more thing," he starts, pausing long enough to make sure I hear him. "You'll have to unload this stuff yourself. I won't be subjecting myself to no Goatman's curse or moon-shining ghosts."

Back at the house, I open the third box of trash bags, having gone through the other two boxes. With so much work to be done, there's no sense in waiting until tomorrow for Tony to bring the rest of my supplies. Rotten food, broken dishes, mildew-stained books, torn clothing, moth-eaten blankets, something that appears to have once been a rat or maybe a squirrel. There's nothing worth keeping. The broken floorboards, termite-infested wood, rat-gnawed furniture and most everything else, I heap into a pile out back. It's tempting to set fire to the whole mess now rather than wait on Tony for the bricks, but the need for sleep wins.

The old army tent from the shack out back serves me well. Despite the condition of the house and obvious neglect of the property, the little shack is in great shape aside from the musty smell that comes from having everything locked up for so many years. Sleep doesn't come easy—the glaring looks from the townspeople are permanently imprinted on my eyelids. The lullaby of their whispering voices finally sings me to sleep, but I couldn't tell you what time. The next thing I hear is the screaming of a car horn telling me Tony arrived just as promised—although he's earlier than I expected.

I pull on my overalls and work boots, wishing I had remembered to buy a coffee pot while I was in town yesterday.

"This is as far as I go, mister," Tony calls to me from the bottom of the long driveway, engine still running. Through the partially rolled-down window of the old truck, his eyes dart around in every direction. It's an amusing sight to wake up to—he looks as if he's expecting something to jump out and drag him underground. Tony keeps that look on his face for most of the day, sitting there in silence while I soak myself in sweat unloading the truck, carrying bricks and lumber up what feels like a mile-long driveway by midday.

"You about done here? I want to get outta here before dark, and I gotta piss something fierce."

Get off your ass and help, you lazy bastard. I nod, unloading the last of the bricks, laying them out at the end of the driveway. Tony is losing his patience, and I don't want to say something I might regret later in case I need him again. I thank him, and he tells me to call him if I needed anything else brought out to the house. I doubt he means it, but I thank him all the same.

I spend the next week fixing leaks in the roof, replacing rotted out floorboards in the bedroom and burning rat-infested mattresses, along with everything else in the heap out back. The night air is still warm, and I don't mind sleeping with the fire pit smoldering through the night, but I miss the firmness of a mattress lined with cool sheets and covered with warm blankets. With the bedroom finished, I spend the next week completely gutting out the kitchen, ripping out the leftover remnants of carpet throughout the house and wishing it were Wednesday already so I can sleep in a warm bed and eat something other than freeze-dried rubber.

The moving truck arrives early in the afternoon, and I'm already covered in paint. Again, I'm forced to unload the truck myself. The delivery men aren't even from this town but say they've heard enough rumors to know better than to even think about setting foot up here. As I'm moving furniture and unloading boxes, I realize the two men sitting in the truck are intent on freaking each other out with the stories they've heard about the property.

I've come to the conclusion that the people around here are all crazy, no matter where they come from. Tales of the Goatman and moon-shining ghosts and dead animals coming back to life—nothing but ridiculous superstition. Hoaxes. How can anyone believe such nonsense? No doubt, a strangeness has come to haunt this town over the last fifty years. It's the townspeople themselves that have gone mad, not some mysterious hole that never existed.

A few minutes before midnight, I sprawl out in bed for the first time in two weeks. Sleep isn't coming as I intended. My mind has other plans. As I lay here staring into the darkness on the ceiling, my body relaxes and soaks in the coolness of the sheets while my mind focuses on Mel Waters and The Hole.

I can hear Art Bell talking to Mel Waters on the Coast to Coast AM Radio back in 1997, but that's not what keeps me awake. The realtor and Tony both offered to let me listen to the recordings, but I told them I had no interest in a fifty-year-old talk show. It's the words of the locals and the visions forming and floating overhead that keep me awake.

"That hole has magical powers, you know."

"That old German gun they found in the dirt by the hole don't even make a sound."

"They say if you set the gun next to a radio, it replays ancient broadcasts."

Magical powers, right. And a 1943 Roosevelt dime—they didn't even make those until 1946. I smiled at the thought of the old woman claiming the gun and dimes were the result of an alternate reality in which the Nazis won the war and created the dimes in Berlin.

Less amusing are the visions forming in the shadows on the ceiling—the hunter's dead dog, the Goatman, moon-shining, mine shafts, lava tubes, civil war slaves, roadblocks and Waters with his IV scars, surgical tape residue, and missing molars. *And what about the Ellensburg Blue Agate, does it even exist anymore?*

My feet involuntarily slide off the side of the bed as I glance at my watch, illuminated by the glow of the nearly full moon creeping in through the window. *3:00 am. Looks like I'm not sleeping tonight.*

Downstairs, my eyes fixate on the gallons of paint lined up against the wall while I wait for the coffee to brew. I grab a brush and hunch over a beige-colored bucket of paint, one hand gripped on the handle. A flash of light jerks me upright, and I spin towards the kitchen window. The bucket hits the cabinet and bounces to the floor.

"What the hell?" I barely notice the beige river flowing across the kitchen floor, mesmerized by the strange black light shining, seemingly, straight up from the ground. I must have grabbed the baseball bat I keep next to the kitchen door in case critters ever try to come inside. I don't remember picking it up, but there it is in my hand as I walk out the door barefoot.

As I walk through the field towards the other side of the property, I'm sure a slug squishes between my toes, or maybe it's a snake. I pay no attention to it as I move toward the black light, holding the bat steadily above my right shoulder. There it is. The light shines up from underneath a nine-foot wide metal lid, like a manhole cover—but not. Is that even a light?

My mind replays the stories of the old well on the property where locals threw garbage, abandoned vehicles, deceased pets and livestock, old tires, run-down appliances and damned if I know what else. No one ever mentioned anything about a light coming up out of it. I hadn't made it this far out on the property before tonight, but I suspect this is the well the locals used as a public dumping ground.

That's one hell of a large well. I creep closer to get a better look at the cover, but my legs are weighted to the ground. Can such a light even exist? It's black, almost like a void—a light of nothingness. Yet, there it is coming up through the ground and around the rim of the metal plate. And it's quiet. Too quiet. A complete absence of sound. As I move closer, the light shines brighter and darker. I can't look away, nor do I want to.

Squatting down close to the ground, right hand numb from gripping the bat, I reach my good arm out towards the rim of the metal plate. I sense something following me, watching me. My head whips around and I look over my left shoulder. Nothing there. I reach out farther. Warm air encircled in ice touches my fingertips as they brush against the metal.

The sound of breathing—no, not breathing, panting—and the steam of hot breath running down the back of my leg hits me. The black light vanishes, replaced by a red glow coming from behind me. Cranking my head around to the right, from my crouched position, my eyes lock on snarling teeth. Blood red eyes meet mine, glaring back at me. Our eyes lock together, seemingly forever.

With snarling teeth pressed against my leg and blurry vision, I try to refocus and break free from the hypnotizing red eyes. The bat swings itself at the snarling teeth as I jolt up and run towards the house, all in one motion. I'm not sure I'm running in the right direction, and I don't care. I just run. The slug squishes through my feet. I must be going the right way. The kitchen door. Did I leave it open? My feet slide across the beige paint on the kitchen floor as I fall on my ass and stumble to my knees. The door slams shut and deadbolts, rattling the cabinets as I push the stove against the door, slip in the paint again and slide down the side of the stove.

What the hell was that?

I'm sitting in a damn puddle of paint. Brought back to reality, I jump up to look for my bat. Damn, I must have dropped it. Where, I don't know. I look through the kitchen window, gazing out over the field. I dismiss the thought of boarding up the windows. The locals already think I'm crazy for buying this place. The black light is gone. No snarling teeth or red glow. Crickets chirp in the distance, and a light breeze passes by. Nothing unusual here. Must have imagined the whole damned thing. Sleep deprivation. Right, that's all it is.

The aroma of freshly brewed coffee fills the kitchen. It's tempting, but I dump it down the drain in favor of the homemade blackberry brandy my sister gave me last year. I've been saving it for a special occasion, and this is as special as they get.

Despite the night's events, I awake with the sun. The empty bottle of brandy sleeps on my pillow. I need answers, and if anyone can tell me what the hell is going on, it'll be Tony. He knows everything about this town's history and must have memorized every story and rumor ever told about this place. He's also the only person around here willing to carry on a conversation with me or even directly look at me. I decide to head over to the hardware store as soon as I find my bat. I can't imagine there'll be anything out there during the daylight, if there was anything out there at all, but I grab the knife off the kitchen counter just in case.

Everything appears just as it should be—there's no sign of anything happening out here last night. The grass in the field is undisturbed, no shining black light, the birds are happily chirping away. If it wasn't for the stove in front of the kitchen door, the spilled paint and missing bat, I would have thought I imagined the whole thing. Maybe I did. The bat isn't anywhere in the field—and neither is the manhole-covered well. Giving up the search, I head back to the house and notice the door to the shack is wide open.

Funny, I thought I locked that. It was no simple task locking up the shack, which required wrapping a large-link chain through the handle, around the side bar twice and back through the handle before clasping both ends together with the padlock. The chain dangled freely from the door handle with the open padlock hooked onto the last link.

With the padlock in my right hand, I use the left to wrap the chain. First through the handle, twice around the side bar and…a sharp, shooting pain stabs through the center my left hand. The padlock hit the ground with a "clink", landing on something other than grass. The skin in the center of my palm caught between the links, pinching hard enough to leave a nasty blood blister. I free my hand and reach for the padlock. Dull, scratched up metal stares back up at me, not from the padlock, but from my bat.

How? No. I don't want to know. With the lock in place, I grab the bat and head over to Tony's Hardware. Tony looks shocked to see me there. Was it the bat? The fact I was still here? The shop is empty this morning so I waste no time asking Tony to tell me everything he knows. He looks away, fiddling with something under the counter.

"Go talk to the crazy old witch lady on Fruitland Avenue."

"I'd rather talk to you. Seems to me you know everything about this town and—"

"Leave me out of it."

"Can you at least tell me where I—"

"You'll know when you see it. I ain't got nothin' else to say." Tony held the front door open. "Best be on your way now."

Tony shakes his head and closes the door behind me. The deadbolt slides into place. I stand there for a moment, ready to knock, wanting him to talk to me, or at least tell me who this witch person is and where she lives. Instead, I head down Fruitland Avenue.

Tony was right. The house is unmistakable. Skulls in various shapes and species, presumably all replicas, litter the lawn, which is more of an herb and weed garden than a lawn. Large oak trees cast shadows on the house. Wind chimes line the gutters and statues with piercing eyes keep guard. A few cats scurry under the front porch as I open the screen door and knock.

"Go away!" A scratchy voice from inside the house.

"My name is Walter Melbrook. I'd like to—"

"I know who you are. Go away!"

"Please, I'd just like to ask you a few questions."

"I can't help you. Now go or be cursed!"

"Look, something happened out there last night. A black light came out of the well and something tried to attack me. When I went out this morning, it was gone."

Silence from inside the house. The doorknob turns slowly, and the hinges creak as the door opens, just enough that I can see her beady eyes peeking through, staring at me through the screen. The woman standing before me isn't that old, but her hair has more rat nests than a horde of swamp rats, and her dress is made of torn rags tied together. She isn't ugly, but I can see why Tony called her the crazy witch.

She says nothing, but I have her attention. I recount every detail I can remember from last night, even slipping through the paint. I stop talking, and I'm not sure she even heard me. Her eyes dig deep into mine as if she's trying to pierce my heart, or maybe my soul, with her eyes.

"The Ellensburg Blue Agate is cursed."

"Cursed?"

"Shh..." A long bony finger presses against her lips and her eyes tell me if I open my mouth again, she'll shut the door. I give her a warm smile as if to apologize, and she continues.

"You see in the blackness what no one else sees. The powers of the stone are strong, but the curse is stronger. It feeds and grows. Its light calls you from the void. The stone has chosen you. Beware the beasts of the underground. They feed on the E-blue, their deadly teeth made from broken shards. You must stop the beasts before their final feeding. After will be too late, for they will release all that lives down in the bottomless hole."

I open my mouth to ask how in the hell I'm supposed to stop something that nearly turned me into a meal. What comes out of my mouth is more of a hissing, guttural *hhhhhh* sound trapped in my throat. The woman stands there, ready to slam the door in my face if I finish the word. Aware of the bat in my hand, I grip it tighter, suck in a deep breath and let her continue in silence.

"Go to the well when the light shines darkest. Remove the sphere and enter the void. Take with you a pickaxe. You must go alone. Find the mother agate and destroy it. Bring none to the surface." The door shut as if it never opened.

I take the long way back to the house, first stopping at Tony's Hardware to buy a pickaxe. The old lady sure sounded crazy, but I buy the pickaxe anyway. I don't have one so why not? I may have a use for it someday. I want to talk to Tony, but the kid standing behind the counter says he left due to a family emergency. The townspeople must really think I'm nuts now—walking down the street with an old baseball bat in one hand and a shiny new pickaxe in the other.

After scraping the beige paint off the kitchen floor, I busy myself painting for the rest of the afternoon and into the evening, trying not to think about the conversation with the witch-lady. Nevertheless, by nightfall, I'm spending more time looking out the damn kitchen window than painting. An hour before sunrise, I crawl in bed. For the next three days and nights, I paint and wait at the kitchen window. No shining black light. No snarling teeth. Just the sound of crickets singing in the wind under the star-lit sky.

Tuesday, more painting—outside this time. And I don't bother waiting tonight. I'm not even sure I saw it before, but I doubt I'll see it again. I paint all the trim on Wednesday. Not much left to do after that. I'll get to the bathrooms and deck tomorrow. Upstairs, I crawl into bed, sliding my hand under the pillow, feeling for the pickaxe. It's still there, and I fall asleep, fingertips rubbing the smooth wood handle.

An hour or two later, my whole body jerks awake and my eyes involuntarily open, staring up at the ceiling. It's quiet. No singing crickets. The wind is still. The moon and stars blackened by the night. I look around and see nothing. Grabbing the pickaxe, I feel my way to the door, down the stairs and into the kitchen. The black light glowing through the window is heavy and dark.

Its light calls you from the void. No, get out of my head! *The stone has chosen you. Go to the well…*

I don't know why, but I'm compelled to go, grabbing the bat on the way out. The light is there, shining darker than before, which means the well is there. My knuckles cramp against the bat and pickaxe, one in each hand. I can't let go, not that I want to, and my grip tightens. Last night's dinner threatens to regurgitate and the tennis ball in my throat strangles me, ready to burst open. I feel the hot breath encircled in ice against my legs. I hear the snarling. I see red. My head is dizzy from spinning in circles. There is nothing there, but I sense it. I feel it. I'm ready to swing at the beast from every direction. It won't catch me off guard again.

Remove the sphere... I bend down and reach out towards the manhole cover with the bat, my eyes unable to focus, waiting for snarling teeth to press against my leg. No snarling teeth. No glowing red eyes. Just quiet darkness, alone with the light. I force myself to move forward, lifting, pulling, pushing at the manhole cover. It doesn't budge. My hands tingle in the dark light, a warm sensation surrounded in ice moves through my veins. I know I should be scared, but it's peaceful and calming like a warm, candlelit bath. The bat and pickaxe slide out of my hands and gently rest at my feet.

With my body fully immersed in the black light, I push all my weight against the edge of the manhole cover. With little effort, the sphere—more like a half-moon that rolls like a sphere—spins then rolls off to the side of the well. Looking down, I see nothing but darkness, emptiness, nothingness.

And enter the void. I'd rather not, but I do.

I slide down on my ass, feet first into the hole. *Shit!* I spin around and reach for the edge. Dangling by my fingertips, I grab for anything within reach—the pickaxe. Kicking and swinging my feet, they hit nothing but air. If this thing has sides, they are nowhere near the ledge. It's too late to climb back up and my fingers slip, grabbing a handful of grass as I fall—no, float—down into the void.

I don't know how far I've fallen or how long I've been down here, staring into nothingness. I must be getting close. Blue agate lined walls appear, moving closer together as I glide further down the well. The stones glow with black light, surrounded by light blue and deep purple rays. A tingling numbness runs through my veins, and every pore fills with an icy warmth. A perfect utopia.

My feet stop me from continuing on the downward journey. I'm standing on a beach made entirely of Ellensburg Blue Agate shards and powdered stone, and I'm brought back to the reality of where I am. I turn on the balls of my feet, looking for a sense of which direction to go.

The mother stone is close. I can feel it. Panting hot breath surrounded by a layer of ice puffs against the back of my legs. I twist my body around. There's nothing there.

The panting moves up my legs, down my arms, around my chest and face. I hear a pack of snarling teeth somewhere in the distance. The pickaxe swings and whirls around into nothingness. The panting and snarling move in closer. The hot breath consumes me. I'm surrounded by hundreds of pairs of glowing red eyes.

"Nooooo!!" The pickaxe swings wildly—left, right, up, down, diagonally, in spirals and zigzags.

Walter's voice trails off, and the weapon falls into a pile of agate dust. The beasts eat their final meal, devouring Walter piece by piece, amputating the limbs first.

The beasts emerge from the well—cows, cats, dogs, chickens, rats, birds, horses, a llama, goatmen, moonshiners—snarling, showing off their E-blue agate teeth and glowing red eyes.

The phone rings at midnight.

"It's done, master. The beasts are free," a scratchy voice on the line proclaims.

"Very well, Maggie. Very well." Tony smiles as he hangs up the phone.

The crazy old witch lady balances the severed head in one hand, and with the other, pats her faithful companion on the head, blood dripping from its snarling, blue agate teeth.

M.J. Sydney

M.J. Sydney is an all-things weird and twisted, horror-thriller-chiller writer living with a vampire, a werewolf, a Mogwai and various fairies, gnomes and woodland creatures in the Pacific Northwest.

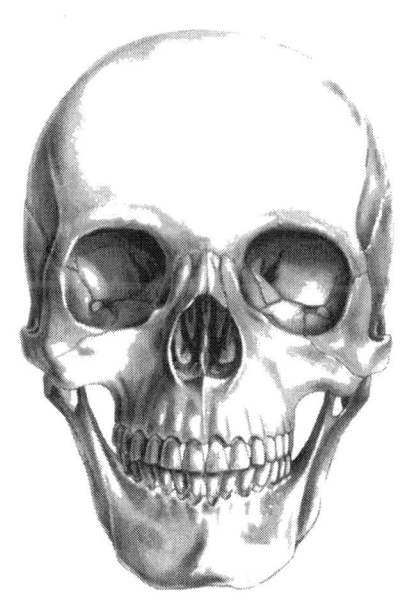

Abandoned

Rose Blackthorn

"This is just stupid."

Charlie happened to agree with his younger sister Ivy, but didn't say so.

"Look, it's going to be fine." Their mother Caroline kept her eyes on the narrow road. Pine trees covered in sweaters of vibrant green moss crowded close to the shoulders, overhanging the winding blacktop lane until they seemed to be driving through a tunnel. "No one is even going to care."

Ivy heaved a theatrical sigh and rolled her eyes.

Charlie watched out the window as they finally began to see buildings. First one, peeking out through the thick forest, then two or three together. It was almost a shock when they got into the town proper, and the pervasive growth of trees and delicate ferns fell back to reveal open sky.

Welcome to Blackwell, population 1128 was painted on a wooden sign at the side of the road. Ivy sighed again.

"Guess they're going to have to repaint it," Charlie said.

Caroline glanced at him with her brows crooked together.

"Now it's 1132," he explained.

Caroline laughed softly. She knew this was a huge change for her kids, and she knew neither of them was happy about it. It didn't help that the town they were moving to was the same as their last name. But her husband Terrence Blackwell had found a good job here and a house they could afford. They were all going to have to adjust and make the best of things.

Dropping down to match the 25 mph speed limit through town, Caroline took the opportunity to look around a bit as she drove. Shops and cafes lined the main street, along with a gas station, town library, and the police station. Everything was quaint, painted white with colorful trim and shutters in green or blue or red. As it was just after noon on a Tuesday, there were no children around except those too young to be in school.

"How much farther?" Ivy asked. She sounded wistful, and her mother glanced back to see her with chin on arm gazing out her side window.

"Not too far," Caroline replied, checking the directions she'd written down. There were three cross-streets on the main drag through town, and she turned left on the second one. After crossing a couple more streets, they started up a fairly steep hill and back into the ubiquitous forest. She checked for signs at the side of the road which was now barely wide enough for two vehicles to pass each other.

When she saw the sign, she smiled. "Here we are," she said brightly and turned right into a driveway. Rather than asphalt or cement, the drive consisted of two well-worn tire tracks with thick furry moss growing down the center.

Charlie read the faded wooden sign as they pulled past, which stated *Ravnensten*. Then they were back in the trees, and as the narrow drive turned right and then left, even the road behind them was lost to sight.

"This is creepy," Ivy said.

"Nonsense," Caroline retorted, taking her foot off the gas pedal to slow as a sharper curve appeared ahead. "Living closer to nature will do us all some good. Being surrounded by concrete and so many people makes us forget how beautiful the world can be."

"As long as we still have Wi-Fi," Charlie muttered under his breath.

The trees opened up again, and in a fairly large clearing stood the house that was now their home. It was two stories, built of wood and stone, with a steeply pitched roofline and many shuttered windows. A low stone fence surrounded it, with a wooden gate opening to the slate walkway leading to the front door. On the far side of the house stood a covered carport. A couple of crows perched on the high ridge of the roof, watching as the car parked and the doors opened.

"Wow," Caroline breathed, gazing at the house. This was the first time she had seen it in person, and Terry's promise that she would be pleased had just come true. The house was twice the size of the one they had left behind, and with the thick forest, they were completely private from any of their neighbors. "Let's go in," she said, smiling at her children, "and you guys can decide which room you want. Your dad said there are three bedrooms besides the master, so you can take your pick."

The little garden gate opened smoothly, and Ivy raced down the stone path to be first to the front door.

"It is kinda cool," Charlie said grudgingly and followed Caroline up the wide steps to the big wooden door. A pane of old-fashioned rippled glass with tiny bubbles and other occlusions was set into the top third of the door, and heavy wrought iron hinges made into the shapes of leaves or wings added gothic grandeur to the entryway.

Caroline used her key in the newly installed modern bolt lock, and let Ivy be the first into the house. While Caroline went to the kitchen first, the kids both ran for the stairs to call dibs on the room of their choice. In the kitchen, she found that the previous owners had updated the appliances, and a heavy granite countertop looked perfect in the wood and brass appointed décor. A stone-inlaid fireplace, the original cooking hearth, was still usable from what Terry had told her. Upstairs, she could hear the muffled sounds of children's feet as they ran up and down the hallway, checking out the bedrooms. When her cell phone rang, she jumped, then laughed and pulled it from her purse.

On the second floor, Ivy had already decided she wanted the front corner room. There were windows on both outside walls, and one of them had a built-in window seat where she could already picture herself curled up with a book. The walls were painted a pale peach color, and the floor was dark-stained wood.

Charlie had also picked the room he preferred. It was at the back of the house, with another bedroom between it and the one Ivy had chosen. The walls were dusky green, and on the back wall instead of just windows there were a set of double doors inset with more of the wavy antique glass like that in the front door. When he opened it, he found a narrow balcony railed with fancy wrought-iron and a view over the back yard and into the forest beyond.

"Charlie!"

He stepped back into the wide hallway. "Yeah, Mom?"

"The movers just called; they're coming through town right now."

Charlie went to the top of the stairs to see his mother at the bottom.

"I'm going to pull the car around into the carport so it's not in their way when they get here," she said. "Will you keep an eye on Ivy? No wandering off, okay? I'm going to need your help with the movers."

Charlie nodded, "Okay."

Caroline smiled and went to move the car.

Terrence Blackwell came home to contained chaos. The moving truck with all their furniture and personal belongings was backed awkwardly along the stone fence. Two movers were in the midst of carrying a couch around the side of the house toward the back patio where the French doors allowed more space to fit the furniture through.

"Honey, I'm home," he called as he came in through the front door. Boxes were stacked in the entryway, and every light in the house was turned on. From the family room at the back of the house, he heard his wife exclaim and then she appeared.

"I've missed you!" she said, greeting him with a hug.

"Daddy!"

He turned to catch Ivy when she threw herself at him, smiling as Charlie loped down the stairs. "I've missed all of you," he said, letting Caroline go so he could hug both his children. "So? What do you think? Pretty cool, huh?"

"It's creepy," Ivy said matter-of-factly. "I picked my room, Daddy. Do you want to see?"

"Mrs. Blackwell?" a male voice called from the family room, and Caroline went to see what the movers needed.

"I'll look in a little bit, Button," Terry said, and raised his eyebrows at Charlie. "You think it's creepy, too?"

Charlie shrugged. "Too early to tell," he answered, then returned his dad's grin.

Terry changed out of his suit, then helped with moving boxes to the proper rooms. The movers handled all the furniture, and Terry happily deflated the camp mattress he'd been sleeping on for the last week. By the time everything had been emptied out of the moving truck it was getting dark.

"I haven't had a chance to get much in the way of groceries," Terry said after the movers left, carefully maneuvering their truck along the narrow curving driveway. "And I can't imagine you're in the mood to cook anything, anyway. But there's a great pizza place in town. Why don't we just order in?"

"So much for my diet," Caroline said.

"You don't need to diet. And I don't know about you, but I'm starved."

"Starved," Ivy agreed.

"Extremely," Charlie added.

"Fine," Caroline sighed. "But see if they have salad, too."

Terry pulled her against his side and smiled. "Whatever you want."

In the morning, Caroline drove the kids into town. She had faxed their records to the school the week before and hoped there wouldn't be any problem with getting them started today. Moving them a month before the end of the school year was hard on everyone, but it wasn't something they'd had any control over. Terry had taken the new job as soon as possible because they needed the money, and once he'd gotten the house Caroline had immediately started packing everything up. The months of unemployment and their depleted savings had meant they couldn't linger even until the kids were done with school.

Because Blackwell was such a small town, all the kids from K through 12 went to school on the same campus. There were two buildings, one which housed classes for the younger children and had playground equipment in a fenced-in area behind the school. The other building was for older students, and according to what Caroline had been told, the cut-off point between younger and older children changed depending on the number of students in each year. For the remaining month of this school year, Charlie would be in the same building as Ivy.

"This is just weird," Charlie whispered to his mother before the vice-principal took him and Ivy to their respective classes. "We haven't been in the same school for two years!"

"I know, but just try to adjust. Things are very different here, but we'll all get used to it," Caroline replied softly, and hugged them both before leaving. "I'll see you when you get home!" she called, and blinked rapidly to clear the extra moisture from her eyes. The school district provided bussing for the kids who lived outside the town proper, so her children would come home on the bus today.

In the car again, Caroline looked around at the idyllic little town. The streets were clean and uncrowded, the air was fresh and flowers bloomed in the parking strip in front of every business. "This is going to be great," she said, urging herself to believe it. After everything they'd been through, her family deserved some happiness.

Charlie soon found out that the kids in school had all been here starting in kindergarten, and being an outsider didn't make him interesting, it just made him a target.

"You moved into Ravnensten house?" one boy asked, a slight sneer pulling his mouth askew. "Guess you think you own the whole town, since your last name is *Blackwell*."

Charlie shook his head, feeling his cheeks burning.

"Weird stuff happens up there," a pretty blond girl added, her blue eyes like ice. "People have gone missing out in those woods. Why do you think your dad got the house so easy?"

"Nothing strange happened since I've been here," he said.

"You'll find out," another boy said. "You might not even last a week."

"Oh, grow up," Charlie said, missing home and his friends more than he wanted to admit. "I'm not some small-town idiot, and I don't believe your stupid stories."

"You'll see," the first boy said, but the pretty blonde girl with the cold eyes just smiled.

When their first day was over, Charlie found Ivy waiting for him in front of the school. Her eyes were puffy, and her cheeks blotched from crying, but she was calm.

"Are you okay?" he asked softly. As siblings, they fought and argued regularly, but here it was the two of them against everyone else, and he didn't like that someone had made her cry.

Ivy nodded, tucking a strand of long hair behind her ear. "I don't have to worry about finding a new best friend," she said, her voice a bit hoarse, "because there's no one here I want to be friends with."

On the bus, Charlie and Ivy sat together, holding hands where no one could see while the other kids talked loudly and pointedly ignored them. When the driver pulled up in front of their driveway, Charlie let Ivy precede him off the bus. He looked back once before it pulled away, and felt a chill when he saw that all the kids, as well as the driver, were staring at them. Then the vehicle pulled back onto the road and was gone behind the intervening pines.

"I hate it here," Ivy said succinctly, and marched down the winding driveway to the house.

Charlie sighed, hitching the bag with his new school books higher onto his shoulder. "Me, too," he said under his breath, and followed her.

Caroline had been busy; after taking the kids to school, she'd stopped and bought some basic groceries so they'd be able to eat at home, secretly dismayed with the lack of variety. Then she'd unpacked all the kitchen boxes and put away the dishes and cookware. When Ivy and Charlie came in, she was upstairs unpacking linens.

"Mom!" Charlie yelled, dropping his textbooks on a kitchen chair.

"Up here," she called, coming to the top of the stairs. "How was your first day?"

"It sucked," Charlie said.

Caroline looked at Ivy as her daughter came up the stairs, noting her puffy eyes, and sighed. "Oh sweetie, come here," she said, pulling Ivy into a hug.

"I'm going for a walk," Charlie said. Before Caroline could say anything, he went through the family room and out the back door, then across the patio and lawn, and hopped over the low stone fence. Within seconds he was among the thick growth of trees that he could see from his bedroom balcony. The smell of pine and the cool shade soothed him, and faster than he would have thought possible he was feeling better. His father had told them the night before that their property extended quite a way into the forest, and Charlie was curious to see how far.

He walked as straight a line as possible, weaving around moss-furred trees both growing and fallen to the forest floor. Delicate ferns were everywhere, even growing on the downed trunks, and he was surprised at the quiet. There was the distant hum of insects and the occasional song of a bird from high above. The damp earth and mossy trees seemed to absorb sound, and even his footsteps were muted. But there were no human sounds at all—no music or voices, or the ever-present growl of car engines that he grew up with. Slanting rays of sunlight rarely made it through the needled canopy, and the hush reminded him of an old cathedral he'd been to once when he was much younger.

The forest climbed steadily up the hill behind the house, and Charlie started looking for the fence his dad had told him marked the end of the property. Rounding a particularly large tree trunk, he was startled to see steps. They were old, covered in moss and half-buried in old pine needles, but definitely broad stone steps. There were about a dozen of them, with no railing to confine them, and at the top was a small building.

"Cool," Charlie breathed, and smiled as he went up the steps. The building stood on a flat expanse of rock, and when he reached the top, he saw that the forest floor dropped away on all sides. On the other side, at the base of the outcrop of granite on which the structure had been built, there was a pool of water surrounded by a low wall or curb. Down the hill past the water, a split-rail fence zigzagged through the trees.

He turned back to check out the building. It was small, with a pitched roof covered in the ever-present moss, and two windows on the side walls that were shuttered and guarded by fancy metal grilles. A door at the front also had a tarnished bronze screen, behind which Charlie saw panels of the same wavy, included glass like that at the house.

There were no signs or plaques affixed to the building, just carvings in the stone lintels and the door frame that looked like stylized leaves or bird wings.

"Like the hinges on the front door," Charlie said, tracing one of the carvings with his fingertips. They were old and weathered, the edges rounded with age. He walked around the building, testing the shutters and checking for any other opening into the apparently abandoned structure, but it was sealed up tight.

The sound of splashing startled him, and he sidled around the back corner to peer down at the little pond.

Below him, perched on the wall was a girl about his age. She put her hand in the water and scooped out a handful which then trickled back through her fingers.

"Hey," Charlie called.

The girl turned to look at him. Her eyes were dark and her expression sad.

"Who are you?" Charlie asked.

She stood, her long dark hair half-covering the white dress she wore. Without a word she turned and slipped through the trees, disappearing from sight.

"Wait!" Charlie looked down, but it was too far to jump, and too steep to climb down. He ran back down the steps and came around the side of the rock platform to the pond. "I'm sorry, I didn't mean to scare you," he called, and tried to follow the way he'd seen her go. There were no tracks, and the thick growth of ferns showed no passage. "Look, I just wanted to say hi. My name is Charlie. You can come back."

He wandered through the trees between the pool and the old split-rail fence but saw no sign of her. Realizing that the beams of slanting sunlight had faded, and it was beginning to get dark, he gave in. Getting lost out here after the sun went down would not be a good idea; plus, he didn't want his parents to forbid him from coming back. He gave one last glance at the enigmatic little stone building, then picked his way through the trees toward the house he now called home. The temperature dropped as the darkness grew, and Charlie wished that he'd worn a jacket.

When he finally made it back to the stone fence, it was to find all the lights on at the back of the house, and his father with a flashlight coming to look for him.

"Where have you been?" Terry asked, relieved that he wouldn't have to go traipsing around in the dark in an area he was not familiar with.

"I just went for a walk," Charlie answered, coming back over the stone wall.

"Your mother was sure you fell into a ravine, or had a tree fall on you," Terry said with a smile.

"Nope, just exploring." Together they walked back to the patio, and Charlie asked, "Did you know there's a little rock building out there before you get to the fence? It's all locked up, but it's pretty cool."

Terry shook his head, letting his son precede him into the back door. "No, I haven't had a chance to scout out any of the property. Although there's supposed to be a stream along the north property line where we can go fishing." He stopped his son in the family room and added, "Your mom was really worried. She said you guys had a hard day?"

Charlie shrugged. He'd almost forgotten about the rotten day at school. "The kids here are jerks. They made Ivy cry."

Terry sighed and put his arm around Charlie's shoulders. "I'm sorry, son. I know this has been hard on the both of you. But it will get better, I promise."

Charlie didn't say anything, but he nodded once, knowing his dad wanted some kind of response.

"That's my boy," Terry said, then hugged him quickly before letting him go. "Better let your mom know you're back."

"Yeah," Charlie murmured, and headed into the kitchen where Caroline was making dinner.

Ivy sat in the window seat, curled up in a ball against the cushions with her favorite threadbare blanket tucked around her. The house was quiet. There was the soft chirrup of crickets heard through the window glass, and occasionally the sound of her mother and father talking from their room, but low enough she couldn't make out the words. Her room was dark but for the soft glow of the kitty night light plugged in near the door. Ivy wrapped her arms around her stuffed bunny, a furry white protector with black button eyes and floppy pink-lined ears. Outside, beyond the low stone fence, shadows moved and danced in the moonlight. She wasn't sure what they were, but knew somehow that they couldn't cross the fence or open the simple wooden gate.

The things outside didn't frighten her because she knew instinctively that she was safe from them. It was the thing crouching at the head of her bed that kept her tucked into the angles of the window seat. It hissed and grumbled softly, waiting for her to cross the room to her bed. Instead, she laid her head against the window and watched the shadows dance.

Caroline was worried, watching her children walk down the curved driveway and into the trees. They both looked tired—more tired than just moving and unpacking would explain. Ivy, in particular, seemed worn out, but when Caroline had questioned her at breakfast, the ten-year-old said everything was fine.

Once the kids were gone, she went upstairs to see what else needed to be put away. She was surprised to see that Ivy's bed was made, standing pristine without a single stuffed animal cluttering it. In fact, the only stuffed animal in evidence was the white rabbit lying on the window seat with Ivy's old blanket.

Charlie's bed was also made, and Caroline put her hands on her hips. She loved her kids, but they were notorious for leaving their rooms a mess, with blankets and sheets trailing off their beds, and books and toys strewn about.

"Well, makes it easier for me, at least for one day," she mused, then went to get a load of laundry ready to wash.

School wasn't any better the second day, and Charlie couldn't wait until the weekend. The thought of going two days in a row without having to deal with the jerks in his class was incredibly attractive.

"Wow, you're still here," a boy named Derek said snidely.

"Must've spent the night hiding in a closet," another boy, Ryan who was the son of the local police chief, added.

"You guys are all full of shit," Charlie retorted. He was tired and not in the mood to deal with their rudeness. "If you're just going to keep being assholes, then don't bother talking to me. I'm not interested."

"Wow, the city boy can swear," the pretty blonde said teasingly. Her name was Tasha, and her father owned the sawmill, which was the largest employer in the area. "I'm so impressed."

"Whatever," Charlie muttered, and pulled out his history book.

When they went to lunch, Charlie saw Ivy sitting by herself picking at the tuna sandwich she'd brought from home. He started across the room to sit with her, not caring about the four-year difference in age, or what anyone thought of him for sitting with his little sister. Tasha stepped in front of him, blocking his way, her cold blue eyes glaring at him.

"You know we're just trying to warn you for your own good, right?" she asked.

"Like you even care," Charlie said.

"No one has ever lived on that property for more than a few months, without something really *bad* happening." She twirled a lock of her hair between her fingers and smiled.

"And what am I supposed to do about it?" he asked. "Do you think I'm here 'cause I want to be? Do you think if I had any choice that I'd be anywhere near this stupid town?"

Tasha raised her brows at his tone and tilted her head. "Have you seen anything strange yet?" she asked. "Animals acting weird, shadows watching you, or people you don't know wandering around? Because that's how it starts—at least, that's what the *last* people said."

Charlie heaved a sigh, aware that other kids were watching them. In the corner, Ivy still picked at her lunch dispiritedly. "Y'know what? I don't care. Just leave me alone." He pushed past Tasha, not caring that he bumped her with his shoulder, and unaware of the angry look she cast after him.

Ivy didn't look up when he sat across from her, but she said, "My sandwich tastes funny."

Charlie just nodded and opened his own lunch.

Charlie washed the dishes after dinner, then went up to his room. Ivy was lying on the couch with their mom, her heavy eyes barely open. Dad had called to say he'd be late, and wasn't home yet. In the privacy of his own room, Charlie got on his laptop and pulled up the search engine. In the text box, he typed *Ravnensten Blackwell Oregon*.

"*History of Blackwell / Ravnensten House was built by Edgar Blackwell Thorson in 1881 above the current location of the town of Blackwell.*" Charlie scanned through the article, looking for information regarding the little stone house he had found, or for any information regarding strange happenings that his classmates kept teasing about. "*The house was named Ravnensten by Edgar's wife Amaranth for the black stone used in its construction…*" The rest of it had to do with the founding of the town of Blackwell and the dates of new construction in town or new businesses that opened.

He tried *disappearances in Blackwell Oregon*, which only brought up missing persons sites for the county and the state. *Weird phenomena* pulled up UFO and bigfoot sightings. From sheer frustration, he tried *stone house Blackwell*.

"*Edgar Thorson commissioned and built the family chapel above Ravnensten House in the woods along with a meditation pond. The family kept the Sabbath in privacy, and their daughter Rowan was laid to rest there shortly before her mother Amaranth.*"

"Whoa," Charlie said. There was a black and white photo of a man and woman in dark, old-fashioned clothing. A second photo showed a girl with long black hair wearing a white dress. A chill caught him as Charlie realized she looked like the girl he'd seen at the pool behind the chapel. "So it's like a mausoleum," he whispered.

The caption below the picture of Rowan Thorson said *Daughter of prominent businessman Edgar Blackwell Thorson dies in accidental drowning.*

"Was it really an accident?" Charlie looked at the door that opened onto the balcony. The glass was too imperfect to be able to see through, but he did see the last evening light through the rippled panes.

Charlie couldn't remember the last time he'd been so happy for a Friday. He felt if he could wish away the next three weeks and just fast-forward to summer vacation, he would do so. The ride on the bus to school was as unfriendly as always, and Ivy seemed to wilt beside him on the hard plastic seat. He hadn't slept much the night before, not even bothering to get under the covers, but he was wondering if his little sister had slept at all. Her usual bright demeanor was completely missing; her face was pale, eyes heavy-lidded over dark half-circles.

"Maybe you should go to the office and call Mom," Charlie said when they walked into school together. Around them, children from the age of six up to Charlie's age of fourteen chattered and made their way to their classrooms. "You look like you're sick."

Ivy shook her head stubbornly. "I don't want to go back to that house until I have to," she whispered, then pulled away from him and trudged to her own class.

Charlie spent the day ignoring all but his teachers. He didn't answer any questions and did his best not to react to anything said to him. By lunch time, Tasha was obviously pissed. She was not used to being ignored by anyone.

"You're such a stupid boy," she hissed when he passed her in the lunch room, "You and your stupid little sister are going to die in that house."

He didn't think. He just dropped his lunch, and pushed her hard with both hands, knocking her onto her butt on the faded linoleum.

She stared up at him, mouth open in surprise while a few kids laughed. "Are you threatening me?" he asked loudly. "Are you threatening my sister? Just because you're some big shot's daughter doesn't mean you have any right to threaten us."

Mr. Perkins, who taught English to the older classes, leaned down to help Tasha up. "Do I need to send you to the principal's office again, Miss Jameson?" he asked pointedly.

Again? Charlie thought, but he didn't say anything.

"No sir," she pouted.

"Fine. Go sit down and eat your lunch then." Perkins looked at Charlie and gestured as though shooing him away.

Charlie didn't wait for anyone else to say anything. He picked up his lunch bag off the floor and went to sit with Ivy.

When they got home from school after the usual uncomfortable bus ride, they found a note tacked to the front door.

"I had to run some papers down to your dad's office. I'll be back as soon as I can. There's a fresh apple-snicker salad in the fridge if you want a snack. Love you – Mom."

Charlie dropped his books on the kitchen counter and looked at Ivy. "I'm going to go for a walk. You okay to be here by yourself?"

Ivy shook her head. "No. I'll come with you."

He grimaced. "I'm just going to walk around in the trees for a while. You should lie down and take a nap."

"I don't want to stay by myself," she whispered.

Charlie didn't want to take her with him, but he couldn't make her stay by herself, not when she looked so miserable. "Okay, but you have to keep up. I'm not going to wait for you."

Ivy left her backpack on the counter next to Charlie's books and walked to the back door. She looked at him, "Are you ready?"

He shrugged and followed her outside.

The walk through the forest took longer with Ivy trailing behind him. A couple of times he thought to snap at her about being so slow, but every time he looked back at her, Ivy's exhausted expression made him bite his tongue. Halfway to the granite knoll, Charlie sat down on a fallen log and patted the space beside him.

When Ivy sat, he asked, "Are you okay? You really look like you feel like shit."

"I can't sleep," she said dully, not looking at him, just staring out at the sea of ferns and moss. "There's a monster in my room, and it sits on my bed."

"There's no such thing as monsters," he said gently.

She turned to look at him, her eyes too bleak for a ten-year-old little girl. "Yes there is. It whispers at me all night, and has glowy eyes and sharp fingers, and it wants me to fall asleep so it can get me. What else could it be?"

He thought about the kids at school, the pretty Tasha with her icy eyes in particular. He knew there were monsters, but not the kind his sister meant.

After a while, they went on, and Ivy was so tired she didn't even show any signs of interest in the carved steps or the stone chapel at their top. Instead, she sat down on the top step, resting her chin on her forearms which rested on her knees.

"I'm just going to walk around," Charlie said, and Ivy nodded once.

He looked more closely at the carvings on the doorframe and lintel, checking for anything that might give him more information. If two people were buried inside, there should have been some kind of marker or memorial, he was sure. But there was nothing that he hadn't already seen. The sound of splashing drew him back toward the pool, and he moved cautiously, not wanting to frighten the girl away again.

She was there, just like the last time. Long black hair trailed down her back, and she perched on the low wall around the pond, her bare feet and the hem of her dress trailing in the water. She swept her hand through the water slowly, lifting a handful to escape through her fingers.

Charlie watched for a long time, but she seemed oblivious.

Finally, moving as quietly as he could, he went back to the stairs so he could circle to the pool. He stopped, looking around. Ivy was gone.

"Ivy?" he whispered, checking the other side of the chapel. She wasn't there. "Ivy?" He spoke a little louder. It didn't matter now if he startled the strange girl; what was important was finding his little sister. "Ivy!" He ran down the steps and around the granite outcrop—and there on the curb surrounding the pool was his sister. Standing in the water before Ivy, hands held out in a gesture of invitation, was the strange girl he'd seen from above. "Hey!"

Both girls turned to look at him, and Ivy blinked as though waking up. "Charlie?"

"Come away from the water, Ivy," he said, moving closer. When Ivy stepped down, the other girl lowered her arms, standing knee deep in the moss-colored pool. "Who are you?" he asked her.

She said nothing, just gazing at him and Ivy.

"Are you Rowan?" he guessed, and she stepped back, deeper into the water. "I don't mean you any harm," he added, glancing down at his sister. She was shaking with cold, and he saw that her shoes were wet.

"You should leave," the girl in the pool said, her voice hollow and sad.

"Are you Rowan?" he asked again.

"I was," she answered, "but we've all been abandoned here."

"What happened to you?" he asked, curiosity welling.

"Charlie, I don't feel good," Ivy said.

"You should go, take her away," Rowan said, stepping backward again. The water was up to her hips now.

Charlie put his arm around Ivy. She was freezing cold, and her teeth were chattering.

"Don't leave her in the house," Rowan called as Charlie led Ivy back around the rock. "Mother lost me, now she wants another daughter."

He stopped, looking back. "What?"

"Abandon hope, all who enter—" Her head sank below the

surface of the water, her black hair floating for a moment like seaweed before disappearing.

"Come on," Charlie whispered, and helped Ivy on the long walk back through the trees.

Ivy's fever topped out at 104 degrees and held there for over two hours. Just about the time that Terry and Caroline had decided to pack her up and take her the fifty-three miles to the nearest hospital, it broke. They took turns sitting with her, checking her temperature to make sure it wasn't rising again, and putting cool washcloths on her flushed forehead. Charlie stayed in his room, trying to find more information online about Rowan or her family, or the house they now lived in.

Once when his dad came out of Ivy's room, Charlie asked him, "Who owned the house before us?"

"What?" Terry was tired and still concerned about his daughter, and looked at Charlie with brows drawn. "I don't know, son. Why?"

"Some of the kids at school said people who lived here before us went missing."

Terry sighed. "Sometimes teenagers have a bad sense of humor. I wouldn't take it seriously, Charlie."

"That little house I found in the woods? It's a mausoleum."

Terry rubbed his eyes. "That's not surprising. I'm sure a lot of people around here in the old days had family cemeteries and such. It was a normal thing back then."

"Something isn't right about this house, Dad," Charlie whispered. "The people who built it, their daughter drowned. And then the mother died, too."

"Charlie, I can't deal with this right now," Terry said, more harshly than he intended. He stepped forward, taking a breath to control himself, and put his hands on his son's shoulders. "We can talk about this tomorrow, okay? Right now I'm just worried about your sister, and I can't worry about anything else."

Charlie clenched his teeth, but let it go.

"Get some sleep. Hopefully, in the morning Ivy will be feeling better. We'll talk then."

Charlie nodded, and stepped back into his room, closing the door.

He awoke sometime later in the dark. Faint moonlight came through the antique glass panes on the balcony doors, printing smudged green-tinged squares on the wood floor. Something tapped on the glass, its rippled shadow indistinct, and Charlie knew that's what woke him. He hadn't undressed for bed, just fell asleep on top of the covers, so he didn't waste any time. He crossed to the double doors quietly and opened one.

Something dark and glossy squawked and fluttered down from the balcony railing. Charlie leaned out to see Rowan's pale face looking up at him.

He went back in and opened his bedroom door. The hall was deserted. The glow of a nightlight showed under Ivy's closed door. Tiptoeing, he went to the stairs, down to the first floor, and out the back door to the patio. Beyond the low wall, near the start of the forest, he saw her white dress. He hesitated. Besides Rowan, there were dark shadowy things that moved and billowed outside the stone barrier. They seemed to whisper as they danced between the fence and the forest. They did not trouble Rowan but gave Charlie the creeps.

"What do you want?" he asked, approaching to within arms-length of the wall, but no closer. Behind him, Ravnensten house waited silently under the waning moon.

"I won't hurt you, Charlie." Rowan's voice was soft and sad, and she didn't try to come any closer. "I can't cross the fence. None of us can." She gestured at the moving shadows around her.

"Fine. You tried to get my sister into the pool with you, so maybe you're not being honest. But, whatever. What do you want?"

Rowan sighed, her expression one of regret. "I was trying to save her. None of us can come inside the wall, Charlie. But she's already in there."

"Ivy? I know she's in there," Charlie retorted. He was tired and irritated, and more worried about Ivy than he would admit even to himself.

Rowan shook her head. "No. Mother. She died inside Ravnensten, and resides there still."

A chill stitched its way up Charlie's spine as he remembered Rowan's words from earlier. *"Mother lost me, now she wants another daughter..."* The wind picked up, cold for this early May morning, and thin clouds scudded across the sliver of moon turning all to shadow.

Ivy opened her eyes. She was warm and snug, tucked into her own blankets in her own bed. Her white bunny was snuggled under the quilt with her, and she smiled. It was nice not to be so shivery cold, so burning hot.

Something whispered and hissed, grumbling softly beside her. Ivy's eyes opened very wide as she remembered where she was, and realized all over again that she was in her bed. She didn't want to but couldn't help it. She turned her head, meeting the cold, glowing eyes that had watched her every night. Long slender fingers that tapered to sharp points brushed Ivy's fair hair away from her pale face. A nightmare visage, all splintered edges and crazed smile, leaned close to nuzzle her cheek. Still weak from the fever, and worn out from nights without sleep, Ivy tried to pull away, to free herself from the tangling blankets and the monster's tight embrace. The black shadowy thing, all that was left of a daughterless mother, pulled Ivy close, muffling her screams, and hummed off-key lullabies until she was silent.

Chief Falk and the three officers employed by the town searched the house and the grounds. They extended the search into the surrounding woods but found no sign of Ivy Blackwell. When Terrence Blackwell insisted, they brought a certified diver up from Grants Pass to check the mossy meditation pool behind the Thorson family chapel. As had happened many times over the years, there were no leads. Just a missing child and devastated parents.

"There has to be something you can do," Terry said, more grief in his voice than he could control.

"We'll keep looking, Mr. Blackwell. But I can't promise you anything." Like all those who had spent their lives in Blackwell, he knew the old legends and scary stories about this place. What he didn't know was why people kept coming to town and buying this cursed house—it wasn't like anyone ever advertised it. It was as much a mystery as the generations of missing kids.

The boy, Charlie, stayed in his room, furious but silent. He was the one who found his sister missing from her bed. He had tried to tell his parents that it was Amaranth Thorson who had taken Ivy. But no one would listen. After all, he was just a kid, who had gone through a lot in the last month. It was only natural that he'd make up a story to explain this disappearance.

In the little girl's room, Mrs. Blackwell lay on the bed, hugging her daughter's stuffed white rabbit. One of its ears had been torn off, as though Ivy had held on to it when she was taken...wherever it was she'd been taken.

Rose Blackthorn is a member of the HWA. Her short fiction and poetry has appeared online and in print with a varied list of anthologies and magazines. Her poetry collection *Thorns, Hearts and Thistles* was published in February 2015, and the novelette *Called to Battle: Worthy Vessel* was published in October 2015. She is a writer, dog-mom, and photographer who lives in the high-mountain desert, but longs for the sea.

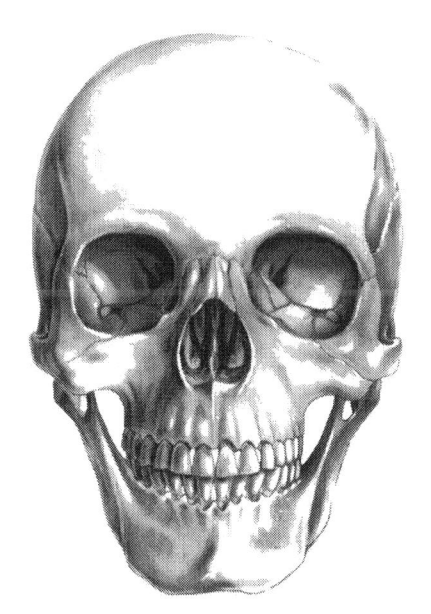

The Call of the House of Usher

Annie Neugebauer

"In this unnerved, in this pitiable, condition I feel that the period will sooner or later arrive when I must abandon life and reason together, in some struggle with the grim phantasm, FEAR." –Roderick Usher

Strange! Undeniably strange and unpredictable that I would be here, now, dragging myself into this clean, brightly-lit kitchen in an ancient, decrepit house that was surely, almost certainly—possibly—never mine. I could not have foreseen it, but I look back so clearly, as if each step led undeniably and irrevocably to the next. As if I might have known, if only…ah, well. There is no use in that. Let me tell you how it began.

I was leaving the library at night after several hours of fruitless attempts to finish my long-belabored novel and having the building closed against me. The unfaltering fluorescence of the place pushed me into darkness, and as I walked to my car in dejected spirits, wondering if the work was perhaps ill-fated and never meant to be, I blinked.

Now, you may wonder at my telling you such a mundanity, but the blink is important here, as this was the first time I saw *Her*.

She came to me in the space before I blinked.

When I opened my lids, she was gone.

I could not have told you more than this, at that point, because there was no more. Simply a blink and Her passing before it. A vague sense of confusion and unease crept into my limbs like the beginnings of catalepsy.

It was nothing, at first, but it continued to occur over the next few weeks, and the recurrence of it began to sink into me. I would almost reach the point of forgetting about Her appearance, and then it would happen again. A blink. Her passing. The vague smell of stale dust. Questions bombarded me with their elusiveness: *What is this, and why can't I see Her fully? Why does she appear so fleetingly? What does she want?* I had no answers—have no answers still—only the dark blur of Her passing with the downsweep of my eyes.

I began to feel crazed with it.

As I attempted to go about my daily life, I found myself expecting Her appearance, yet she never came when I was ready—when I thought to trick Her into revealing herself. At times when she was at the forefront of my mind, I would squint slowly, hoping to maintain Her image, but she eluded me. I developed an odd sort of dread in Her coming. I feared Her.

I became strange, keeping my eyes open for as long as possible between blinks, hoping to ward Her off with my constancy.

Even my friends could not understand my pervading sense of dread, or my desire never to be left alone. They would lean in too closely, sometimes, and tell me I was getting carried away. When they were inches from me, I would blink, thinking to face Her with a witness present. But of course, she did not appear then. I was ready then.

She only came when I was alone.

I did not have to be in the solitude of my city apartment, although she often swept by there, appearing in my periphery as my eyelashes came into view, but disappearing before I could look—leaving only the elusive scent of dust in her place.

She was slow-moving, but fleeting. She pulled at my hairs one by one, making the dryness of my eyeballs prick in anticipation, but she never came then. Anticipation wracked me.

I was mad with it.

My loved ones began to avoid me just as I avoided long empty stairwells. Somehow, I knew that she would chase me then, nipping at my heels and slinking along the flights above me in a dark smear, gaining as I ran.

I avoided parking garages, too, along with alleyways, empty fields, and swimming pools at night. She became the obscured shape beyond the shower curtain. The skin on the back of my neck. The billow of air behind the drapes. She was everything that frightened me, but hidden. The more I avoided Her—my eyes spread open like two biopsied tumors—the more she pursued me in the corners of things.

And I could not avoid my home forever.

Safe havens became a bane for me. Solitude is Her bedfellow. I sought the bright lights of 24-hour diners, the curious glances of bystanders, the ever-beating pulse of humanity. But they stared at my overly wide eyes, just like my friends. They turned away from the dryness of my refusal to blink. They whispered behind their hands, and she was there, too. She was just beyond the space they looked away from, hollowing me.

About this time, when my irrational fear (for that is what I told myself the fear was, in the light of day when reason seemed a possible feat once more) had taken hold of my sanity and begun pushing me to believe and do things that I would never have thought myself capable of, I got a letter by post. This was singular, as very few people use paper mail in these modern times, so I opened it with haste and was more than a little surprised at its contents, which read something thus:

> *Brother,*
> *You are wanted at the site of our family estate. I fear it lies in utter disrepair, but I doubt not that you possess the facilities and wherewithal to make it a source of family pride once again.*
> *I can picture you as you read this—pale, smooth brow furrowed in confusion even as your dark, dry eyes widen in disbelief; but I assure you it is true. We are indeed the last of the line of the House of Usher. Do not deny your lineage.*
> *Enclosed you will find directions to the estate, which lies some distance from your current home. I will be waiting for you here. Until then.*

The letter was unsigned and undated, and at first, I dismissed it as some type of hoax. For you see, I was and have always been an orphan. I have no parents, sisters, or brothers to call my own.

So how then, could I receive such a correspondence? And yet, the speaker of the letter described me so accurately and had alluded to my ability to rehabilitate an old building. I was currently doing exceedingly well in the field of historical housing reconstruction. I checked the envelope again, and indeed, it was addressed to me.

A strange sort of hush fell over my apartment at this time, and I felt as though I were not alone. I whirled, half expecting to see the author of the letter standing behind me, but there were only shadows and the soft shifting of the vertical blinds as the fan sent wind around the room.

I could still feel eyes on me. *Her* eyes. I could not allow myself to blink. She would be there. Oh! She would be there!

With all of the false bravado I could muster, I spoke into the empty room. "Who are you?"

The blinds rustled. I clenched the letter in my fist.

"What do you want from me?"

I thought...I thought I saw something move from behind the long white lines of the blinds in front of the sliding glass door. Her.

She didn't speak—she never speaks—but I heard Her still. Not in words, but in knowledge. *Go*, it seemed to say, *or I will show you.*

"No," I groaned, clutching the letter to my chest, my eyes beginning to water. I would have to blink soon. I thought I smelled dust.

The blinds bulged outward as if a human form was pushing forth, and I screamed.

"Stop! Please. I will go. Just leave me. Leave me!"

There was soft, metallic clinking as the strips fell back into place. I blinked, once, and they were as they had been—flat—with only the slight breeze of the ceiling fan shifting them back and forth.

I wish I could adequately describe to you the sense of doom I felt at my decision to obey this mysterious letter from a sibling I never had. In that moment, I had no choice. I was compelled by my own dread. Compelled to seek a fate that could only condemn me. I was forlorn.

In the days that followed, She did not return. I began packing my things. My friends could not understand my reasoning. "A change of pace," I told them, and in my slightly less harrowed mind, I began to believe myself. I saw that I had become deeply disturbed, that I was giving in to fears and delusions no grown man should suffer and that they seemed to be rooted in *place*. Never mind that She had followed me everywhere. I simply needed something to believe, and at this point, "a change of pace" seemed sufficient.

Besides, country air has long been believed to aid ailing minds.

And country it was—wild, abandoned countryside that had not seen the tread of man for some time. It was with great difficulty that I made my way across the desolate terrain. Thankfully, I had only myself and my meager possessions to attend to.

I finally came upon the site described in the letter, and I almost turned back without pause. The choice of the word "disrepair" seemed generous, given the state of shamble and decay below.

I stood at the edge of a deep hollow—a valley, of sorts—at the bottom of which lay the remains of what I could only assume had once been the House of Usher. Which meant that the mucky gorge in which it lay must have once been the tarn indicated in the directions. If it had ever been full of water—which I found difficult to picture, as it had a mansion in it now—the water must have been the darkest shade of brown. Or perhaps gray, or a combination of the two mired together with a strange phosphorescent green pulsing from within…

I blinked. Where had that image come from? I glanced out of the corners of my eyes, almost expecting to see the dark flash of Her, but there was none. She had not come to me since my decision to travel here.

The day was oppressively hot for mid-autumn, and even the rapidly-overtaking evening didn't bring relief. A bead of sweat fled down my forehead as I studied the destitute structure.

It was large and looming in spite of its location below me, and in its damaged lines, I saw a gracefulness that might once have been stately, if not beautiful. Now it sat hunched in upon itself, like an animal that was broken but still deadly. Its simple stone façade was overspread with flora of a dismal green color, and an odor of dank rot emanated from the whole in a wave of heat as if the thing were *living*.

On either side of a wide, jagged split running the whole length of the façade were two glassless windows that gave the appearance of dark eyes.

As I stared down at them, they seemed to stare up at me. Blank, vacant, dark. Never blinking—like my own.

In one of them, I saw a faint movement of light. At first, I supposed it to be Her. She haunted my eyes, why not the eyes of this building? But that, I realized, was an irrational thought. Nor did I have feelings of unease as I invariably did when she was around. I thought there must be someone within the fallen house.

I glanced around the perimeter of the gorge in hopes of spotting signs of my so-called sibling who promised to be waiting for me. I could now see the moon rising in the pale sky, as if a sliver of fingernail balanced on the dead, pointed branch of a gnarled tree. Night was falling. I knew I must go further or retreat.

Having in mind that brief glimpse of life within the dead eye windows, I decided to see if the writer of my letter was indeed within the dwelling.

As I descended the steep walls of the old tarn, I was surprised by the dryness of the dirt. The smell and appearance of moisture seemed to be a false one. By the time I made it to the half-open doorway directly in the path of the large fissure splitting the house in two, my nostrils were coated in fine dust.

I walked inside.

I was at once struck by the enormity of the space. The house was even larger within than it appeared to be from without. In spite of the cracked ceilings, walls, and floor, the arrangement of the vast entryway seemed orderly—as if the house had split and the inhabitants had fled, leaving the room untouched. A thick layer of pale dust covered almost every surface, but some trick of physics had left one thing clean near to gleaming on the far wall: a family crest.

I walked across the floor, careful not to step in the crack which looked deep enough to wrench an ankle, and stared up at the magnificent crest displayed in the place of prominence. It was whole, placed directly over the crack that split the wall. I knew not what held it in place. The image was crowned with the helmet of a knight, and above that scrolled the words, "The Ancient Arms of Usher." So I was at the correct place. The family must have been very old indeed to use the word "ancient" on an object that itself seemed to be so.

"Hello?" I called out. "Is anybody here?" My voice echoed around the building with surprising clarity, making me wince. "I have come based on a letter…"

I took another careless step forward when something at my foot caught my eye. It was some bundled shape, seeming almost to hover over the two-foot crack in the floor. I shifted my position to lean over it, attempting to decipher its form. I squinted into the dimness of the room, and all at once the shape made itself clear to me.

It was a corpse—no, two corpses. Lying together toe to toe, head to head, wrapped in one another's arms.

I thought to scream, but my breath was suddenly a noose at my throat. I widened my eyes, staring down at the dead balanced so precariously over the fissure.

It was a man and a woman. Obviously young in life, ancient in death. Something about the state of the air here—perhaps the lack of moisture, although I am no chemist—had preserved the corpses surprisingly well. Both were pale-complected, although the skin had withered with time. Both had airy raven tresses, although death had drawn them unnaturally thin at the decaying scalps. They each had coins placed over their eyes, which I found singular, as it implied that someone had found them here and chosen not to bury them.

But it was the woman who caught my eye. Particularly, her cheeks, which somehow gave the illusion of a slight flush, even after all these years. And her lips seemed curved into the subtlest of smiles, as though content to be wrapped in her lover's arms for eternity.

I found myself entranced by this. By her strange sort of smirk. By her long, curling hair. By her preservation.

I knelt at her side, unthinking, and reached out one hand to brush the pale pink that coated her cheek. The very tip of my longest finger scarcely brushed what I must have only imagined to be warmth when the whole of both corpses collapsed in on each other, toppling over the edge and into the fissure below. The flesh and clothes on them turned instantly to powder.

I was left kneeling there, my hand still held in mid-air as if to caress her cheek, blinking at the little poof of dust that reached my face, and staring at a pile of so many indistinguishable bones.

All I could see was one skull—hers based on the dark curls I could just make out against the dirt below—looking up at me with dark, hollow eye sockets like empty windows. The coins had fallen off, winking at me from the depths. I shuddered and stood abruptly.

What had I done? I was preparing to leave immediately, ashamed of my desecration at this strange place, when I saw the white sheet of paper taped to the inside of the front door. I walked over and pulled it down. It read thus:

Brother,

If you are reading this, you have made it safely to the House of Usher. Welcome! I am sorry to say that I have been called away. But I have prepared a room for you on the second floor, and although (as you can see) the house is in shambles, this particular room is nice enough to inhabit while you begin your restoration of the family estate.

Enclosed you will find the deed to the property; sign it and all is yours. Do not wait for me. I will return as soon as I can. Until then.

Again, it was unsigned and undated. Unable to resist my curiosity, I went up the grandiose staircase to see the room in question.

It was indeed a nice room, overly spacious, gothic, and unnervingly clean. As it suddenly began to rain, I decided that I would stay the night before heading home.

One night turned into many. I slept better here, in this ancient home I'd never known, than I had anywhere else I'd ever stayed.

Over the next few months, I did begin reconstruction of the estate, which cost me hundreds of thousands of dollars, but I had that money to spare, and I soon grew passionate in my attempts to put the old mansion to its former magnificence—with some modern additions for comfort. My supposed sibling never returned, but neither did *She*, and as the project neared completion, I grew to like it here. I began to feel more like myself than I ever had before.

When the final stained glass window was installed and polished, the ultimate chandelier electrified and gleaming, the new kitchen completely modernized and galvanized, and the last floorboard mended and re-stained—the bodies left between the joists and boarded over—I sold my apartment in the city and signed the papers my "sibling" had left me.

The House of Usher was officially mine.

I felt at home. I was not just the owner of the house, but the rightful master. I walked down the stairway, and the walls seemed to stand straighter in salute. I opened doors, and entire rooms seemed to sigh in relief. I drew drapes closed, and the fabric seemed to billow out to caress me in a loving embrace.

I began to write again. The words came fervently, feverishly—as if in a dream. Every evening, I sat at a large oak table that I had restored into a desk and wrote for hours in one of the upper chambers. I came within pages of finishing my novel, my life's work. I was ecstatic.

And then things begin to change.

The words slowed, began hiding. I found myself restless and discontent. After a few nights of this block, I started moving about the estate, trying to find desks, counters, or fainting couches that would bring back the spark of creativity inside me. The doors that had once welcomed me now banished me from their presence. The stairs thrust me downward. The very carpets seemed to crawl underfoot, leading me to one place. A new place. The only place I'd yet to try writing.

A seat directly over the bodies under the floor.

Here, sitting ramrod straight against the hard-backed chair, I was able to write once again. But this time, my progress was not met with relief and joy, as before, but rather with a bitter sort of weariness that I could not talk myself out of. Begrudgingly, I abandoned my spacious writing desk and returned to this uncomfortable spot in the middle of the main entry every night.

Days blurred by in a greasy smear. One night, I noticed that there was a small crack making its way down the wall with the family crest on it. I blinked, surprised that the new plaster had weakened so quickly, and She was there. Just beyond my periphery. A feeling. A whiff of dust.

"It is just the shadows," I told myself, but I put my writing away and moved the chair against a far wall.

The Call of the House of Usher

But the next night, I returned. I had to; I could not write anywhere else. The crack in the wall had begun to split the gleaming floorboards. And it was no illusion. This time, I blinked and saw the dark flash of Her hair as she turned away.

Fool! I could have known. I should have known! I never should have signed the papers to this house. I would have done better to sign my soul to the devil—and perhaps I have! I should have listened to my sinking gut and *seen* that *She* was luring me here, that She would return.

Now I am alone here, destitute and stranded, and my beloved mansion has become what my loathed apartment once was: Her domain!

She comes to me in the space before I blink. When I open my lids, she is gone.

I do not know why I call her "She." A fall of hair? A glimpse of skirt? A flash of feminine smile? It is beyond me. My vision cannot reach Her.

She is not a ghost.

Ghosts are cold, pale things that long to be seen. She is darkness. She is the shadow behind the door as I turn to lock it, receding when I put light upon it. She is ever-taunting.

I quit writing. I quit blinking. My eyes begin to ache with a familiar dryness, like when the corpse dust puffed into them.

But when I sleep, she reaches me, like two long hands of smoke running through my hair. She brings me nightmares—terror of inconceivable means—but when I wake up, warm and sweating and shaky, she is gone before I can pin Her down.

I have stopped sleeping.

Insomnia is a dark, unnatural thing. I seek it frantically, as I sought Her in the beginning before I learned to loathe Her. Before she ripped away my sanity when I wasn't looking.

But even insomniacs eventually sleep between heartbeats. That space is like the space between blinks, and she finds me. I am unprepared for Her—as she likes—so she tugs organs around in my body while it sleeps against my will. I awake screaming, and still I cannot see Her face.

I see more of Her, though.

Every visit, brief and shadowy, further cements the impression of Her in my mind. She runs quickly even as she paces solemnly by, Her skirt floating behind Her like a cape. But Her head always turns away as I look at Her, a wash of dark hair flinging me the vestige of dust before she dissolves and I am left trembling.

I cannot go on like this. My body begs for rest—demands it—but my heart tremors and rebels at the thought. It is too dark here. I begin to see Her in every corner of my overly large chamber. She awaits me beyond the flickering of every period-accurate, candle-lit sconce.

With one hand I pry my left eye open, the right closing in relief, and crawl on hands and knees from my room down the long, winding staircase that I helped to rebuild, across the beautiful floorboards that the bodies rest under, and into my contemporary kitchen—the shadow of Her nipping at my heels like a wave of air.

I reach tile. It is bright here. No shadows. I installed fluorescents in this room alone. But as my left eye twitches for moisture, my right catches glimpses of Her.

She is growing bolder.

The lights in the kitchen flicker, once, and I scream.

She cannot have me.

With my last ounce of strength, I force my eyes open wide like a lunatic and grab for the sharp, gleaming kitchen knife. When the steel shifts, she flashes through it, running, Her hair flipping around to cover Her face.

I can feel my eyes closing against my will.

Without another thought, I plunge the blade into my chest.

The dull hilt protrudes as I collapse on my side, my eyes finally closing for good, and I seek peace.

But there is dimness. She is here, no longer running.

She has no need to chase me anymore. I am Hers.

She turns, finally standing in the vision of my inner eyes, still. Her long, dark hair flares once more, and she is facing me.

Except she has no face.

There is nothing there but shadows, a pit of unknown where the pale oval of skin and blushing cheeks should be.

I try to scream, but I no longer have a body.

She has no mouth, but I hear laughing. She is still laughing, still smiling in Her faceless face as she approaches me slowly.

And I no longer have eyes to open.

Annie Neugebauer is a novelist, short story author, and award-winning poet. She has work appearing in over fifty venues, including *Black Static*, *Apex Magazine*, and *Fireside*. She's the webmaster for the Poetry Society of Texas, an active member of the Horror Writers Association, and a columnist for both Writer Unboxed and LitReactor. She's represented by Alec Shane of Writers House.

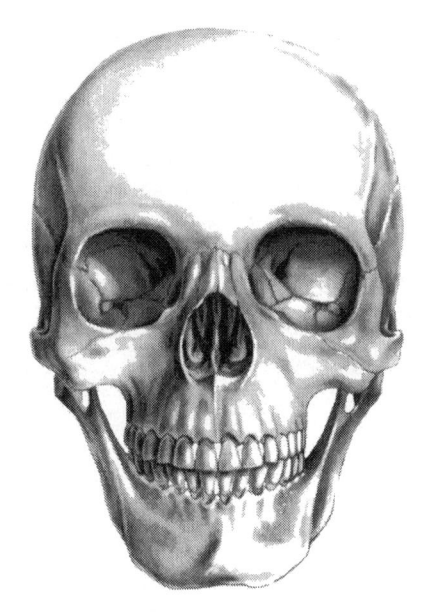

Ravens

Elaine Cunningham

People move to the suburbs to get away, am I right? Safe neighborhoods, good schools, backyard barbeques, Little League, and yadda yadda are great if you have kids—and I don't, as far as I know—but let's not lose sight of the frickin' point. When you stop getting away with the things you do, you've got to get away from them.

So I bought a house in the suburbs last month in a place that, lemme tell you, is about as far away from my old life as I'm likely to get without a kayak and a dog sled. The house is this little blue box with wood shingles on the walls instead of the roof, what people around here call "a Cape." It sits in a little New England town that's straight out of a freaking coffee table book. Seacoasts around every other corner, white steeples on the churches. That sort of thing.

Bottom line, this town is about the last place anyone would look for me. Sure, Rhode Island used to have a pretty decent organization, but crime went to shit after Ray Patriarca's day. Business is still being done around here, don't get me wrong, but nobody's got a reason to be looking for a low-level, burned-out soldier from New Jersey.

And I fit in pretty good, if I do say so myself. Probably half the names in the phone book end with a vowel and my accent is close enough to the blue-collar Rhode Island natives that it doesn't raise eyebrows.

So anyway, here I am. At first, it was mostly okay. The neighborhood is quiet. Lots of kids around, but they're usually being driven to tennis lessons and soccer games. The two kids across the street don't have much to say. They go to the Baptist school in town, which probably explains why they look at me like they're mentally reciting the Commandments and expecting me to break one of the top ten any minute.

Okay, sure—maybe I'm a little paranoid. Truth is, those kids seemed a lot more spooked by the nice suburban mom next door to them than the ex-mob guy across the street. But where I come from, paranoia's a pretty important part of the package. On top of that, I had this situation to think about.

Thing is, there was something wrong with the house. The first night I slept there, no problem. But the next night I had nightmares for the first time since I was a kid. Real spooky shit, and so real it took my eyes a while to adjust after I woke up. I'd be sitting bolt upright in bed, sweating like a pig, and still seeing this transparent, half-rotted corpse sitting in the bedroom chair, swinging slowly around to face me and taking its own sweet time to fade away into moonlight and shadows. I guess when dreams are vivid enough, it's like looking at the sun: even after you look away, it takes a while for the spots to disappear.

Anyway, the dreams were so freaking real that for a while I shrugged off everything else that was happening. Weird thumps and creaks? Hey, it's an old house. Murmured conversations I couldn't quite make out? The TV was on—if not mine, then probably a neighbor's. Lying in bed and hearing people I'd silenced whispering together in the corners? I must be asleep and dreaming. Waking up gasping for air, feeling a black cloud pressing down on me like it was trying to smother me in my sleep? Just another bad dream, most likely due to all the Portuguese food I'd been eating recently—spicy sausages like chouriço and linguica, high-voltage soups, snail salad. I mean, snail salad? That has to be worth a nightmare or two, am I right?

Things went on like this for a while, and frankly, I was starting to get a little ragged around the edges. Then one night I turned out the lights and was beating the pillow into a more comfortable shape when I heard this crash downstairs. Not a coffee mug falling off the counter sort of crash. This sounded like someone had picked up a pool table and thrown it down an escalator.

There was no way I could write this off as a dream, so I pulled out the gun I kept under the mattress (old habits again) and got ready to take care of things. I don't scare easy, but my heart was pounding, and the back of my neck felt cold and prickly. But I pulled my shit together and went downstairs for a look around.

Nada. Zip. Zilch.

Everything was perfectly in place. The doors were all locked, none of the windows had been opened or broken, and the alarm system (top of the line, and about half the price of the damn house) hadn't been triggered.

By this time, I was seriously spooked. So after I checked everything three or four times, I went upstairs and threw some clothes in a suitcase. I grabbed a bottle of scotch on the way out. There was no freaking way I was going to get any sleep in this place tonight. Or maybe ever.

As I pulled out of the driveway, I noticed the lights were on in the suburban mom's house. Kind of strange, seeing that it was past two in the morning. But as I drove past, I noticed that the lights were not actually in the house, but sort of around it. And the closer I got, the brighter they seemed to get.

But by that point, I was already way past my weirdness threshold and didn't have much brainpower to spare on this. So I drove about fifteen minutes to a town that had less scenic charm and more strip malls, and I checked into a motel behind the Bugaboo Steakhouse. I figured if there were any ghosts hanging around, they were probably beef cattle, and since I hadn't personally killed any of them, they had no call to be pissed off at me.

Yeah, that's right: ghosts. Because at that point, there wasn't much sense in denying what was going on. I'd bought a haunted house. The question was, what the hell was I going to do about it? Complain to the real estate agent? Get myself a lawyer and sue the old owners? Check the Yellow Pages to see how Rhode Island was fixed for ghost busters? I mulled it over for a while, then, thanks to the scotch, I managed to get a couple hours of sleep.

The next morning was Monday, and it was one of those bright, crisp New England mornings that almost made a hangover worth having. As I drove up to the little blue Cape, the setup seemed so freaking normal that I felt like a complete moron for thinking…what I'd thought the night before. I figured that since I was a reasonable man, there had to be a reasonable explanation for all this.

The suburban mom who scared the crap out of the Children of the Corn was in her front yard, digging in one of the flowerbeds. Her house was basically a plain, off-white box—the real estate guy had called it a "Federal-front colonial"—but the little gardens all over the yard made it less boring than it could have been. She looked up when I got out of the car and waved. For no reason I could think of, I started to walk over.

My neighbor wasn't any more impressive at close range. She was on the wrong side of forty, close to my height—just short of six feet—and probably a good twenty pounds heavier than me. She was wearing black jeans and a black tee shirt. Probably she thought black was slimming, but there's only so much you can expect from a color.

Her hair was short and not quite red. No makeup. Glasses. A few silver rings. Pretty average stuff, except that she was barefoot, and her tee shirt read, "If I wanted your opinion, I'd read your entrails."

I was starting to see where the kids next door were coming from. But she was walking toward me now, and I figured what the hell. She introduced herself as Frances Connolly and told me to call her Frankie, and I gave her the name I was using these days and told her to call me Bobby.

"Connolly—isn't that an Irish name?" I observed. The king of small talk, that's me.

She smiled a little. "Connolly is my husband's family name. I was born Franceska Kwitowska, which should explain a few things."

Couldn't argue with that. I knew some Polacks back in Jersey, and she would have fit right in with the kielbasa crowd.

"How are you settling in?" she asked. "I've been meaning to do the welcome thing, but the last two or three weeks have been fairly hideous."

"You got that right," I agreed with feeling.

Apparently, I put a little too much feeling into it because her gaze sharpened. "Anything I could help you with? Starting out in a new place can be tough, and this town has more red tape and strange bylaws than most."

I was about to say thanks but no thanks when she moved her left hand. It wasn't like, this big gesture or anything, but for some reason, it drew my eyes to one of the rings she was wearing. It was that star in a circle thing you see in movies about werewolves and devil worshipers.

"A pentagram," I actually said that out loud—again—before I could think. A couple of weeks without much sleep had taken more of a toll than I'd thought.

Frankie got this schoolteacher look on her face. "Strictly speaking, it's a pentacle. The suffix 'gram' indicates writing, as in 'telegram.'"

Like I give a shit. I was a lot more concerned about what this meant for me. I was having a hard enough time sleeping, without knowing that someone in the neighborhood was chanting over chicken bones every full moon.

"A pentacle, huh? So you're…what?"

"Careful."

That wasn't what I was expecting to hear. I must have looked confused because she pulled a silver chain out from under the tee shirt and showed me a little twisted horn made from red coral. That, I knew. It was a charm against the *mallochio*—the evil eye. A lot of people I used to know wore it, but they're all Italian. It was a tradition, that's all. An ethnic thing. Something told me Frankie had a different view, and since she was still wearing the schoolteacher look, I figured she planned to tell me about it.

But like I said before, I'd already had all the supernatural shit I could handle. So I said, "Yeah. Well…Nice to meetcha and so on, but I've got to get to work."

She nodded and went back to her flowers, and I headed into Hell's Little Outhouse to get ready for the ten-to-six shift at Lombardi's Volvo. Hit the shower, put on the shirt and tie, take out the trash for Monday pickup—that routine.

Work was the usual civilian bullshit, and afterward, I stopped by the Italian deli to pick up dinner. I got home to find trash scattered all over the front yard. My first thought was that maybe my ghosts had started working days. But of course, there was no lid on the trashcan. I'd thrown the plastic bags in and hadn't given it another thought. There were a lot of trees in this town, so there were probably animals and shit around.

Frankie wandered over with a plate of something. "A belated welcome to the neighborhood."

I looked down at a dozen or so chocolate cookies, big suckers that had little peanut butter cups stuck in the middle and melted chocolate drizzled over the top. They looked pretty good, assuming there was nothing funky mixed in. Eye of newt, human blood—things like that.

"You shouldn't have gone to the trouble."

She shrugged. "I always seem to be baking something. I have kids. They have friends. Every one of them could polish off this plateful without stopping to breathe." Her gaze shifted to the litter scattered over the grass. "Yikes. You know what will stop that?"

"A lid for the garbage can?"

"Well, that too. But if you have to put out extra garbage bags some weeks, take a couple pieces of bread, tear them into small pieces, and scatter them near the trash. In fact, do this every trash day. The ravens will eat the bread and leave the trash alone."

"Ravens."

I must have looked skeptical because she gave this little shrug to let me know she realized how that sounded.

"They're extremely intelligent birds, and if you pay attention, you'll notice some pretty interesting behaviors. For example, if you pay 'protection bread,' they'll leave your trash alone. I've even seen them chase other birds away from it."

It sounded to me like someone had watched *The Sopranos* a few times too many. "Protection bread, huh?"

"It's a figure of speech. But yeah, ravens are sort of like suburban mafia."

"How about that."

Maybe she noticed my lack of enthusiasm, but she didn't let it slow her down. "They have close-knit family groups, and if anyone messes with one of them, the others can hold a serious grudge. I read a story about a woman who found a baby raven who'd fallen from the nest. Its leg had been mangled in the fall. The bird couldn't survive in the wild, so she took it to a wildlife shelter. A small flock of ravens dive-bombed her, squawking in protest. They followed her car for a couple of miles before she lost them. And for years after that, they'd be watching for her and would mob her whenever she came out of the house. They never bothered anyone else in her family."

This was really out there, but to my surprise, I was starting to get interested. "No bird is that smart."

She turned and pointed to a big tree, the one the real estate agent had told me was a maple. Why, I couldn't tell you. In case I wanted pancake syrup, maybe?

"Every Monday morning, there's a raven perched in that tree waiting for me," she said. "When I come out of the house, he lets out a loud series of caws. The call is repeated from a tree not too far away, then another a little farther, and so on. On a quiet morning, you can hear the relay go for quite a ways. Ravens gather in those two trees and wait until a certain number arrive—usually no fewer than six."

"You're telling me they communicate?"

"Of course they do, and not just with other birds. In the wild, ravens sometimes form partnerships with wolf packs. Ravens are the eye in the sky, and the wolves are the muscle. If ravens fly over carrion or a wounded animal, they'll find the wolves and lead them to the food. In return, the wolves let the ravens eat alongside them when they make a kill."

It was enough like the system I grew up with to make sense. "As long as nobody eats alone, everybody eats."

"That's a good way of putting it. My ravens have this down to a routine. They take turns, some eating, some standing sentry. Same thing, every Monday morning."

"So how do they know it's Monday?"

She lifted one eyebrow. "That's the day people in this neighborhood put out trash cans."

"Oh. Right."

Frankie chuckled and gestured with the cookie plate. "Do you want me to take this in for you? Here—let me take that bag so you can open the door."

Since she was determined to be helpful, I gave her one of the deli bags and dug my keys out of my pocket. I unlocked the door and held it open for her. There's a little table in the hall. She took two steps toward it and stopped dead, like she'd run into a wall I couldn't see.

The cookie plate clattered to the floor, and she probably would have followed, if she hadn't caught herself against the table. I've never seen the color drain out of someone's face like that—not when they were alive, anyway.

She turned around and pushed past me. Once outside, she sank down onto the stairs, breathing slow and hard. There was a wheeze to her breathing that I recognized from way back. My brother had to use an inhaler when he was a kid. The sound was comforting, in an odd way. Familiar. I sat down beside her and waited for the worst of it to pass.

"Asthma?"

She nodded. We sat there like that until she got her breath back, and then for a while longer. I was pretty sure she got a whiff of one of my ghosts, but if there's a good way to start a conversation like that, I sure as hell didn't know it.

"Maybe you're allergic to something in the house?"

"Oh, there's definitely something in that house." The expression on her face made it plain that she wasn't talking about dust, pollen, or cat dander. "Not that I'm surprised."

"Why's that?"

She grabbed the railing and pulled herself to her feet. "Let's talk somewhere else. My house is pretty well protected."

I doubt that meant the same thing to her as it did to me, but I was interested enough in what she had to say to follow her across the street and through the attached garage. There was a small bundle of dried herbs on either side of the door leading into the house. She took one of them off the hook and waved it over her head, then she crossed herself with it like a good Catholic—only she used five points instead of four—and brushed at her shoulders like she was flicking off dandruff. She did the same to me, which gave me the feeling that I was going through some kind of decontamination process.

We went inside, and Frankie nodded toward the kitchen table. I took a seat and looked around while she got out mugs and put the kettle on.

A pair of Siamese cats slinked in. One of them jumped up on the table and gave me a long, flat stare—the kind of look I used to give people to let them know I had orders to shoot if they pissed anyone off. There's a reason why I don't much like cats.

The place seemed pretty normal, except for a dark painting hanging on one wall—a portrait of a barefoot woman drawing a circle around a small fire. Smoke rose from the flames in hazy curls that seemed to be shaping up into something pretty fucking significant. Several ravens gathered outside of the circle, maybe waiting for the smoke to get its spooky shit together.

"That's a Waterhouse print," she told me as she gently shoved the cat off the table and set a steaming mug in its place. "But you didn't come here to talk about art. Let's focus on your problem."

"You said you weren't surprised there was 'something in my house.' Why not?"

"This part of Rhode Island has been settled for over four thousand years. There are a lot of weird things around. Some are recent and fairly mundane—for example, there's a black bear buried behind the house two doors down from you. I get a sense of it from time to time."

"You get vibes from a dead bear? So you're like, a medium?"

That amused her. "Thanks for the thought, but I've got another twenty pounds to go before I'm down to a large."

"No, what I meant was—"

"I know what you meant," she said, still smiling. "Ever heard of self-deprecating humor?"

"Oh. Right."

"But to answer your question, no, I'm not a medium, and I don't want to be. For one thing, I'm still working out what I believe about all that. I don't know if it's possible to talk with the dead, but I'm pretty damn sure that I don't want to. With my luck, I'd be hearing from dead telemarketers at all hours."

By now I was starting to get a feel for Frankie's sense of humor: pitch black, delivered with a straight face and a bone-dry tone. At least I hoped it was a sense of humor. With this conversation, it was kind of hard to tell.

"I had the same problem when I moved into this house," she went on. "Nothing quite as specific as you have, but a lot of negative energy. It took me a while to get the place cleansed and warded. Protected, in other words."

I thought about the dim light that had lingered around the house the night before, and how it seemed to get brighter as I got closer. That raised some interesting questions, but for the moment I was more interested in getting rid of my ghosts than figuring out why I was setting off magical alarms.

"So, how do you set up this protection?"

"It depends on what the problem is. Give me your hand."

After a short hesitation, I held out my left hand, palm up. She dropped a small, smooth, very shiny black stone into it.

"That's polished hematite. I found it when I was breaking sod for the garden out back. Hold it tightly, and tell me what you feel."

I clenched my fist around the stone. It gave off a slightly fizzy energy. It was sort of like holding a damp Alka-Seltzer tablet, only it was hard and dry. Slightly freaked, I put the stone on the table. Frankie picked it up and dropped it into a little silk bag. She added a couple shakes from one of the salt shakers on the table, pulled the bag's drawstring shut tight, and tossed it onto the kitchen counter.

"Hematite absorbs negative energy. And let me tell you, it works. I learned that a few years back, when I was visiting my parents in Florida. I love my father dearly, but he's one of the most negative people I've ever met. A couple of days into the visit, my sister-in-law took me to a New Age shop. I tried on this little black ring, not knowing what it was. Suddenly I felt this whoosh, like something had pulled a plug, and all the tension and bad energy drained right out. Needless to say, I bought the ring." She paused long enough to send me another of those half smiles. "The ring shattered on my finger when I was on the way to the airport. Apparently, Dad had exceeded its capacity."

I didn't believe a word of it, but it was a pretty good story. "So you're saying someone buried a hunk of hematite in the back yard to keep away negative energy?"

"Actually, it's not a bad precaution. My guess is that there's enough psychic energy in this area to magnify whatever people bring with them."

I wasn't sure I liked the sound of that. "For example…"

"I started work on a book about Stregheria—that's hereditary Italian witchcraft—shortly after we moved in. There were a few strange occurrences, but mostly just a lot of unexplained tension in the air. I planted rue and fennel by the doorways and set up a Lare shrine inside, and things calmed down." She gave me a small, one-sided smile. "There's still a lot more dust generated by this house than any rational explanation can justify, but things could be worse."

For a while, I sipped at the coffee and tried to make sense of this. The woman was a fruitcake, make no mistake about that, but I knew enough crazy people to realize that being nuts didn't mean you couldn't also be right. Maybe she really was some kind of psychic.

On the other hand, how good could she be, if she'd let a guy like me into her house?

"You have a very strong affinity for death," she announced casually.

Her timing was too good to be accidental. Surprise made me jump, and coffee sloshed over my hands and onto the table. Frankie handed me a paper napkin and waited while I mopped up and pulled myself together.

"That's an interesting theory," I said cautiously. It also raised an interesting question: if she was some kind of psychic, how much did she know about me? And how much of a problem was that likely to be?

Frankie took a sip from her mug. "Green tea," she said sadly. "I'm decaffeinating. There ought to be a clinic for it, or at least a goddamn patch." She took another swig of the tea, then pushed the mug aside and got down to business. "There's a dark presence in your house—most likely more than one presence. But you already know that."

There wasn't much sense in denying it, but I shrugged and gave her a look that suggested we should move on.

"I never got a strong read from that house before, but it's possible that the entities were already there, and the kind of energy you brought into the house gave them the strength to act out. Sometimes houses are quiet until someone with an affinity for death moves in. I've seen it happen."

"So you're saying I bought a haunted house?"

"Possibly," she said, drawing the word out to add emphasis. "But if I had to guess, I'd say that whatever I sensed in there followed you here. The energy in this area gave it, or them, enough of a boost for you to see what has always been there."

Okay, that was just fucking creepy.

She took one look at my face and pushed a plate of cookies toward me. "Chocolate," she said. "Best coping mechanism I know. Seriously, Bobby, don't overthink this. Forget about how they got here. The question is, how do we persuade them to leave?"

"We?" I said around a mouthful of cookie. "How is this your problem?"

"When you have kids, everything is your problem," she snapped. "What if your house guests decide to wander? Because sometimes they do. I lived next to a seriously haunted house right after I was married. The things that went on…"

She shook off the memory and reached for a coping mechanism. "No ten-year-old needs to deal with that. Besides, what are neighbors for?"

As God is my witness, I had no idea how to answer that question. The whole suburban neighborhood thing was new to me, but I was pretty sure cookies and witchcraft wasn't the usual welcome package.

I drained my coffee mug to buy some time to think. "So what should I do about the house? Call a priest?"

Frankie smiled and shrugged. "If you feel more comfortable going that route, sure—give it a try."

"Or…"

She sipped her tea and considered. "It's odd that ravens came into the conversation earlier. A lot of the old religions considered them to be psychopomps—that's a sort of messenger that can move between this world and the spirit world. Some people thought ravens carried souls to the next world. Their presence on the battlefield was considered a blessing, as well as a practicality."

My patience was starting to wear thin. "This is freaking fascinating, but it doesn't solve anything."

"You know," she mused, "it just might."

The "protection bread" I could almost see, but this? I pushed back my chair and stood. "Thanks for the coffee."

Frankie rose with me. "Meet me in my front yard next Monday morning, just before dawn," she said. "This time of year, that's around five o'clock. Not many people are awake at that hour, so we should be able to wrap things up without raising too many questions."

The Siamese, who'd been sitting by Frankie's chair listening to all this, narrowed his blue eyes and let out a long, rusty meow. It was, hands down, the most sarcastic sound I have ever heard.

I tipped my head toward the cat. "What he said."

Frankie ignored us both. "Leave all your doors and windows wide open and come into my yard. The wards on it are pretty good. The ravens will do the rest."

"Sure," I said, which struck me as a pretty good way to go. Fairly polite, but it didn't make any commitments. Fact was, I had no intention of carrying out some half-assed exorcism. I left with a half dozen cookies and a private vow to forget all about this conversation.

Things didn't work out that way. Over the next few nights, I had plenty of reason to think about Frankie's offer. When Monday rolled around, I woke up before dawn pretty much the way I'd been waking up every morning, not to mention several times a night: drenched in sweat and fighting my way free of tangled sheets.

After I'd beaten back the latest nightmare, I noticed the faint, gray light rimming the window shades. Morning was just about here. I glanced at the clock. It wasn't much past five, so I just lay there for a while, waiting for the now-familiar panic to recede, and my pounding heart to crank down the volume.

As the thumping in my ears faded to manageable levels, I became aware of the noise outside—a chorus of rough caws, growing louder by the moment.

I swung out of bed and stumbled over to the window. Frankie was standing in the middle of her yard, wearing some sort of long, black dress. There was a silver chain around her neck, and hanging from it was a large cloth bag. She was barefoot—big surprise—and looking up into the maple tree.

I followed her gaze, and my jaw dropped. The branches were black with birds—big, sleek birds that scooted down along the limbs as they made room for the newcomers flying in from God only knows where.

Just then Frankie looked over to my window, and even from this distance, I could feel her eyes on mine. There was something in them that made me begin to understand why the ravens came to her call.

There had to be something to what she'd said; otherwise, how'd she manage to recruit all these birds?

On the other hand, it looked like a scene from a Hitchcock movie out there, and if my memory was holding up, that movie didn't end real well.

I was still mulling this over when something changed in the air around me. There was this electricity in it, like the supercharged, super-still feel the world gets just before lightning strikes. The bedroom was still fairly dark, and in the shadows, something started to rustle and whisper.

Suddenly one middle-aged Polish-American witch and a few hundred ravens sounded like a much better bargain than whatever was stirring inside the house.

I moved away from the window long enough to pull on a pair of pants. Open the windows, she'd said, so I threw that window wide open and moved on to the next one. When all the bedroom windows were open, I went to the next room, working my way downstairs. The dark energy grew stronger with every step, pressing in on me from all sides like a smothering cloud. It was stronger than it had ever been, and it was starting to feel so familiar that I could give it a name:

Unfinished business.

Whatever was in my house had a score to settle with me, and apparently they'd decided this was the time to do it.

Once the house was wide open, I ran across the street and realized too late that I was barefoot. I sort of hopped my way across the rough pavement and loose stones to the Connolly's yard. Frankie gave me a distracted nod and swung one arm like a sidearm pitcher firing off a high fastball. She finished off with a sharp snap that left her pointing at my house.

What happened next brought to mind the starting gun at the New York Marathon. Hundreds of birds leaped off the branches and headed straight for the little blue Cape. That was pretty bizarre, but I was nowhere near ready for what happened next:

The windows started to slam shut.

Ravens pulled up short as best they could, but some of them whapped into the glass and slid down the side of the house. There were enough birds still on the wing to circle the house like a dark tornado, and it occurred to me that their shrill, harsh cries were getting loud enough to wake half the town. Weirdly enough, no one else seemed to notice. The neighborhood houses stayed dark, and a passing dog casually lifted his leg on some bushes and trotted on. Apparently, Frankie and I were the only ones seeing this particular freak show.

She didn't much like what she saw. Her face creased in a frown, and she let out a string of words I was trying to get out of the habit of saying. She took off for her garage at a run, calling for me to follow.

I closed my mouth, which had been hanging open like I was some small-town tourist who'd just gotten a sales pitch from a Times Square hooker, and I followed her into the garage. She was taking a solid-looking shovel off a wall rack of tools.

"The entities in that house are stronger than I thought, and they don't want to leave," she said. "Windows and doors are portals, in more ways than one. If the ravens can't get through, we're screwed. We've got to open the windows or break them. Grab something."

I looked around and noticed a black leather sports bag someone had dropped in the middle of the garage. The zipper was half open, and a bat handle stuck out. I pulled it out and hefted it. It was one of those fancy new metal bats, dolled up with metallic blue paint.

Frankie snatched it out of my hands in mid swing, looking more shocked by my choice of weapon than by anything that had happened so far. "Are you kidding? There's no exorcism in baseball!"

She threw the shovel at me, grabbed another, and ran across the street, ducking this way and that as she made her way through the feathered wind tunnel that was still circling my house.

I've had some strange moments in my life, but nothing like the feel of all those black wings sweeping past. The weird thing is, none of them actually touched me. It was like the ravens were only halfway into the world, or maybe halfway out the other side.

I made it through the raven swarm without completely freaking out and tried the front door. It wouldn't budge. No luck with the windows, either—the place was locked down tight. So I swung the shovel at the dining room window, bracing myself for a shower of broken glass.

That turned out to be a mistake. Something behind the window—or maybe in the window—make it act more like hard rubber than glass. The surface gave a little, but it didn't shatter or even crack, and the shovel rebounded so hard it flew out of my hands. I lost my balance, overcompensated, and fell face-first into the unbreakable glass.

Holy shit, that window was cold!

I stumbled back, surprised that my skin didn't stick to it, like my brother's tongue had stuck to the stop sign that one winter he was young and stupid enough to take a dare.

I looked around for Frankie. She wasn't doing much better. Her first attack on the house sent her reeling back hard enough to land her on her backside. She pushed up from the ground, grimacing in pain, and reached into the cloth bag she wore like a necklace. She took a handful of whatever was in there and flung it at the window.

A small dust cloud hit the window, and the glass immediately blew inward. Ravens flew in right behind, streaming past Frankie as she hurried to the next window and did the same thing there. She started around to the back of the house, then spun on her heel and yelled at me to get over into her yard.

Too late.

The first wave of birds burst out of the house, dragging behind them an invisible cloud of cold and darkness and rage and despair. As it swept over me, I remembered why I'd decided to get out of the family business—every fucking moment and every bloody detail that had led me to that decision. Let's just say it was a bad few moments, and leave it at that.

Fortunately, it was over pretty quick. Just like that, the ravens were gone, including the ones who'd pancaked themselves against the house. The neighborhood was as quiet as a church, and I noticed that the grass was cool and damp. I didn't remember falling to my knees, but there I was.

Frankie stumbled over and sank down onto the grass beside me. A long moment of silence passed, broken only by the yap of someone's dog a couple of blocks away, and the faint echo of the raven chorus.

"Well, that should do it," she said.

I had to grin. She sounded like a roadside mechanic telling me my muffler ought to hold until I got the car to the nearest Midas.

Come to think of it, that's exactly what it sounded like—an admission that we had a fix, but not a solution.

"So...what next?"

Frankie took off her glasses and began to massage her temples with both hands. She looked very tired, not to mention several years older. I guess she'd been hit pretty hard by the psychic shit left behind by all those bad men I'd turned into dead men.

Several moments had passed before she spoke. "The stuff I threw at the window had salt in it, so you'll want to dig out the soil around the windows and have it taken to a landfill. Not much will grow in salted ground. Once you replace the soil, I'll tell you what things to plant. If they grow, it'll help." She shrugged and sighed, then admitted, "Not much, but some."

"So what'll help a lot? What'll keep…stuff like that out of the house?"

Frankie met my gaze. "You could move."

That, I didn't see coming, and it hit me pretty hard. I hadn't realized until this minute that I was actually starting to like the ditzy broad. She'd stood with me, better than any longtime friend I could name. I couldn't blame her for giving up on me, but still.

"You could move," she repeated, "which would probably solve the problem in this particular house. And maybe the next place you go would be better for you. Maybe the energy levels will be low enough to keep something like this from happening again. But if you want to make sure, you need to go back to wherever you came from. Face whatever there is to face, make whatever restitution you can. Then it'll be over."

That was a true statement if I ever heard one. If I went back to Jersey, I'd be dead, which is about as "over" as it gets.

Or so I'd always thought, up until, say, last month.

I flopped back to lie on the grass, one arm flung out wide and one thrown over my eyes. All of a sudden I felt more tired and hopeless than I'd ever been.

The soft rustle of skirts and a creak of protest from middle-aged knees informed me that Frankie was leaving. I guess I was okay with that, seeing there wasn't much more to say.

Fact was, I was pretty sure I understood the problem. I didn't need a witch to tell me my karma was fucked beyond recognition.

Maybe she sensed what I was feeling, because I heard her hesitate. After a moment, something cold dropped into my palm. I felt the faint fizzling energy, and I closed my fist around the hematite stone.

The tingling increased until it took all my strength to hold my hand closed over the vibrating stone. It felt good—scary, but somehow cleansing. After a while, I stood up and clenched my other hand around that fist, determined to let the stone suck as much negative energy out of me as it could.

By then Frankie was long gone. The sun was up. Her family would be awake soon, and she'd have the usual mom stuff to do. That was okay—what I was doing now, I could do alone.

So I held onto that stone until senses I didn't know I had screamed at me to drop the thing. Not quick enough. The stone shattered, and black shards burrowed deep into my hand. Blood welled up from several small wounds in my fingers and palm, like scattershot stigmata.

Suddenly I understood why Frankie had given me the stone. As she'd mentioned earlier, there was only so much negativity a chunk of hematite could hold.

I walked over to the nearest broken window and let a drop of my blood spill into the tainted earth. It seemed like the thing to do. Blood calls out for blood. I might not know shit about magic, but some things I know.

So I walked around the house, making small offerings to appease the dead. Fortunately, the place was small. I managed to squeeze a drop or two by each window and door before the bleeding stopped.

I was sitting on the front step, picking out the last of the stone shards with a pocket knife, when a sharp, grating call came from the maple tree. I glanced up. One of Frankie's ravens was back, and damned if he wasn't looking right at me.

There was a very familiar expression in his black eyes, and I could almost hear the feathered motherfucker saying, "Not bad, kid, but you might want to take out a little extra insurance, if you get my meaning."

Yeah, I got it. So I went into the house for the rest of the garlic bread I'd had last night. It was trash day, and apparently, the ravens and I had this little arrangement.

Elaine Cunningham is a *New York Times* bestselling author whose publications include 20 novels, over 4 dozen short stories, poetry, non-fiction, and a graphic novel. She is best known for her work in licensed settings such as the Forgotten Realms, Star Wars, and Pathfinder Tales.

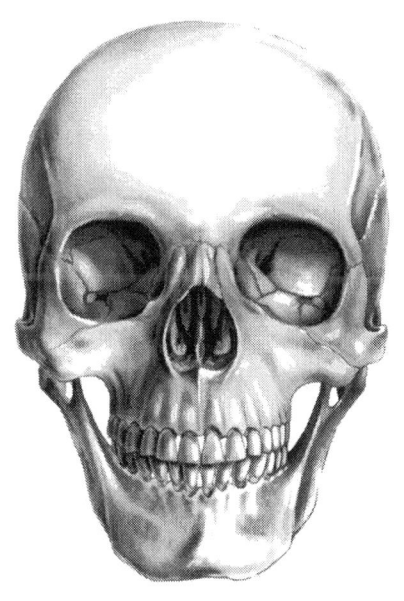

Foxford

Sandra Kasturi

Furred shapes move in the darkness near the platform, waiting for the last train. Fog muffles their sharp barks.

Eleanor really should have known better. The whole day had started unpleasantly, and even though she ought to be used to it by now, the gnawing misery she felt in the presence of her half-sister still surprised her. It was just like when they were children—Frankie shredding an entire shelf of her mother's books and then blaming it on her; Frankie stealing her dessert; the non-stop teasing; the list was endless. Eleanor had spent most of her grade school years with a persistently nervous stomach and endless visits to doctors, and now, when she really was too old for this sort of thing, there was that familiar intestinal lurch. The taste of the infinite barium shakes of her youth filled Eleanor's mouth every time Frankie walked into the room.

In Oxford, beautiful, peaceful Oxford, Eleanor had finally felt like she belonged somewhere, yet here was Frankie ruining it, like she ruined everything. And Bill was worse.

Eleanor had been working on her thesis in England for a year now, and she would have thought her half-sister might have grown up a little since she'd been away, but Frankie was still her usual childish self. And now she was dragging Bill along with her, their new relationship excluding everyone but themselves. Their visit was almost over, but Eleanor had already had enough.

Frankie and Bill were terrible guests, rendering Eleanor's small flat even smaller by their tiresome boisterousness and constant complaints, rabbiting on and on about, among other things, water pressure and English food. At the moment they were whinging about the fact that their hair dryer and shaver plugs didn't fit into the outlets.

"I told you it was a different voltage system," said Eleanor with a sigh, but Frankie had scurried back into the bedroom to sulk.

Eleanor lay back down on the narrow sofa and wondered again what had possessed her to agree to this two-week visit. But she knew—it was their mother, still recovering from Frankie's father's death—who desperately needed some peace and quiet, even for a short while.

I need to get them out of the flat, thought Eleanor. Or I'm going to lose my mind. London. I'll take them to London. She called out to Frankie with the proposal.

"I'd love to go to London. But don't you have more research to do?" She came out of the bedroom and stood in front of the window, brushing her silvery blonde hair.

"Well, yes," said Eleanor, "but I can do that tomorrow. Or the next day."

Bill grinned and smoothed his thumb and forefinger over the new, ratty-looking mustache he was cultivating. "I didn't think

Nervous Nelly wanted to brave London again after the Heathrow craziness."

Eleanor had never told Frankie how much she hated the crowds of Heathrow and London, although she had said as much to her mother in an email. She looked at her half-sister. Would her mother have told Frankie? Or had Frankie read her mother's e-mail? It wouldn't surprise her. And Frankie, of course, would have told Bill.

When did he get so nasty? she thought. Was it always like this, or is it just this trip? Maybe it's Frankie. The two of them together. She looked away.

"Come on, Bill. You know Eleanor doesn't like crowds. Or new places," said Frankie.

"Oxford's hardly new to me anymore. And neither's London. It would be silly for you to come all this way and not see London properly,"

"Very silly," said Frankie.

"Very silly, very silly, very silly!" shouted Bill. He grabbed Frankie by the hands and twirled her around in the cramped room until they nearly fell on top of Eleanor on the sofa, laughing. Bill pulled Frankie to him and started kissing her on her thin mouth.

Eleanor stood up and said, "I'm going to run a few errands. I'll meet you at the train station at 11:00 if you want to go. If you're not there, I'll go to the Bodleian and do some work. You two can do whatever you like."

"Ooooh, we can do whatever we like," said Bill, looking down at Frankie. "Did you hear that?"

Frankie pulled his head down to hers again.

Eleanor dressed in the bathroom, grabbed her purse and slipped out the door.

She and Frankie had never been close. Eleanor had been ten years old when her mother remarried, and Frankie had been born a year later. She'd felt completely disconnected from the pink, squalling creature, who reminded her of nothing so much as some new species of naked mole rat, and retreated further into the books she loved.

And Bill…Bill had been so nice in Toronto during grad school; she had even thought at one point he might be something more than a friend. She'd had no idea he and Frankie had even met, much less become involved. When Bill said he'd dropped out of the graduate program and wanted to visit, she'd felt a clutch in her heart. That was before she'd known Frankie was coming too.

Bill had turned into a real Nipper. Not a Biter—which is what her mother called men, in her still-strong Welsh accent—nothing so dangerous, but like some annoying and relentless little sharp-toothed creature.

Her father, on the other hand, had apparently been all Bite. Her mother said so over and over again. "Nell, lovey, watch out for those men, they're real Biters. Just like your father." Eleanor wasn't quite sure what she'd meant, but assumed some unnamed violence, some unspecified cruelty—truth be told, she didn't remember her father at all, and her mother had never even told her his name. But if her mother had meant for her to avoid all entanglements, she succeeded, at least until Bill came along…and even then it had just been a friendship. He probably hadn't even realized she'd once had other ideas. Now, in England, she was glad it hadn't come to anything.

As for Frankie…Frankie had been born with a set of mean little teeth.

The train picks up speed and dives into thickening fog rolling in from the north, turning the falling darkness a silvery gray. Strange, furred shapes keep pace.

To Eleanor's surprise, Frankie and Bill did meet her at the station, and the hour-long ride up to London was uneventful. She didn't sleep like she usually did in trains, only managing a kind of fitful doze, the clacking of the wheels echoing like the snap of teeth as she drifted in and out of peculiar dreams.

The other two had chosen a seat ahead of her, and Eleanor heard their whispering every time she lurched into wakefulness.

Paddington Station was a crowded nightmare, but Eleanor

Foxford

plastered a falsely serene smile on her face and walked ahead of Frankie and Bill. They skittered forward to catch up, and she could have sworn she saw a look of disappointment on Frankie's face. Perhaps they'd assumed she'd be hapless and needing to be led, and had been looking forward to abandoning her in the crowd and then teasing her mercilessly about it later?

I've been living in Oxford for a year, Eleanor thought. Do they really think I can't even manage some minor travel on my own? Idiots. She smiled. A genuine one, this time. She caught Frankie looking at her, a puzzled frown on her narrow face. Frankie's eyes were too close together, Eleanor realized. Why had she never noticed it before?

"Let's go on the London Eye," said Frankie.

"Oh, our Nelly-Nell doesn't like heights, does she?" said Bill.

Eleanor, who usually didn't, perversely said, "I think I can manage."

Bill grinned and said, "Oh, yes, *let's*."

Eleanor beamed throughout the entire whirling ride on the London Eye, pointing out landmarks. Frankie looked like she had swallowed a wasp.

"Tell you what," said Eleanor when they were back on the ground, "I want to have a look at some historical buildings and do a lot of boring stuff. Why don't you two go shopping, and we can meet up later? Maybe at a pub?"

Frankie was about to protest, but Bill interjected: "Sure. I know just the place. It's called the Fox's Head. Victoria Road, near Queen's Park station. I read about it on the internet. Think you can find it?"

"I live in England, Bill. It's no problem. I'll meet you at the Fox's Head at six o'clock."

"Sure," said Frankie.

"Whatever," said Bill.

"Bye, then," said Eleanor, and walked off. Only another three days.

The fog completely blankets everything for miles, but Eleanor, sleeping deeply, is oblivious to it. In her dreams, the sound of the train's wheels turns into sharp barks and the train furs over into a river of steel-grey foxes speeding northward, carrying her with them on their backs, like a queen being brought to her rightful throne.

Eleanor decided to become the complete tourist and wandered the streets, looking into shop windows and even venturing into Harrods where she allowed the perfume girl to spray her with an exotic musky scent. She took a ride on a double-decker and bought a map and a paper at a news agent's, finally settling down to a proper cream tea in a forgotten little café and enjoying herself hugely, despite not having seen any of the important things—the Tower Bridge, Big Ben, the Beefeaters. Well, she was here for another year at least. There'd be plenty of time for that.

"Will there be anything else, dear?" asked the elderly café lady.

"No, thank you." Eleanor looked up, and she saw something in the corner of the shop—something furry that darted out of sight. "Er, I'm so sorry, but you don't have mice, do you? I thought I saw…"

"Well, dear, sometimes you can't avoid 'em in big cities, you know. But mostly the foxes do take care of 'em," said the old lady.

"Foxes?"

"Yes, dear. London has red foxes everywhere."

The train slows and Eleanor wakes with a start at the change in its rhythm. The lights in her carriage have dimmed and several flicker. Outside is nothing but darkness and fog.

She looks at her watch. It is very late.

"That can't be right," she says. The trip back to Oxford should only have taken an hour.

The train slows further. A tree branch brushes against her window, and Eleanor jumps. Why would anyone plant trees so close to the track?

The train comes to a halt. Eleanor can almost distinguish the platform outside, and a sign that says "—xford," and then something else underneath it.

Oxford, she thinks. She picks up her purse and moves toward the door. The rest of the train carriage is empty. Frankie and Bill are nowhere in sight.

Having asked at the Tube station and consulted her map, Eleanor found Queen's Park on the Underground without difficulty. Victoria Road, lined with knobby, still-bare plane trees, was only another block away, and the Fox's Head was right on the corner.

The pub's weathered sign swayed as the wind sprang up. It was a bit odd—Eleanor had expected one of the famous red foxes of London—but the sign had the painted head of a big gray fox, teeth showing, red tongue hanging out lasciviously. Its eyes were bright and full of mischief.

Frankie and Bill were already at a table, barely visible in the dim interior, two pints in front of them.

"Eleanor," called Frankie, and waved her over. "Did you have a nice day?" she asked as Eleanor sat down.

"Lovely. Have you been waiting long?"

"Not long," said Bill, casting a sly glance at Frankie. "See anything good?"

"Not much. The usual tourist stuff. Maybe a fox. Just walked around a bit," said Eleanor. "I'll have a vodka and orange," she said to the barmaid.

"*What* did you say? A *fox*?"

"Yes, London has foxes everywhere, didn't you know? Hence the pub, I guess. But they're red foxes, not gray ones," said Eleanor.

"Oh, yes, *hence*," said Frankie.

The barmaid returned with the vodka and orange.

"Excuse me, but could you tell me why you have a gray fox on the sign? I thought it was only red foxes in London," said Eleanor.

"Well, it is, usually," said the barmaid. "The landlord got the sign from up in Wales. Says it's one of the *milgwn*."

"Mil-what?" said Frankie.

"*Milgwn*. It's a Welsh word. Means these enormous gray foxes up in Wales that have magical powers or some shite." Another punter caught her eye, and the barmaid moved off.

"Aren't you Welsh?" asked Bill.

"Our mother is," said Eleanor.

Frankie chimed in, "My father isn't. But Eleanor's father might be. She doesn't know, of course, since she doesn't know who her father is, poor lamb."

Eleanor looked at Frankie calmly and said, "No, I don't." Frankie actually looked faintly ashamed and studied her pint carefully, a red flush moving up her ears. "I have to go to the loo," said Eleanor. She got up and went to find the toilets.

When she got back, they were gone. She fumed as she paid the bill, which, for goodness sake, also included champagne of all things; they must have downed it lickety-split while waiting for her to arrive. A hundred and twenty pounds! That was…what? Nearly two hundred dollars? Eleanor could hear their giggling squeals outside, fading into the distance as they scampered off. She'd go back to Paddington Station and then Oxford on her own. She'd had enough of their selfishness and bad manners. If they got stuck in London on their own for the night, so be it.

She thought longingly of the drama-free past year in Oxford, which had been glorious.

"Nasty little vermin," she muttered, doing a passable imitation of her mother's Welsh accent. *Better watch it, or I'll bite back.* Now where had that thought come from? She wondered.

Outside, it wasn't quite full dark. Eleanor kept thinking she saw movement out of the corner of her eye, but when she looked there was nothing. There seemed to be more shadows in the alleys and along the sides of buildings than there should have been, all of which were blurred along the edges. Maybe vodka and Welsh mythology were a bad mix.

From Queen's Park to Paddington, Eleanor didn't see Frankie or Bill anywhere, but what did it matter? They could go their own way. Maybe she wouldn't move back home after her second year at Oxford. Maybe she'd just stay permanently. She smiled at the thought.

Paddington Station wasn't crowded. She fed her return ticket through the machine, and the turnstile opened. The lights flickered, and the very air grew dimmer.

A man in a conductor's uniform shouted, "Last train to Foxford, departing now from platform seven!"

Eleanor ran up to him. "What did you say? Oxford?"

"This is the train you want, ma'am," said the conductor, and handed her into the carriage. His accent was thick and barely intelligible.

Eleanor sat down in the last seat. Up ahead she spotted a silvery blonde head and a dark one, close together, whispering. Frankie and Bill had made the train after all.

"All aboard to Foxford," said the conductor, but Eleanor was already nodding off.

Eleanor steps onto the platform. It is very cold, and she can't see much in the fog. Frankie and Bill must have gone ahead. The platform doesn't look anything like the one they'd left from that morning. She walks up to the sign. Part of it is obscured, but she can still make out that it says "Foxford," not "Oxford." She inhales sharply. She has taken the wrong train and now she is lost in the dark. She squints at the sign again. Eleanor can't read the smaller writing underneath, but she does recognize it. It's Welsh.

Her watch isn't wrong—she's been on the train for hours. She's in Wales. Eleanor shivers. As she stands there wondering what to do, the train starts up and speeds off into the darkness without her.

From somewhere in the fog comes a series of sharp barks.

The fog swirls and pulses. Eleanor clutches her purse and stands very still. The barks come again, closer.

The fog in front of her parts, and standing there is one of the most enormous foxes she has ever seen. It is almost the size of a small pony. It gives that high, barking yip and looks right at her. More foxes emerge from the fog, though none are quite as large as the first.

The great king fox barks again, and she swears it almost sounds like words. His dark eyes are upon her, and she feels something strange. Not fear, but the start of something else—the pulse of excitement, of blood calling to blood. The other foxes surge toward her, a relentless gray tide. She feels them against her legs, hot, lithe bodies and coarse fur. They mill around her, noses touching her knees.

She looks down. She is stranded in a sea of furred creatures, all of them eerily silent, looking at her expectantly. She offers one hand to them. The king fox steps forward and licks her. His tongue is rough and warm. The other foxes shrug closer. They lick at her legs and feet. Wherever their tongues touch, she changes. Her shoes disappear, her skirt vanishes, her skin turns dark, furring gray.

Eleanor drops her purse and falls to all fours. The foxes lick her clothing away until she is new-minted, a clean animal, gray coat gleaming as the fog lifts and the moon comes out.

She sniffs the air. She can smell two-leggers close by. A male and a female. The scent of their fear wafts deliciously on the wind. A part of her is reminded of something, something to do with family…but she pushes it aside. She lets out a bark and surges to the head of the skulk, next to the king fox. He barks at her in return, and all Eleanor's milgwn brethren flow forward, together in joyous pursuit, teeth white, red mouths open and ready.

Sandra Kasturi is an award-winning poet and writer, with work appearing in various venues, including ON SPEC, Prairie Fire, several Tesseracts anthologies, Evolve, Chilling Tales, ARC Magazine, Taddle Creek, Abyss & Apex, Stamps, Vamps & Tramps, and 80! Memories & Reflections on Ursula K. Le Guin. Her two poetry collections are: *The Animal Bridegroom* (with an introduction by Neil Gaiman) and *Come Late to the Love of Birds*. She is also the co-publisher of ChiZine Publications, winner of the World Fantasy, British Fantasy, and HWA Specialty Press Awards.

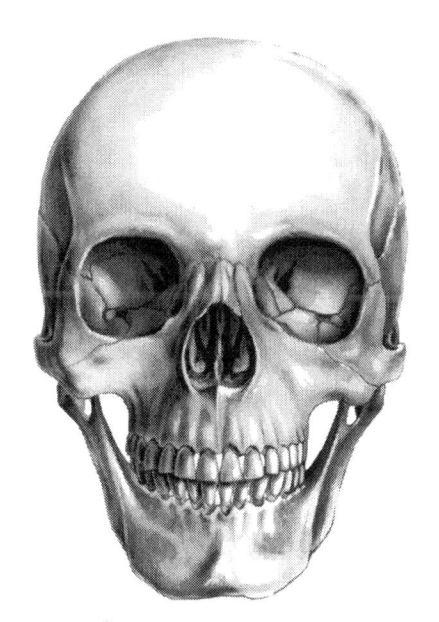

The Root

Jess Landry

The journey up the mountain had been as treacherous as I had imagined—of the seven local men I hired for a petty sum, only myself and three others reached the highest point any man in known history had set a weary foot upon. I could tell the three remaining grunts were fearful; at the last rest point before our final ascent, they conversed anxiously amongst themselves in their native tongue, a language unfamiliar and vexatious to my ears.

I watched as their apprehensive eyes searched wildly in every passing snow drift for the winged demons of local tall tales that supposedly stalked the mountainside, demons that craved the flesh of man. Sitting apart from their musings with no desire to consort, I chortled at the thought of their local legends while my body trembled in the sub-zero temperatures. Were these men so blinded by ancient folklore that they did not see the opportunity that presented itself? It was no matter, soon I would have all the secrets the mountain kept hidden for myself.

My gloved hand found its way into my coat pocket, and I pulled out the very reason I had come to this desolate area and risked my life by setting foot on this supposedly accursed rock—my golden coin. Although the shimmer had faded considerably over the decades since its discovery (mostly in part from old age and my family's ceaseless fascination with it), the intricate symbols that had been painstakingly etched on were still somewhat coherent.

One side had an etching that was unmistakably the mountain I now sat upon in a frozen state—a mammoth formation that lay hidden within the deepest, most barren region of the Himalayas; the summit of the behemoth splitting off into two sharp and ragged peaks that resembled horns, as though the Devil himself had sought to create a gaudy shrine to his most distinguishable features. Some weeks earlier, I had discovered that the impoverished few that inhabited the region had an immeasurable fear of the mountain. Most able-bodied men I had approached with my translator rejected my generous monetary offer in exchange for safe passage up the peak, often mumbling "Raksasa Pahada" as they walked away. *Raksasa Pahada*, I had learned, meant Devil's Mountain. Yet on this coin I saw no impending doom, no intimidation from Lucifer himself, only the promise of what lay within—on the coin, where the two peaks joined at their base, there appeared to be a mouth that led into the pits of the mountain, and from that mouth radiated signs of a great light; a light that, no doubt, led to what the other side of the coin presented.

The etchings were somewhat worn down as I flipped to the other side, yet it was as clear as the snow was white that a vast treasure had been depicted. There appeared to be mounds upon mounds of what were surely more coins like the one I held in my frozen hands, with what I assumed to be three larger mounds standing tall at the head of the pack, although the bottom of the coin was slightly faded. The chamber in the image seemed to stretch beyond the size of the coin, leaving my imagination to fill in the blanks, as I had done many times in my childhood; stealing the coin from my sleeping father, the only time I could get close enough to press its reassuring cold metal to my warm skin. I closed my eyes for just a moment and held the coin close. In that moment, I was young again; floating upon a sea of gold, scooping at the treasures with warm hands, tossing my coin into a pile of its kin—there would be no need to have one prized possession when I could have thousands. I opened my eyes and found myself smiling. I glanced over to the hired help and they were watching me with a look that transcended language, it was a look of profound distrust.

Conditions grew for the worse, the higher we ascended. The frigid wind picked up speed, the cliffs and sturdy grips grew steeper and more far between. One more hired helper was lost to the unforgiving elements of the mountain before our remaining trio reached where the two peaks met.

The two horns of the mountain were lost in the dense fog and cloud above. The snow and wind howled and cursed in the darkening sky as we stood in awe of its mammoth features. The entryway stood menacing and comfortless, a hole of endless night, its blackness contrasting against the white snow and gray rocks that surrounded it. A wind noticeably cooler than the one affixed to us on the mountainside seemed to be exhaling from the hole, yet the coolness was no mask for the abhorrent melody of smells that accompanied it: bile, filth, rot, and decay blended with other unfamiliar scents. I had anticipated a warm and not so putrid victory within the depths of the Devil's Mountain, but what was warmth and pleasant smells when I would have the frozen touch and metallic perfume of thousands of coins? I reached into my coat pocket and felt the uneven roundness of my coin. That was all the warmth I needed.

"Right then," I motioned my remaining help to the opening. "In you go."

There was a confused glance between the two men, one tall and one fat. The latter nudged at the former to speak on both their behalf.

"Doctor Shaw, please," the taller one spoke in the finest broken English he could muster. "No. No farther."

"Yes, farther," I mocked. Tall and Fat would be going into the mountain if I had to drag them both by their frozen ears. "If you want to get paid, you'll step in. Do you understand? PAID."

They exchanged worried glances, but nodded in unison. Money, I had found in my travels, was a language every man understood. Fat reluctantly went first, lighting a torch from one of the many bags he carried as he did. It nearly extinguished where the path of the mountainside wind met the interior wind, fluttering for a just moment, then regaining its strong flame. From a few feet inside the hole, he turned back to face us, no doubt to ensure he was not alone. Tall lit his torch and joined Fat. The power of both their torches illuminated the deception of the entrance—the walls towered far beyond the reach of the light. I waited somewhat impatiently before both men turned a corner, the light still strong enough for me to locate them. When I did not hear any screams, I followed suit.

A sufferer of claustrophobia I was not, but venturing deeper into the increasingly tighter corridors of the mountain, I may have easily became afflicted. After some hours of downward trailing caverns and some narrow ledges that Fat struggled to get across, we were at the point where the only way through was to squeeze by with our backs tightly pressed against the icy mountain walls, leaving no room for the multiple bags I had intended to fill with treasure. Up ahead, Tall, whom I had placed in the front (with Fat struggling to push his gelatinous body through the cramped space in the back), let out a cry of what was, no doubt, elation—the narrow passage opened up rather abruptly into a monstrous chamber. We had descended into the very bowels of the mountain. Not wanting to waste a single moment, I pushed past Tall to behold the magnificent hollow innards of Raksasa Pahada. What a sight it was: a delicate golden light shimmered off every surface like light reflecting through water, rendering the torches practically useless; hieroglyphs by the thousands had been etched painstakingly onto the mountain walls, surely the same artist as the one who etched my coin; and just ahead of where I stood, an ancient staircase pieced together step by individual step followed the curves of the mountain to nearly fifty feet below, the last step meeting the chamber floor. My eyes hunted the path of the staircase and saw that only a few short paces from the bottom step sat an archway leading deeper into the mountain. The brilliance protruding from the archway seemed to be the light of the sun itself. My treasure.

In my excitement, I grabbed hold of Fat's torch, who was only now exiting the tight space, and threw it down into the pit below where it hit the ground hard some fifty feet below yet remained illuminated. Both men let out a shocked gasp as the sound of impact echoed throughout the chamber, growing louder as every ripple climbed until it abruptly stopped above us where the golden shimmer met the darkness that surely led to the horned peaks high above. I sensed the anxiety of my two helpers and stood as quietly as they did for a moment, searching the hollow for any winged demons or other cave-dwelling creatures that enjoyed the taste of a man's flesh. None seemed apparent.

"Very well, let's move on," I chimed to Tall, but his mind was elsewhere. He was studying the ancient drawings etched on the walls, his fingers tracing them with a nervous pace. Every drawing seemed to render his state more and more agitated. As the treasure was no doubt within reach, I pushed the man aside and went on without him, motioning for Fat to follow me if he anticipated payment. Without warning, Tall grabbed hold of my wrist with a much stronger grip than I predicted from a man of his size. Taken aback by his unexpected action, I struggled to pull free, but his grip was too powerful. The man began screaming incomprehensible words at the fat man and myself, pointing upwards into the darkness where the warmth of the golden shimmer could not reach. He then frantically pointed towards a certain glyph, but I had no time to study it. He was dragging me back to the claustrophobic corridor when our eyes met amongst his hysteria. Money may be a language understood by all men, but so is fear, and I had never seen fear before as I did in his eyes. For a moment, just a brief moment as we held our gaze, I felt it, too. But as the moment grew, his eyes began to shimmer. Such a delicate golden shimmer, like the morning sun passing over a serene pond. In the reflection of his wide, fear-stricken eyes, it illuminated every surface just enough for safe passage to the source—my treasure. My coins. No need to have one when I could have thousands.

I had no choice but to shake Tall loose, a task on the archaic staircase that had but one end result. With my free hand, I lunged at the torch he still carried, catching him off-guard. As he stepped back from my sudden movement, his foot met the edge of the landing, slipping off. In a daze, he dangled nearly fifty feet above the solid ground; all that could save him from meeting his fate was the grip he held on my wrist. He released the torch for leverage, the flames popped and fizzled as it hit the stale air with speed, dropping next to the torch I had tossed moments before. I couldn't understand a word Tall was saying, I assumed he was pleading for his life. Desperation had swept over his features; he was a man terrified, not a man ready to die. He tried frantically to get his free hand latched onto something solid, but the staircase protruded from the mountain walls some distance and had no visible supporting structure underneath; the man was grabbing at nothing but air. I grimaced in pain as he attempted to grip both hands around my wrist, yet as he searched for steadiness, I sensed a moment, just a brief moment, where his grip loosened and I could squirm free. Without hesitation, I seized it. Our eyes locked as he fell to the ground. I turned away before witnessing the carnage. Lying on my back, gasping at the cold air, my gaze found the hieroglyph he had been so adamantly pointing at. It was the image that had been etched on the back of the coin that I had assumed to be piles upon piles of riches with three prominent mounds as the main focus. I sat up and squinted at the image - no, now that I could see it clearly, it appeared to be something slightly different. Yet before

I could determine what the difference was, Fat caught my attention. He was breathing quite heavily but remained unmoved from where he originally stood, except to raise his hand and point skywards. His eyes were fixated to the darkness where the golden shimmer had no sway, and only the darkness reigned.

"You there," I called out, realizing I did not know the man's name. "Come help me up, would you?"

The man frantically looked back and forth, meeting my eyes and then the darkness. Was it a trick of the shimmer or was the man weeping? At that moment, as I lay against the cold, undisturbed earth, I came to realize a few things: first, in the hustle of all that had just occurred, I had not noticed the delicate shimmer (that surely was from my treasure) had begun to pulsate ever so slightly, as though a feather had landed on a pond causing a ripple; second, after simply lying on the ground in silence, attempting to regain my breath, I had not heard the sound of the tall man's body hitting the floor; third, and most important, upon realizing the lack of the sound of impact, another noise seemed to resonate throughout the chamber—the impossible sound of thrashing wings. A cacophony of horrible, reptile-like screeches from above and below filled the hollow cavern, knocking Fat to his hands and knees in prayer. I spun my head around just in time to see the doll-like body of Tall flung high into the black obscurity, and from where the cusp of the shimmer met the darkness, I saw a large claw emerge to grab hold, and slightly above that claw, the shimmering face of the devil himself.

The fear I had felt for that brief moment in Tall's eyes coursed back into my veins, my immediate reaction was to flee. Fat was still in prayer with his eyes shut tight as I sprung up to my feet and ran down the aged staircase as expeditiously as I could. Fat only caught wind I had left when I was nearly two-thirds of the way down. In his panicked and foolish state, he quickly gave chase. I kept my eyes focused not on him, but under the staircase, an area where the delicate shimmer dared not venture, leaving the busy shadows as a hiding place for everything that lurked below, and the shadows certainly seemed busy.

As I approached the archway, with nearly every breath eliminated from my body, its framework came into view. It was an immaculate display in the style of the etchings on my coin, hundreds of hieroglyphs seemed to adorn the edges that appeared to be made of marble that gleamed from the light source beyond it. More shrieks echoed out and with one final push, I dove head first into the warmth of the ethereal light, into the open arms of the treasure's glow. It took me a moment to catch my surroundings, but one thing was certain—the chamber was striking. It stretched further than my cold eyes could see, with mounds upon mounds of exactly what I had come for—golden coins ripe for the taking. I could do nothing but smile as fear vacated my body. All the years I had invested into what my colleagues had deemed 'unrealistic fantasies', all the uncertainty my father had placed in me when I had inherited the task of finding the lost treasure now sat readily at my toes. I had done it, it was mine.

A scream from not so far behind interrupted my moment of beauty. I turned to see the fat man bloodied and crawling forward, gripping the fine craftsmanship of the archway to pull himself in, his actions sullying its delicateness with his gore and filth. He reached out for my hand, no doubt pleading for salvation in his native tongue, but I had come too far to be any use to him and his wounds. With a sluggish kick, I pushed the man's mangled body away from the archway. He rolled a few feet towards the center, near the fading torches. When he came to a stop, there was a moment of unanticipated silence, as though the things that dwelled beyond were not sure how to proceed. No doubt they had never had their meal handed to them. The sound of heavy footsteps echoed from outside the archway; I stepped back behind the safety of the walls, keeping the fat man in my sights. From the shadows of the far wall underneath the staircase, one of the creatures stepped out from its hiding spot. Just like the creature from above, it had the face of what could only be the devil—a face that had human features which were horrifically amalgamated with those of a vampire bat. Its razor-sharp teeth were too large for its mouth, it had no choice but to keep it open, giving off the illusion of a diabolical smirk. Its nose was nothing more than a deformed, hollow snout. Its red eyes bore no pupils and looked of pure evil, and protruding from its head were two raggedly sharp horns that mimicked those of the mountain top. Its body was that of a sickly, pale man; it walked on its contorted back legs like an unsteady child, legs that gave way to its clawed feet, with a pointed tail dragging behind. It slinked cautiously toward Fat (who was curled up in the fetal position and deep in prayer with his eyes closed yet again), its serrated claws clicking against the solid earth floor. His prayers grew louder as the creature drew closer, and from my hidden corner, I watched it all unravel. The creature steadied itself on its hind legs, like a lion preparing to pounce, yet as it did, a creature nearly triple the size of the small one swooped down from above and into view. It shrieked at the smaller one as its claws gripped onto the man, dear Fat who had ceased praying and now met his fate. He turned his head in my direction, the light from the treasure chamber hitting his face, highlighting the sweat and crimson that ran down softly. With that, the gargantuan creature took off; the fat man's screams faded as he was carried higher and higher into the darkness above.

I had unwittingly shifted from my hiding spot to watch the fat man's demise. When he was out of view, I averted my gaze to the small one. It was watching me. Startled, I fell backward onto the cool ground. The small one seized the chance and crouched over onto its four limbs, slinking towards me like a proud cheetah. I hastily searched my surroundings; although the room was vast, there was nowhere I could hide from this creature. All I could think to do was fight.

The creature was steadily approaching the archway when it came to an abrupt stop. It sniffed at the elaborate markings on the marble doorway and released a growl unlike anything I had heard before. It stood up on its hind legs, glaring at me as it let out a piercing shriek. It then raised its frail arms, flaunting its underdeveloped wingspan and its clawed hands. The small one took off erratically to the shadows under the stairs; a feeble attempt to no doubt to show the fully grown creatures above that it was growing fearless. I remained unmoved. The iciness of the ground had seeped through my winter coat and now chilled my entire body. Or was this chill the feeling of death releasing its hold on me? The creature had approached me but turned away at the arch. Could this room be protected? Was I safe to enjoy my treasure? I had to be.

With the commotion beyond the archway at an end, I cleared my mind of all that had just occurred and fixated my energies on what lay ahead. It was much colder in the beautiful chamber than it had been in the mountain's hollow, the walls were thick with layer upon layer of ice, surely built up over the years, even centuries, of undisturbed peace. My breath materialized heavily in front of me as I walked over the endless mounds of coins, humming pleasant melodies from my childhood. There was so much to think about—what would I do with the treasure? Sell some of the coins to museums for a hefty sum, no doubt, but would I keep the rest for myself? Perhaps fill a room in Mackenzie Hall with the remaining coins and lay among them for the rest of my years? Might be wise. And the creatures, they would be no issue as long as the workers extracting the coins remained in this room; surely a way out of the mountain existed somewhere in this chamber. There simply had to be.

I had wandered deep into the beautiful chamber, so deep that I could not see the archway anymore. Every mound and every wall looked the same, there had been no distinguishable landmarks during my trek, no way of knowing how far I had traveled. For a moment, just a brief moment, I felt the fear rising from within me, forcing itself up through my body and into my throat. I harbored a scream that I dared not cast away, no need to raise alarm. I swallowed my dread and sat down near the base of a high mound of coins to think, the shimmer reflecting warmly in my eyes. Surely another door existed within this room, I would simply have to find it. I grinned to myself with the slight regret of letting Fat and Tall go so easily, their assistance would have been needed at a time like this. But now was the time to get my hands dirty and when I reached the cool surface air, I would have to put the events of the day in proper order, so as no one would deem me a suspect. Not that they would, once they saw my riches for themselves, all men could be easily enticed with the promise of money.

I put my gloved hands in my coat pockets in a feeble attempt to warm them. My right hand touched upon the familiar edges of my golden coin. I pulled it out of my pocket and studied it for a moment; the one side with the distinguishable features of the mountain's peak, and the other side, somewhat faded, but no doubt depicting the very room I sat in. With not so much as a blink, I tossed my coin onto the mound behind me and ran my hands through the pile I sat at the bottom of. I could feel the chill of the metal penetrating my heavy gloves as I continued to run my hands through, causing small avalanches of golden delight. A shimmer, unlike the others, caught my eye. At the top of the mound, one coin seemed to outshine its brethren. My curiosity got the better of me, and I crawled on hands and knees like a child unable to walk. The coin appeared to be wedged within its kin and try as I might, the coin would not move. I brushed the other coins aside to clear room around it, but most of them seemed to be in the same predicament. I moved in for a closer inspection of the edges of the coin, removing my gloves and attempting furiously to dig my bare fingers beneath it with no luck. I stood up in unbalanced frustration and began kicking and kicking, until finally, the coin came free and flew to the base of the mound. I laughed cheerfully to myself and childishly slid down the hill to my new prize. Its shimmer was ten times brighter than any other coin in the room, and its etchings were perfection. On one side, the Devil's Mountain shone its wonderment into my ecstatic eyes, the etching of the light escaping from the center seemed to radiate a glow on its own. On the other side, the three mounds of riches were more detailed than I had ever imagined, every pile seemed a precise depiction of what surrounded me. Yet as I studied the coin, I noticed one detail that had not been present on my old, worn coin. The three mounds in focus, near their base, each had one open eye. Surely I was seeing things, mounds of riches could not have eyes.

Just then, a hint of warmth oozed onto my ankle, causing me to fling myself forward. I looked up in time to see a flow of black ooze seeping from the top of the mound where I had kicked the coin free. Then, the mound began to move. Coins shook loose from all around where I sat, as though a volcanic eruption were about to take place. The floor around me shook, too, and for a moment, just a brief moment, it seemed as though the other mounds were moving. I retreated backward, not taking my gaze off the unnatural movements until I hit the thick layers of the ice walls. Before my very eyes, the golden hill I had sat upon just moments before was now transformed. The mound was kin to the large winged devil I had watched from beyond the archway, the only difference being the creature had coins upon coin embedded in its back, in its wings, and in its horned head. It rose up from its disturbed slumber, and the sound of little metallic avalanches rang through the room, as the beast shook itself clean. It shrieked as it rose, enticing the others to rise with it. I could not move; I could not think. There was nothing for me to do, no other options but to watch; watch as the red-eyed devil opened its eyes, sniffing at the putrid air with its hollowed out nose; watch as it turned its wretched smiling face towards mine; watch as it went on its two legs and slinked towards me while the others rising from their slumbers took notice and followed suit. A group of three had gathered around me, sniffing and smiling. Then, like a pride of lions, they attacked with perfect synchronicity.

I awoke sometime later to darkness. The events of the day seemed like a bad dream, and it took me a moment before I realized it had been no dream. I tried moving my limbs but was met with such resistance that I ceased immediately. I felt as though I had been buried alive; unseen forces weighed heavy against my body, and when I inhaled, I breathed in only the sweet perfume of metal. I attempted

The Root

to scream, but my wail was no sound that could come from a man. It echoed through my heavy grave, reverberating a familiar tune. Panicked, I attempted yet again to move my limbs. The fear I had absorbed earlier from the tall man stretched through my extremities, breathing new life into them, and with some effort and immense pain, I was able to free my right arm. I used my shaking hand to pick away at what encompassed me while clearing a passage for my head. The sounds of the small metallic avalanches made no guesses necessary—I was entombed in my treasure. I began digging furiously around my head, my arm aflame with agony until the golden shimmer of the room pierced the darkness. Coins hurtled past my face, the disharmony of their landslides caused crushing pain in the back of my skull as the now still chamber came into view. I was only able to clear enough coins away to grant one eye the gift of sight, but that was all I required. My hand, still digging at the coins surrounding my face, was not my hand. It looked sickly, it looked pale. My fingernails had fallen off and from the opened wounds so grew the tips of serrated claws. My breath grew rapid as I brought my maimed hand to my head, pricking my fingers on the needle-fine horns that protruded from my skull. Anxiety swept over me, could this actually be happening?

My panicked eye then caught a glimmer from the only golden mound in my view. At its base, a red, pupil-less eye watched me; an eye that had appeared so evil, so furious before now studied me quietly, as I had studied my coin for so many years. Its eye observed me for a moment more, our stares interlocking, but at that moment, I perceived hints of emotion—of empathy, of melancholy. Then, it closed its eye gently, slipping back into a tranquil slumber.

It was then that I knew: money was a language we all understood.

Jess Landry is a graphic designer by day and a writer by night. You can find some of her work online through SpeckLit, EGM Shorts, and The Sirens Call. She currently resides in the icy wastelands of

Jess Landry

Winnipeg, Manitoba with her husband, daughter, and two cats. Follow her on Twitter @jesslandry28

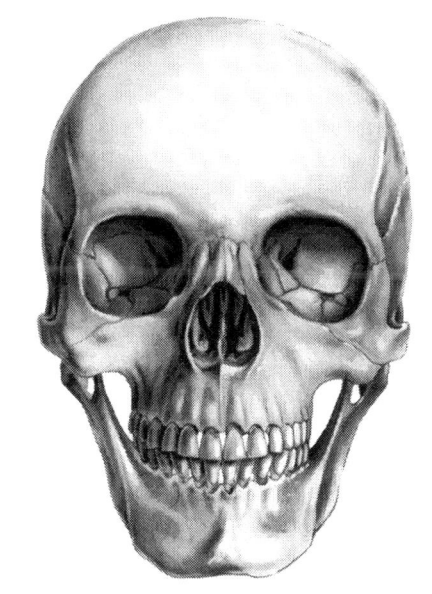

Long Time, No See

Sarah Hans

Ayida's eyes were blank. She was only a child the first time I met her, still unfinished, but even so, I saw the space where a soul should be. My skin prickled when she looked at me with her vacant face.

"Your daughter will become a powerful *mambo*," I told her mother in the marketplace. "You should let me take her for training right away."

"How can you know such a thing?"

"I can see it when I look at her. I can read the bones," I offered, reaching for the pouch at my side. "The *loa* can prove my words."

"That's silly superstitious nonsense."

Bile-flavored rage bubbled up in my throat. "I've built my life around such silly superstitious nonsense." I bit back further angry words. "Let me show you, please. The *hounfour* is right around the corner. It will only take a few moments, and it could change your daughter's life." Still, she hesitated, so I pressed on. "My name is Erzulie Tio, and I've been reading the bones since I was not much older than your girl."

"Erzulie Tio? I've heard of you."

Of course, she'd heard of me. "From your neighbors?"

"Yes. They said you freed their son from a demon."

"Not a demon, a Petwo loa. But yes, I coaxed the spirit from the boy. Let me read the bones for your daughter. You're part of our community now, so your spiritual welfare falls to me."

She licked her lips, conflicting beliefs warring on her face.

"Mama, please?" The girl turned those big, empty pools up to her mother and the woman at last smiled and nodded.

"Yes, alright."

I brought them to the hounfour and cleared a circle on the dirt floor, squatting beside it. "What's your name, child?"

"Ayida Fazande," she replied, kneeling and watching my hands with intense interest. I drew the bones from their pouch, and she asked, "Are they real bones?"

"*Yapok* knuckles." I held out my palm studded with bones. Each knuckle was marked with mystical symbols.

"They look like dice." The girl's mother inspected the bones too, leaning down over her child. They looked so much alike, mother and daughter, nearly identical, Ayida the smaller and less scarred version.

One soul can't inhabit two bodies.

"Please stand back, Mrs. Fazande."

She smiled and took a step back, saying, "Call me Lourdes."

I muttered a quick prayer to Papa Legba and threw the bones into the circle. They scattered and rolled like they always do. I prepared to announce the fate I'd already determined for Ayida, but my breath hitched in my throat as the scattered knuckles told me a story. A story of power. A story of blood. A story of the terrible things that lurk in the darkness. Shrill screams made my ears ache and my nose burned with the stench of searing flesh. And through it all, there was Ayida Fazande, flames dancing in her eyes.

"Erzulie? Erzulie are you alright?" Lourdes Fazande stood over me. "Should we get the doctor?"

I was prone on the floor, and the fire was gone. "No, no, I'll be fine," I assured her, sitting up. I scanned the room for Ayida. The girl was standing in the doorway, her empty eyes wide with fear and staring at me.

"What happened?" Lourdes asked, offering her hand to help me climb to my feet.

"The loa spoke," I replied, still watching Ayida.

"What did they say?"

"Your daughter has power. She is destined for…" I shook my head, conflicted. "…greatness. I should begin her mambo training immediately."

"Mambo training? If she's destined for greatness, then she can do better than this." Lourdes' gesture swept over the hounfour. The mud-and-straw walls, the swept dirt floors, the glassless windows. Her gaze even included me, in my simple cotton dress, barefoot and childless. "I want more for Ayida than this life."

A matter of disappearing chickens brought me to the Fazande's doorstep not long after our first meeting. Neighbors had complained to me that their fowl were missing. I'd discovered the birds deep in the forest, following a trail of feathers and blood, thinking perhaps a wild dog was the culprit. Instead, I found headless chicken corpses, a circle of blood, and dirt tamped down by dancing.

My feet carried me to the Fazande's house. Lourdes and Ayida were working in the garden with the rest of the family. When Lourdes spotted me, she called for all the children to hide in the house.

"What are you doing here? We don't want to talk to you!" She brushed sweat from her forehead, leaving streaks of dirt, squinting against the bright sun.

"I found dead chickens in the forest," I blurted. "Someone has been stealing them from your neighbors and using them for…for Vodou rites."

"What does that have to do with us?"

"I think it was Ayida."

Lourdes scoffed. "Ayida knows less than nothing about your Vodou rites."

"Your daughter is special."

"I know. That's no reason for me to send her with you."

"You must." I looked up at movement on the porch. Ayida stood there, staring. I suppressed a shudder. "There's something…I didn't tell you."

Lourdes followed my gaze and shouted for Ayida to get back in the house. "This thing you didn't tell me, is it something that will convince me to send Ayida with you?"

"Yes. She's…"

"You should have told me before. Now I don't believe you. Now I think you're desperate."

"I am desperate. Your daughter…"

"No. I can't make it any clearer. You should go before Papa comes home."

"Your papa respects me. If you won't listen, he will."

"Papa also owns a gun. Are you willing to take the chance he'll side with you?"

My retort was interrupted by a warm, salty breeze and the distant rumble of thunder. Both Lourdes and I turned to the horizon, where dark clouds boiled. We nodded to one another, an unspoken agreement that our human concerns could wait in the face of the coming storm.

I hurried back to the village. My neighbors were boarding up their homes and shops. With the help of a few neighborhood boys, I just managed to get the windows of the hounfour shuttered before the rain arrived.

The word "rain" is barely sufficient to describe a summer storm in Haiti. "Torrent" is a better word. The world was silenced and stopped by the force of the winds and the huge, pelting droplets. Even the human smells that always surrounded us, odors of sweat and garbage and cooking and sex and birth and death, were obliterated by the clean, fresh scent of water.

Alone but for a few guttering candles, I used the time to sweep the floors and clean the walls with my special tonic. The room filled with the scents of pepper and herbs, backed by the cleanliness of vinegar, the scent of a room purified both physically and spiritually. I always found comfort in that scent, because it reminded me of the mambo who trained me, who taught me to brew the tonic from wine, and cast the bones, and pray to the loa. I could feel her beside me, singing as I worked, and I felt less afraid.

I prayed for a while, seeking guidance from the loa, but the guidance never came. Eventually, exhaustion won out over my vigil, and I curled up on my cot in the back of the hounfour. Lulled by the grumble of thunder and the tap of rain against the aluminum roof, I dozed.

Pressure against my throat startled me awake. Ayida's face loomed in my vision, her mouth twisted into a snarl. Her small hands were about my neck, strangling me. I shoved her back and sent her sprawling across the dirt floor.

"What are you doing?" I croaked, rising from the cot.

Ayida crouched on all fours like an animal. She bared her teeth and growled at me, snapping at the air. Her eyes were full of blind rage.

I fumbled for the bottle of tonic and the broom. Ayida lunged at me, and I poked her in the belly with the broom, keeping her away from me, while I called for Papa Legba. "Take this loa from this child," I called, and splashed the tonic at the girl.

Ayida screamed and covered her face, crumpling to the floor. I dropped the broom and wrapped one arm around her, still clutching the tonic bottle in my other hand and calling for Papa Legba. "Call the loa back across the divide, Father of the Crossroads! Release this girl!" I sprinkled more tonic onto her hair, the scent of pepper and vinegar surrounding us like a caustic cloud. My eyes burned, and I squeezed them shut.

Thunder exploded all around us, and Ayida shrieked with fear, writhing in my grasp. I wish I could say that it was my tonic that drove the loa away, or perhaps the intervention of Papa Legba, but I have to give credit to Agau, the spirit of thunder. His voice rolled and clashed and encompassed us for a few moments, as if the house were in the center of the storm. His brutality was so frightening that the loa gripping her body fled, and Ayida went limp in my arms when the thunder had passed.

I lowered the girl to my cot. She whimpered and curled into the fetal position, tears streaming down her face to leave silvery tracks across her dark skin.

"I'll get you some water." I rose, but her hand shot out and grasped my arm. "What is it, child?"

Her voice was small and distant when she spoke. "Can you make them stop?"

"Make who stop what?"

"The loa. Can you make them stop?"

My chest felt tight in sympathy. "With training and hard work, yes. Together, we can make them stop."

She released me, and I went to find her water. She stayed the night in the hounfour, draped across my lap, and I sang her the songs of the mambo while I wiped the tonic from her face with a wet cloth.

The thunder gradually grew less and less fearsome until it stopped altogether, and not long after, the rain stopped as well. The crickets and frogs returned to their chirping and buzzing. I threw open the shutters to greet a hot morning that was quickly becoming stifling.

Ayida was asleep on my cot, and I was boiling plantains for breakfast when Lourdes Fazande appeared. She threw open the door, glanced about, issued a strangled cry of relief, and ran to her daughter. Behind her followed her father, an imposing farmer holding a gun, and two of the young men who worked on his farm.

I nodded greeting to the men. "You'll find the girl unharmed."

Kneeling by the cot, Lourdes checked her daughter for injuries. "Her face is swollen. What did you do?"

"A loa was riding her." I gestured to the now-empty bottle of tonic on the floor near the bed.

"Mama? Mama, Erzulie Tio hurt me." Ayida's voice sounded nasal and strange, but Lourdes didn't seem to notice.

"What did you do?" Lourdes demanded of me as she pulled her daughter to her feet and clutched the child to her side.

"I defended myself and saved her from the loa. Nothing more."

"She hurt me," Ayida insisted. She pushed away from her mother. "She touched me *here*." She cupped her nether regions.

Lourdes's mouth puckered in fury. "This ends now. If you touch my daughter again, I'll kill you. Do you understand?"

"She came to *me*. I didn't take her, and—"

"I don't care! If she comes to you again, if you so much as speak to her in the marketplace, I'll make you wish you'd never been born. Come, Ayida." She grabbed her daughter's hand and tugged her toward the door.

Ayida didn't move for a moment. Dark intelligence flickered in her eyes. Her lips curled into a sneer. "*A pi ta*, 'Zulie. See you on the other side."

The trek through the jungle was not an easy one. It required the better part of a day and a full pack of supplies. When I finally approached the clearing where an old man crouched over a fire pit, the afternoon was preparing to give way to evening.

"Erzulie Tio! *Sa fè lon temps nou pa we!*" The man squatting by the fire stood and waved. His voice was the same booming bass I remembered from years gone by, though he was no longer the towering giant of a man he once was. Twenty years ago, I had likened my friend to a wild boar, substantial and intimidating, but now he reminded me more of an ancient tree, with brown limbs so frail they looked like they might break in a strong wind.

"Manno Roche!" I called. "*Bonswa*, my friend." We met halfway between the path and the fire pit. We clasped hands, and Manno pulled me into his embrace. I kissed his cheek and then, overwhelmed by emotion, I planted another kiss firmly on his mouth.

He laughed. "I'm happy to see you too, Erzulie." He turned to the house. "Sylvenie! Come quick, it's Erzulie Tio!"

Manno's wife emerged from the house. She had barely aged since our last encounter, still beautiful and shapely. She smiled reluctantly and waved from the porch but didn't approach.

"What brings you all the way out here?" Manno asked.

"Let me sit and have some water and I'll tell you."

We went to the porch, and Sylvenie brought us a table, two small chairs, and a big pitcher of water. I drank and made small talk, asking about their life in the jungle, and then when I had recovered my breath, I told them about Ayida Fazande.

When I finished, Sylvenie disappeared silently into the house. Manno sat back in his chair and stared off into the distance for a few moments before speaking. "You're sure it was Baron Kriminel?"

"No one else calls me 'Zulie."

Manno stared at his own hands. "What do you want me to do?"

"I want to call Agau."

"Are you mad? I can't call Agau. Look at me, Erzulie. This body couldn't stand to be mounted by Papa Legba. Agau is brutal. You're asking me to sacrifice myself."

"Then I'll do it. You do the ritual, and Agau can mount me instead."

Manno studied me closely. "These visions really have you spooked, to offer that."

"I'm desperate. And Agau frightened the loa once before…I believe he could do it again. Maybe permanently."

"You used to hate being ridden."

"I still hate it. Ever since…" I swallowed against the lump of fear in my throat.

"Ever since we tried to call Baron Samedi and got Kriminel instead."

I grimaced. "But I don't see what choice we have. The alternative is unthinkable."

Sylvenie brought us wooden bowls full of rice and beans. "I forbid either of you to make a decision on empty stomachs."

I accepted the food and watched as my friend's wife handed him a bowl and spoon and lovingly kissed his forehead before retreating into the house.

"She seems sad," I offered.

Manno frowned. "She is sad. She has always been sad, my Sylvenie. She has always known a day would come when someone would need the Vodou, and it would be my undoing. She knows this will probably kill me."

"Not if I let the loa use my body."

"Even if you let the loa use your body, Erzulie. The cancer has taken its toll. There's not much left of me to give."

I had no reply to that, so I ate instead. We sat for a long time, watching twilight conquer the jungle, listening to the birds grow quiet and the insects grow louder. Eventually, our bellies full, we set the bowls aside, and Manno sighed.

"Did you bring a chicken?"

"I can't ask for your life. If I had known…"

"Let my death be a sacrifice. Soon I'll be going to see Baron Samedi either way. It might as well be in service to a greater purpose."

"But Sylvenie…"

"Promise me you'll take her back to the village with you. Don't let her stay here when I'm gone."

Numb, I could only nod. "There's a chicken in my pack."

"And what about the girl?"

My gaze settled on the tree line. "She'll come. Baron Kriminel and I have unfinished business."

We built a massive bonfire in the fire pit. Manno sacrificed the chicken and smeared its blood on my forehead and chest. He sat beside the fire with a pair of drums and beat frantic music while

Sylvenie and I danced. We pushed ourselves past the point of exhaustion, chanting and singing even when we were out of breath. Eventually, after hours of this, I felt myself step from my thrashing body, and I knew the time had come for Agau to mount me. The sacred trance had removed my doubt and fear, leaving me apathetic, vacant, ready to be ridden.

I felt Agau's spirit thrumming in my bones, his consciousness filling me until it felt like he would split my skin. But then, suddenly, I was empty, and my own soul snapped back into my body. I collapsed to the ground, disoriented. "Agau! Agau, come back!" My voice was hoarse with overuse.

Manno slid off his chair onto the ground and began to convulse. Sylvenie and I ran to his side and tried to protect him from hurting himself. His body became stiff and for a moment, I feared he was dead. But then he relaxed in our arms and sat up.

He laughed, and it was a sound like rocks rubbing together, low and gruff. When he spoke, his voice was even deeper and more resonant than usual. "*Bonswa*, my chickadees. I'm hungry."

Wiping tears from her cheeks, Sylvenie went to fetch food.

"You were supposed to take me," I told Agau. "Why didn't you take me?"

"I don't want to mount you. I want to *mount you*!" Manno's hands pressed the flesh of my thighs, and his mouth went for my neck.

Desire surged through me at the feel of his callused fingers and hot breath on my neglected skin, but I pushed him away. "No! We're not here for that! We're here to talk about a girl. Ayida Fazande."

"Hungry." He reached for me.

"Sylvenie is bringing food."

"Not just for food, woman!" He pulled me to him roughly.

"First we talk about the girl." I pushed away and rose, stepping back from him.

"First we sate my needs." He stood as well, grabbing at me again. "I am the god of thunder. You called me here. Now you will do as I command."

He chased me around the fire, growling and grunting until Sylvenie appeared with plates laden with food. He crouched over the plates and shoved handfuls of chicken and rice into his mouth, eating loudly and with no care for manners.

"We called you because we need you to protect Ayida Fazande," I said as he ate, careful to stay an arm's length away from him.

Manno's eyes—Agau's eyes—locked on mine. "And what will you give me in exchange? My protection comes with a price."

"I'll marry you. No loa has ever claimed me."

"Baron Kriminel says otherwise."

"Baron Kriminel is a liar."

He smiled. "That much is true. But I don't want you. You're too old." He glanced at Sylvenie.

She gasped. "I'm already married."

"I would claim you only once a week."

Sylvenie turned to me. "This was not part of the bargain."

"You can have her once a month and me as well," I offered.

"And the girl."

I shook my head. "I can't make that bargain. Ayida is too young. And her parents aren't here to bargain for her."

"All three or nothing at all." Agau tossed chicken bones into the fire.

"No bargain." Ayida appeared just outside the ring of light cast by the fire. She was filthy, her clothes caked with muck and body smeared with what might be blood or might be something else. Her voice was still high and nasal.

"Ayida!" I took a step toward her and then stopped, catching myself. "Baron Kriminel."

"Aren't you clever." Kriminel stepped into the firelight, walking with a masculine swagger. Ayida's arms were riddled with bite marks—human bite marks—probably from her own mouth.

"What have you done to her?"

Kriminel chortled. "What do you care? The girl is an empty vessel, waiting to be filled. No soul, or such a tiny one that it's inconsequential. She's barely more than an animal, and you sacrifice those to my kind regularly."

"She's a person, and you're hurting her."

Kriminel ignored me and instead turned to Agau. Manno stood, towering over the tiny girl even in his decrepit state. "Baron. I see you're still mounting children, like a pathetic weakling."

Ayida's body moved faster than any serpent I've ever seen. With a growl, she barreled into Manno and knocked him to the ground. Screaming, the two loa fought each other, punching and kicking and biting, abusing the human bodies they possessed.

"We have to stop them!" Sylvenie cried.

"Get more food!" I told her. She ran for the house.

I grabbed the bottle of tonic from my pack and doused the fighting loa with the liquid. They both screamed and reeled away from one another. "Stop this!" I shouted. "Agau, do you see now why I want protection for the girl? She's too easy for the lowest of spirits to mount."

Agau glared at me through red-rimmed eyes. "I don't care about the girl. I don't care about any of you!" His voice boomed, startling birds in the jungle to take flight in a flurry of wings.

Baron Kriminel laughed, a sinister sound that made me shiver. "Your gambit to save the girl has failed. But I will offer you a bargain even if he won't."

Sylvenie appeared with bowls of food and laid them at the feet of the two loa. They both squatted and used their hands to scoop pork and plantains into their mouths. "What bargain do you offer?" I asked breathlessly, terrified of the answer.

"Marry me as you should have done twenty years ago."

The world was suddenly hazy, my vision a tunnel. "What would be the terms?"

"You'd be my wife. You'd do my bidding. You'd let me mount you whenever I choose. In exchange, I'll leave the girl alone."

Sylvenie moved beside me and laid a gentle hand on my arm. "You can't do this, Erzulie. To be married to Baron Kriminel would be the cruelest fate I can imagine."

I remembered the stink of burning flesh and the piercing screams of my vision. "There are crueler fates." I turned to Kriminel. "I'll marry you if you'll give the girl your protection. No loa are to mount her, ever, for the remainder of her life."

Kriminel stood, his mouth smeared with grease. "You would make this bargain for her?"

"Not only for her."

"No!" Agau threw his bowl aside like a petulant toddler. "The women are mine. I will protect the girl! Not you, pathetic scum." He advanced on Kriminel.

I called for him to stop, but it was too late. This time, Agau wasn't interested in a brawl. He laid his hands on Ayida's shoulders. His mouth opened, and the sound that emerged was thunder, but louder than any thunder I'd ever heard, so loud it shook the ground. Ayida struggled for a moment, and then her eyes grew wide and her body went limp.

Agau gently laid her on the ground. "Baron Kriminel is no match for the god of thunder."

I hurried to Ayida and laid my hand on her chest to be sure she was still breathing. When her ribcage rose and fell I let out a laugh that was half relief and half disbelief. "Thank you," I breathed to Agau, hardly believing I'd so narrowly missed such a terrible future. Ayida was safe; we were all safe.

"Don't thank me yet," Agau replied. Manno's arms opened, and he smiled lasciviously.

Sylvenie and I went to him without hesitation.

In the morning, Sylvenie and I awoke in Manno's arms. His mouth curved in a beatific smile, but his body lay stiff and cold. I covered Manno's still form with the blanket, my mind still hazy with memories of the night before, memories of skin and mouths and hot, wet darkness. Sylvenie smiled, though it was full of sorrow, and I couldn't help smiling myself.

Ayida was sitting on the porch.

"*Bonjou*, Ayida," I said quietly, cautiously.

"*Bonjou*, Erzulie Tio," she replied, turning to look at me. Gray clouds roiled behind her eyes, dark with the promise of rain.

I breathed a sigh of relief. "Let's go home."

Sylvenie took my hand. "You know that it's not over, don't you? You've deceived Baron Kriminel twice now. He'll come for you again, as soon as he has a chance."

I nodded, squeezing Sylvenie's fingers and reaching for Ayida's hand. "Agau saved me this time. Next time, I probably won't be so lucky."

"Then why do you smile, Erzulie Tio?" Ayida asked, and I noticed that her voice sounded deeper and more resonant than it had before.

"Because you are safe, Ayida, and that's all I wanted."

As we made our way into the jungle, hand-in-hand-in-hand, I could have sworn I heard the gods laughing.

Sarah Hans is an award-winning editor, author and teacher. Sarah's short stories have appeared in about twenty publications, but she's best known for her multicultural steampunk anthology Steampunk World. Sarah's next project is an anthology featuring characters with disabilities called Steampunk Universe.

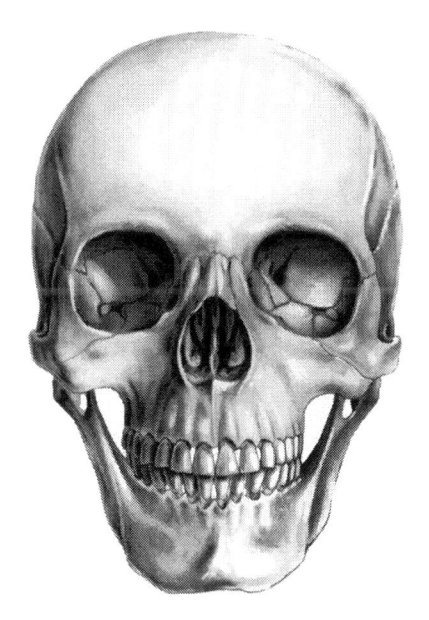

Saving Grace

Lillian Csernica

"Papa says the pilgrims are fools, too vain to see the holiness of the relics in their own lands. Do you think so, Katarina?"

Yvette sat at her dressing table while I combed her hair. The beautiful golden strands spilled between my fingers as I ran the ivory comb through them. My sweet little mistress, as fair as I was dark, the only sun I would ever see.

"I think it is good for people to travel, my lady. They go home with new eyes." I parted her long hair down the middle of her head and pushed each side off over her shoulders. "Tell me, are there priests in this party? Monks, perhaps?" I had sensed nothing, but I had to be certain.

"Papa did not say so. Only a scholar, some merchants, and two women."

I let out a small sigh. Perhaps the evening's feast would not be the ordeal I had feared.

"I do not think Papa will let you stay away this time," Yvette said. "Papa says we must show these Germans all the grace they will never achieve."

My relief vanished. "Surely your father would not ask me to forsake my prayers?"

Yvette lapsed into silence, her eyes on her hands where they fretted with each other on her lap. I loved her most in these still moments. At fourteen, the Lady Yvette de St. Martin was just reaching ripeness. Blushes warmed her fair cheeks. Her eyes were not the empty blue of so many girls, but hazel, wondrous and complex, flecked with bits of gold and dark green. In her eyes, I saw the forests of my homeland, so far away in the cold north. No wolves stalked through those imaginary trees. Yvette was a beauty, with none of the calculating edge that so marked the catty witches of the French King's court.

After braiding both sides of her hair and binding them, I trapped each in turn in the little cages of golden wire that hung from the golden fillet. I smiled. The young never tired of inventing new styles. My own hair I bound back into one braid, with only my carnelian combs for ornament. They were all I had left of my mother. The Tatars had taken the rest.

Yvette reached into her jewel box to select the brooch that would fasten her mantle. She cried out and jerked her hand away. On her forefinger, a red spot swelled into a fat drop of blood.

"Hush, *ma petite*. It is nothing." I took her hand between mine and bent over it so she could not see the hunger in my face. I opened my mouth and let my tongue lick up the blood. It was only a little scratch. I straightened and let the trickle of blood run down my throat, fighting down the temptation to squeeze her finger for more. "There now."

I turned away to hide the sudden heat in my face and rummaged in the jewel box. I chose the brooch her father had given her last spring. Four small emeralds surrounded a fat sapphire. It would suit the bliaut Yvette wore, made of wool dyed a deep blue. Over it lay a cotehardie of forest green. A girdle of lapis set in silver hung round her narrow waist. I pinned the brooch to her the shoulder of her cotehardie and dropped a light kiss on her forehead.

"All is well, my dear. Your mother will be the only one to better you tonight."

Yvette walked to the door. It opened ahead of her reaching hand. In the doorway stood her father, Sieur Etienne de St. Martin. He was a slender man in his thirtieth winter, elegant in a long houppelande of green velvet. He would have been handsome but for the harsh lines around his dark eyes.

I curtsied. "*Mon seigneur.*"

He ignored me and spoke to Yvette. "Are you ready, my sweet? Our guests have bathed and dressed. It should be safe to sit near them now."

Yvette giggled against the back of her hand. "Do they smell so bad, Papa?"

"After two months' hard travel, their horses stank less than they. But they are fit company now." He deigned to look at me. "And what of you, Mademoiselle? Will you join us?"

"*Mon seigneur*, I have no stomach for the richness of your table this night."

"Fasting again? I wonder you don't starve to death."

I tasted the last bit of blood on my tongue and felt a little dizzy. I often wondered where I gained the strength to hold back my hunger. One glance at my precious Yvette and I knew. The instant I fell to that temptation, I would lose her forever. The scorn in Etienne's eyes prompted me to further my excuse.

"The kitchen maid's mother lies dying. She asked me to pray for her."

"I see." His tone was cold. "Some peasant slattern means more to you than your proper duties as a member of my household."

"No, Papa!" Yvette cried. "Katarina would not—"

"Be still!" He glared at me. "You turn the child's head to thoughts of nunneries with all this fasting and praying. You will join us at table."

"As you wish." I curtsied, bowing my head to hide my anger. If my patience was not so essential to survival, nor so tempered by the passage of ten decades, I think I might easily have slain this pompous farm boy in the first hour of our acquaintance.

He turned to leave, offering his hand to Yvette. Her brow creased with worry for me. She knew I would suffer for my obedience. I took up my basket of needlework and followed them out into the passage.

Sieur Etienne led us into the Great Hall. He nodded to the steward, who called the hall to order. Sieur Etienne presided over a large household. The Great Hall of the Chateau was crowded, filled with shouts and the clattering of crockery. There were servants, villeins, grooms, and the usual assortment of lesser staff. The noise subsided as all present rose from their benches to bow their heads as their Sieur passed by.

The Dame Clarisse stood by her place at the high table. Five years older than Etienne, she kept her beauty intact through a ruthless regimen of bathing and ointments. When silver had begun to dull the gold of her hair, she risked her lord and master's rage by dying it black. Now, not even the most milk-pale babe could match the whiteness of her fair skin with all that black hair framing it. She took care to dress in hues that heightened her pallor, midnight blue, scarlet, charcoal gray. A clever woman, Clarisse. What a pity she had no greater ambitions.

The pilgrims also waited at their places. Three months past, a half-starved band of mendicant Franciscans begged hospitality of us. Their very presence in the Chateau gave me a fearsome headache. As I approached, I eyed the pilgrims, seeking any source of that same unbearable pain. The four men wore the tunics and hose of merchants, somewhat tattered by travel. The two women huddled together. The fur lining their cotehardies marked them as noblewomen. A fat and florid man in the black robe of a scholar stood behind the chair to the right of Sieur Etienne's place. The scholar merited greater honor than the noblewomen? They must have been sent on the pilgrimage to atone for some crime, most likely an excess of the flesh.

Sieur Etienne seated himself. His chair was immense, a broad high-backed thing of black walnut and oak, draped in soft furs. Dame Clarisse and Yvette sat in smaller chairs. I took my usual seat, a little stool just behind Yvette. The stool's lower height permitted me the concealment of shadows thrown by the enormous candlesticks on the table.

"Good pilgrims," Sieur Etienne began. "Let me welcome you to this table. May we give thanks to Our Lord for seeing you safely to our door."

The chaplain stepped forward to ask the blessing. Several of the pilgrims crossed themselves. I closed my eyes, but still I felt the sting of it.

"Allow me to present my wife, Dame Clarisse Gastineaux, and my daughter, the Lady Yvette."

"Blessed Sieur." The scholar bowed. "Much kind words have I heard of this house, but that angels lived here, I did not know."

Dame Clarisse laughed, head held high. I felt the urge to join her. The scholar's French was atrocious, marred by his accent and clumsy grammar.

"You are too kind, Herr Doktor," Sieur Etienne said. "My dears, this man is Doktor Schwartzen, well learned in theology and a frequent visitor to the University of Paris."

"Do you know much of Heaven, Herr Doktor?" Yvette asked.

"Not as much as I would like, Mademoiselle."

Yvette sighed. "I want so very much to go there."

Sieur Etienne and Dame Clarisse exchanged a smile. Sieur Etienne reached across to pat Yvette's hand.

"Let the Doktor enjoy his meal. You may ask him your questions afterward."

"Yes, Papa. Forgive me, Herr Doktor."

"Not at all, dear lady. I will be happy to tell you everything I know."

His ingratiating tone vexed me. I watched his beaming smile, the way his sausage fingers toyed with the scrip hung round his waist. Here was a man far too puffed up with himself.

Kitchen boys carried out loaves of bread and dishes of butter. Another group brought huge wooden platters of roast pig, lamb, and beef. They returned bearing trays piled with chicken and duck. Sieur Etienne desired a reputation throughout France for hospitality bettered by none but King Philip himself. At Sieur Etienne's nod, the lutist began a song about some recent war.

Eating knives flashed and glittered along the table as the pilgrims filled their bowls. Cupbearers poured rich red wine into their goblets. I watched it splash out of the mouths of the wine jugs. Too long, too long since I sated the hunger wakening within me. I was more than foolish to let myself taste that drop from Yvette's finger. I knew I would be required at table, with temptation all around me. Perhaps I could escape to the kitchen and find one of the animals not yet butchered. I raised my hand to touch Yvette's sleeve. Before I could ask her permission to depart, the fat Doktor spoke.

"Will you have nothing, Mademoiselle? Not even a sip of wine to toast our good fortune at finding such a magnificent welcome awaiting us?"

His eyes moved over me, noting every detail of my appearance. Despite the heavy comfort of my rust-colored bliaut and black cotehardie, I felt naked, exposed. His searching look roused the fear in me, such fear as I had not felt since the night my damnation began. I clung to Yvette's sleeve.

"You must excuse my daughter's nurse, Herr Doktor," Sieur Etienne said. "She fasts more than the strictest Order."

"Katarina makes an excellent governess," Dame Clarisse added. "She is a model of piety for Yvette, fasting and praying, sometimes all night long."

Sieur Etienne snorted. "Better still, she saves me the trouble of paying some convent a ridiculous dowry, just to teach Yvette what she can learn at home."

"'Katarina'?" the Doktor mused. "You are not of German blood?"

"She comes from the lands the Tatars ravished," Sieur Etienne said. "I believe the University has some record of that invasion?"

"Indeed." A note of wonder crept into the Doktor's voice. "Stronger than most men she must be, to survive a journey all the way to France."

"She came to us the victim of violence while on a pilgrimage much like yours." Sieur Etienne smiled a smug, possessive smile. "We consider ourselves fortunate to have such a rare treasure for Yvette."

The pilgrims looked on me with new respect. I did not want them to look at me at all. Sieur Etienne enjoyed flaunting me before his guests. His praise was no more sincere than my curtsies.

"Truly this is a blessing," the Doktor said. "So much would I like to know about your land. Let us drink now to the kindness of Our Lord."

Sieur Etienne watched me out of the corner of his eye. He had presented me to his guests as what amounted to his court holy woman, so I could hardly refuse to join in that toast. In truth, he mocked what piety remained to me. I raised my goblet and allowed the Doktor to pour only a little wine into it.

"And to Sieur Etienne," I said. "For all his many kindnesses. May his memory be eternal."

None of them would recognize the last remark as the traditional prayer offered at the funeral rite of my people. I did not honor Sieur Etienne. I wished him dead.

When the pilgrims had finished gorging themselves, Sieur Etienne patted his lips with his napkin and rose. He offered his hand to Dame Clarisse, then addressed the pilgrims.

"If you will join us in the oriel, there will be sweetmeats and cordials."

They sprang up and loped after him like so many dogs wriggling for scraps. Greasy-fingered, unwashed, crawling with vermin and so ignorant they could not even read the Scriptures, these people were little more intelligent than the farm animals they fed on. Yet the Kingdom of Heaven was theirs, thanks to souls like jewels shining in the dung heaps of their filthy bodies. Long past were the days when I was allowed the comfort of tears, but the grief that was their source consumed me.

The oriel lay next to Sieur Etienne's quarters at the opposite end of the Great Hall from Yvette's rooms. The pilgrims followed Sieur Etienne, Dame Clarisse, and Yvette into the little hall that would take them to the oriel. I let my basket fall off my knee and knelt to gather up my needles and thread. Yvette glanced back and gave me a little nod. She knew I had endured all I could stand. Now I could escape to the stockyard and sate the fury building inside. The last of the pilgrims trailed out. I turned toward Yvette's rooms and hurried off. I had taken two steps when a hand grabbed my elbow.

"Mademoiselle Katarina! Will you not join us?"

The Doktor. His winy breath in my face angered me. How easy to break the arm that restrained me, then move on to his neck.

"Come now," he said. "Most grateful would I be to hear of the customs in your land. Are you not of the Eastern Church?"

"Herr Doktor." I struggled to keep my voice down. "You will take your hands off me this instant."

He clucked his tongue. "Sieur Etienne will not be pleased to hear of such rudeness to his guest."

He dragged me along with him down the hallway and into the oriel. Yvette looked up in alarm. She sprang to her feet, ignoring her mother's staying hand.

"Herr Doktor!" Yvette cried. "This is the hour of Katarina's prayers. I must insist you release her this instant!"

"Blessed Sieur." The Doktor's grip did not slacken. "Certain questions I would like to put to Mademoiselle Katarina about her homeland. That is not too great a request, I hope?"

Sieur Etienne looked at me. I did my best to conceal my loathing for the Doktor. If Sieur Etienne saw it, he'd give the Doktor free reign to vex me as long as he liked.

"What say you, Mademoiselle?" Etienne asked. "Will you deny our guest this paltry favor?"

I yanked my arm free from the Doktor's grip and curtsied. "*Mon seigneur*, the wine has been too much for me. I beg you, permit me to retire."

Sieur Etienne smiled. "What you need, Mademoiselle, is an evening out of your cell. Doktor, you may proceed."

"But Papa!" Yvette pushed between me and the Doktor, giving the Doktor a scathing glare. "If Katarina is ill—"

"Yvette." Dame Clarisse pointed to the empty chair beside her. "You will obey your father's wishes."

Yvette met her mother's cold blue stare. For a moment I hoped she'd argue. She took her seat and sulked.

"Excellent." The Doktor settled into his own seat and cast a look around the room that commanded the attention of all the other pilgrims as loudly as a spoken order. He turned his false smile on me. "Mademoiselle, you have not answered me. Are you of the Eastern Orthodox Church?"

"Here in France, I find it wiser to blend my faith with the laws of the Crown." He could say little enough to that without leaving himself vulnerable to attack.

"I have seen the crucifixes of Russia. They are most splendid. Perhaps you would be kind enough to let me see yours?"

"Herr Doktor. In my country, we do not display our family treasures to the pawing of every tourist who knocks on our doors."

He laughed, a hollow little chuckle meant to distract attention from the angry flush that added to his already red cheeks.

"But you do wear a crucifix?"

"All good Christians wear crucifixes."

"Surely you attend morning mass, and receive Holy Communion?" He stalked me with these questions. What was he hunting for?

"You are aware of the tension between the Churches at present?" I asked.

"I am."

"Then you will understand me when I tell you I cannot receive Communion at a Roman Catholic altar. To do so without discernment is to risk spiritual harm."

"You are well-educated, Mademoiselle, to understand such a fine point of theology."

"No one wants to be called heretic."

"True, true. May I ask how long you have been in France? To have traveled such a long way, you look very young."

"Sieur Etienne has been kind enough to give me shelter these four winters. As to the time before that, I cannot say. When the bandits attacked my party, they struck me such a fierce blow on the head my memory is not what it was."

"Poor Mademoiselle! Such a life you have led."

I smiled, letting him think I meant it for him. It was a good story. I spent quite a lot of time in Venice thinking it up before I made my way to France.

We moved on to happier topics. He asked for descriptions of vestments, details of services, points of doctrine. The other pilgrims asked about trivial matters, court gossip and fashions and the bloody truth about the Tatars. It warmed my heart to speak of my homeland. Perhaps this was a reward for my patience with the Doktor.

Sieur Etienne beckoned Yvette. She rose to stand before him. He kissed her forehead.

"Off to bed, my sweet. The hour is late."

"Yes, Papa. Come, Katarina."

No words were more welcome to me. I rose to follow her out. The Doktor stepped in front of me.

"For indulging my curiosity, I must thank you, Mademoiselle. Please, take this."

He seized my hand and crushed it between his own. Pain seared my palm. I screamed, tugging at my hand. The stink of my burning flesh filled the room. With my free hand, I lashed out, striking the Doktor across the face and knocking him backward. Embedded in my palm was a silver holy medal of the Virgin Mother. I dug my nails into the wound and tore the medal out, then flung it away from me and ran. Yvette kept shrieking my name. The pain, the horrible burning pain made me deaf and blind to anything but escape.

Once in Yvette's room, I fell across the bed, so weary from fighting the hunger and now exhausted by the agony torturing my hand. A part of my mind screamed at me to think, to plan. In that moment I could do nothing. My safety, my peace, my adopted child all forsaken because of that damned German's insufferable curiosity!

The door burst open. Yvette slammed it behind her. She dragged a large chair over to the door and wedged it beneath the knob.

"The Doktor!" She threw herself at my feet and hugged my knees. "Oh, Katarina! He said you're a monster, that you're unholy because the blessed medal burned you. How can he say such things?"

She looked up at me, baring the length of her white throat. Blood would save me now, enough blood to give me back my strength and all those other hideous powers that became mine when I lost my soul. The pain made my hand rise toward her. I could almost taste the hot gush of blood. I turned my hand to grip her hair—the brand of the holy medal stared up at me. The Most Holy Theotokos, Mother of God, Protector of the Holy Child. I thrust Yvette away. I could not deny my beloved child her right to the Kingdom of God.

I heard a commotion out in the hallway. Sieur Etienne and the Doktor shouted as they hurried toward us.

"Out of your gown!" I cried. "Quickly!"

Yvette pulled off her fillet and let her braids spill out of her crispinettes. She tore the brooch from her shoulder and threw off her cotehardie, then held her arms out to me. I tugged her bliaut off over her head. The thud of boots approached the door. Yvette stood shivering in her thin cotton chemise. A heavy fist hammered on the door.

"Yvette! Let us in!"

"Papa, I am not dressed. I've torn my gown and Katarina must mend it."

The door thumped inward, hitting the chair. Another heave and the chair grated backward. The door opened a few inches.

"Papa!" Yvette wailed. "You yourself told me no man can be allowed to see me like this until my wedding night!"

"Do not be afraid, child," said the Doktor. "We will save you from her!"

"Yvette!" Sieur Etienne shouted. "Take the cross above your bed! That will keep the creature from you!"

"Papa!" Yvette burst into tears.

Another loud thump against the door and it swung inward, shoving the chair aside. The Doktor's fat face appeared around the edge of the door. Yvette shrieked. I yanked a blanket off the bed and threw it around her shoulders. She huddled against me.

"How dare you!" I cried. "How dare you burst into the private chamber of this lady!"

Sieur Etienne stepped through the doorway. "You will release my child this instant!"

"I would never harm Yvette, no matter what this oaf has told you."

"Herr Doktor, you will hold the monster at bay. If anything happens to my daughter, I will have your head."

The Doktor set a bag on Yvette's dressing table. Even from several feet away, I could feel faint heat from it. In there would be my doom. He opened the bag and took out a long bodkin. The light from the oil lamps played along its silvery length. Next, he brought out a crucifix. I forced my eyes open against the sting of it. He reached in once more and withdrew a little phial. The heat from it streaked across the room and seared the very air I breathed. Holy water. Real fear seized me.

"*Mon seigneur*," I began. "I will do as you say. I ask only that you allow my lady to dress and depart. She is too young to witness such a thing."

Sieur Etienne looked at the Doktor, who wore a smirk of triumph. He nodded.

"So be it," Sieur Etienne said. "Yvette, you will gather your clothing and go to your mother's rooms. Stay there until I send for you."

Yvette turned a fearful look on me. As little as she knew, she understood terrible events were about to take place. I collected a bundle of fresh clothing, tucked it under her arm beneath the blanket, then looked down into my beloved's eyes for one last time. Tears welled there.

"Shh, *ma petite*, all will be well." I reached up to take the carnelian combs from my hair and pressed them into her hand. She bowed her head and hurried out, the tears streaming down her cheeks. I let out a long breath and steeled myself for the next step.

"*Mon seigneur*, will you not go with her? She cannot be allowed to walk the Great Hall without an escort, not dressed as she is." I put enough lurid implication in my voice to spur Sieur Etienne into motion. I knew what lurked behind his pride in Yvette. My deepest regret now was leaving her at his mercy. He hesitated in the doorway, looking at the Doktor.

"Go," the Doktor said. "I will hold her here."

I bowed my head in all humility. The door closed behind Sieur Etienne. The Doktor gave me that revolting smile.

"Very clever have you been, to disguise yourself for so long. Only a man of my education would know the signs and how to investigate."

"I doubt you would recognize pig dung if you fell in it."

His smile grew. "I have questions for you, many questions. You will answer all of them, or I will see you staked out in the courtyard so the entire household may watch the sun burn the flesh from your unholy corpse."

"Am I to believe you will not do exactly that no matter what I tell you?" It would take Sieur Etienne some time to walk Yvette all the way to her mother's chamber.

425

The Doktor picked up the phial of holy water. "You will remain where you are unless I command otherwise."

"Of course. I am hardly the ravenous monster you think me."

He took two steps closer to me. "Your skin is not so pallid as I have read."

"Sieur Etienne keeps many farm animals. They serve my needs."

"You have never touched the girl?"

"Never. Not once."

"I am impressed. I had no idea your kind could resist the slightest temptation."

"Count yourself lucky I'd drink the blood of a rat before I'd stoop to German swine."

"You *dare*—" He jabbed a finger at me. I grabbed his wrist and jerked him forward, away from his precious weapons. He raised the holy water. What a pity he'd corked it so tightly. I struck his hand and sent the phial flying. It smashed against the far wall. I threw him head first into the opposite wall. His skull cracked against the stone, and he slid down to the floor. I dragged him over onto his back and stared down into his piggy little eyes. He was only dazed. Good. I wanted him to know what was about to happen.

"Thanks to you I must leave my Yvette. With all my heart I wish on you the anguish I have known!" I shook him. "Are you listening, Herr Doktor? This should answer all your questions!"

I shoved his chin up and sank my teeth into his fleshy neck. I rejoiced at the feel of hot blood spurting against the back of my throat. I drank until my shrunken belly could hold no more, then hauled his body up onto my shoulders and staggered out into the hallway. With my elbow, I nudged open the panel to the garderobe, then stuffed him down the shaft. His feeble cry stirred my heart to nothing but contempt. When he woke to the hunger and found himself buried in a winter's worth of filth, his screams would bring Etienne and his knights. They would burn the monster as he meant to burn me.

I ran back to Yvette's room and gathered up my books, my

needlework, and the few gowns and pieces of jewelry Yvette had given me. I threw it all into my traveling bag, dragged on gloves to conceal the brand, and slung my heaviest cloak around my shoulders.

I stopped a few feet from the Doktor's bag and the painful items laid beside it. The sensible thing would be to throw them all after the body. The agony they would cause him would make his torment all the worse. I turned away. Monster I might be, but defiler of the sacred I was not.

I crept out into the hallway. Sieur Etienne's voice boomed from halfway across the Great Hall, ordering the servants to make ready a bonfire in the courtyard. My revenge would be complete indeed if I could rip his throat out, but that would ruin Yvette's future. I ran down the hall to the right, through the pantry and buttery to the stair that wound down the outside of the wall. With every step, the infernal speed came back to me until I was a blur streaking past the stupid faces of the startled kitchen boys. I shot down the stairs and out the back door, headed for the stables. I could not rely on my demonic speed alone to carry me out of France.

The stable door stood open. I kept to the shadows and slipped inside. A harness jingled ahead of me. The shadow of a cloaked figure moved in one of the stalls. I slipped up behind the shadow, silent as a ghost. The horse shied. I raised my hand to strike. Before my hand could fall, the figure turned. Its hood fell back.

"Yvette!"

Her hair was a wild yellow tangle. Tears still streaked her face. Beneath her cloak, she wore nothing but the chemise. She threw herself into my arms.

"It's not true!" She sobbed. "Papa said you're evil, and the Doktor had to kill you! It can't be true!" She looked up at me and her eyes widened. She touched my chin. Her fingers came away red. "*Mon Dieu*, Katarina! What have you done?"

"I saved my life."

She stared at me. "Then—it's true?"

"That God has cursed me? That much is true."

My heart shattered inside me as I waited for the horror and revulsion. Instead, Yvette held me tighter.

"I don't care! You're my friend. You've always been my friend!" She handed me the reins of the harness she had put on her favorite mare. "Take Eugenie. I will order the guards to open the gate."

"*Non, ma petite*. They would punish you. I cannot bear that."

I clasped her to me in a last desperate hug, then swung up into the saddle. Yvette opened the stall door and stood aside as I urged Eugenie out with my knees. I leaned down to touch Yvette's cheek.

"They will tell you horrible things about me. I ask you to remember I have always loved you, and never once did you harm."

Yvette held my hand to her cheek. "*Je t'aime, cher* Katarina. God be with you."

My little child loved me, even knowing what I was. I reined Eugenie around and nudged her with my heels. She cantered toward the Chateau's gatehouse.

"Open the gate!" I cried. "The Lady Yvette lays dying. I must fetch the abbot!"

"We have heard nothing," answered the guard.

"Do not question me! If the child dies unshriven, Sieur Etienne will send your souls to join her!"

The guards dragged the enormous doors inward. I glanced back and saw lights flaring everywhere inside the Chateau. Sieur Etienne and a party of knights charged out of the Great Hall.

"Close the gate!" Sieur Etienne roared.

I kicked Eugenie. The already nervous mare leaped forward and carried me through the gap so narrow my shoulders scraped the sides. I looked back one last time. Yvette ran out of the stable to wave to me. I drank in the sight of her, then turned my face to the bitter wind and galloped away.

Lillian Csernica's fiction has appeared in Weird Tales, Fantastic Stories, and DAW's The Year's Best Horror Stories XXI and XXII.

Born in San Diego, Lillian is a genuine California native. She currently resides in the Santa Cruz mountains with her husband, two sons, and three cats.

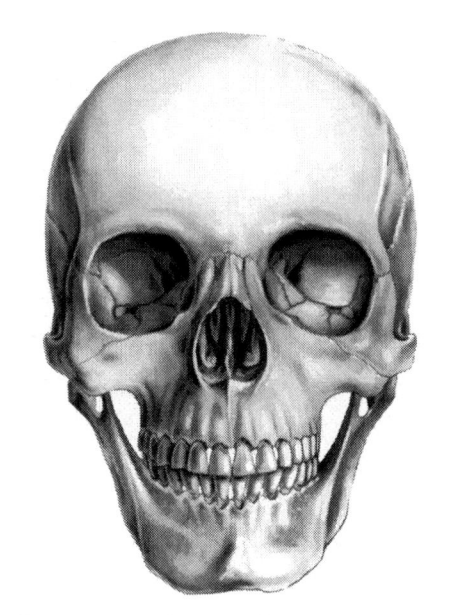

Millie's Hammock

Tory Hoke

The noise wakes Millie with a start. Short and sharp, so thank the Lord it's no midnight earthquake or LAPD helicopter. The Oteros' beagle, maybe? Or Cupcake the possum? Millie grips her bed's handrail, pulls herself upright and tries to place the sound.

It happens again. In the yard, distinct through the open window, bark three hard beats of a human cough. Her weak heart races, but she prays for calm. She didn't make it to eighty-three to be scared to death by a cough.

She puts on her trifocals and parts the blinds. It's a man. He's rocking in her hammock, his sour booze stink in the air, his empty booze bottle on the grass. Outrageous. She struggles to her feet. She could call the police, maybe, or the Oteros next door. Then again, the

Lord is with her. Why should she need to be rescued?

The man in the yard groans and turns over. Poor thing. The hammock was Wilson's, God rest him. Of course, it would attract some poor homeless fella. Private yard, no dog, no lock on the gate; might as well be a Red Roof Inn.

She calls out, "Young man!"

The coughing chokes off.

"This is my house and my yard," she says. "You can stay if you like, but don't you leave that dirty bottle on my lawn." She takes his silence for agreement. "Close the gate when you go."

Millie shuts the window and lowers the blinds. Her bare foot oversteps the rug and, with a scraping sound, lands on the rough, ruined patch on her hardwood floor. The sensation lingers. Even as she settles back in bed, her foot feels numb and slightly soiled, as if it's been licked by a cat.

Thank God for the dry hammock, the open gate, the nice old lady who's leaving Simon alone. They stole his sleeping bag. Without it, the underpass is torture. They stole his three dollars, too.

He brushes flakes of blood from his coat. At least the bottle is finished, and the devil is fed. At least tonight there's sleep, six hours at least. Sleep is relief. Sleep is escape, for a while.

In the morning, Millie pulls on her Easter-pink housecoat and hobbles to the yard. The gate is closed. The hammock is empty. There's no trace of the coughing man. Did she imagine him? Under the lemon tree, she picks up Cupcake's bowl and shakes off the lace of black ants. It would be a setback if she imagined him. If she had a setback, Anthony should know. But there was a bottle! A bottle would be proof. She searches the yard and the driveway and the recycle bin, and under the lid it's there: a handle of Boxwell's vodka. *Thank you, Lord.*

Reassured, Millie fixes an oatmeal breakfast and takes her morning jumble of pills—meloxicam and Plaquenil for her arthritis,

0.5 mg extended release Pramipexole for Parkinson's and bipolar depression, 500 milligrams valproate for mood stabilizing, and 200 milligrams of the new Prozerpine anti-psychotic—all sorted in an organizer the size of Texas toast. She changes into her lavender suit, settling the elastic waistband where her waist used to be. At eleven o'clock, Anthony pulls up in his Pontiac wagon and beats her to the door, toting groceries, the spitting image of Wilson at that age—long-jawed, rangy, and bald at the crown. He puts away the milk and smoothes the tuck of his button-down shirt.

"Morning, Ma." He stoops to kiss her cheek. "You ready for lunch?"

"Morning, baby. Almost."

As she disappears to the bedroom, Anthony counts the pills in her organizer and asks, "What's new?"

"A man slept in the hammock last night."

"What? Homeless guy?"

"I told him he could stay if he cleaned up after himself."

"You talked to him?"

"Sure. Through the window."

"Ah, Jeez." Anthony approaches as she rifles through her dresser. "Ma, you can't—"

"I'm doing better, aren't I? The house is tidy, isn't it? But not too tidy. I know you don't like that, either."

"A man isn't some animal you can just leave a bowl for. He could be a drunk or a crack addict casing the place—"

"You'd be surprised what I know. Let your mother do what she wants." She checks her top drawer for the third time. "I can't find my handbag. Tell Dr. Nawadi I'm off my rocker again."

Anthony musters a laugh. "Actually, there's something I want to talk to you about."

Morning sun flogs the Third Street Promenade. Simon's stomach threatens to dump out, but he keeps his cup rattling. People rush past with smoothies and coffees and glossy shopping bags. His lips are chapped. His hands are chapped. He whistles a jumpy tune in a minor key. It's the only song he knows.

Across the promenade sits another panhandler. Wheelchair. Camo pants. Sign says he's a vet. He's fifty-something, dirty, matted, and maimed. If Simon makes it to that age, that's how he'll look. No chance of that, though, ha ha. They don't speak to each other. What would they say? Like two corpses at the bottom of a cliff: *higher than it looked, huh?*

He counts six dollars from his cup. It's no use until it's $10.58, enough for a handle of Boxwell's, his ticket to the end of the day.

He tongues his front gums. He misses those teeth. Devil took them. Without them, there's no work in the front office. His back throbs. Devil took that. Without that, there's no work in the warehouse. His head hurts. Devil took that, too. All that's left is Beg, Drink, Feed.

A pigeon with a missing toe limps by, and the devil rumbles its demand. There's no hope in resisting. Shaking in every limb, Simon pockets his cup and follows the pigeon up the alley, away from witnesses.

Holding a brochure and an egg salad sandwich, Millie waves goodbye as Anthony backs down the driveway. The brochure says "Palm Village" and has two smiling seniors on it. She buries it in the kitchen trash.

At least the sandwich is useful.

At sundown, under the lemon tree, Millie rattles a fresh bowl of cat kibble. On the high back wall, Cupcake the possum waddles out of the ivy and blinks.

"Ebenin'," she says, slurring. The end of the day is the hardest. "E-ve-ning."

Cupcake bares needle teeth and hisses.

"Oh, shush. You don't mean it."

On the hammock, Millie leaves the egg salad sandwich, a pen, and a note.

I'm glad you feel safe here. Stay until morning. I can help you. - Millie

She takes the evening pills: Pramipexole, valproate and Prozerpine, and drowsiness, the cost of the Prozerpine overtakes her by 7:00 PM. Millie settles into bed with her Episcopal Daily Reader, listening for clanking gate or creaking hammock, but her bed is soft and warm, and sleep soon drags her under.

The whoop of a cop car wakes him. Park bench. Cold. It does get cold in LA. Cops peer at Simon from their cruiser. "Don't make us get out of the car, buddy."

He nods. Clutching his Boxwell's, he shoves up from the bench and shambles off.

Was it Lindblade Road last night? Herbert Street? Walking makes him feel like he's going to fall off the earth, makes it hard to concentrate. He grips the sidewalk with his toes. Finally, there's the house—yellow stucco, spider plants, unlocked gate. There's food on the hammock. A note, too. Sweet old lady. He reads and eats and drains the bottle. Sleep is coming. Sleep is on the way. He lies down and shuts his eyes tight.

Something small and furry rustles the ivy beside him. *No, no, no. Don't let it hear that.* The devil rumbles its demand. *Please, not here. Not tonight.* The devil rumbles louder, cranking the winch in his skull, dragging him toward the ivy, the hissing, the black glittering eyes.

Wrapped tight in a pink housecoat, Millie hefts the lid on the recycle bin and finds two vodka empties and a plastic clamshell. On the hammock sits her note, folded back into a triangle. The sight of strange handwriting makes her heart leap.

Millie, I did this. I didn't want to. There is a devil in me and I can't get it out. I'm sorry I'm so sorry

Did what? As she turns to the house, her foot knocks something stiff and gray. Her stomach drops. Cupcake. Flies hop in his empty eye sockets. His skull is skinned, his guts are gone, and from his backbone trails white tissue like untied shoelaces. Black ants march over the cat kibble stuck in his teeth.

"Poor boy." She bends carefully, joints cracking. "Poor sweet boy."

She needs the spade. The spade is in the garage. The garage remote is in the kitchen. Nothing worth doing is easy. The door grinds open to shine daylight on an arsenal of abandoned tools: half-barrel planters, orange camping rope, a push mower. She takes the shovel and pats the pegboard's his-and-hers hedge shears. *Wish you were here, Wilson.* He was the strong one. He always knew what to do.

She whistles a disjointed tune in a minor key. It's been a long, long time since she's thought of it.

Burying Cupcake leaves her damp and shaky. Her back will pay for this tomorrow. After a nap in the living room, she makes two turkey sandwiches—one for her, one for the coughing man—and writes another note.

I forgive you. Stay and let me help. - Millie

Disgusting. Disgusting. Simon didn't even clean up the remains. Too sick when he woke. Too jittery. All he could do was write the note. Millie deserved better, but he can't do better. It's time to end this. It's time to try again.

On Venice Boulevard, he rattles his cup. As soon as he has two dollars to show, he limps down the block to J&D Liquor, where a Mexican clerk with a linebacker neck gives him the evil eye. Simon holds up the money, a show of good faith, and swerves down the housewares aisle—detergent, Windex, cat food, and a row of little bleach bottles along the floor. Two dollars will buy him one bottle. One bottle isn't enough to be sure. But if he goes back out, he might lose his nerve.

Here. It has to be here.

Simon squats out of sight then unscrews a bottle and tips it down his throat. It pours like oil and tastes like table salt, swimming pool, chemical burn—angry, unnatural. Eyes streaming, he replaces the empty bottle and opens another. His face tingles. His fingers go stiff, and he fumbles the third bottle loud enough to hear. The clerk spots him in the fisheye mirror, snatches up a broom, and hurtles down the aisle.

"Stop that!" yells the clerk. Simon holds his ground, downing the third bottle with noisy chugs. "Are you crazy, borracho?" The clerk belts him with the broomstick. The bottle drops. Simon scrambles for the door, woozy from the poison, herded by blows. "Get out of my store." The clerk's voice has as much fear as anger. "Out!"

Simon flings down the two dollars, lurches into the parking lot, and stumbles around the corner to the alley. Can't risk a do-gooder interfering, not when he's so close. He slides down the wall into a fetal position as the bleach blots his mind. He can keep it down. It was enough. Sleep is on the way forever.

No such luck. Simon's gut jackknifes. He flips to his knees as his gorge surges, and the bleach shoots out his mouth and nostrils. It bounces off the concrete and back in his eyes. Every nerve shouts fire. He moans and drools, rocking like a bear. His skin prickles. His vision tunnels to red, and then to nothing.

"Not again."

The devil cramps his gut again. He pukes out the last of the bleach. Tears and snot patter like rain into the puddle of expelled bleach. The devil straightens Simon's back and pistons his legs. Blind, deaf, dumb, Simon careens forward, desperate and helpless, as the devil pilots his body toward the intersection. Gravel crunches under his feet. Sidewalk. Tires. Honking. The sounds swerve to the left.

Here comes that disjointed, chromatic tune. Is it outside? Is it inside? Time snarls. Traffic noise coils like a maze. Everything is shut off. Nothing is in reach. Simon scrabbles the walls of his mind for purchase like a crab in a bucket, but his mind wears down. Exhaustion sets in. Dragging one thought toward the next is like hanging bricks on a string until the strength to lift them drains out, and in the dregs, there is only pain, only hell.

And the devil marches him on.

When Millie opens the organizer for her evening medicine, she finds five pills in her morning slot. *Dumb, dumb, dumb.* She forgot them. That's what happens when a morning is busy. Is it better to take them or skip them? She can't remember.

She calls Dr. Nawadi, but his voicemail picks up. Her speech is poor this time of day; a recording might be hard to decipher. Dr. Nawadi might misunderstand. Misunderstanding makes people anxious. Anxious means interventions. She hangs up. She could call Anthony, but she's not supposed to forget pills. Forgetting makes him anxious. An anxious Anthony means more brochures.

Judicious, she takes the evening pills only, clicking the morning lid closed on five pills.

Anthony calls her after dinner. "Did you take your medicine?"

"Of course." Most of it.

"Did the homeless guy come back?"

"Yes."

"What'd he do?"

"Nothing. Anthony, this is my home. I'm perfectly able to deal with a stranger. I left him a sandwich."

"Ma."

"He's harmless."

"You don't know that."

"I'm doing the Lord's work. You'll see. I can't do the Lord's work in Palm Village."

A glass of milk is just the thing before bed, but the milk is spoiled. Chunky. Didn't Anthony just buy it? She dumps it down the disposal, and the sour rotten stink makes her gag. She cracks the kitchen window for some air and happens to glance out.

Outside, in the driveway, in the gathering dark, there's a man. Bent under a stained overcoat, he stands in profile, facing the road, weaving figure-eights on his feet. He's younger than she guessed, with a month's growth of beard, and very thin. There are strange pale streaks down the front of his body like he fell face-first in glue.

She drops the carton in the sink with a soft, hollow *thop.*

"Young man?" she asks.

He turns toward her, but their eyes don't meet. A bang shakes the house like a Mack truck hitting a speed bump. Millie grips the sink. The window judders at her. Another bang. An earthquake? No. The man is still on his feet. He steps toward the window. His jaw drops and his head lolls back. In the depth of his throat, two eyes glint like pinpricks of flame. She staggers back, and they track her.

Another bang. The driveway is empty. The kitchen is pitch dark. The oven clock says she's lost an hour.

She knows what this means.

"Rapid cycling." That's what Dr. Nawadi called it when she scrubbed the floor with salt until the finish came off, trying to purge the house of evil. The memory used to embarrass her, but it feels all right now. It makes sense. Her mind doesn't play tricks. It sees through tricks that others play.

Millie pulls down her family Bible and opens the Book of Mark. "'Those who believe…will drive out demons.'" She leafs the pages backward. "'For nothing is hidden except to be revealed.'"

She opens every window in the house. She has nothing to fear. *Bear ye one another's burdens, and so fulfill the law of Christ.* Beyond the hedge, the Otero children squeal. A Harley-Davidson prowls by with a *blatt-blatt-blatt*, and an emerald figeater beetle buzzes the screen. This is right. This world is brighter, better. *For he is not the God of the dead, but of the living.*

The devil drops him. Simon collapses, grabbing at air. The swollen meat of his face hangs loose and heavy. It's dark everywhere. Is it night? His fingers scrabble on pavement—a driveway—and up the black border of his vision—a fence. Yellow stucco. Spider plants. Hammock. Help is here.

He guzzles water from her garden hose and sprays down his aching face. Millie can save him. Millie can help him die.

There's a knock at the kitchen door. Millie opens it to find a man, haggard and reeking and soaking wet. In his swollen purple face, his eyes float like raw eggs.

"Help me, Millie," he says.

She takes his hand.

Simon ratchets the shower dial to scalding and stands face-up under the spray. The tiny bathroom fills with steam. Sick, he props himself on her bathtub grab bar.

Millie knocks. "Simon?"

"Yes?"

"I found you some clothes. I'll leave them here."

"Thank you."

"Anything else?"

"I'd kill for a shave."

"Wilson's kit should still be under the sink."

The DTs set in and jitter his hands and make shaving a blood-spattered challenge. Months of matted hair accumulate in the sink.

His belly rumbles. Time is short. Time is always short.

Simon comes out barefoot, nails trimmed, face shaved, dressed in Wilson's clothes—beige knit slacks and plaid madras shirt. What a difference a day makes! He could be anybody's child.

Millie's dragged the recliner to the middle of the living room, opposite the couch, where her Bible and pink-handled hedge shears are waiting. Simon's old rotten clothes sit folded in a grocery tote on the kitchen counter. They're not hers to throw away.

She holds out ten feet of camping rope, a noose tied at each end. "Are you ready?" she asks.

"What's this?" asks Simon.

"I'll guide you. Take a seat."

"I've tried hanging. It doesn't work."

"What?"

"The devil stops me. It always does."

"Oh, Simon. We're not going to kill you." She lowers herself on the couch, grimacing, and rests the orange double-noose by the hedge clippers. "We're going to get the devil out."

Simon slaps his hands on his head. "The thing in me is real. It can hurt you. It will hurt you." He snatches up the grocery tote of his old clothes. Of course, he thinks she's crazy. Why wouldn't he? "This was a mistake. I'm sorry. I shouldn't have come back. I need my shoes. Are my shoes in here?"

She whistles for Simon the tune Wilson taught her, a disjointed melody in a minor key.

It works, of course. Simon freezes, eyes wild, braced for disaster. "Where did you hear that?"

"Wilson."

"Where did he get it from?"

"Same place you did, I expect."

"That song. That awful song. It..." He taps his chest. "This thing whistled that song at me for months."

"And one day you whistled back."

He drops the tote. "I thought I was the only one."

"Why on earth would you think that?"

He sinks onto the couch beside her. "I came to one night with a busted table and a busted head. Before, things were okay. I mean, I was drinking, but I could function. But after..." He shakes his head like there's water caught in his ear. "It won't even let me die, Millie."

"I know." She rests her hand on his shoulder. His bones feel light and sharp as a bird's. "That's how we draw it out." She drops one end of the camping rope behind the couch and offers him the other.

"You can kill this thing?"

"No, unfortunately. But we can prune it."

"Prune it?"

"Whenever it starts to get too big. Help me with this? Put one loop through the other, like a big belt. The couch is our anchor."

He takes a hangman's loop.

"Forgive me," says Millie. "That's the only knot I remember. Wilson always did this part."

Simon crouches, chest to floor, to pull the second loop from under the couch, and he threads it through the first. He hands the loose end to Millie. "That's your seat," she says, pointing to the recliner. He sits. Millie passes him the hedge clippers. "Cut your throat."

"I thought—"

"Lure it out, and live."

Simon takes the clippers and holds them at arm's length like a stranger's baby. "Pink," he says. Noose in hand, Millie braces against the couch. Simon opens the blades and touches them to his throat.

"You're sure this will work?" he asks.

"It always has."

"How many times?"

"Hundreds."

He squeezes the handles. The blades pinch, drawing blood. He flinches back, pupils dilated, breath shallow. His heart pounds hard enough to rock him.

"This is a lot harder sober," he says.

"The only way down is to jump."

He yanks the handles apart and thrusts his neck between them.

The devil's arm shoots from his mouth and swings for the shears. It's a rope, a tentacle, a roiling whip of layers on layers of glittering black ants. It reeks of sulfur and roars like a sandstorm, caustic, overwhelming. The arm smacks Millie across the face. Ants knock loose and crumble into ash.

Simon chokes, his air squeezed off. Millie lassoes the hand. It bucks. The knot tightens. Simon pitches forward. The couch hops, bouncing Millie. She braces a foot on Simon's chest. The arm creaks and stretches. Simon gags, clippers shaking in his fists.

"Cut it off," says Millie.

He lifts the blades. Veins bulge in his distended neck. The arm frays, fingers of ants plucking backward at the knot. Millie shoulders the nylon rope, winching the arm higher. The couch rocks onto its back legs.

"Do it, child!"

Simon plants the clippers on the arm and claps the handles together. The blades shear sheets of ants, and ash pours out, but more ants flood from Simon's mouth to stanch the wound. The arm slashes at Millie, ripping her housecoat. Simon's vision sparkles silver. His hands sway, uncoordinated.

"Again!"

He hacks the arm again. It splits. The flailing end ebbs to a single thread. Simon opens the clippers for the last time, blind, suffocating. Millie yanks down her loop, pushing the arm between the blades. Simon chops. The blades meet. The arm bursts into soot. The stump disappears down Simon's throat as Millie's couch topples backward.

The stink and the ash and the adrenaline subside. Simon rolls to his elbows, cradling his savaged face, barking wet coughs from the depth of his lungs. He crawls around the couch to where Millie lies upside-down, and he collapses beside her. The stillness of the house soothes them.

"It was real," says Millie.

"Yes," rasps Simon. "It was real."

"I knew it. I know it." She labors to sit up and falters, gasping. "Lord help me. I broke something."

Simon rallies upright. "What should I do?"

"Call my son. His name is Anthony. His number's in the phone. Oh, please don't let it be my hip."

Simon stumbles to the kitchen to fetch the cordless, dials, and holds it to her cheek. A man's voice says, "Ma?"

"Anthony." Millie's breathing turns shallow. Pain takes hold. "Come get me. I've had a fall."

"Be right there, Ma," he answers, voice raised but steady, a good son, a good man. Simon hangs up. The truth of their situation rises with a blinding glare. Millie squints her mind's eye into it, muscling her way to understanding.

"They're going to put me in a home," she says. "Last time I was in a hospital. They gave me lithium. Made me a zombie. But you'll tell them, won't you? Tell them it was real."

Simon tucks a couch cushion under her head. "Millie, they're not going to believe me either."

"What do I do, Simon?"

"Tell them it was an accident. It didn't happen. I wasn't here."

"You are here."

"Yes. But no one besides us needs to know."

She snatches his shirt, shaking in every limb. "I'm not ready. Lord forgive me, I'm not ready at all."

He kisses the back of her hand. "Then be willing."

Millie relaxes, pressing her body to her cold floor. It's real. It as real as anything she knows.

"Take the clippers," she says.

Simon waits under a street light, rubbing his arms against the chill until a Pontiac pulls into Millie's driveway. As Anthony's long loping figure hurries out of the car to the house, the younger man turns up the street and disappears into the night.

Under a friendly mid-morning sun, Simon climbs the circular driveway to the Palm Village awning. He scratches his stubble. With his clean shirt, he passes for a landscaper, even if his hedge clippers are pink. As long as he stands straight and keeps moving, no one will stop him.

He follows a "Transitional Care" sign to the back of the facility, where a familiar Pontiac sits parked. He works his way down the hedges, stealing glances into rooms. At last, he finds Millie, tucked in floral sheets on a reclining gurney. Anthony sits nearby, sipping a foam cup of coffee.

Simon crouches and pulls a few weeds while a ponytailed nurse comes and goes. When it's clear, he taps the window, smiles, and waves. Anthony looks up, confused, and politely waves back. Millie looks up, too. Her head bobs with fatigue, but her eyes sparkle. She knows him. She remembers him. She made it through. Tough old bird.

Monday he'll find out if they're hiring.

He presses his palm to the window and leaves a print—a sigil. He hopes she understands.

He descends the driveway, back straight, and jaw set. His shower and shave will hold another three days. His clothes may last a week if it doesn't rain. Respectable fades fast.

There are plenty of his kind in Santa Monica, off the cliff but not yet corpses. Walking toward Venice, clippers cocked on his shoulder, he whistles the tune he knows best. Few will recognize it, but one will be enough. One and one makes two. It takes two to fight a devil.

And the devil is on the mend.

Tory Hoke writes, draws, and codes in Los Angeles. Her fiction has appeared in Strange Horizons, Pseudopod, and Drabblecast, and her art has appeared in Apex, Spellbound, and Strange Horizons, where she now serves as art director. She's editor-in-chief of sub-Q, the pro magazine for interactive fiction.

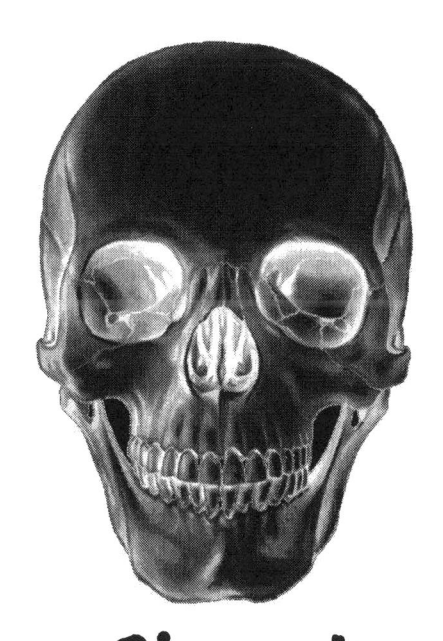

Changed

Nancy Holder

The vampires invaded New York the night Jilly turned sixteen. She was pacing in front of a club called Watami, waiting for Eli to show, eager to see what he had bought her. He was late, and she knew it was Sean's fault. Sean wouldn't want to come, because it was Jilly's birthday and Sean hated her. But Eli would make him do it, and they would show and she would wonder all over again why Eli couldn't love her like that…and how he could love someone who didn't like her.

Then, out of nowhere, the place was swarming with white-faced, bone-haired, bloody-eyed monsters. They just started *attacking*, grabbing people and ripping open their throats—dancers, drinkers, bartenders, and her three straight friends: Torrance, Miles, and Diego.

She still had no idea how she'd gotten out of there, but she called Eli first and then her parents. *No service, no service, beepbeepbeep...* no texting, no net; no one could freakin' communicate.

She was Jilly Stepanek, lately of the Bronx, a semi-slacker who wanted to go to film school at NYU once she got her grades back up. She had been a neo-goth, into Victorian/Edwardian clothes and pale makeup without the Marilyn Manson vibe, loved steampunk—but now, she was just another terrified chick on the run from the monsters. Used to be the monsters were in her head; now they were breathing down her neck in real time.

No one stepped forward to represent the vampires or explain why they had taken over the boroughs like the world's worst gang. There were no demands, no negotiations, just lots of killing and dying.

In less than a week, drained corpses—the homeless, first—littered the streets of Manhattan, SoHo, and the Village. As far as Jilly could tell, none of them rose to become vampires themselves. Maybe all the movies weren't true; maybe once they killed you, you were just dead.

The vampires had hunting animals, like falcons, that dug into their white arms. They were all head and wings, with huge whited faces and bloodshot eyes and teeth that clack-clack-clacked like the windup false kind. Blood dripped and splattered onto the ground from the places the bird-suckers gouged their claws into their masters' arms, but—she observed fearfully from as far away as possible—either the vampires couldn't feel it or they liked it. Maybe it was their version of cutting.

The bird-suckers swooped and pirouetted across the night clouds, tearing the city pigeons to pieces. A few nights of slaughter and they owned the skies. A few nights more, and there were no wild dogs on the island of Manhattan.

Three nights after her birthday, a vampire attacked and killed her father; its vampire-bird ran her mother to the ground while they ran out of their house. Jilly screamed for her mom to run faster, run faster, oh, God, but it swooped down on the back of her mother's head and started pecking and tearing. Her mother fell; her eyes were open but she wasn't seeing a thing. Blood from her neck gushed onto the sidewalk beneath a lamp post, and it looked as if her shadow was seeping out of her body.

Hiding in the bushes, heaving, Jilly waited it out. Then she ran the other way, wearing nothing but a long black chemise, some petticoats, her boots, and a long black coat she had bought at a garage sale.

She tried to get to Eli's row house, but whole blocks exploded right in front of her, and others whooshed up in flames like paper lanterns. Weeping and gasping, she phoned him over and over; she texted with shaking hands. *No service, no service, beepbeepbeep.*

She raced in circles to get past the fires as the smoke boiled up into the dotted clouds of clack-clack-clacking birds.

By the fourth day after her birthday, the streets were a real jungle. The survivors were as vicious as the street dogs the vampires-birds had eaten: hoarding food and threatening to kill each other over safe places to sleep and water bottles. She had some experience with hostility, from when she had gone drug-mad. Rehab and a lot of love had redeemed her, but the old lessons were not forgotten.

Dodging fiends and madmen, she stole tons of phones—or maybe she only took them, since there was no one left alive in the stores to ring up sales—but there was really, really, really no service. Trying to find one that worked became an addiction. At least it gave her something to do—other than hide, and run.

Her therapist, Dr. Robles, used to caution her to ease up, not use her busy brain quite so much. He said she had to let go of loving Eli because people who were gay were gay; there wasn't going to be a change of heart no matter how much she wanted one.

She tried to find a cybercafé that the vampires hadn't gutted, but there were none to be found. She broke into the office buildings and tried their computers, but they were fried. She wondered how the vampires did it. Must've been part of their plot to take over the world.

Just like the vampires, she slept during the day, in the brightest sunlight she could find, her black coat covering her like a shroud. Even though she had never been a Catholic, she prayed to the God of the crucifix, because crucifixes could hold the vampires at bay. She wanted to pray in St. Patrick's Cathedral but it was too dark and enclosed; she could almost hear the vampires hissing in the chapels lining the sanctuary. Her lips were cracked and chapped, and she was filthy. But maybe God would help her anyway.

Please, God, please, God, please, God, please, God, please please please don't let Eli get burned to death or sucked dry by the demons...Amen.

High rises burned down to ash, cars exploded, and the vampires capered on stacks of the dead. And Jilly staggered through it like the last victim of the Apocalypse. No one hooked up with her and she didn't make any effort to take on a sidekick or become one. She had to get to Eli; at least she could die with him.

So she kept skirting the crazily burning buildings in her tattered bad-fairy gear, the indigo in her hair bleached by the sun and coated with dirt. She showed people the photograph of Eli she always carried in her coat pocket. *No, Jilly, no Jilly, no Jilly, no Jilly, no no no sorry, loser.*

She kept waiting for the fires to burn down, burn out. The smoke lingering in the air smelled like someone barbecuing rotten hot dogs; she felt it congealing in her lungs and coating her skin.

Five days after her birthday, she was so tired she could hardly breathe anyway, which was a sort of blessing because maybe she would die and then she could just stop everything. Escaping the bad was also one of her habits. She felt empty, outside and in, just a husk. If a vampire tried to suck her blood now, it would probably find nothing but red powder.

She really thought that the time had come for her to die. She thought about her parents, and her friends, but mostly she thought about Eli Stein. He had been her first and only love, before he had realized he was gay. She still loved him; she would always love him, no matter what form his love for her would ever reach. *Brain brain, go away, obsess again some other day...*

He was crazy-mad for Sean instead, and she hoped...

No, she couldn't even think that. If she went anywhere near praying for something to happen to Sean…

You are evil, Jilly, and you deserve to die.

Beneath her coat, she fell asleep and dreamed of Eli, and Sean; because in the summer after tenth grade that was who they were. EliandSean, like one person, like the person she had hoped to become with him. Once Eli had found his other half, they had come to her house almost every day, because they could hold hands there.

They could brag about their slammin' skillz on their skateboards and video games like any other teenage boys, and they could flirt with each other and sit on her couch with their arms around each other while Jilly's mom brought them sodas and grilled cheese sandwiches. They were amazed and delighted by the acceptance they found in Jilly's house. Tolerance, in her house, came after a hard struggle, won by determined parents who never let go of Jilly, even after she ran away with a biker, shaved her head, and told her shrink there were no bones in her hands.

Now, everything was crazy in a new way; taggers wrote VAMPIRES SUCK over every surface there was, and people tried to share whatever information they'd learned about them: They were mindless, they were super smart; they had a leader—it was all random. The lured you in with dark sexuality. They attacked you like animals without a plan. It had something to do with global warming; they were terrorists. They were created by the government.

She saw plenty of them. White-faced and leering, they darted down streets and stared out of windows, like terrible Will Smith CGI effects. She didn't know how she'd avoided being killed by all the near misses. One thing she did know, they were more like people than beasts.

Just very evil people.

Their birds were the mindless attackers, but the vampires themselves listened to music and went joyriding on motorcycles and kept the subway people alive just so they could go on rides; *it was a dead world now, after all.*

After another near miss—a vampire turned a corner just ahead of her, and she turned on her heel and ran, hard—she broke down weeping, her thin stomach contracting; and then God must have taken the hint, or felt guilty, or whatever, but He/She/It/They did something miraculous:

It began to rain. Hard. Buckets poured down from Heaven as if old lady angels were washing their doorstops; gallons and rivers tumbled onto rooftops and treetops like the tears of all the New Yorkers who'd died; like all the blood that had gushed out of the necks of the dead.

And the rain toned down the fires just enough that she soaked her coat and then raced through the fire line, arriving on the other side into some kind of hellish otherworld; everything was covered with gray and white-bone ash: trees, buildings, abandoned cars, rubble. She shuffled through the layers of powdery death.

And then, there it was. *There it was...*

Eli's row house. With the formerly turquoise paint and the American flags and some kid's ash-colored tricycle overturned in a pile of ash like strange granular leaves. Then she thought she saw a shadow move across the window and she stared at it for a long time, because she had actually made it, and in her heart she'd expected to find no signs of life.

There were no more shadows and she wondered if she had gone crazy or died or imagined the whole thing. By then, Jilly was certain the dead could be as crazy as the living. She staggered up the stoop stairs, kicking up layers of death that made her gag and choke.

She knocked on the door, but no one answered, so she tentatively pushed it open.

Eli and his father faced each other in the living room with the old tapestry of the Jews at Masada hanging over the upright piano. Eli looked taller and much thinner, his dark hair long as ever, and he had a semi-beard. He looked like a leftist rabbi in the NYU sweatshirt she had given him. Mr. Stein was still Mr. Stein, in his navy blue sweater and dark trousers.

Mr. Stein was shouting. "You stupid faggot, you're going to die out there."

"Just shut up!" Eli shrieked. "Stop calling me that!"

"Eli," she whispered from leaning on the doorway. "Eli, it's me." They both turned.

"Jilly!"

Eli whooped, gathered her up, and hugged her against himself. She felt as light as a desiccated leaf, unbelievably dizzy, and reeling with pure joy Eli was safe, alive, and with her. He'd been here, in his old house, living indoors with his parents.

"Oh my God, Jilly, are you okay?" he said; and then, before she could even answer, he asked, "Have you seen Sean?"

"No," she said, and he deflated. She saw the misery on his face, felt it in the way he nearly crushed her.

In the kitchen, his gaunt, black-haired witchmother was *cooking*, as if nothing had changed. They had electricity and gas, and Jilly smelled the hot food—onions, meat—her mouth began to salivate. She burst into tears and Eli held her tightly, swaddling her into himself. He smelled so good. So clean. Almost virginal.

His father's eyes bulged like an insect's and he glared at Jilly, as if she were an intruder.

"I've been trying to get here," she said in a shaky voice. "Everything was on fire. And then the rain came."

"The rain," Mr. Stein said reverently, glancing at the tapestry.

"Now we can go look for Sean," Eli said.

"Don't you speak that name," Mr. Stein snapped.

For God's sake, why do you care about that now? she wanted to snap back at him. But instead, she took Eli's hand and folded it under her chin. She saw the layer of ash-mud on her hands and wondered what she looked like. A zombie, probably.

"I was just about to leave, to search for him," he said, bringing her knuckles to his mouth. He kissed them, then laid her hand against his cheek. His tears dampened her skin like more rain. "He called just before it happened, from midtown. I don't know what he was doing there. We had a fight. I was lying down."

Weren't you going to meet me at the club? More pieces of her broken heart fell away with the realization he'd forgotten.

Eli searched Jilly's face with his fingers and she felt each brush of his fingertips begin to close the wounds that the long days and nights had cut into her soul. There was no one she loved more. She would go to her grave loving Eli Stein.

"Of course you're not leaving now. Look at her. She looks like she's dead." Mr. Stein had never liked her. Not only was she formerly known as a mad slut, but she wasn't Jewish, and her family had given Eli and Sean safe harbor to commit their carnal atrocities.

"You need to fix the door," Jilly said. "Or at least lock it."

"I thought it was locked," Mr. Stein said. He looked at Eli. "Did you unlock it?" He walked over to check it, passing so close by Jilly that she had to take a step out of his way. He grabbed the door, she heard a click, then he turned his attention on the knob.

"It's broken." He glared at Eli. "Did you break it?"

"Dad, why would I do that?" Eli asked.

"Maybe vampires tried to get in last night," Jilly ventured. "You need to put up some crucifixes. They really do work."

Mr. Stein crossed his arms over his chest like an angry child. "Not normal," he muttered.

"Dinner is almost ready," Mrs. Stein announced from the kitchen, smiling weakly. Jilly wondered where on Earth she'd found a brisket. In the still-working refrigerator of their house, she supposed.

Eli gave her a look that said, *My parents have lost their minds, obviously.* He had some experience with mental illness, since he was her best friend.

She didn't smile, even though, as usual, they were thinking the same thing. Today, it wasn't funny. She didn't know who was crazy and who wasn't.

"You could take a shower, Jilly," Mrs. Stein continued.

Jilly was too weak and exhausted to take a shower. But Mrs. Stein gave her some mashed potatoes and a piece of cheese and the food energized her just enough to stagger into the bathroom. For the first time in weeks, she was a few degrees less afraid to be enclosed in a small room; to take off her clothes; to stand vulnerable underneath a stream of water...

...and then Eli was in the bathroom, taking off his clothes, too. He climbed into the shower and wrapped his arms around her, sobbing. She started to cry, too, naked with the boy she loved who did not want her the way she wanted him; they clung to each other nonetheless, and mourned.

"He's out there," he said. "I know he is. I feel it."

She turned around and leaned her back against his chest. It was so unreal the she was here. To just walk through their door...

"Your parents are probably out there having a fit," she said, her eyes closed as she savored the pleasure of mist, and warmth, and Eli.

"Are you crazy? They're probably dancing in circles. 'He's in there with a girl! Maybe he isn't gay, he's not a faggot!'" He mimicked his father's voice perfectly. Then he added softly, "What about your parents?"

She raised her chin so the water would sluice over her face. Her silence was all he needed.

"Oh, Jilly, Jilly, God, what happened?"

"I can't talk about it." she swallowed hard. "Please don't say anything. I'll never stop crying."

He laid his hand over her forehead. "I'll only say this; they were so good to me. And in Judaism, goodness is a living thing." he whispered.

"Thanks." She licked her stinging lips again.

Head dipped, he turned off the water. Then he toweled her off and retrieved some neatly folded clothes set out by his mother in the hall. A pair of sweat pants swam on her and belled around her ankles. There was a black sweater, no bra, not that it particularly mattered.

He put his clothes back on, laced his fingers with hers, and took her into his room. There were pictures of her everywhere—at school, at their first Broadway play, holding hands in Central Park. The ones of Sean outnumbered them, though. First there were a lot of pictures of just the two of them, Eli and Sean, the brand-new boyfriends; and then, of Eli, Sean *and* Jilly, as Eli brought the two "together"—mugging for the camera, practicing for a drama skit, their very silly trip to a book signing at Forbidden Planet. Sean looked pissed-off in any picture she was in. Didn't Eli notice?

She stretched out on the blue velour bedspread, feeling as if she had just set down a heavy load of books. It was incredible to her that he had been sleeping on this wonderful bed, in his own room. She didn't even know if her building was still standing. She could go back, get more clothes, get her valuables and money.

Eli would go with her. They could look for Sean on the way...

She dozed. Eli spooned her, holding her; each time she inhaled, he exhaled. It had been that way in the early days, for them. When Sean came along, he added something new; a literal breath of fresh air. Even Jilly had been charmed by the surfer dude who'd lived in L.A. and knew movie people who might be able to help her. He talked about working as a stand-in. He hung around stunt men. His uncle had rented out his surf shop as a movie set.

But once he was sure of Eli's love, he changed. She saw it all happen. Eli didn't. Maybe changed was the wrong word; around her, he became chilly and disinterested, and she knew he was never going to introduce her to anyone in the industry.

But Eli didn't see it.

Sean had actually been a kind of vampire. He sucked up anything he wanted; he drained Eli's friends and classmates by using them to advance up the social ladder, then blindsided them with his snotty I-am-mean-and-because-I-deserve-to-be-you-must-permit-it attitude. She could almost predict when he'd show his other face. Jilly's mom used to say they should give Sean the benefit of the doubt because he had been through a lot. Any guy who was gay had suffered. So they had to be nice to him, even though he was a total jerk. She knew what her mom was not saying: *We put up with your bad behavior. Welcome to the real world—the one that does not revolve around you.*

Her mom would never say anything like that, of course.

Because she was dead.

But she had never talked like that, not even when Jilly was the most drug-crazed; she had said that Jilly was hurting.

But even when Jilly was at her worst, she still would have done anything to help Eli become more, and more, and more of all the wonderful things Eli was.

"God, I'm glad you're here," he whispered, nuzzling the back of her head. She cried some more, and he held her.

There was a soft knock on the door. Mrs. Stein whispered, "It's dinner time."

Jilly was starving, and the smell of food was making her clench and unclench her hands. But Eli had fallen asleep with his arm over her. She tried to figure out a way to slide out from underneath him without waking him up. She couldn't manage it, so she stayed beside him. Her arm began to ache. Her stomach growled.

As she contracted and released her muscles, trying to keep the blood circulating, she heard Mrs. Stein crying. It was a high-pitched, irritating kind of weeping, and it set Jilly on edge.

"No one is coming to help us!" Mrs. Stein cried. "No one."

Jilly, hungry and despairing and exhausted, listened to the rain, and imagined New York City going up in steam. Then she let herself go fully to sleep for the first time since she had turned sixteen.

The yelling jerked Jilly awake.

"You will die!" Mr. Stein shouted from downstairs.

"Stop yelling!" Mrs. Stein was crying again. "You'll drive him away, the way you always have."

"What!? Drive away? Didn't you hear what he just said? He's leaving anyway!"

Jilly groaned, feeling in the bed for Eli, realizing he'd gotten up. His parents were trying, in their way, to tell him that they loved him and didn't want him to risk his life by leaving their home. She felt the same way. She didn't want to get out of bed. She knew Eli so well, knew they were going to leave as soon as she emerged from the bedroom—*maybe we can eat first*—and it wasn't going to be a graceful exit.

"It's because they blame you for not fixing me," Eli told her as they left his parents' house. It was still raining; Mrs. Stein had given them parkas with hoods and umbrellas. The rain seemed to have cleared the sky of the vampire's birds of prey. Another miracle.

At least they had eaten some breakfast first—last night's brisket, and pancakes. And blessed coffee. While she'd been on the street, she'd heard a story that one man had knifed another over the last cup of coffee in a pot in a diner.

She didn't say anything. She couldn't forgive Eli's parents for being so narrow-minded as to pick a fight with their son and his best friend, when they might never see either of them alive again.

She adjusted the heavy backpack, filled with extra clothes, shampoo, toothbrushes, and toothpaste. Eli was carrying the heavier one, packed with food. He had a small satchel over his shoulder too, packed with photographs of Sean, seven of them, as if someone might not recognize him in the first six. Sean was weird-looking, in her opinion, with almond-shaped eyes and a long, hooked nose in a long, narrow face. So he wasn't handsome, he wasn't nice, and there were other gay guys in their school if Eli wanted a boyfriend. Gay guys who liked Jilly a lot. Unfortunately, Sean was the guy for him.

Eli groaned when they reached the pocket park, site of their first make-out session, after her birthday party in the eighth grade. She'd been so excited and happy she hadn't slept all night.

"Even the trees got burned up," he said. They walked close together, holding hands. She had a strange floating sensation; if he hadn't held onto her, she thought she might have floated away from sheer fear.

They passed dozens of burning buildings, sizzling and steaming in the rain. The subway station split the sidewalk; by mutual unspoken consent, they gave it a wide berth. Darkness and seclusion—perfect vampire territory.

Shadows and shapes moved in the alleyways; they walked down the center of the street, gripping each other's hands. It was strange, but Jilly was more afraid with Eli there than she had been by herself. She didn't think she could stand it if something happened to him. He was so nervous; he was broadcasting "come and get me" to anyone interested in easy pickings.

He pulled a cell phone out of his parka and dialed numbers, listening each time. Finally, he grunted and put it back in his pocket, and moved his bangs out of his eyes. Her heart stirred, and she touched his cheek. He smiled distractedly; she knew he was glad she was there, but it was Sean he most wanted to see.

She used to have these long conversations with her girlfriends about if Eli would ever come back to her. Eli had been her actual boyfriend for two years. They had made out all the time, but never gone any farther than that. They'd been too young. Then he and Sean had found each other…or rather, Sean had found him. Sean had moved from L.A. to New York and zeroed in on Eli, even before Sean was sure Eli was gay. So Eli had given Jilly the "we can still be friends" speech.

Only in their case, it was true. They were excellent friends. They thought alike, read alike. He thought NYU was a great goal. He talked about going there too. They both hated sports.

And Sean, who was a jock, hated that.

He never said a word about it to Eli. As far as Eli was concerned, Sean loved Jilly like a sister. Had used those exact words, in fact, the one time Jilly tried to discuss it with him. But when Eli wasn't paying attention, Sean zinged her out with vast amounts of passive-aggressive BS—veiled threats and lots of snark. He picked fights just before they were supposed to meet her somewhere—like Watami. Being somewhere in midtown when he was supposed to celebrate with her was classic Sean, King of Bitter Homosexuality.

Eli brushed it off, refused to agree to her reality. So she didn't bring it up again, ever. She didn't want to give Sean the ammunition for an "It's either her or me" speech.

As they walked out of the burn zone, the sky began to darken, and a rush of resentment soared through Jilly. Her tired body was aching for Eli's soft, clean bed. She wanted to take another shower, and brush her teeth for a year. She didn't want to be risking her life, or Eli's, for someone who hated her.

Her mind was trying to figure out what life would be like if they found Sean. And then, before she knew what she was doing, her inside voice escaped. "Watami. The club. Maybe he went there."

He looked at her. "He wasn't going to go. And he'd come to my house first, or try to get to me through our friends." And they did have other friends, gay friends, who envied them for having Jilly's family to hang with.

"Okay, never mind. Maybe he went to school."

Eli raised his brows. "Maybe." He smiled. "It's big. Maybe they're doing like a Red Cross shelter there." He hugged her. "You're a genius, Jilly."

Too smart for my own good, she thought. The old Jilly, pre-rehab—the one without the boundaries—might not have suggested places to look for Sean. But Jilly was a good, nice person now. Maybe that was why he didn't love her. She wasn't edgy enough. She could change...

But he can't. He is gay, she reminded herself.

It was nearly dark. It was very dangerous to be out like this; she'd seen vampires leap from shadows and drag people away. Sometimes they growled; sometimes they were silent. Jilly had been sleeping next to an old lady in a store one night. In the morning, all that was left of the lady were her shoes. Jilly had no idea why she herself had been left alive. Maybe the old lady had been enough?

They met a man on the street a few blocks from the school named Bo. He staggered when he walked and he talked very slowly. There was a scar across his face from the slice of vampire fangs.

"They have to feed as soon as they change," he told them. "The vampire who tried to kill me was brand new. There was another one with him, the one who made him into a vampire. He was laughing.

My friends staked him. They don't change to dust."

Then he staggered on.

"Wait!" Jilly cried. "Tell us everything you know."

"The new ones are the worst," he said. "They're the most lethal. Just like baby snakes."

Now, as the gloom gathered around them in the rain, they hurried to their old high school. There were lights on, and shadows moving in across the windows. Neither spoke as they crossed the street and walked past the marquee. The letters had been stolen; there was no school news.

Rose bushes lined the entrance. She couldn't smell their fragrance, but the sight of them, drenched by the downpour, gave her a lift. The double doors were painted with crosses; so were the walls and windows. The taggers had written VAMPIRES SUCK GO TO HELL VAMPIRES on the walls.

There were two guards at the door—a male teacher named Mr. Vernia and Jilly's English teacher, Mary Ann Francis. They hugged both Eli and Jilly hard, asked for news—asked how it was—then ushered them in.

It smelled, and the noise was deafening. Students, adults, little kids, and teachers—everyone was milling around. People who hated her ran up and hugged her, crying and saying how glad they were that she was alive. She realized she and Eli should have eaten a good meal before they'd come in. If they opened up their pack now, they would have to share.

Is that so bad, sharing?

"Jilly. Eli," their principal, Ms. Howison, said when she spotted them. There were circles under her eyes and deep lines in her forehead. She looked like a skeleton. "Thank God."

Ms. Howison had tried to keep her from coming back to school after rehab. But crises did strange things to people, didn't it?

Eli skipped the pleasantries and pulled out all his pictures of Sean. Men and women, computer nerds and cheerleaders, carefully examined each one—even if they knew exactly who Sean was—

before passing it on. No one had seen him.

Jilly was too tired to stay awake any longer. Principal Howison promised her that all the doors and windows had been covered with crosses, and the ground was dotted with garlic bulbs and communion wafers. Jilly wondered if the rain had dissolved the wafers. How many molecules of holiness did you have to have to keep the monsters at bay?

Bazillions of cots were set up in the gym and sure enough, there were Red Cross volunteers. Eli and Jilly pulled two cots together, stashed their packs underneath, and lay down in their clothes. It was better than what she'd been sleeping on before she found Eli, at least.

Eli touched her face with his hands. "I'm so glad you're here."

"Me too," she said, but what she meant was, *I'm so glad you're with me.*

Eli fell asleep. She looked at the diffused light drifting across his face, making him glow. She wanted to kiss him but she didn't want to wake him; correction, she didn't want him to wake up and remind her he didn't love her *that way.*

Then she heard someone crying. It was muffled, as if they were trying not to make any noise. She raised her head slightly, and realized it was Ms. Howison.

Jilly disentangled herself from Eli slowly. Then she rocked quietly onto her side, planted her feet underneath herself, and sat up. She walked over to where the woman was sitting in a chair, facing the rows and rows of cots. She looked as if she'd just thrown up.

"Hey," Jilly said uncertainly. "Ms. Howison?"

"Oh, God," she the principal whispered, lowering her gaze to her hands. "Oh, God. Jilly. You're still here. I was hoping…" She turned her head away.

"What?" Jilly asked.

She took a deep breath and let it out. She was shaking like crazy. "I need you to come with me for a second."

"What's wrong?"

"Just…come." The principal wouldn't look at her. Jilly shifted.

"Please."

Ms. Howison got up out of her chair and walked out of the gym. The overhead fluorescents were on. Jilly followed her past the coaches' offices and then into the girls' locker room, past the rows upon rows of lockers, and then through another door into the shower area.

Ms. Howison cleared her throat and said, "She's here." Then she stepped back and slammed the door between herself and Jilly.

Jilly tried to bolt.

Sean was there, and he was a vampire. All the color in his long, narrow face was gone. His eyes looked glazed, as if he was on drugs.

And she should know.

He grabbed her, wrapping his arms around her like a boyfriend; she smelled his breath, like garbage. He wasn't cold; he was room temperature. She was completely numb. Her heart was skipping beats.

She wet her pants.

"I'm glad to see you too," he said.

She set me up. She gave me to him. That bitch.

He wrapped his hand around her bicep and dragged her forward. She burst into tears and started wailing. He clamped his other dead hand over her mouth so hard she was afraid her front teeth were going to break off.

"Shut up," he hissed, chucking. "I've wanted to say that to you forever. Shut up, shut up, shut up."

She kept whimpering. She couldn't stop. Maybe he knew that as he dragged her along with his hand over her mouth. His fingernails dug into her arm and she knew he had broken the skin, but she didn't feel it.

He walked her into a storage room where they kept cleaning supplies—brooms, mops, big jugs of cleaner. She started screaming behind his hand, and he slapped her, hard. Then he slammed her against the wall. With a gasp, she bounced back off and fell on her butt.

He slammed the door, leaving her in darkness. With a sob, she crawled to it and started to pound on it.

"*Don't,*" he hissed on the other side.

He's going to get Eli, she thought. *Oh, God, he's going to vampirize him. That's what he's here for.*

Maybe he will let me go.

But why would he? He was the King of Bitter. And she would never leave without Eli.

She fumbled around for a light switch, found one, and turned on the blessed, wonderful light. Her arm was bleeding and it finally began to sting. She didn't know if she wanted to feel anything. She wondered what it would be like when he—

The door burst open, and Sean came back inside. His eyes were glittering. He looked crazy. "Eli says hi."

"No," she begged. "Don't do it. Please, Sean. Don't change him."

Sean blinked at her. Then he laughed. "Honey, that's what love is all about, don't you know?"

She doubled up her fists and bit her knuckles. He lifted a brow.

"I smell fresh bloo-ood," he sang. "Yours. It smells *great.* If you were alone in the ocean, the sharks would come and chew you up. Alone in the forest, it would be the wolves. Alone in the city—it's us."

Vampires. "How...did this happen to you?"

He ignored her. "I'm going to give you a choice, girlfriend. The choice is this: You can change, or he can change. The other one of you...is blood in the water." He moved his shoulders. "I'll let you pick."

She stared at him. "What are you saying?"

"God, you are so stupid. So incredibly, moronically stupid. I could never figure out why he loved you." He shook his head.

What did it matter, she wondered, *when Eli still loved him more?*

"Does it even matter which way I choose?" she said. "You don't even like me." Of course he would change Eli and let her die.

"Maybe it doesn't. Maybe I just want to see what you'd say," he told her. "I'm giving him the same choice."

She stared at him in mute terror.

"I told him that I would change you if he asked me to."

He folded his arms across his chest and leaned against the back of the door. He didn't look much different at all—he was still the same surf-charmer Sean.

"You know I'll say to change him," she said. What did she have to live for, after all? Only Eli. And if he were gone...

"Be right back," he said, turning to go.

"Why are you doing this?" she asked.

He didn't turn back around, just looked at her over his shoulder, as if she was a nuisance.

"I don't know why he's loyal to you. He doesn't love you the way he loves me."

"But he loves me," she said, as she realized. "That's why..."

He turned around and stared at her. The expression on his face was the most frightening thing she had ever seen. She took another step back, and another. She bumped into the wall.

He raised his chin, opened the door, and left.

She paced. She thought about drinking the cleaner. She tried to break the mops and brooms to make a wooden stake. She couldn't so much as crack one of them.

She fell to her knees and prayed to He/She/It/Them: *Get us out of here get us out of here, come in, God, come in, over...*

The door opened, and Sean came back in, grinning like someone who had finally, really, totally gotten what he wanted. Triumph was written all over his face. He looked taller. Meaner.

Ready to kill her.

"Eli will be changing," he said. "GMTA. You both made the same choice."

She jerked. *No, he wouldn't.*

"And you'll be his first meal. Have you ever seen a newly changed vampire? All they want to do is suck someone's blood. That's all I wanted to do."

"You're lying," she said. "Eli would never..."

But Eli would. He hadn't even asked her if she wanted to leave his parent's house to help him look for Sean. He had put her in harm's way, for Sean. He didn't love her the way he loved Sean. Lovers did things differently than friends.

"If it makes you feel any better, he feels terrible about it." Sean sneered at her.

"His going to hate you for making him do this," she said. "He'll never forgive you." She was talking to a vampire. To a vampire who was going to kill her. To a gay vampire who was going to turn Eli into a gay vampire.

She felt reality begin to slip away. *This wasn't happening.*

"I'm going to get him now," he said, going for a smile, not quite pulling it off. Irritated, he slammed the door.

She stood as still as one of the mops she couldn't turn into a vampire stake. Her heart hammered in her chest and she had no idea how she could hear all that thumping and pumping because she was

at the door

at the door

at the door

pounding and screaming, begging to be let out.

Ms. Howison was going to have a change of heart and rally all the people in the gym and rescue her.

Sean was going to open the door and take her in his arms, and tell her that he'd been so mean to her because he actually loved *her*, not Eli. That he'd only pretended to love Eli so he could stay close to her. And that he wouldn't kill either of them, not if Jilly didn't want him to.

Sean was going to tell her that he was sorry, both of them could be changed, and they would go on as they were, as a trio, only nicer, like Dorothy, the Tin Woodsman, and the Scarecrow.

Sean was going to see some other hot guy on the way back to Eli and fall in love with him instead, change him, and leave.

Eli was going to escape, and find her, and they would get out of New York together.

She pounded on the door as she remembered the night Eli had confessed that he had met someone else...a guy someone else...and he had cried because he didn't want to hurt her, his best friend.

"I will always love you totally and forever, I promise," he had said.

The door opened, and she scrambled backward away from it as fast as she could. Her elbow rammed into a container of cleaner. *Throw it at them. Do something. Save yourself.*

Sean and Eli stood close together. Sean had an arm around Eli, and Eli had on his baggy parka. Eli, as far as she could tell, was still human. His bangs were in his eyes.

He was looking at the floor, as if he couldn't stand to look at her.

"No," she whispered. But it must have been yes, he must have told Sean to change him. Sean was going to change Eli, and then he was going to kill her.

Her heart broke. She was on the verge of going completely crazy, all over again.

Sean took a step toward her. "If it makes you feel any better, it's going to hurt when I change him," he promised her. He sounded bizarrely sincere.

He shut the door. The three of them stood inside the cramped space. She was only two feet away.

Sean placed both hands on Eli's shoulders and turned Eli toward him. Tears were streaming down Eli's cheeks. He looked young and scared.

Sean threw his head back and hissed. Fangs extended from his mouth.

And Eli whipped his hand into the pocket of his parka, pulling out a jagged strip of wood—

—Yes!—

—and he glanced at Jilly—

—Yes!—

—and as Sean prepared to sink his fangs into Eli's neck, Jilly rammed Sean as hard as she could. He must've seen it coming, must have guessed—but Eli got the stake into him, dead center in his unbeating heart.

Sean stared down at it, and then at Eli, as blood began to pour down the front of him. Then he laughed, once, and blew Eli a kiss.

He looked at Jilly—gargled, "Bitch," his throat full of his own blood—then slid to the floor like a sack of garbage, inert, harmless.

Eli and Jilly stared at him. Neither spoke. She heard Eli panting.

Then Eli gathered her up. Kissed her.

Kissed *her*.

They clung to each other beside the dead vampire. And Eli threw himself over Sean, holding *him*, kissing *him*.

"Oh, my God, Sean," he keened. "Oh, God, oh, God. Jilly." He reached for her hand. She gave it to him, wrapping herself around him as he started to wail.

After he wore himself out, she tried to get up, thinking to see if there were more vampires, to check on Ms. Howison and the others, but he held her too tightly, and she wouldn't have moved away from him for the world.

He held Sean tightly too. "I can't believe it. How evil he was." Eli's voice was hoarse from sobbing.

"I know," she said. "He was always—"

"Sean wasn't even in there. When you're changed, the vampirism steals your soul," Eli went on. "You're not there. You're gone."

Tears clung to the tip of his nose.

"Sean loved you, Jilly. He told me that a million times every day. He was so glad you're my best friend."

She started to say, "No, he hated me," but suddenly she realized: that was going to be his coping mechanism. He was going to believe from now on that the Sean he knew and loved would never have made him kill his best friend.

She put her hand on the crown of his head and found herself thinking of the tapestry of the Jews at Masada in his parents' living room. It was a pivotal moment in Jewish history, when cornered Jewish soldiers chose to leap over a cliff rather than submit to Roman rule. Mr. Stein talked about it now and then, and sometimes Jilly had wondered if what he was saying was that Eli should take his own life, rather than be gay. She couldn't believe that, though, couldn't stand even to suspect it. The rigidity of the adult world was what had made her crazy. The unbelievable insanity of Mr. Stein, who condemned his own son just because Eli couldn't change into a heterosexual Jewish warrior and defy the invading sin of misplaced lust. At least, that was what her therapist had told her.

"You are brilliant, and you're so…*much*," Dr. Robles had declared. Dr. Robles, her savior. "People don't change, Jilly. They just see things differently than they used to, and respond according to the way they already are. It's all context. Reality. Is. Context."

Dr. Robles had saved her because he didn't try to change her. So she had never tried to change Eli.

She took a deep breath and thought about her hopeless love for him.

And something shifted.

Her love was not hopeless. She loved him. It didn't have to break her heart. It didn't have to do anything but be there.

Be there.

So she said, "Sean loved you so much." Because that's what would help *him* the most.

"Thank you," he whispered. "He loved you too. And I love you, Jilly." He looked up at her, broken and crumpled like a rag—the boy she kissed in the eighth grade, a thousand million times, almost until her lips bled.

"And I love you," she replied. "I love you more than my own life. I always have." It was right to say that now. People didn't change, and love didn't, either. Where Eli was concerned, there was no context.

"Thank you," he said. No embarrassment, no apologies; their love was what it was. Alone in a closet, with a dead vampire, hiding in a school because the rest of the city was overrun by vampires…

She laid her head on his shoulder, and he laced his fingers with hers.

"Happy birthday, sweet sixteen," he whispered. "My Jilly girl."

"Thank you," she whispered back. It was the best present ever.

After a while, they opened the door. The sun streamed through, and for one instant, she thought she heard the trilling of a lark.

Then she realized that it was Eli's cell phone.

Beepbeepbeepbeep. This is God, Jilly. I'm back on the job. Amen.

Nancy Holder is a NYT bestselling author of approximately 80 novels and 200 short stories. She writes a lot of tie-in material for Buffy the Vampire Slayer, Crimson Peak, Ghostbusters, and other "universes." Her most recent horror novel is a YA thriller titled The Rules. She has received 5 Bram Stoker Awards for her horror fiction and is a board member of the Horror Writers Association. Socialize at @nancyholder.

Thank you for reading our *Digital Horror Fiction* anthology, **Killing It Softly,** and for supporting speculative fiction in the written form. Please consider leaving a reader review so that other people can make an informed reading decision.

Find more great stories, novels, collections,
and anthologies on our website.
Visit us at DigitalFictionPub.com

Join the Digital Fiction Pub newsletter for **infrequent**
updates, new release discounts, and more:
Subscribe at - Digital Fiction Pub

See just some of our exciting fantasy, horror,
crime, and science fiction books on
the next page.

More from Digital Fiction

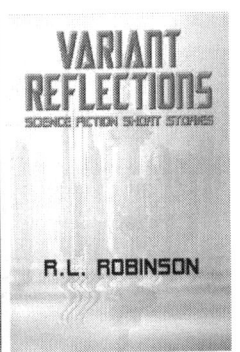

Copyright

Killing It Softly
A Digital Horror Fiction Anthology of Short Stories
Executive Editor: Michael A. Wills
Managing Editor: Suzie Lockhart
Copy Editor: S. Kay Nash

These stories are a work of fiction. All of the characters, organizations, and events portrayed in the stories are either the product of the author's imagination, fictitious, or used fictitiously. Any resemblance to actual persons or ghosts, living or dead, would be coincidental and quite remarkable.

Killing It Softly – A Digital Horror Fiction Anthology of Short Stories. Collection copyright © 2016 by Digital Fiction Publishing Corp. Stories: Torn Asunder © 2016 Rebecca Snow, Lambent Lights © 2016 H.R. Boldwood, Nosophoros © 2016 Christine Lucas, What the Rain Brings © 2016 Gerri Leen, Taking it for The Team © 2016 Tracie McBride, Here We Go Round © 2016 Rie Sheridan Rose, Songs for Dead Children © 2016 Aliya Whiteley, Music in the Bone © 2016 Marion Pitman, All of a Heap © 2016 Jenner Michaud, Traitorous, Lying, Little Star © 2016 Suzanne Reynolds-Alpert, Truth Hurts © 2016 Carole Gill, A Trick of the Dark © 2016 Tina Rath, Abysmoira © 2016 Airika Sneve, Skin Deep © 2016 Carson Buckingham, Orbs © 2016 Chantal Boudreau, Rule of Five © 2016 Eleanor R. Wood, Guilty by Chance © 2016 Nidhi Singh, Ecdysis © 2016 Rebecca J. Allred, Coralesque © 2016 Rebecca Fraser, The Funhouse © 2016 Jo-Anne Russell, Graffiti © 2016 K. S. Dearsley, Complete © 2016 Amanda Northrup Mays, Ellensburg Blue © 2016 M.J. Sydney, Abandoned © 2016 Rose Blackthorn, The Call of the House of Usher © 2016 Annie Neugebauer, Ravens © 2016 Elaine Cunningham, Foxford © 2016 Sandra Kasturi, The Root © 2016 Jess Landry, Long Time, No See © 2016 Sarah Hans, Millie's Hammock © 2016 Tory Hoke, Changed © 2016 Nancy Holder, all published under license by Digital Fiction Publishing Corp., Cover Image Adobe Stock: Copyright © 91583310. This version first published in print and electronically: October 2016 by Digital Fiction Publishing Corp., Windsor, Ontario, Canada—Digital Horror Fiction and its logo, and Digital Fiction Publishing Corp and its logo are Trademarks of Digital Fiction Publishing Corp.

All rights reserved, including but not limited to the right to reproduce this book in any form, electronic or otherwise. The scanning, uploading, archiving, or distribution of this book via the Internet or any other means without the express written permission of the Publisher is illegal and punishable by law. This book is licensed for your personal enjoyment only. This book may not be copied and re-sold or copied and given away to other people. If you're reading this book and did not purchase it, or it was not purchased for your use, then please purchase your own copy. Purchase only authorized electronic or print editions and do not participate in the piracy of copyrighted materials. Please support and respect the author's rights.

DigitalFictionPub.com

Made in the USA
Middletown, DE
12 October 2017